The
Tiara Club

Chetco Community Public Library
WITHDRAWN
Brookings, OR 97415

WITHDRAWN

Beverly Brandt

The Tiara Club

St. Martin's Griffin

New York

Chetco Community Public Library
405 Alder Street
Brookings, OR 97415

THE TIARA CLUB. Copyright © 2005 by Beverly Brandt. All rights reserved. Printed in the United States of America. No part of this book may be used or reproduced in any manner whatsoever without written permission except in the case of brief quotations embodied in critical articles or reviews. For information, address St. Martin's Press, 175 Fifth Avenue, New York, N.Y. 10010.

www.stmartins.com

Design by Kathryn Parise

LIBRARY OF CONGRESS CATALOGING-IN-PUBLICATION DATA

Brandt, Beverly.
  The Tiara Club / Beverly Brandt.—1st ed.
    p. cm.
  ISBN 0-312-34122-9
  EAN 978-0-312-34122-0
  1. Young women—Fiction. 2. Beauty contests—Fiction. 3. Women investors—Fiction. 4. Gulf Coast (U.S.)—Fiction. 5. Female friendship—Fiction. 6. Beauty contestants—Fiction. 7. Conflict of generations—Fiction. I. Title.

PS3602.R3635T53 2005
813'.6—dc22

                                                          2004065822

First Edition: July 2005

10 9 8 7 6 5 4 3 2 1

To Kim Cardascia,
for being such a fabulous editor . . . and for loving this book!

Acknowledgments

As always, I'd like to thank my agent, Deidre Knight, for all she does to help keep me sane in the sometimes insane world of writing.

I'd also like to thank my friends and fellow authors Alesia Holliday and Katherine Garbera for the countless hours spent talking about our books, our lives, and our business. I wouldn't want to be in this game without you!

A big thank-you to everyone who works behind the scenes at St. Martin's Press to produce, promote, distribute, and otherwise support my books. I hope when you see the books on the bookshelves that you get as much of a thrill as I do!

To Jill Conner Browne, the author of the Sweet Potato Queens books—you're my hero! Thank you for writing such hilarious books and making me wish I could move to Mississippi to be one of your friends. I love your message of empowerment, of settling for more (if the story about Funkdog in *The Sweet Potato Queens' Book of Love* doesn't make you cry, I don't know what will), and of filling your life with great food, great men, and great friends.

But, most of all, I'd like to thank all the readers out there who love what authors do as much as we do.

The
Tiara Club

One

Georgia Elliot raised the hood on her plastic poncho and pulled the elastic strap of her safety goggles to take up the slack at her temples. The strap pulled out several strands of curly blond hair as it tightened around her head. Wincing, Georgia picked up the tongs next to the burner in front of her and gingerly poked at the can immersed in simmering water. With one gloved hand, she inched the flame up a notch and watched the bubbles appear on the surface of the water.

She glanced at a timer as the seconds ticked by.

A blue-lined pad of paper lay open on the counter behind her. Georgia turned, picked up the pencil lying next to the pad, and scribbled a note. *8:24 P.M., humidity 86 percent, raised heat to approx. 98° C. No sign of imminent explosion.*

Finally, after three months of experimentation, she was going to have her first success. Tonight, there would be no metal fragments to pick out of the ceiling, no oozing goo dribbling down the walls.

She glanced at the timer again. Only four minutes left to go.

"Georgia, come quick," a voice suddenly shouted from the sitting room. "We're going to be on TV."

Startled, Georgia poked her head out of the kitchen and into the parlor, where the other five members of the Tiara Club were gathered, sipping frosty banana–cream pie martinis and staring intently at Georgia's old thirty-eight-inch console television. Callie Walker Mitchell—Georgia's best friend since kindergarten, when the Walkers moved from

Birmingham, Alabama, to Ocean Sands, Mississippi, and bought the old Hiram Purdue place next door to the Elliots—aimed the remote control at the TV, pressing her right index finger on the volume button while shushing the occupants of the room.

"Shh, shh," Callie said, gleefully shifting her weight from one foot to the other in a perfect imitation of what Georgia termed the "tee-tee dance." Georgia had baby-sat Callie's four children often enough to know that in anyone under ten years of age, the tee-tee dance required immediate action, but she assumed that her best friend's bladder was not what was causing her to jump up and down so frantically.

"What is it?" Georgia asked, glancing back at her timer to see that she had two more minutes left before her experiment could be deemed a complete success.

"Just listen," Callie answered, clicking the volume up.

Georgia peered at the television screen as a commercial ended and the cameras cut to a sterile studio kitchen. A granite-topped counter was artistically decorated with gleaming produce and several woven baskets. An eight-burner gas cooktop that Georgia would have given her Shrimp Festival Princess crown for was flanked by a built-in cutting board, a deep-fat fryer, and a professional-grade KitchenAid mixer. Twin ovens, a microwave, and a Sub-Zero refrigerator were set in a wall lined with maple cabinets. It was a gourmet cook's dream. Georgia was so busy drooling over the equipment that she hadn't noticed the host of the show, who had entered the set and was looking into the cameras with a smile that didn't quite make it to his bright blue eyes.

"Welcome back to *Epicurean Explorer*. This is Daniel Rogers and today we're exploring products that promise to save you time and money . . . but do they deliver? I must admit that I think a good cook can get by with nothing more than a great set of knives and some decent pots and pans, but there are companies out there that manufacture gizmos that exist for tasks as simple as removing the seeds from lemon juice or separating an egg—both of which you can do just as easily with an ordinary sieve. For today's show, we went through our viewer mailbag and decided to put some of your favorite gadgets to the test. We were intrigued by a product mentioned in this letter from a Ms. Callie Mitchell in Ocean Sands, Mississippi."

Daniel Rogers picked up a folded sheet of white paper from the counter in front of him and started to read as a collective murmur of surprise went up among the group in the parlor.

"Ms. Mitchell writes, 'I love eating supper with my family because it gives us all a chance to catch up on what is happening in one another's lives. However, as a single mother of four young children, I was finding it impossible to make time for this nightly ritual. Impossible, that is, until my friend Georgia Elliot introduced me to an amazing new product called the Miracle Chef. The Miracle Chef enables me to make a delicious, nutritious, four-course meal in less than thirty minutes. Now I have time not only to make supper for my family, but to enjoy eating with them as well. I'd love it if you would dedicate one show to this miraculous product. Yours truly, Callie Walker Mitchell.'"

Daniel Rogers stared at the piece of paper in his hand for a moment before turning his head to look right into the camera. Georgia watched as his lips curved up in a slight smile, his teeth white and even. Several strands of dark brown hair lay on his forehead, as artfully arranged as the waxy yellow squash and polished red apples on the counter in front of him.

"Well, viewers, Ms. Mitchell is going to get her wish. *Epicurean Explorer* is traveling down to Ocean Sands to pit man against machine."

"Isn't this exciting?" Callie said with a wide grin as the TV show host paused.

"You knew about this?" Georgia asked incredulously.

"Yes. Daniel called me last week to discuss the cook-off. Can you imagine? A TV star called *me*. I darn near peed my pants. You can't imagine how hard it's been not telling y'all, but I wanted to keep it a secret until tonight."

"Well, I'm definitely surprised," Georgia said, turning her attention back to the television when Daniel Rogers spoke again.

"I'll go head-to-head with the Miracle Chef in a five-part cook-off series, where I plan to prove that a good cook can whip up a four-course meal in less than thirty minutes *without* spending money on these so-called miracle gadgets. Remember, folks, if a product seems too good to be true, it most often is." With that, he tossed Callie's letter back onto the counter and flashed his movie-star smile at the cameras before picking up another piece of paper.

Georgia's teeth snapped together as she drew up to her full five-feet-eight-inches and glared down at the television screen. "Why that arrogant son-of-a-Yankee. He has no idea what the Miracle Chef can—" she began, only to gasp when a loud *boom* sounded from the kitchen behind her.

Five of the six women gathered in Georgia's sitting room dove for cover. Having survived several of these disasters in prior months, Georgia merely ducked, putting her arms over her head for protection.

"Oh, honey, you did it again," raven-haired Kelly Bremer said from beneath the coffee table, shaking her head.

Georgia turned and looked at the mess in her kitchen, at the light brown goo oozing down her normally clean white kitchen cupboards. With a heartfelt sigh, she walked to the stove and turned off the flame under her saucepan.

One of these days, she was going to get this right. One of these days, she'd find the perfect combination of timing and temperature that would produce the silky caramel that only a slowly simmered can of Eagle brand sweetened condensed milk could provide. She knew other women who could whip up the perfect treat without having can after can blow up in their faces, but, so far, success had eluded her.

A glob of sticky caramel dropped from the ceiling and onto the hood of Georgia's plastic poncho as she reached into the sink for a washrag.

"Want me to get the ladder?" Callie asked, peeking into the kitchen.

"I still have my raincoat in the car from last time. Should I get it?" Deborah Lee Tallman offered.

"I brought some praline sauce from that gourmet shop on Main Street. You know, just in case this happened again," Kelly said, crawling out from under the coffee table.

The other two members of the Tiara Club, Sierra Riley and Emma Rose Conover, headed for the linen closet, where Georgia kept her washrags and dish towels. They'd experienced the fallout of enough of Georgia's experiments to know the drill.

"This is all that arrogant Daniel Rogers's fault," Georgia grumbled, swiping at another glob of caramel that dripped from the ceiling onto her head.

"He was a mite rude," Callie agreed, gingerly stepping into the kitchen to help her friend clean up the mess. "But, really, what does it matter? So what if he thinks he can beat the Miracle Chef? We'll prove him wrong. Besides, you know that I appreciate it. I'm so glad you found it for me. I even tried to get one for my cousin, but the shop on Main said they'd never heard of it. Are you sure you don't remember where you bought it?"

Georgia busied herself with removing her safety goggles, taking great care not to yank out any more clumps of her hair as she did so. She set the goggles on the kitchen counter, rinsed out her washrag, and tackled another smear of caramel before answering, "No, I don't remember. And I think it's a bad idea for this TV show to come here to Ocean Sands. I mean, can this guy even find a Miracle Chef to use on his show?"

Callie breezily waved her hand in the air, dismissing Georgia's concerns. "Oh, don't worry about that. I told him I'd be delighted to let him use mine. I'm actually glad the Miracle Chef is so hard to find. My cousin turns pea green with envy every time I use it. Since she's the one always braggin' about how *her* husband would never run off and leave her for another man, I'm actually kind of glad she can't find one."

Georgia gently squeezed her friend's arm. Callie had taken her husband's defection over to the gay side with remarkably good humor, especially since before Jim left her, he quit a lucrative job in banking to join a cult, thus drastically reducing the amount of child support he was able to provide. Overnight, Callie had gone from being a pampered former beauty queen with four lovely children, a nanny, a full-time maid, and a seat on the board of the Junior League to a former beauty queen with four lovely children, a full-time-plus job, and a dwindling bank account that only stayed in the black by occasionally selling off pieces of the family silver.

"Look, let's just leave this mess for now. I can clean up after y'all leave," Georgia said.

The Tiara Club members protested and refused to adjourn to the sitting room, for which Georgia was secretly grateful. The true test of friendship, she figured, was in who stayed behind to help clean up after a party was over. It looked like all the members of their little group passed that test.

Georgia and Callie were the founding members of the Tiara Club, a group they'd laughingly formed one night after a few too many martinis. Their membership, they decided, giggling over the memory of putting glue on their behinds to keep their swimsuits from creeping and taping their breasts together to create the illusion of cleavage, would consist of recovering beauty queens who had survived the pageant circuit. Deborah Lee Tallman, Kelly Bremer, and Emma Rose Conover (who was also Georgia's cousin) had dabbled in the beauty pageant ring but hadn't gone all the way to the Miss Mississippi competition like Callie and Georgia had done in their prime. Sierra Riley was a pageant virgin and a relative newcomer to the South who taught first grade at the school where Callie's twin boys were currently enrolled. Callie had figured any woman who could cheerfully handle thirty hyperactive six-year-olds every day ought to qualify for Tiara Club membership, whether or not she'd ever set foot on a runway.

The main goal of the group, as far as anyone could tell, was to drink their way alphabetically through the sixth edition of *The Bartender's Black Book*. After two-plus years of meetings, they were only just getting started on the B's, with tonight's featured drink being the banana-cream pie martini. With more than 2,600 drink recipes, Georgia figured the club would still be going strong when all the members were well into their eighties. That is, if their livers held out that long.

So far, in addition to sampling six versions of the Alabama Slammer, three Bahama Mamas, and thirteen various B-number-something drinks, the Tiara Club had been through one birth, four divorces (one each for Callie and Georgia, and two for Kelly, who insisted that there was a vast difference between getting a man and actually *keeping* him for any length of time), fourteen funerals, countless church potlucks, and twenty-three weddings. With Callie's own wedding just three weeks away, that last number would go to twenty-four—with all of the members of the Tiara Club playing a part: Callie as bride, Georgia as maid of honor, and the rest of the group as bridesmaids.

Oh, yes, and they'd survived four explosions while Georgia continued trying to perfect her caramel-making process.

"So, how are the wedding plans coming along?" Sierra asked, tentatively swiping at a brown spot on Georgia's pad of paper.

Georgia wasn't sure whether the wistful note she heard in Sierra's voice was there because she was disappointed that there would be no homemade caramel again this evening, or if it was Callie's impending nuptials that had her feeling blue. Sierra and her boyfriend, Tim, had been living together for more than five years now, but as far as Georgia knew, Tim had never once asked Sierra to marry him. Of course, it was possible that he had and that Sierra had turned him down. Georgia didn't like to pry, so she'd never broached the subject with the Tiara Club's newest member.

Callie responded with one of those laughs that wasn't really a laugh and said, "Let's just say it's a good thing this is my second trip down the aisle. I have much lower expectations this time around."

Deborah Lee's hand flew to her throat, looking as horrified as if Callie had just admitted to disliking grits or fried okra. "That's a terrible thing to say," she whispered.

Georgia had to turn away to hide her smile. Deborah Lee liked to believe they all lived in a world of cotton candy clouds where everyone was sweet to everyone else and fairy tales really did come true. Of course, since she had married her high school sweetheart twenty-five years ago and they were still disgustingly happy together, Georgia allowed that maybe in Deborah Lee's world, all of that was true. For the rest of the Tiara Club members, however, life hadn't always been so kind.

Callie's laugh was genuine this time as she gave Deborah Lee's shoulder a friendly squeeze. "Oh, you know what I mean. It just isn't as important to me this time that I have the perfect wedding. With trying to fit everything in between the kids and the dress shop and cooking and cleaning and all, it's inevitable that things are going to fall through the cracks. And that's fine by me. Trey assures me that our honeymoon is going to be heaven, and that's all that really matters."

"I don't know," Kelly said, grabbing a carrot stick from the vegetable tray Georgia had set out earlier and doing a surprisingly good imitation of Bugs Bunny as she loudly crunched off the tip and leaned back against the doorjamb. "I've never had any trouble with the wedding ceremony or the honeymoon. It's the actual marriage part that disagrees with me."

"Oh, you're awful," Deborah Lee said, throwing a wet dish towel at her friend.

"Besides, I'm sure Georgia can give Callie a few tips on what *not* to do to make her marriage to Trey a success," Emma Rose added.

Georgia shot her cousin a "knock it off" look from across the room. She didn't understand why Emma Rose continued to make a big deal out of the fact that Georgia's best friend was marrying her ex-husband. After all, it wasn't like Callie had stolen Trey from her. Their marriage had broken up long before Callie had even come back to Ocean Sands after her own marriage had ended in such disaster.

Always the peacemaker, Deborah Lee ended the awkward silence that had descended upon Georgia's kitchen by cheerfully announcing, "Well, it looks like we're all cleaned up here. Why don't we take our drinks out into the parlor, hmm?"

Georgia looked around her gleaming kitchen. This was certainly one way to keep the place spotless month after month. "Thanks y'all. Let me whip up another batch of martinis and then we can—"

Her telephone rang, startling her. She picked up the receiver as her friends filed back into the sitting room. "Hello," she answered, pressing the phone to her ear and reaching for her own half-full martini glass.

"Georgia, honey, it's Mama. I'm so sorry to call. I know you've got your girlfriends over there."

Georgia smothered a sigh. Mama called nearly every time the Tiara Club got together, and she always apologized as sweetly as if this were the first time she'd interrupted her daughter's girls' night in.

"That's all right, Mama. Is something wrong?"

"Oh, dear, I know this is silly, but . . . well, I'm feeling so lonely to-night. Ever since you moved to your own place, I just can't help but wonder what the good Lord has planned for the rest of my life. Surely, He can't mean for me to live alone for many more years. I just don't think I can bear it."

Georgia flicked open the kitchen curtains and looked down the quiet, oak tree–lined street where her old Victorian house was located. She could see the lights on in the second-floor-bedroom window five houses down and across the street where her mother lived. If the apron strings were any tighter, Georgia would have been strangled by now.

She was tempted to ask her mother why, after living alone for the past eleven years, she couldn't seem to adjust to being by herself. But she knew it wouldn't do any good. Mama would just go on about how Georgia was all she had left in the world.

It was an awful thing to know she was being manipulated but not be able to do anything about it. The pattern had been established so long ago that Georgia didn't know how to break out of it. Even this small re-bellion of moving into her own home after her divorce was final four and a half years ago seemed too much for Mama to bear. She had ex-pected her daughter to move back home after her marriage to Ocean Sands's golden boy had ended. Instead, Georgia had bought this house on the same block as her mother, hoping that Mama's protests would die down after the first few months.

They hadn't.

Georgia looked out over her front porch and frowned into the dark-ness. She loved this old house, with its creaky front steps, wide-plank pine floors, and doors that didn't quite fit right after a century of set-tling. No matter how much her mother complained, she couldn't give up her home—or the small measure of freedom she had gained by liv-ing alone. Georgia was a devoted daughter, but she had already sacri-ficed enough for her mother's happiness.

Still, the despair-filled tones of her mother's pleas had her worried, so she knew she might as well give in right now. There was no use try-ing to cajole Mama out of a full-out mope. Georgia knew from experi-ence that it wouldn't work.

She poured her martini down the drain and rinsed out her glass. "All right, Mama, I'll come on over. How about if I bring my copy of *Miss Congeniality*? We can curl up on the sofa and have some popcorn and it'll be just like going to the theater."

"That sounds delightful, dear. I'll go get my air popper out of the cupboard. You know how much healthier it is to make popcorn that way. We girls have to watch our figures, don't we?"

Georgia cringed when her mother actually giggled. She'd been "watching her figure" since she was four years old and a Little Miss Pageant judge had taken Mama aside after one event and told her that Georgia would have placed higher in the competition if her legs weren't so pudgy. It was all celery sticks and raisins after that, except for the occasional cookie Daddy slipped her behind Mama's back.

Muttering something appropriate, Georgia ended the call and went into the parlor to face her friends. "Sorry, guys, but I have to go. Mama's in one of her moods again. Y'all are welcome to stay, though. I've got plenty of vodka and banana liqueur left."

Callie delicately covered a yawn with the back of her hand. "Well, I don't know about the rest of you, but I'm ready to call it a night. Caroline was up three times last night with a tummy ache and I've got an early morning tomorrow. Besides, I'm sure the kids have about wore my former mother-in-law out by now."

"I think I'll be going, too," Kelly agreed. "I've got a busy week ahead. Might as well make tonight an early night. It's the last one I'll have for a few days."

Sierra and Deborah Lee made similar comments about turning in early, leaving Georgia's cousin Emma Rose as the only one who didn't voice an eagerness to end the evening. Still, she didn't protest as the group headed out the door and into the warm night. Georgia waved good-bye to all but Emma Rose and Callie, who both lived just down the street from Georgia and her mother. Emma Rose had never moved out of her mother's house—both she and her brother, Beau, had lived under the same roof nearly all their lives. Callie, on the other hand, had spent a good decade away from Ocean Sands when she moved away to attend college with Georgia at Ole Miss, and then later when she married and moved to a posh neighborhood in Jackson. Her divorce had brought her back to Ocean Sands permanently two and a half years ago, when she, her children, and her ex-mother-in-law moved into the house her own parents had bequeathed to her after their death.

As she, Callie, and Emma Rose walked down the street, Georgia couldn't help but think that this was why the South was so steeped in tradition. When you lived in the same house your own parents had grown up in, doing things in new and different ways just didn't seem natural.

Georgia stopped to give her cousin a quick hug when they passed the gate that marked the entrance to the Conover home. The springs creaked like they always did when Emma Rose pushed open the faded white gate, letting out the scent of blooming yellow roses and cigar smoke.

"Well, hey there. What are you pretty girls doing out this time of night? Don't you know that wolves go on the prowl when the moon comes out?"

Georgia rolled her eyes skyward as Emma Rose's brother, Beau, stepped out of the shadows of the Conover's wide front porch. In true mocking-Southern-gentleman form, he leaned up against one of the columns flanking the steps, causally crossed his legs at the ankle, and took another deep pull on his cigar, letting the smoke out in a thick cloud as he exhaled.

"I don't think we're in any danger of being waylaid by scoundrels," Georgia said dryly.

"I'm the only one here who's not directly related to you, and it's been a long time since I needed protection from the likes of you," Callie added.

"Ouch," Beau said and then grinned, his teeth gleaming white in the darkness.

Georgia often thought that her cousin looked like just what she expected the devil might if he came to earth, with his perfectly tanned skin, jet-black hair, and dark, unfathomable eyes. He was handsome as sin and, according to rumor, had tempted a good measure of Ocean Sands' females into bed with him. The four members of the Tiara Club who were not related to Beau, however, seemed immune to his charms; a fact for which Georgia was grateful, since she knew her cousin had no intention of sticking with any one woman longer than it took cream to curdle in the icebox.

"Besides, I heard that you and Miranda Kingsley are an item. Doesn't that take you out of prowler mode, at least for a week or two?" Georgia asked, folding her arms on the top of the fence as if she had all evening to stand around needling her cousin. Which she did. Mama would be fine. Just knowing she had ended Georgia's fun would be enough to settle her down.

Georgia winced at that ugly thought. She knew her mother didn't exactly have her "moods" on purpose, but the timing of her lonely spells certainly did seem suspicious.

Beau's smile turned to a frown as he exhaled the last of his cigar smoke, tossed the butt down, and ground it into the dirt with his heel. "How in the world did you know about that? I just asked her out today at lunch."

Beside her on the sidewalk, Callie gave a mocking laugh as she answered Beau's question with one of her own. "Don't you know you can't keep secrets in this town?"

Georgia looked down at the leaf-strewn path leading up to the Conover's porch and then up at the lighted second-story window of her mother's house. Then she glanced back at her own house, with its cheery Chinese-red painted shutters and darkened attic. And as she and Callie waved good-bye to Emma Rose and Beau and turned to make their way down the quiet, tree-lined street, all she could think was, *Yes, when it's important enough, you can.*

Two

"Genteel poverty is not what it's cracked up to be," Georgia muttered under her breath, looking from the bill in her hand to her computer screen and back. She'd set both herself and her mother up on on-line banking years ago, without bothering to tell Mama she was going high-tech. Since Vivian Hughes Elliot had no intention of ever, in her entire life, interacting with—*shudder*—bill collectors, it was just as well that Georgia didn't mind the task of dealing with her mother's finances. At least, she didn't mind it when there was enough money in her mother's accounts to pay her bills, that is.

Georgia sighed and picked up the cordless phone on the desk in the attic that she'd converted to a home office/laboratory. Mama answered the phone on the fourth ring, sounding as if she had just meandered into her house from an afternoon spent sipping sweet tea on a rocker on her porch.

"Ms. Vivian Elliot speaking. How may I help you?"

Georgia resisted the urge to roll her eyes at her mother's exaggerated Southern drawl. Mama sometimes acted as if she were the mistress of some sprawling plantation where servants hovered around every door, waiting to do her bidding (Georgia was certain that Mama had changed her imaginary minions from slaves to paid servants several years ago in order to be politically correct). The truth was far less appealing. Vivian Elliot lived in a hundred-year-old home that was badly in need of repair, without the funds necessary for more than the occasional patch job. Her "help" consisted of a neighborhood teenager who cleaned her house every other week for ten dollars an hour, and her daughter, who kept her sidewalk swept clean of fallen oak leaves and mowed her grass whenever the need arose. But Mama, with her delusions of grandeur, treated her old house as if it had housed presidents and foreign dignitaries, which Georgia supposed wasn't too far from reality—Ms. Vivian had entertained decades of Junior League presidents and Miss Mississippi hopefuls from outside of Ocean Sands, which she considered to be the same as foreigners.

"Mama, it's me," Georgia said into the phone. "Why do you have a bill from Russell's Stationery for three hundred dollars?"

"Because I needed some note cards printed up and Russell's does a better job than that new place on Post Street. I tried the Post Street store a few months ago, if you recall, and their work was sloppy. I refuse to use them again, even if they are less expensive."

Georgia sighed into the receiver. "Why can't you just use the prepackaged cards from Walgreen's? That would be a whole lot cheaper than having personalized cards printed up. My wedding invitations barely cost three hundred dollars."

"Yes, and look how that marriage turned out. Besides, you insisted on using recycled paper," Vivian said with a quiver of distaste, as if her daughter had written her invitations on old cardboard boxes in crayon instead of having them printed on perfectly nice ecru paper. "We've had this conversation before, dear. A proper Southern lady does not buy generic note cards from the drugstore. A proper Southern lady has cards embossed with her initials and lightly scents each page with her favorite fragrance before she drops it in the mail. This lends a personal touch to every note she writes."

"Well, as charming and delightful as that sounds, you can't afford such luxuries. Daddy didn't leave you with enough money to last forever and, at this rate, you're going to be completely broke well before you're eligible for social security. It won't hurt you to cut back on little things like personalized stationery."

"It's those 'little things,' as you call them, that set a true lady apart from the rest," Vivian answered sharply. "It's having finger bowls at each place setting for supper and knowing the proper fork to use for your shrimp and slipping a thank-you note in your host's mailbox as you leave so they'll receive your note first thing in the morning. Those are the things I taught you, the things my mama taught me, and I cannot—I *will* not—give them up."

Georgia sighed again. Loudly. "Well, then you're going to have to think of some other way to cut corners. I'm doing what I can to keep us both afloat, but I can't do it if you don't stop spending more than I bring in."

"You could always move back in here with me," Vivian suggested smoothly, as if she had been waiting for the opening. Which, of course, she had been.

"I'm not going to argue with you about this, Mama. I am a grown woman and entitled to live in my own home. If Trey and I were still married, I'd be living with him right now, so you'd have to come to terms with being on your own. This is no different."

"I never did understand why you divorced that boy," Vivian said, completely changing the subject.

Funny how Mama's memories of the circumstances of her daughter's divorce had changed once Trey Hunter had been elected mayor of Ocean Sands. Before that, she had no problem recalling that it had been Trey who had divorced her daughter and not the other way around. After Ocean Sands' golden boy had been sworn in as mayor, however, Vivian started remembering things a bit differently.

Not Georgia. She still remembered it all quite clearly; her now-ex-husband laughing at her attempt to finish college. His final, hurtful comment: "Who needs brains with a body like yours?"

But Mama didn't need to know all that. Or perhaps Georgia feared that if she were to tell her mother the truth, she wasn't certain whose side Mama would take. In any event, all she said was, "My divorce has nothing to do with your finances, Mama. Can you please just try to rein in your spending for a while so we won't have to make a trip up to the county courthouse to file for bankruptcy? I sure would not want word of that getting around."

Vivian gasped in horror as if Georgia had just announced to a set of pageant judges that the way to end the world's overpopulation was to perform involuntary abortions on pregnant women—clearly an answer that would sabotage her bid for the all-important crown. "No. Surely we won't have to take such desperate measures?" her mother asked, her voice trembling.

Georgia choked back a laugh at her mother's response—the exact response that she had hoped to elicit, she might add. "No, we don't need to start making dresses out of the drapes just yet, but you do need to be more careful about how you spend your money. Otherwise, we might just have to consider less palatable alternatives."

Mama made an agreeable-sounding noise and hung up the phone, presumably off to find her smelling salts before she fainted at the thought of the scandal that filing for bankruptcy would create. Georgia shook her head, then blew an errant curl out of her eyes. She suspected her little lecture would work for a few weeks, and then her mother would resort to her usual spending habits, which Georgia liked to think of as the "fiddle dee dee, I'll think about that tomorrow" financial plan, which only worked if your first name was Scarlett and your last name was O'Hara. Oh, yeah, and only if you existed in fiction.

Georgia was spared any more nasty fiscal surprises when her front doorbell sounded. She wasn't expecting company, but she welcomed the interruption. Before coming upstairs to pay bills, she had taken a pitcher of tea off her sunny back porch and put it in the icebox. Now, with the sun nearly set, a glass of chilled iced tea with company would be a nice start to her evening.

Georgia padded downstairs in her socks, being careful not to slip on the smooth hardwood floor. She knew her mother would admonish her for not changing into "proper" shoes before opening the door, but Georgia figured that whoever was arriving unannounced would just have to take her as she was.

When she opened the door, she had a split second to wish she had a whiff of her mother's smelling salts, because the sight of the movie-star-handsome man standing outside on her front porch nearly made her drop to the floor in an old-fashioned swoon. She recognized him

immediately as Daniel Rogers, the insulting host of that Food TV show
Callie had been watching the other night. She had heard somewhere
that most celebrities were less good-looking in person, but that was certainly not the case with Daniel Rogers. His brown hair looked softer
and shinier, his blue eyes nearly aquamarine in the fading sunlight. His
face was all strong angles, like Rock Hudson or Cary Grant back in
their glory days. He wore a pair of off-white linen slacks topped with a
silvery blue silk shirt, and on his feet were a pair of the softest, buttery
tan leather loafers that Georgia had ever seen.

If this guy wasn't gay, he'd taken his makeover from the Fab Five of
Queer Eye for the Straight Guy fame very seriously. No heterosexual male
she knew could pull off the linen trousers/loafers with no socks look
like this.

Georgia swallowed, trying to get some saliva back into her suddenly
dry mouth, and said the first thing that came to her mind, "Mr. Rogers,
I presume?"

The corners of his perfect, not too thin and not too thick, mouth
curved up in a slight smile and he held out a hand by way of greeting.
"Yes. And you're Georgia Elliot, friend of Ms. Callie Walker Mitchell,
and inventor of the Miracle Chef."

Georgia's still-dry mouth dropped open with shock—an expression
her mother would have admonished with her usual, "Close your mouth,
dear. You weren't raised by Yankees." She felt as if her heart had stopped
beating in her chest.

This couldn't be happening. Daniel Rogers had no idea how critical
it was that no one in Ocean Sands—or anywhere else, for that
matter—discover her secret. If word got out, her life would never be the
same.

Recovering as quickly as possible, Georgia blinked and cocked her
head, smiling up at her handsome visitor. "Well, you've got one part of
that right. Callie Mitchell has been my best friend since we were five
years old. But I'm afraid you're mistaken about me inventing anything.
Why, I'm a member of the Junior League, I work at a little gift shop
over on the corner of Park and Main, and I've got my hands full takin'

care of my ailing mama. Even if I had the inclination to be an inventor, I surely don't have the time."

She fluttered her lashes up at Daniel Rogers and put one pink-fingernail-polish-tipped hand on his forearm. She felt his muscles tighten under her fingertips as he narrowed his eyes at her in disbelief. But before he could say anything further, they were interrupted by the sound of a man clearing his throat.

Daniel stepped to one side and turned toward the sound. A young man wearing a ragged blue uniform with tarnished gold buttons and wielding a musket that was nearly as tall as he was stood on the porch steps.

"Excuse me," the young man said, taking his hat off and shifting his weight sheepishly from one foot to the next. "I think I'm lost."

"I believe you're looking for twelve *South* Oak Street. This is twelve *North* Oak Street," Georgia said, stepping around Daniel and walking to the edge of the porch. "The street changes from North to South at Main, so if you'll just go back to Main and continue on for about a block, you'll find the Hall House there on the left."

"Thank you, ma'am," the young man said, doffing his navy blue cap as he turned to leave.

"You're welcome. Tell Miss Beall that Georgia Elliot says hey, would you?"

"Yes, ma'am," the young man said.

"What was that all about? And how did you know where that man was going?" Daniel asked, his gaze sliding from the retreating faux soldier to Georgia and back.

Georgia looked at him for a moment, considering the idea that had just come to her. She desperately needed Daniel Rogers to believe that she was a simple girl—a simple girl incapable of anything more than being able to serve tea to her guests without spilling it in their laps or cutting the crusts off her tomato sandwiches without written instructions. A simple girl who could *not* be the inventor of a product he had exposed on national television.

Daniel Rogers was just about to discover the lengths she would go in order to keep her secret from getting out. She hadn't kept it buried this deep for this long just to have it exposed by a perfect stranger who wanted nothing more than to show off his cooking skills in front of a live audience.

The stakes on her end were much greater . . . and much more personal.

Hopefully, though, deterring him would only take one small ruse. It had been her experience that men like Daniel Rogers—sophisticated, linen-trouser-wearing men who were not from the South—found the Southern obsession with all things Civil War related to be completely ridiculous. Since ridiculous was exactly how she wanted Daniel to perceive her, she figured she'd be smart to take advantage of the opportunity that fate had presented her.

"I don't think I can explain it," she said now, blinking up at him flirtatiously. "Why don't you come on down the street with me and I'll show you?"

He looked at her warily for a moment, then obviously decided he had nothing to lose by following her. Georgia started down the steps, cringing when she realized that she was still wearing just her socks with no shoes. She made sure she was on the far side of the sidewalk as they passed Mama's house. It was bad enough that she had greeted a stranger like that, but to be walking around town in broad daylight in her stocking feet would give her mother fits.

"Nice evening," she commented as an oak leaf drifted by her head on its way to the ground. A soft breeze blew, rustling through the dry leaves like a thousand wind chimes. There was a slight nip to the early autumn air, but Georgia loved this season. Unlike other parts of the country, the falling leaves were not the harbinger of month after month of gray skies and freezing rain or roads blocked for days by snowstorms. In Ocean Sands, winter meant bright blue skies and temperatures that almost never dipped below fifty degrees. It wasn't unheard of for her to wear short sleeves at Christmas, although that was the one day a year when she wished for New England–like weather.

"It is a nice evening," Daniel surprised her by agreeing. She wasn't sure what she'd expected—perhaps a comment about how much less humid it was in L.A. or some snide remark about old Mr. Talmadge's Buick cruising down Oak Street constituting a traffic jam or something.

It didn't take them long to get to Main Street, and once they did Georgia could see the hushed crowd standing on the sweeping lawn of the Hall House.

"It's much better to have an address on the south side of the street," Georgia remarked in an offhand manner. Indeed, Main Street was the dividing line between houses of a more palatial nature than those of Georgia and her mother, who lived north of Main. Of course, when Daddy had been alive, they'd lived on South Oak, in the house right next door to where Callie now lived, just across from the Hall House. Their fortunes since Daddy's death had definitely taken a turn in the wrong direction, Georgia thought, glancing across the street to the white columns flanking the doorway of her childhood home. It was a three-story Georgian (of course), far larger than their small family had ever needed, with leaded glass windows, black shutters, and a second-floor "pontificating balcony" from which Georgia and Callie, dressed up like mini Southern belles, used to wave down to their imaginary suitors when they were little girls.

"So I gathered," Daniel murmured beside her, stopping at the edge of Miss Beall's lawn to watch the goings-on.

The crowd, dressed in costumes from the 1860s, had parted, leaving a pathway for the navy-uniformed soldier who had mistakenly arrived on Georgia's doorstep to walk through. The young man knelt and laid his musket down on the steps. Then he reached into the gap between two buttons on his jacket, pulled out something shiny, and held it aloft. Just before the sun dipped below the horizon, it glanced off the metal object, blinding anyone who was looking directly at it at that exact moment.

The crowd gasped, and Georgia, shielding her eyes from the glare, choked back a distinctly unladylike snort of laughter.

"What is that he's holding?" Daniel whispered from beside her, apparently caught up in the drama of the moment.

"A fork," Georgia whispered back. "Repoussé, made by Kirk. It's one of the oldest silver patterns still made today."

Daniel turned to her, his big-screen blue eyes narrowed skeptically. "All of this fanfare for a fork?"

Georgia smiled. "It's a reenactment."

"A what? I thought you said it was a Re-poo-something-or-other."

"Repoussé," Georgia corrected, lifting one hand to brush a wayward lock of hair from her eyes. "That's the name of the silverware pattern, but what's going on here is a reenactment."

Daniel shook his head, as if trying to clear out the cobwebs clouding his brain and making this all sound like so much nonsense. Georgia bit back a grin. Her plan was working perfectly.

"You see, during the War of Northern Aggression—that's the Civil War to you Yankees—the Union soldiers marched through the South, burning the homes of our people, raping our women, and stealing our possessions. When Miss Beall's mama—she was young Miss Hall back then; this was before she even met Mr. Beall, whose family owned a string of mercantile stores in Ohio and, unlike most Southerners, was spared financial ruin in the War. He traveled down to Mississippi with a friend a few years after the war ended and was captivated by Miss Hall's ingenuity, not to mention her legendary beauty."

Georgia paused to take a breath, glancing up at Daniel from under her lashes to see if he was following her story. He seemed to be, so she continued, "Anyway, when Miss Hall heard the troops were heading toward Ocean Sands, she refused to bury her things or run like so many others had. Instead, she brought out all her finery—her best table linens, her great-grandmother's china, and the family's treasured silverware—and she proceeded to make the finest feast those boys had had in years. She threw open the doors of Hall House and invited the enemy in.

"Well, I can tell you, the commander of the troops was suspicious at first, but it didn't take long for him to be overcome by the smell of Miss Hall's roast ham and sweet-potato pie. His boys dug in and flat-out gorged themselves and, afterward, the story goes that you couldn't even walk across the lawn without tripping on a sleeping Yankee.

"The next day, the commander gathered his troops, and I heard tell that there were tears in his eyes when he kissed Miss Hall's hand before marching off. I think if he hadn't known a union between them would be doomed from the start—him being a Yankee and all—I think he would have asked Miss Hall to marry him that morning." Georgia sighed, caught up in the romance of the story that most likely had very little basis in reality, but sounded much cleaner and prettier than the truth had undoubtedly been.

Daniel slid his hands into the pockets of his trousers and rocked back on his heels, a smile playing about that perfect mouth of his. Georgia got the distinct impression that he was laughing at her, but she pretended not to notice.

"That doesn't explain the fork," he said, turning his head just a bit to watch the soldier kneeling down in front of an ancient woman who stood on the wide front steps of the pinkish brown colored house wearing full hoopskirts and a frilly purple hat.

"We-ell," Georgia said, dragging the word out so that it sounded like two. "Two days after the troops left, Miss Hall was taking a lie-down in the heat of the afternoon when she heard a knock at her front door. She could only afford to have her servants come in for half days, so she herself crept downstairs to see who was at the door. She was alone in the house, with no one around for miles, you see, so she was mighty frightened."

"Mighty frightened?" Daniel repeated, raising his eyebrows.

Georgia figured then that she might be piling it on a bit thick but could hardly change horses midstream, as it were, so she widened her eyes innocently and continued, "Why yes. During the War, all manner of horrendous things happened to our women, especially ones living alone with no sort of male protection." Georgia feared that her mascara might be falling off in clumps with all the eyelash batting she was doing.

"Sounds like Miss Hall was doing just fine," Daniel remarked dryly.

Georgia couldn't help but grin, so she coughed to cover her response. "Yes, she wasn't *entirely* helpless."

"Women like that never are."

Georgia coughed again, covering her mouth with one hand. "Oh, excuse me," she said, once she'd smothered the urge to laugh.

"All right, so our intrepid heroine is huddled behind the door of the family mansion, nearly shaking her knickers off in fright. What happens next?"

This time, Georgia cleared her throat to stop from laughing. "Well, it wasn't exactly like that."

"No? Do tell."

"Typically, these reenactments attempt to be as historically accurate as possible, but the police told Miss Beall a few years ago that she had to stop acting out the story as it really happened. Seems they started worrying when she shot Sheriff Mooney in the foot while she was trying to prove to him that her revolver wasn't loaded."

"That would definitely cause me to worry, too," Daniel agreed.

"Miss Beall insists that she would have missed him entirely if he hadn't leapt off the sofa when she pulled the trigger, but the sheriff contends that if he hadn't moved, she most likely would have shot him in the gut."

"Sounds like Miss Beall takes after her mother."

"You're not the first to draw that conclusion. But getting back to our story, Miss Hall was no quivering miss just waiting for the Yankees to come slaughter her while she slept—"

"Do you think they would have rung the doorbell if that had been their intention?" Daniel interrupted smoothly.

Georgia allowed herself a small smile at that. "Most likely not, but you never know with Yankees. They can't be trusted."

"So I've heard," Daniel said, looking completely serious.

"In any event, Miss Hall was taking no chances, so she pulled out the revolver she always kept under her pillow and then whipped out the pistol she kept strapped to her thigh—"

"She slept with a pistol strapped to her thigh? That brings a whole new meaning to safe sex," Daniel said.

Georgia bit her tongue and pretended that Daniel's comment had gone over her head. "It was wartime. She was only doing what she had to do to protect herself."

"Right. Of course. What's the difference, by the way?" Daniel asked. "I mean, between a pistol and a revolver."

Frustrated that he wouldn't let her finish her story, Georgia resisted the urge to frown at the man standing beside her. Instead, she just said, "I don't know. May I finish?" a bit more peevishly than she probably should have, and nodded her satisfaction when Daniel took his hands out of his pockets, waved them in the air, and said, "By all means. Go ahead."

"Thank you. Now, as I was saying, Miss Hall crept downstairs with her revolver in one hand and her pistol in the other. Slowly, so as not to let the varmint out on the front steps know she was coming, she let herself out the side door—the one the servants used to bring food into the kitchen without having to drag things through the house and risk soiling the carpets—and came around to the front to surprise whoever was at the front door."

Daniel looked like he wanted to say something, but he refrained, so Georgia continued, "So, she peeks out around the corner of the house, but instead of seeing a full battalion of Union troops like she'd expected, there's just this one lonely young man, looking all nervous and worried and wringing his hat in his hands until it nearly fell apart right there on Miss Hall's front porch.

"Miss Hall still didn't trust that the soldier didn't mean her any harm, but he sure didn't look like someone she should fear, so, keeping her guns trained on the young man's back, she positioned herself out of sight behind a shrub and called out for the man to identify himself. That poor boy nearly dropped dead right then, hearing a voice coming from out of nowhere and not knowing that the lady of the house had snuck up behind him. He threw his hands in the air, dropped his musket on the steps, where it clattered to the ground, and pulled this silver fork from out of his uniform."

"I knew you'd get around to the fork if I just waited for it," Daniel said, raising his fist triumphantly.

Georgia scowled. "Of course I was getting around to the fork. Isn't that the point of this whole story?"

Daniel was shaking his head. "Honest to God, I really wasn't sure."

"Hmph," Georgia snorted.

Daniel put his palms up in surrender. "Okay, okay. I'm sorry. So what's the rest of the story? Did the commander send this lad back to

Miss Hall's with a new salad fork to show his undying devotion to the lady? Was the commander really a Confederate spy, and there was a coded message hidden in the hollow stem of the fork? What?"

Georgia crossed her arms across her chest and continued scowling. "Are you making fun of me?"

Daniel smiled down at her and Georgia found herself rooted to the warm sidewalk, struggling to draw a breath. She felt the same as she had the day she and Callie had climbed out of Callie's second-floor bedroom window and into the magnolia tree in the Walker's backyard. Always the first one to try something dangerous, Georgia had shimmied backward out the window and onto the wide limb of the tree, but hadn't figured on the slope of the limb or the slipperiness of the tree's bark, both of which combined to make her slide down the branch, lose her grip on the tree, and fall to the ground with a heavy thud, knocking all the air out of her lungs. She lay on the hard ground, staring up at the puffy white clouds in the sky, wondering if she was going to die from lack of oxygen. She had finally gasped like a dying fish, sucking in a lungful of air while Callie worriedly paced beside her, afraid her friend was genuinely hurt but equally afraid her parents would kill them both if they found out what the girls had been up to in the first place.

"Are you okay? Your skin seems to be turning blue," Daniel observed, his smile turning to a concerned frown as he reached out to touch her arm.

Georgia jerked in a breath as his warm fingers closed over her skin. She felt a sudden jolt of electricity, as if her heart had just been shocked back to life after a cardiac arrest. Then she started coughing, patting her chest with one hand as oxygen returned to her lungs. "Yes, sorry. I'm fine. I just . . . breathed in a bug, I think," she said, using the first excuse she could think of aside from admitting that she had been struck dumb by this man's good looks. For heaven's sake, it wasn't like Daniel Rogers was the first handsome man who'd ever smiled at her. As a former beauty queen, she'd been squired around by some of the most attractive men in the country, if not the world.

Chiding herself for acting like a starstruck teen, Georgia cleared her throat one final time and turned to watch as the reenactment wrapped up, with the crowd applauding and clapping the Union soldier on the back as he collected his musket from the steps.

"So how did the story really end?" Daniel asked after it quieted down a bit.

Georgia tried to recall what she had been saying when she'd lost her breath—and apparently, her mind, as well. "Oh, yes, the reason for the young man's return. Seems this youth had become accustomed to the thieving ways of the—"

Daniel held up a hand to stop her. "Don't say it. The Union soldiers weren't the only ones who committed atrocities during the Civil War."

Georgia conceded the point with a nod. "All right, then, let's just say the lad had seen the riches of his Southern brethren and had learned that none of his fellow soldiers seemed to mind helping themselves, so he figured he might as well join them."

"That's better."

"Hmm. Well, so this boy, being welcomed into the home of a proper lady and served the best of what she had to offer, had not realized that the typical lack of morals he had applied to earlier situations would not be acceptable here. When his commander found out that the soldier had stolen one of Miss Hall's serving forks, he ordered the youth to march back to Ocean Sands without delay and return it. Whether the boy learned the lesson of proper gentlemanly conduct or not, I couldn't tell you. But at least Miss Hall got her fork back."

"Did Miss Hall shoot the kid?" Daniel asked.

Georgia's horrified look was probably all the answer Daniel needed, but she elaborated anyway, "Why, of course not. No lady would dishonor herself by killing a man who had come to right a wrong. Besides, the boy had thrown down his gun. Miss Hall would never have shot an unarmed man in the back like some coward. Well-bred Southern ladies just don't do things like that."

Daniel went in for the kill before Georgia even realized his true intent. She was so lulled off guard by his seeming interest in the story of Miss Hall's role in the redemption of the Union soldier that she had completely forgotten that she was only using the reenactment to distract him from his original line of questioning. That's why it took her by surprise when he turned, flashed his Hollywood smile at her again, and said, "Is that why you won't admit to inventing the Miracle Chef, Miss Elliot? Because that's also not the sort of thing well-bred Southern ladies do?"

Three

"Well, aren't you just like a hound dog with a juicy ol' bone," Georgia said with a lilting laugh once she had regained her composure.

Watching her, Daniel tried not to be impressed by her act. After all, growing up in Hollywood with parents who were famous actors, he'd seen his fair share of chicanery. Still, Georgia Elliot was pretty damn good at seeming to be no more than a beautiful airhead whose only skill was outrageous flirtation.

Too bad he wasn't buying it.

Before he'd even called Callie Mitchell to talk to her about the letter she'd sent in to *Epicurean Explorer*, he'd Googled the Miracle Chef to find out as much as he could about the product. When the search returned no results, Daniel had been puzzled. He'd thought for a moment and then surfed to Williams-Sonoma to see if they carried the product. When that turned up nothing, he tried Sur La Table, Chef's Choice, and then Cooks' World.

Still nothing. But no way was he giving up. He tried several more cooking stores, all with the same result.

"What sort of company makes a product that isn't available anywhere?" he grumbled, then had an idea. He looked up the URL of the United States Patent and Trademark Office and clicked the link to go to the official government site to do a patent search on the Miracle Chef. He typed "Miracle Chef" into the keyword box and limited the date range to search only the years 1976 and above. His curiosity nearly got the better of him when he saw that patent information was available going all the way back to 1790. It sure would be interesting to see what sorts of inventions people had come up with over two hundred years ago, but he needed to stay focused on the task at hand.

The patent search was amazingly easy. And fast. After the hour he'd spent fruitlessly perusing on-line kitchen-supply stores for the Miracle Chef, he'd expected his search at the U.S. government site to take days, not seconds. In fact, he'd almost relished the idea of having to dig through an archaic, labyrinthine set of data to finally discover the origin of this so-called miracle product. To his disappointment, the information on the patent holder of the Miracle Chef popped up almost immediately.

The patent was held by one Georgia Marie Elliot in Ocean Sands, Mississippi.

Daniel stared at the name of the inventor for a moment. Georgia Marie Elliot. He wondered why Ms. Elliot hadn't told her best friend that she was the inventor of the timesaving gadget. It was obvious from Callie Walker's letter that she didn't know her friend was behind the Miracle Chef's creation.

Propping his feet up on an open drawer, Daniel leaned back in his chair and skimmed the patent application. Then, unable to resist a good mystery, he went back to Google and typed "Georgia Marie Elliot" in the search box.

The soles of his Italian leather loafers hit the floor after he clicked the link to the first result. He was certain he looked like some kind of cartoon character—staring as his computer screen with his eyeballs bulging and his mouth wide open. This was even more of a surprise than discovering that Ms. Elliot was the Miracle Chef's inventor. He supposed he expected that Georgia Elliot would be a stout, bespectacled, elderly woman, and that the link he had just clicked would lead him to some university's science department.

Instead, his screen displayed the image of a woman about his age with teased blond hair and exotic-shaped brown eyes. She was wearing a dark blue one-piece swimsuit and was smiling into the camera with the practiced ease of someone who had done this sort of thing a million times before. A white banner was slung diagonally from her right shoulder to her left hip, with "Shrimp Festival Queen" written in bold red letters. Some sort of crown was perched atop her head, winking and glittering in the lights overhead.

Just then, his watch had beeped and he realized that he was going to be late for dinner with his parents and his sister Kylie, who was visiting from Seattle with her husband and their triplets.

Hurriedly, he had shut down his computer and grabbed his keys from the top drawer of his desk. Callie Mitchell's letter spun slightly on his desk as he got up and headed toward the door, but Daniel's mind had still been on Georgia Elliot—the secret inventor trapped inside the body of a beauty queen.

He'd told himself before flying to Mississippi that his main reason for coming to Ocean Sands was not to meet the mysterious woman who had invented the Miracle Chef, but to get his hands on one of the damn things so he could prove to his viewers that his skills as a chef were superior to some stupid machine. But now, with the patent holder standing right there trying to "aw, shucks" him into believing she didn't know what he was talking about, Daniel was even more intrigued. And, while Georgia's "hound dog with a bone" comment was—he was certain—her ultrapolite way of telling him to mind his own damn business, she had no idea how accurate a description that was for him when he wanted to get to the bottom of something.

However, it looked like his sleuthing would have to wait, because the beautiful Ms. Elliot had turned her back on him and was walking away. In two strides, Daniel caught up with her, again casually sliding his hands into the pockets of his slacks.

"So, how long have you lived here in Ocean Sands?" he asked.

Her answer, when it came, sounded reluctant, as if she'd rather not have answered, but felt compelled by politeness to do so. "All my life, except for the three years I lived in Oxford while attending Ole Miss. The University of Mississippi, that is."

"Only three years? You must have worked your, um, fanny off to graduate that quickly," Daniel said, impressed.

"I didn't graduate," Georgia said shortly, with no further explanation.

"Oh." Daniel didn't know what else to say, but was saved from thinking up another topic of conversation when someone called Georgia's name from across the street. Beside him, Georgia hissed in a breath as if she'd just been caught with her hand in a forbidden cookie jar.

Ah, yet another mystery, he thought, turning toward the sound of the woman's voice.

A stunningly beautiful woman who appeared to be in her midforties came wafting down the wide steps of a graciously decaying Victorian home and stopped on the bottom stair, obviously waiting for them to come to her.

Georgia looked as if she were mentally calculating the distance to her own house and thinking about making a run for it, so Daniel put a hand firmly under her elbow to stop her from bolting. He guided her across the street, feeling her reluctance grow with every footstep.

As they got closer, the older woman started shaking her head, raising one hand to her throat as her head moved from side to side.

"Georgia Marie Elliot, you tell me right now that those are not socks that you have on your feet," the woman said.

Daniel looked down at Georgia's foot, noticing for the first time that she wasn't wearing any shoes.

"There's no need to cause a scene, Mama. I don't believe the head of the Social Register was lurking around Miss Beall's reenactment, waiting to catch me outside without my shoes on."

Mama? This was Georgia's mother? Daniel's own mother was no slouch in the looks department, but over the years she had become rounder and softer and less . . . glamorous than she had been in her youth. But this woman looked as if she were probably still fighting off the advances of college guys.

It wouldn't win him any points with Georgia or get him any closer to solving the mystery of the Miracle Chef to stand there gawking at her mother though, so, instead, Daniel held out his right hand and said, "I'm Daniel Rogers. Pleased to meet you. And you can blame me for dragging your daughter outside like this. We were interrupted by a Union soldier who came knocking at her door and I just had to know what was afoot. Miss Elliot was kind enough to show me to the performance and remained there to tell my poor ignorant self the story of the stolen fork. I'm much obliged to her, and apologize if I've embarrassed her—or you—in any way. My folks always did say that my curiosity had the upper hand over my common sense. Sadly, they're right more often than not." He added his most charming, self-deprecating smile for good measure, and was not surprised when Georgia's mother clasped his hand warmly in both of her own.

"My dear boy, I hardly think anyone would ever label you poor or ignorant. Now, why don't you come on in and let me get you a glass of lemonade. Or maybe even a cocktail if you're so inclined. After all, it *is* past five o'clock and the evening is perfect for a well-aged Scotch, don't you think?"

Daniel inclined his head. "Yes, ma'am, I do believe a glass of Scotch whiskey would go down nicely this time of day. While we're at it, maybe we can have ourselves a nice chat about your daughter. Did you know she in—"

"Insisted that Mr. Rogers stay for supper," Georgia interrupted smoothly, with a not-too-gentle but surreptitious shove that had Daniel nearly tripping over his own feet. "Unfortunately, he has other plans for the evening. Isn't that right, Daniel?"

"No. Actually I have nothing on my schedule until the morning, with the exception of finding myself a place to stay for the night. I greatly appreciate the invitation, Miss Elliot." He turned to Georgia's mother and added, "Unless you mind, of course, Mrs. Elliot?"

The older woman reached out and put a hand on his arm, gently pulling him next to her on the porch step. "Why, of course, I don't mind. I'd love the company. Ever since Georgia moved away, I'm alone more nights than I care to admit. Now, please, do call me Vivian, won't you? Mrs. Elliot makes me sound like somebody's mother."

"You *are* somebody's mother. And, for God's sake, I only moved across the street," Daniel heard Georgia grumble behind him as he led Vivian up the stairs and opened the screen door, motioning for the two women to precede him into the house.

————

Georgia used her big toe to push the porch swing backward, then pulled her leg up under her as the swing gently rocked back and forth. What the world could use was a self-rocking swing, one that, once set in motion, wouldn't stop until the user turned it off. Hmm. There had to be a way to make something like that work. Maybe if—

"You're being awfully quiet," Daniel said, interrupting her thoughts.

Georgia took a sip of the white wine her mother had poured her. Vivian herself had opted for Scotch, as had Daniel, who looked every inch the wealthy Southern gentleman, sipping whiskey on the front porch of her mother's home. Before she could respond, her mother laughed and said, "My Georgia has always been a bit of a dreamer."

Acknowledging her mother's comment with a small smile, Georgia put her foot down and stopped the swing. "Yes, that's true enough. I suppose I ought to get dinner started if we want to eat before midnight. Is anyone opposed to fried chicken? I set some to soaking in buttermilk last night for supper tonight. But I suppose I could whip up some pasta instead, if that would be more to your liking."

"Fried chicken is fine with me, dear," Vivian said, knocking back a healthy swallow of her drink.

"That's fine with me, too. But you know, what I'd really like to see is how you'd cook that in that Miracle Chef you gave to your friend Callie Mitchell. You wouldn't happen to know what I'm talking about, would you, Vivian?"

Georgia dribbled wine down the front of her dress as her hand jerked in surprise. Swearing under her breath, she dabbed at the moisture with the embroidered linen cocktail napkin her mother had pressed into her hand along with her glass of wine. Damn him! Why couldn't he just let it go?

"Mama doesn't know anything about the Miracle Chef," she said, glaring at Daniel Rogers.

"What's this you're talking about?" Vivian asked.

"The Miracle Chef," Daniel repeated before Georgia could think of a way to shut him up. "According to the patent information I read on-line, it's a system that cooks with pressurized dry steam. I'm not exactly sure what dry steam is, but Ms. Mitchell claimed that it could cook a four-course meal in under thirty minutes—a pretty amazing feat if you ask me. However, since Ms. Mitchell seems to be the only one in possession of this elusive product, I have no way of seeing how it works in person."

"I know where you can get one," Vivian said, sipping her Scotch and looking from Georgia to Daniel and back again.

"Where?" Daniel asked.

"Mother, I don't want—" Georgia began.

"Georgia has one," Vivian interrupted, either ignoring or not sensing her daughter's warning tone. "Why, just the other night she made homemade chicken and dumplings, string beans, and the best apple cake I've had in years. All in the time it took me to finish writing up the week's batch of thank-you letters."

Daniel's gaze was steady on Georgia's. "I would greatly appreciate a demonstration of this miraculous product. You might even say that it would be the highlight of my trip to Ocean Sands. Aside from meeting you lovely ladies, of course," he added, bathing them in the glow of one of those charming smiles of his.

"Go on and get that contraption, dear. You can't disappoint him. He's our guest."

"Our *pest* is more like it," Georgia muttered under her breath, low enough so that only Daniel could hear.

Then she put her wineglass down on one of the glass-topped patio tables. There was no use arguing. She hadn't realized that Mama had paid enough attention the other night to realize that she was late getting supper ready and had brought her Miracle Chef over to get herself out of a jam. On the nights they dined together, Mama liked to eat supper at eight o'clock sharp. Last week, Georgia had been working on a new project and had lost track of the time. Rather than just toss together a salad and make up some lie about being on a diet (a lie she knew her mother would use as an excuse to watch every ounce of fat Georgia put into her mouth for the next twelve months, at least), she grabbed her Miracle Chef and set off down the street to start supper. Mama must have noticed the product's name imprinted on the bottom of the unit when she'd helped to dry the dishes.

Georgia had found that her mother tended to be observant at all the wrong times.

Like when she broke a nail and didn't have time to repair it before an important social event. Mama noticed that. But when her daughter's husband had walked out on her and her heart was broken, Vivian had barely even acknowledged that, except to tell her that it wasn't ladylike to cry in public and that people would only forgive her that sin during the first month after her breakup.

"Let me escort you back to your house," Daniel offered, setting his own glass down next to Georgia's wineglass before standing and smoothing his palms down over his fashionably wrinkled trousers.

"No, that's all right. I believe I can safely make my way across the street and back. But thank you," Georgia said, struggling to keep her tone polite and not sarcastic. "Why don't you stay here and keep Mama company? As she said, she's unbearably lonely now that I've moved away."

With that, Georgia stalked off to do her mother's bidding, frustrated to be trapped in the patterns of the past, but unwilling to change her own behavior and break free of them. She supposed that was the basis for most traditions—the good ones and the bad.

In less than five minutes, she was back on Mama's porch with the Miracle Chef in hand and a pair of shoes on her feet, only to find that Daniel and her mother had gone inside.

Probably up in the trophy room, Georgia figured, letting the screen door bang behind her as she let herself into the house. She refused to go up there, heading instead for the kitchen to get started on supper. She set her Miracle Chef on the large butcher block in the center of the kitchen and looked at it, a sense of pride welling up in her chest.

She had invented this. Her. Georgia Elliot. Former beauty queen, dreamer, college dropout.

And the real miracle was, it worked. She had tinkered with it for nearly a year, testing everything from the exact size of the pressure-release valve in the lid, to the interlocking removable pans, to the best metal to use as the base material. Month after month she'd tested different variations of her invention, all in her spare time after work and

Junior League and the Tiara Club and taking care of Mama whenever she felt lonely, which was remarkably often for a woman with Vivian Elliot's social connections.

Georgia could still remember the look on Callie's face when Georgia had told her that she had a surprise for her friend. Callie had been complaining since moving back to Ocean Sands that she never had time to make a real supper for her family anymore. Georgia, seeing so many busy families drift apart because they didn't eat together, had vowed that this wouldn't happen to her best friend. So she'd tinkered and tested until the Miracle Chef was perfect. Then she'd found a manufacturer who could turn out as many Miracle Chefs as she wanted and had one made for Callie, who loved it nearly as much as Georgia did.

She hadn't said anything the night of the Tiara Club meeting, but she'd called the manufacturer last week to do another small production run for her so she could give Deborah Lee, Sierra, and a few other friends Miracle Chefs of their own. She still wasn't quite sure how she was going to give them their gifts without telling them where she'd gotten them, but she was certain she'd be able to think up something when the time came.

Resisting the urge to stroke the smooth metal of her first real professional-grade invention, Georgia turned to the icebox and removed the plastic tub of chicken she'd prepared the night before. She needed to drain it and pat it dry before dredging it in the egg wash and cornmeal crust she liked, but first she'd better get the okra to cooking. Otherwise, it would be hard and tough and nobody would be able to eat it.

Georgia rocked back on her heels, blinking.

Of course, she thought, smacking her forehead with the palm of one hand. If the food she made this evening tasted awful, Daniel would never air the Miracle Chef cook-off on his show. It would just make him look foolish. And the bottom line was, she couldn't afford to let her secret get out, no matter how proud she might be of her invention.

She eyed the chicken on the counter, planning her next move. If Mama's food tasted bad, she'd know that Georgia had sabotaged the meal, but if only Daniel's food was horrible, he would think that she and Mama just didn't know the difference. Heck, he probably already thought Southerners couldn't tell the difference between cabbage and caviar. She would just be reinforcing his opinion, thus convincing him that Callie's glowing recommendation of the Miracle Chef was completely unjustified, which would, in turn, convince him to go back to California, where he belonged.

A slow grin spread across her face—a grin she was quick to extinguish when she heard footsteps in the dining room that adjoined the kitchen. Whirling around, she turned and opened a cabinet door, reaching up on her tiptoes to grab a set of bowls off the top shelf.

"Here, let me get those for you," Daniel offered, striding across the kitchen to take the wobbling glass bowls out of her hands.

He was standing close to her, his front nearly touching her back, and Georgia could feel the heat from his body reaching out to envelop her. His chest was hard against her shoulders, his arms muscular and strong where they brushed hers. Trapped between him and the counter, Georgia stood frozen by the nearly overwhelming desire to press herself to him, but, before she did anything stupid, Daniel stepped back and set the bowls on the butcher block next to the Miracle Chef. Their contact had lasted only a second, but it left Georgia desperately trying to calm her pulse and steady her breathing.

She closed her eyes, trying to erase the feel of his body against hers.

"Is something wrong?" Daniel asked, and Georgia opened her eyes and turned to find him watching her with a frown.

She looked out the window, saw the neighbor girls riding their bikes in the yard next to her mother's, innocently laughing as they raced after each another in the dry, crackling grass. Georgia drew in a deep breath and cleared her mind of all its carnal thoughts. "No, everything's fine. I assume Mama showed you the trophy room?" she asked brightly, reaching into the refrigerator for the bottle of wine and pouring herself and Daniel each a glass.

"The trophy room?" Daniel asked, absently picking up his wine.

"The shrine where Mama pays homage to all things beauty pageant," Georgia elaborated. "Mama thinks there's no higher calling for a girl than to prance around a stage in a swimsuit with a tiara on her head."

"I heard that," her mother said from the doorway of the kitchen.

"I figured you might."

"Say what you will, those pageants paid off. I met your daddy through the Miss Mississippi competition."

Georgia heaped a cupful of cornmeal into one of the mixing bowls and then added a spoonful of salt before glancing up at Daniel and filling in the details of the story she'd heard over and over since birth. "Daddy's company was one of the sponsors of the pageant that year and he got some free tickets. He brought along one of his clients, who took one look at Mama and decided to meet her backstage after the competition was over."

"He didn't even care that I hadn't won," Vivian added with a tinkling laugh.

Cracking two eggs into a separate bowl, Georgia continued, "Daddy arranged it so he and his client could meet Mama after the show, but once he met her in person, he was determined to have her for himself. He lost that client, but he and Mama were married less than two months later."

"Georgia's daddy was a very single-minded man," Vivian added, stepping into the room and hefting a heavy scrapbook up onto the butcher block next to where Georgia was busily engaged in whisking the eggs.

As Vivian proudly showed Daniel clippings of her pageant career, Georgia patted the chicken dry with paper towels and laid each piece on a platter in preparation for dredging in the mix.

"Do you prefer breasts or thighs?" she asked in an attempt to make sure she only sabotaged Daniel's part of the supper.

Daniel choked on his wine, covering his mouth as he sputtered and coughed. "Excuse me?" he asked when he could finally speak again.

Georgia looked from the pictures of half-dressed women her mother was proudly showing off to Daniel's mottled red face and realized that he hadn't known that she'd been talking about supper. Chuckling, she pointed to the platter of meat. "I meant the chicken."

Daniel grinned, his blue-green eyes sparkling with humor. "Of course you did. Well, I'm a thigh man, myself. I think breasts are highly overrated."

Georgia looked down at her own barely-B cups and hid a smile. "Thighs it is," she murmured, letting her mother drag Daniel's attention back to her prized newspaper clippings.

She dredged each piece of meat in a mixture of egg and buttermilk, then dragged it through the bowl filled with flour, cornmeal, and spices. When only the two remaining thighs were left to coat, Georgia turned her back to her mother and Daniel and surreptitiously added a cup of salt to the breading mixture. During the Miracle Chef's cooking process, the extra salt would leach every extra ounce of moisture out of Daniel's chicken, leaving it as dry as the county would be if Reverend Jackson had his way. When the last two pieces of chicken had been coated, she neatly arranged them in the bottom section of the Miracle Chef. She decided to pass on the okra and make a simple green bean and tomato mixture instead. That would be easy to overcook because Mama liked her vegetables as bland and slimy as possible and Daniel would most likely blame it on the Miracle Chef. She'd finish it off with undercooked grits (she'd leave hers and Mama's in for a few minutes more after scooping some out for Daniel) and a pineapple upside-down cake with a little added surprise.

In less than an hour, Daniel Rogers would be convinced that taking on the Miracle Chef would be a complete waste of his time.

Four

"Your chicken looks a little dry," Georgia said, sounding concerned.

"No, no, it's fine," Daniel insisted, reaching for a glass of water to wash down the leatherlike meat. A sort of tasteless porridge that he assumed was supposed to be grits had spread into a puddle on his plate, encroaching on the red-and-green slop that he guessed had once been green beans and tomatoes. Without a doubt, this was one of the worst meals he'd ever eaten.

Of course, his opinion may have been a bit skewed. When he was growing up, the family cook was more likely to pack his lunchbox with coq au vin than PB&J, and Kraft macaroni and cheese was something he only learned about during college.

Still, this meal was nearly inedible, and it was only Daniel's good manners that kept him shoveling one forkful of the awful food after another into his mouth.

"There's plenty left if you want seconds," Georgia offered with a smile.

Daniel fingered the edge of the napkin that lay across his knees and studied the blonde sitting across from him. She *had* to be pulling his leg, right?

He watched as she brought a hand up to smooth back a wayward curl. He would have expected her fingernails to be long and painted a bright red like her mother's, but instead, her nails were short, neatly trimmed, and painted with a demure pink polish. She had a small, slightly upturned nose, marred by a smattering of freckles across the bridge that he figured a heavier hand at the makeup table would hide. Obviously, she wasn't as concerned with covering her every flaw as her mother, who had hidden even the tiniest laugh line on her face.

"So, what did you think of our town's little reenactment?" Vivian asked, setting her knife on one edge of her plate and putting a microscopic bite of food into her mouth.

"It was interesting. I've heard about battle reenactments, but not ones like that."

"Yes, it's pretty silly isn't it?" Georgia asked, as if prompting him to mock the event.

"I didn't say that," Daniel insisted.

"We know a lot of outsiders like to think Southern traditions are ridiculous."

Daniel cocked his head and smiled across the table at Georgia. "Do you know who I am?" he asked, seemingly apropos of nothing.

Georgia finished chewing and swallowed, wiping her mouth with her own napkin before answering, "You're the host of *Epicurean Explorer* and the bestselling author of several food and travel books. I read your latest and enjoyed it very much, by the way. *I'm in Brussels, Where Are the Sprouts?* wasn't it?"

"Amusing title," Vivian interjected.

"Thank you. But that's not what I meant. My parents are George and Elizabeth Rogers. Hollywood's golden couple. I grew up watching people getting paid enormous sums of money to pretend to be witches or cowboys or space aliens—or sometimes all three at once. If you think the retelling of a story from the Civil War is going to faze me, you don't know who you're dealing with." Daniel took a bite of his chicken as if to prove the point.

"I didn't know that," Georgia admitted reluctantly.

"Then you're the only one in America who doesn't. Believe me, it's a lot easier to hit the *New York Times* bestseller list when your parents are household names." Knowing that he was on the verge of sounding like an ungrateful whiner—everybody get out your Kleenex, poor little rich kid Daniel Rogers can't touch anything without it turning to gold—

Daniel put his napkin on the table and stood up. "Are you ladies finished? Let me take your plates into the kitchen."

Georgia waved him back down with an odd sort of look on her face, as if she wanted to say something but wasn't certain that it would be polite. "I'll take care of these. I've got to get dessert anyway. Would either of you like some coffee? I can brew a pot while I'm up," she offered.

"I'll take a cup. But are you sure you don't want me to help?"

"Georgia can handle it. She's very efficient," Vivian answered before her daughter could. "We'll take our coffee in the living room. I'll show you some of my favorite video clips from our pageants."

Georgia groaned loudly enough for Daniel to hear, but Vivian had already left the room, obviously excited about getting to show off her treasures to a newcomer.

"Please, tell her you don't want to watch those things," Georgia said, stacking her mother's nearly full plate on top of her own.

"Oh, I don't mind. Remember, I'm a guy. Looking at beautiful women isn't exactly a hardship for me."

Georgia looked up as Daniel smiled at her. She shivered at the force of all that male attractiveness being directed at her from such a short distance away. This guy was dangerous—both because he knew the secret she most needed to keep buried and because she was more fascinated by him than she'd been by any man since her husband had divorced her nearly five years ago. But then again, what was the harm in that? Most likely, Daniel Rogers would be gone by this time tomorrow. What could it hurt to stop fighting the attraction between them? After all, it wasn't as if they were going to forge a lifelong bond in the next hour or two before he left her mother's house and, more than likely, was out of her life forever.

So Georgia allowed herself to smile back at him, even sashayed a bit as she walked past him into the kitchen. Then she spied the cake cooling on the counter and gave her reflection in the mirror a wry grimace. Once Daniel tasted her sorry excuse for a dessert, he'd probably not even wait until tomorrow to leave Ocean Sands.

Which is exactly what you want, right?

"Of course it is," Georgia muttered under her breath as she pulled the carafe out of the coffeemaker and turned to fill it with water. And it was more than just that she *wanted* him to go, she desperately *needed* him to leave Ocean Sands exactly the way he'd found it.

In no time at all, the smell of freshly brewed coffee filled the air. Georgia piled three plates of whipped cream–topped pineapple upside-down cake on a tray with silverware, napkins, and everything she needed to serve coffee. As she entered the living room with the carefully stacked tray, Daniel immediately stood up and offered to relieve her of her burden.

Although he seemed bent on destroying her life, Georgia had to admit that he had impeccable manners.

"I've got it," she assured him, setting the tray down on the coffee table and immediately handing him the plate of cake that she'd set nearest the uppermost left edge of the tray. She poured them all cups of coffee before handing her mother a plate of dessert and taking the last piece for herself.

Her mother ignored the cake, picking up her coffee instead as she excitedly scooted to the edge of the wingback chair she was sitting in and turning up the volume of the television. "Oh, look. Here we come."

Georgia took a bite of cake and watched Daniel out of the corner of her eye as he raised his fork to his lips. His eyes were transfixed on the TV screen where Georgia and Vivian were walking down a runway wearing clear acrylic high heels and matching emerald green, one-piece bathing suits. The sashes cutting diagonally across their torsos were labeled "Ocean Sands" in green ink.

"Last year's mother-daughter Christmas pageant," Georgia supplied helpfully, taking another bite of her cake.

"You guys still do these things?" Daniel asked, lowering his fork back to his plate without taking a bite.

"Of course we do. Why wouldn't we?" Vivian asked with a slight frown in his direction.

Daniel cleared his throat. "Well, I just assumed after a woman reached a certain age, she stopped entering beauty pageants, that's all."

"Oh, no. Mama plans to be entering pageants until she's Miss Beall's age, don't you?"

"I don't know why I shouldn't. After all, I'm just as pretty as the day your Daddy and I met. Why should I let a silly thing like the calendar stop me from winning competitions?"

Georgia scooped up a giant forkful of whipping cream and stuffed it in her mouth, studying Daniel as he watched her and her mother giving their rear views to the judges. He seemed mildly shocked, which annoyed her for some reason.

"It's not pornography, you know," she said.

Daniel gave his head a small shake and lifted his fork again. "Of course not. I'm sure you and Vivian get a lot of enjoyment out of this sort of thing."

"Pageants are not for fun. They're a way of life," Georgia said softly, just as Daniel took a big bite of his cake.

He chewed once and then stopped, and Georgia nearly burst out laughing at the look on his face. Instead, she bit her bottom lip and attempted to look concerned. "What? You don't like my pineapple upside-down cake? It's my great-grandmother's recipe."

Daniel swallowed his cake without chewing it again. Picking up his napkin, he dabbed at his lips. "It's very moist, but . . . ah, don't you think it tastes a bit like chicken?"

Georgia had to fight to keep the smirk off her face. Well, yes, *his* piece might have just the slightest bit of poultry flavor. Especially since she'd doused it with canned chicken broth before serving it to him. She forced the corners of her mouth down in a sincere worried frown. "Why no, I don't think so at all. Are you certain? Maybe you should take another bite just to be sure?"

Daniel glared at her suspiciously and said, "No, that's all right. I'm perfectly convinced that something is wrong here."

Georgia lowered her gaze to her mother's cherry hardwood floor and followed the pattern of the pretty pink-and-blue Oriental carpet under her feet. "I'm sure you're right," she said, folding her hands together on her lap. "You know, that Miracle Chef probably makes it so that the food you cook on the top layer absorbs the odors of the foods cooked underneath it. Mama and I have most likely become accustomed to it. It's not like we're fine gourmet chefs like you." She looked up and blinked innocently. Yeah, that's right. They were just a couple of dumb Southerners who could barely boil water without a recipe.

"Uh huh. Well, I do believe it's time that I should be going. I appreciate your hospitality and all, but I need to find myself a hotel and get settled in for the night."

"Yes, you'll want to be nice and refreshed when you go back to L.A. in the morning," Georgia agreed, standing up to show Daniel to the door. She couldn't believe her plan had worked so beautifully. It just went to show you, it was much easier to go along with someone's expectations than to try to change their minds about a thing. Once she'd realized that Daniel's real goal in all this was to prove the Miracle Chef was worthless, all she'd had to do was give him the evidence he was already expecting to find.

It was just like when she'd tried to go back to school after she and Trey got married. She'd dropped out of Ole Miss years before, but was confident that she could pick up where she had left off. Instead, she'd floundered for the first few weeks, then flunked her first Discrete Mathematics test.

"Well, honey, what did you expect? Someone as pretty as you doesn't *need* to be smart," Trey had said. Then he'd nuzzled her neck, and Georgia realized that her husband had married her despite her brain, not because of it. Treating her academic failure as if it were what he expected—as if it were what she should expect from herself, as well—undermined her already fragile self-confidence and she quit. It was easier to become the pretty, frivolous wife Trey wanted her to be than to fight him and her own self-doubts every step of the way.

"If you don't have a hotel booked, you should just stay here."

Her mother's words ripped Georgia out of her fog of remembered hurt. She looked up to find that movie star smile of Daniel's spreading across his face, and she wanted to throw herself down on the hardwood floor and pitch a good old-fashioned screaming fit. Damn Mama, anyway.

"Yes, then you could see *all* of Mama's videos, even the ones from her early years," Georgia said, hoping that would convince him to find shelter elsewhere.

Daniel's smile widened into a flat-out grin. "See, I keep telling you that watching beautiful women parade around on a stage is not something I consider a bad thing. You don't seem to be getting that."

Georgia tried not to bare her teeth when she smiled back. "Fine. Go ahead. Stay here. Watch beauty pageant videos to your heart's content. Mama, the guest room's all made up. I made sure there were towels in the bathroom and clean sheets on the bed after Aunt Joyce and Aunt Margaret visited. You should be all set. You two have fun now, you hear," she called, waving as she picked up the Miracle Chef that she'd washed and set in the front hall earlier.

Mama let her go with a soft "good night," but Daniel followed her out into the hall.

"I don't suppose your mother has any videos of you doing the pageant circuit, does she?" he asked, grinning down at her wolfishly.

Georgia clutched the Miracle Chef to her chest, the metal rim of the lid digging into her collarbone. "Yes," she answered quietly. "She does. You should ask to see the ones from when I was four. Those are my favorite."

Then, without giving him a chance to respond, Georgia turned on her heel and let herself out into the dark night.

Five

"Good-bye, Mrs. Jackson. I'll see you in an hour," Sierra Riley said, pushing the classroom door closed behind her and ruefully shaking her head. As if one solid oak door could contain the exuberant squeals of the six-year-olds shut inside the room. She passed the door leading to the teachers' lounge and briefly considered stopping in the lavatory to try to do something with her hair, but figured it was just no use. She almost always kept her unruly mass of red hair clipped back in a ponytail. She had enough to worry about, keeping control of her first-graders, she didn't have time to worry about her errant hair as well. Besides, no amount of primping would put her in the same league as the women she was going to meet.

Sierra sighed and tugged her pink blouse back into place. She didn't know how the Southern beauties who made up the Tiara Club always managed to look so poised and graceful. She felt like an unattractive klutz next to them.

Ah well, why should her life in Ocean Sands be any different than anywhere else? She was an outsider wherever she went; the new kid in town always doing her best to fit in. Or, barring that, to at least remain unnoticed, because in the half a dozen towns where she'd moved growing up, getting noticed was not a good thing. Getting noticed got you picked on and harassed and sometimes even beat up. Although those times were decades behind her, Sierra hadn't outgrown the feeling that she would never belong, no matter where she lived.

Which was why Callie Mitchell's easy friendship had come as such a surprise. Sierra had met Callie last year, when her oldest son, Jimmy, was in Sierra's first-grade class. They'd struck up a conversation over cupcakes at the Ocean Sands Elementary School's Halloween party, and Callie had invited her to lunch the next week. That lunch had led to another, and then another, and Sierra had been more than a little surprised when, less than a year later, Callie asked if Sierra would do her the honor of being one of her bridesmaids. And with Callie's acceptance came the invitation to join the Tiara Club, where, once again, Sierra struggled not to feel like an outsider among the group of former beauty queens.

As she pushed open the door to Callie's dress shop, Sierra figured she should just give up all hope of trying to fit in with this crowd. She was a good ten pounds heavier and four inches shorter than anyone else in the room. She must have been a fool to agree to come down to the shop while the rest of the Tiara Club were here doing the final fitting of their dresses for Callie's wedding. Four of Callie's five bridesmaids were stripped down to their underwear, lounging around the dress shop as if it were a bordello.

The women all seemed to be talking at once, and Sierra could only make out snippets of the conversation, words like "Hollywood" and "supper" and "reenactment" being bandied about.

Just then, Callie stepped out of the back room, her arms filled with an acre of midnight blue satin.

"Oh. Hey, Sierra. Come on in," Callie said when she saw her hovering near the door as if she were about to bolt.

Georgia, Emma Rose, Kelly, and Deborah Lee looked up from their conversation and Sierra was warmed a bit by the friendliness she saw in their eyes. She didn't know quite why she always expected them to suddenly turn on her, as if they were only pretending to be nice to her until they'd lulled her into thinking they actually liked her, only to rip their masks off when she least expected it.

"Hey," she said back, stepping farther into the shop.

"Georgia, you're up first," Callie announced, dropping the load of dresses on a table near a squat set of steps placed in front of three full-length mirrors.

Georgia Elliot, Sierra decided as she dropped her shapeless tan bag on the floor and slid into a chair, was every man's fantasy girl come to life. With the exception of her smallish breasts, she was perfect. Wildly curly blond hair, long legs, elegantly slim hands and feet, one of those cute little upturned noses, almond-shaped dark eyes. But the funny thing was, she acted as if her looks meant nothing. Which, Sierra supposed, could be because Georgia was so accustomed to being beautiful that she took it for granted. But Sierra didn't think that was it. It was more like Georgia didn't give herself any credit for how she looked at all.

"Ew, you need to take the hips in a bit. That flare right there makes her butt look enormous," Kelly Bremer said.

"Got it," Callie noted, taking a pin from the cushion at her wrist and using it to mark several places on the satin dress draped over Georgia's body.

Sierra sat in her chair and blinked in openmouthed shock as Georgia's friends picked apart the fit of her dress. Even sweet-tempered Deborah Lee surprised Sierra by standing back and remarking critically, "And it's too loose in the chest. If you don't take it in, she'll end up lookin' like a boy."

Rather than act insulted, Georgia obediently twisted and turned until no part of her anatomy had been spared. It was only as she stepped down off the dais that Georgia noticed the green pallor of Sierra's skin.

"Are you all right?" Georgia asked before turning to Emma Rose and ordering, "Run and get her a Sprite, would you? I think she's going to be sick."

Sierra blinked several times and then sat up straight, suddenly feeling the need to fan her warm face. "No, that's all right. I'm fine," she said, putting a hand to her mouth and mumbling through her fingers.

"Honey, what's wrong? You look like you've seen a ghost." Deborah Lee sat down on the arm of the love seat next to her and patted her arm.

"You're not pregnant, are you?" Callie asked, eyes wide.

Sierra swallowed and hastily stood up. "God, no. Don't even *think* that. Tim would kill me if I got pregnant," she said, turning just in time to miss seeing the narrow-eyed looks being bandied around behind her back.

"Then what's wrong?" Emma Rose asked, returning from the back room with a Dixie cup full of bubbling soda.

Sierra gratefully took the cup Emma Rose offered and slowly took a sip. She didn't understand this. How was it that they could all be so mean to Georgia and then act as if nothing was wrong? Uncomfortable with the other women's scrutiny, Sierra looked down at the beige speckled carpet beneath her feet. "Um, it's nothing really. I just thought . . . uh, that maybe you all were being just a little . . . I don't know. Harsh, maybe?" She looked up and gave a sort of fake laugh to cover her discomfort. "I guess it's just the schoolteacher in me. I want everyone to play nice."

Georgia looked at Emma Rose, who gaped back at her. Similar looks were exchanged between Kelly and Deborah Lee, and Callie and Georgia, before they all started to laugh. And not nice little ladylike chuckles, either. Big, snorting, back-slapping guffaws.

"What?" Sierra asked, knowing there must be some private joke that she was missing.

Callie straightened up and wiped her eyes, attempting to get her breath back. "Oh. I'm sorry. We're not laughing at you," she said, stopping to wipe her eyes again.

"Yeah," Sierra said more than a little peevishly, dropping back into the chair she'd vacated moments before. "You're laughing with me. I get it."

Callie scooted Sierra over with her hip and put an arm around her shoulders. "No, don't get mad. I really am sorry. We forget sometimes that you haven't spent years up on the auction block like the rest of us. Believe me, what Georgia just went through is nothing compared to the things pageant judges say about you."

"We're all used to being picked apart, right down to the color nail polish we choose to wear," Emma Rose agreed, coming over to perch on the arm of the chair beside Sierra.

"If you're even the tiniest bit bloated, you can bet some judge is going to notice and mark you down on your score sheet," Deborah Lee said.

"I once had a judge take points off because he thought my toes were too long," Georgia added with a shrug, plopping down on the sofa across from her.

"I got ten points deducted for a mole on my shoulder," Kelly added.

"I didn't make it to the final round of one pageant because one judge thought my ears weren't big enough," Callie tossed into the mix with a "bet you can't top that" look in her eyes.

As the women tossed out successively more outrageous "flaws" they'd been criticized for, Sierra started to laugh. Soon, her eyes were running and her sides beginning to hurt. She threw her hands up in surrender. "Okay, okay. I'm beginning to understand," she said. "I have a newfound respect for beauty queens. How you all can come out of that experience with even a smidgen of self-esteem left is beyond me."

Georgia smiled at her as she stood up and began to dress in what Sierra assumed were the clothes she'd worn to work that morning. "Well, one thing I'll say for beauty pageants—after years of being subjected to such intense scrutiny, you learn how to smile and make everyone believe you're having the best day of your life even when your world is falling apart."

And with that, Georgia waved to her friends and left the dress shop, leaving Sierra to wonder if Georgia Elliot's seemingly perfect life maybe wasn't so perfect after all.

Daniel had one last person to see before he could deem the Miracle Chef matter a complete debacle. Standing outside Callie Mitchell's faded gray house, he yawned and rubbed the back of his neck.

Georgia Elliot's mama sure was enthusiastic about her beauty pageants. Last night after Georgia had left, Vivian had shown him tape after tape, saying after each one, "You can't go to bed yet, I'm working up to the Miss Mississippi competition. You've got to see that." Contrary to what he'd told Georgia, Daniel actually didn't much care to watch endless hours of beautiful women doing nothing more than strutting across a stage. Yes, these young women were bright and talented, but it was a bit like watching golf, except the players in the beauty pageant wore swimsuits instead of plaid pants.

He'd woken up later than usual this morning—not surprising since his body's internal clock was still two hours behind—only to discover that Callie Walker Mitchell, whose glowing letter had unwittingly set this whole thing in motion, had already left for work. Tracking her down was laughably easy. He'd asked the woman who answered the Mitchell's phone where Ms. Mitchell worked and she told him he could find her at Callie's Couture on Main Street.

When he arrived at Callie Mitchell's place of business, however, he was met with a roomful of women being fitted for their bridesmaids' dresses—it seemed like there were at least half a dozen of them in varying states of undress when he'd walked in the front door. He was shooed out amidst a cacophony of squealing and giggling (one of the bridesmaids had even managed to slip her telephone number into his jacket pocket, Daniel noticed later as he was fishing around for his keys) by Ms. Mitchell herself, who looked quite harried but said she'd be delighted to talk with him about the Miracle Chef. Did he mind dropping by her house after work? Say 5:30ish?

So, here he was, dropping by her house. Daniel glanced at his watch. 5:30 on the dot.

He rang the doorbell again and heard a variety of thumps and bumps from inside the house, but the door did not open. Daniel raised his hand to knock on the door when it was flung open from inside and a streak of white came barreling out and crashed into his legs, sending both he and the white streak careening backward. Daniel landed butt-first on the porch with a grinning imp of a girl tangled around his legs.

"Are you okay?" Daniel asked, once he'd managed to get his breath back.

"Caroline, where are you?" someone called from inside the house.

The little girl—Caroline, Daniel presumed—quickly extricated herself from their tangle of limbs and made as if to dash off the porch, but Daniel grabbed the back of her white dress before she could do so. He hadn't been around kids that much, but he guessed that this child, who couldn't be more than two or three years old, probably shouldn't be allowed to run out into the street.

The girl squealed with laughter, put her hands in the air, and in a split second, she was gone, leaving Daniel sitting on the porch, dumbly holding her dress in one hand.

He looked up as Callie Mitchell burst through the front door, her thick auburn hair floating around her as if she were the model in a shampoo commercial.

"Caroline, get back here," Callie shouted to the naked girl who was streaking across the front lawn with childlike abandon. Without pausing, she said, "Hello, Daniel. Please do come in. I'll be right with you." Then she took off across the lawn after the errant child.

Daniel watched as the little girl evaded capture for several more minutes. Then suddenly, she stopped, crouching down in the grass as if trying to get a closer look at something.

"Caroline, no," Callie said, stopping ten feet from the girl. "We've talked about this a hundred times. This is totally inappropriate behavior and you know it."

The child grinned up at her mother. Then she started peeing.

Daniel turned away, smothering a laugh. He heard Callie's long-suffering sigh, even from twenty feet away, and guessed this was not the first time her daughter had engaged in such "totally inappropriate behavior."

A few minutes later, Callie had the child by the hand and was leading her back up the porch steps. Daniel handed her the girl's dress as they passed and noticed that Callie wouldn't meet his eyes. Her cheeks were bright red as she took the dress and mumbled, "Thank you."

Daniel followed Callie and the naked child into the house. "Don't worry about it. I have a sister exactly like her."

"Does she pee on the lawn, right in full view of all your neighbors?" Callie asked dryly.

"Not anymore," Daniel answered, closing the front door behind him.

That elicited a chuckle from the girl's mother. "At least I can hope that this one will outgrow it, too. I'll be right back. Please make yourself at home," she said, waving him into a tidy living room before disappearing down a hall with the now docile toddler behind her.

Daniel seated himself on the couch and quickly took in the room, which looked as if it had been transported directly from a decorator's showroom. There were knickknacks in all the appropriate places, small touches like a shallow bowl filled with decorative pinecones on the coffee table and never-to-be-lit candles arranged artfully on the mantle. This was not a room that people actually lived in, more a parlor than a living room, Daniel thought.

Callie Mitchell entered the room bearing two tall glasses of what Daniel guessed was iced tea.

"I thought you might like some tea," she said, proving his guess to be correct as she handed him a glass. Smoothly, she pulled two coasters seemingly out of nowhere, placed one directly in front of him, and then set her own glass down on the other.

"Cute kid," Daniel said, taking a sip of his iced tea.

"She's a devil in the guise of an angel, just like her daddy. Don't let those big brown eyes fool you."

Daniel laughed. "Like I said, I have a sister who's just like her. She looks at you, all innocence and light and then—wham!—she's landed you right in the middle of one disaster or another. I feel sorry for her husband. I don't think he knew what he was getting into. For instance, she got pregnant last year, but could she just have one baby? No-o. Not even twins for my little sister. She went off and had *triplets*. Can you imagine?"

"Bless her heart," Callie said, leaning forward to take a drink of tea.

Daniel wasn't sure exactly what that expression meant, but assumed Callie was agreeing with his assessment of the situation. "Precisely," he said. "So, is Caroline your only child? I know you said in your letter how many children you have, but I've forgotten."

It was Callie's turn to laugh. "Heavens, no. Besides my little hellion, I've got the twins and my oldest. He's seven. The twins are six."

"Wow. You have your hands full."

"That I do," Callie agreed. "Fortunately, all but Caroline are in school full-time this year, so that makes things a little easier. I could never do it without my mother-in-law. With one person, you just don't have enough time to do all that needs doing. Not with me working a full-time job. That's why I love the Miracle Chef. Now I have the time to cook supper for my family, which I think is really important. Before, I just couldn't do it—at least not the way I wanted to. Growing up, I remember sitting around the supper table talking to my parents about things that had happened that day. As I got older, I didn't appreciate it. I mean, my friends got to eat TV dinners in their rooms while I had to actually eat with my family. Yuck." She smiled wryly.

Daniel nodded. "Yeah, I'll bet most teenagers feel the same way— like being with your parents is punishment for something."

"Exactly. But looking back, I see that it forced me to interact every day with the people who cared about me the most. Some of my friends could go for a week without really talking to their parents. By then, they had time to erect that parental deflection shield that all teens have so that when problems arose, their parents were the last to know. I don't want that to happen with me and my children."

"That's understandable," Daniel said, remembering all the nights he and his sisters had eaten dinner alone while their parents were off filming in one exotic location or another. He loved his parents, had no deep childhood scars from being "forced" to eat gourmet meals without them, but he did admit that he had not turned to his folks for help when he'd been faced with the typical teen struggles because he had sometimes felt as though they were merely polite strangers who occasionally lived in the same house.

"If you'd like to see the Miracle Chef in action, why don't you stay for supper? I'll warn you that it gets a bit hectic around here at mealtimes, but if you're up to the challenge, so am I," Callie offered as she smiled at him and lifted her iced tea in a mocking salute.

"You're on," Daniel said, knocking his glass against Callie's to seal the deal.

Georgia finished tying the blue tulle bow on Mrs. Rydell's gift for the upcoming nuptials of Callie Mitchell and Trey Hunter and wondered how many more of Ocean Sands' residents were going to ask for her advice about what to get the couple for their wedding. Not that she hadn't expected to be asked for her opinion.

She *was* Callie's maid of honor after all. In a place like Ocean Sands, where the population was reaching fifty thousand but it still felt like a small town, attendance at social functions would be close to zero if the hosts started excluding exes and outcasts.

At first, of course, Callie's relationship with Trey had been a bit awkward for Georgia. Even though Callie hadn't been living in Ocean Sands while Georgia and Trey were married, and it had been nearly three years since the divorce when Trey and Callie started dating, there were still some situations that even the best of friends struggled to deal with. For her part, Callie had even gone so far as to ask Georgia's permission for she and Trey to date. And Georgia, whose misgivings had more to do with her ex-husband's personality traits than any lingering feelings she might have for him, felt the gracious thing to do would be to give her consent and let Callie find out for herself what a dud Trey could be.

Only, she hadn't. Or maybe Callie was just willing to overlook the aspects of Trey's character that had driven Georgia crazy in return for a husband. Now that Trey and Callie were engaged, it was something Georgia really couldn't ask Callie about without seeming petty and jealous.

Which she was not. She was merely concerned about her best friend's future happiness, but it was only in hindsight that she realized she should have voiced her concerns when Callie had first approached her about dating Trey. With only a few weeks left until the wedding, it seemed a bit too late to be bringing up objections now.

"There you go, Mrs. Rydell. My mama's motto is that no home is complete without a deviled egg plate. I'm sure Callie will be delighted with it," Georgia said, pushing the neatly wrapped box containing a Waterford crystal deviled egg plate across the counter.

Mrs. Rydell balanced the package under the same arm that carried her massive pocketbook. "Thank you, honey."

The bells tied onto the front door of the Uniquely Yours gift shop jangled and Georgia looked up to see her cousin Emma Rose enter the store, excitement shining in her eyes.

"Hey Georgia. Mrs. Rydell," Emma Rose said, stopping to feign interest in a set of vegetable-shaped porcelain bowls.

"Hey Emma Rose. How's your mama?" Mrs. Rydell asked. "I never see her down at the club."

"The club" was the Ocean Sands Golf and Country Club, of which both Mrs. Rydell and Emma Rose knew Emma Rose's mother was not a member because, although her pedigree was impeccable, her reputation was not. The dark side of living in the same town your whole life, Georgia thought, was that it was impossible to escape the sins of your father . . . or your mother, as the case may be. Mrs. Rydell meant the question as a put-down and everyone present knew it.

Twin circles of color appeared on Emma Rose's cheeks and Georgia feared that her cousin might be tempted to brain Mrs. Rydell with the cute eggplant-shaped bowl that Georgia had just unpacked that morning. In order to avert such a disaster (especially since Georgia knew she'd have to charge Emma Rose for the piece if she broke it across Mrs. Rydell's mean-spirited thick skull), Georgia stepped out from behind the cash register and went to stand next to her cousin.

"My aunt is fine, thank you. She's just been busy helping Beau with the restaurant and doesn't have much time left for socializing," Georgia said.

"The restaurant" in this case was actually a bar that served hamburgers and fried catfish to help soak up the alcohol consumed by the establishment's patrons. Emma Rose's brother, Beau, had bought the place—aptly named the No Holds Bar—seven years ago, when the previous owner decided he'd had enough of trying to handle the local drunk and disorderlies. Beau, having personal experience with being drunk and disorderly himself, had no such difficulties. So now, whenever Aunt Rose needed some extra spending money, she strapped on an apron and sashayed her way down to her son's "restaurant" to pick up some cash as a waitress.

"Well, you tell your mama we miss seeing her down at the club." With that, Mrs. Rydell waved her fingers in a toodle-loo gesture and

backed her way out of the gift shop with the newly purchased deviled
egg plate beneath her arm.

As soon as the front door whooshed closed, Emma Rose childishly
stuck her tongue out at Mrs. Rydell's retreating back.

Georgia threw a comforting arm around her cousin's shoulders. "Just
let it go. You know Mrs. Rydell's been mad at Aunt Rose since they
were sophomores in high school and Mr. Rydell asked Aunt Rose to the
prom instead of her. It's nothing to do with you."

"That's easy for you to say," Emma Rose said, shaking off her
cousin's arm. "Everyone thinks your mama can do no wrong when all
she's done is prance around in swimsuits and evening gowns all her life.
My mama isn't so much different. She just doesn't wear a tiara while
she's sleeping with *her* lovers."

Rather than be offended, Georgia laughed and shook her head.
"Oh, honey, that is not the visual image I want of my mother. Come on,
now, you didn't come in here to talk about our mothers. What's up?"

At Georgia's question, a fraction of Emma Rose's former excitement came back into her eyes. "Did you know that movie star's in town?
The one who said he was going to do that cook-off show here in Ocean
Sands? He walked in on us down at Callie's shop this morning after you
left. Callie told him to go over to her house later tonight after she closed
up shop. Want to come with me to see if he's there?"

Georgia blinked back her surprise. She had assumed that Daniel
Rogers would leave first thing this morning. She should have called her
mother to make sure he had checked out of Hotel Vivian and gone
straight to the airport. She had not counted on him being so tenacious.

Damn the man anyway. Why couldn't he just go away and leave
things just as they were?

"He's not a movie star," Georgia grumbled. "He's the host of TV
show."

"Whatever. He's still hot." Emma Rose shrugged and traced the top
of a bowl shaped like a tomato with her index finger.

"What makes you think he hasn't left already?" Georgia asked, ever
hopeful.

"There's a rental car parked on our street. It's been there all day."

"Well, that could be anyone's," Georgia argued.

Emma Rose's gaze shifted to an iced tea pitcher before she answered. "It could. That's why I called Deborah Lee's cousin Marlene down at the car rental agency. She's the one who told me that Daniel Rogers flew into town yesterday afternoon and rented the very same car that's parked on our street."

Rats. If Daniel was still in town and had gone to see Callie this morning, that meant he hadn't given up. But really, what did that matter? So what if Callie told Daniel in person that she loved her Miracle Chef? It wasn't like Daniel was just going to believe her without seeing—

"Come on, Emma Rose. Let's get over to Callie's," Georgia said, grabbing her pocketbook from behind the counter. It was 6:45, fifteen minutes before the gift shop was supposed to close, but Georgia couldn't worry about that now. This was an emergency.

Dragging her cousin behind her, Georgia locked the shop's front door and made a beeline for Emma Rose's old Honda Accord. She had walked the three blocks to work this morning, but riding back with Emma Rose would be faster. Impatiently, she waited for her cousin to unlock the car, shifting her weight from one foot to the other. The pale pink skirt she was wearing swished around her legs like affectionate felines coming in for a rub.

It didn't take more than a minute for them to get from Main Street to Oak, but it felt like hours to Georgia. She'd be fine if Daniel hadn't somehow insisted on a demonstration of the Miracle Chef's abilities from Callie. But if he had, Callie would surely oblige, and Daniel would know he'd been had last night.

Georgia pushed open the Honda's passenger side door even before Emma Rose came to a complete stop outside Callie's house. She raced up the front steps and was just about to fling open the screen door when a man's voice stopped her.

"I've been expecting you," he said, the words followed by the creak of wicker as he got up off the chair on Callie's front porch.

With her hand still on the screen door, Georgia turned and did her best to stop the sharp intake of breath at the sight of him. Emma Rose was right. He *was* hot. And just looking at him made *her* hot, which really annoyed her. There was nothing as irritating as wishing someone would just go away, while at the same time wishing he'd stick around so you could ogle him at your leisure.

Today, he wore a pair of black slacks and a shimmery silver shirt that clung to his body. He looked as if he had just stepped off the cover of *GQ* and onto Callie's porch, with every detail, right down to his neatly trimmed fingernails, perfectly in place.

Next to him, Georgia felt like a beautiful swan that had been turned back into an ugly duckling. She glanced down at her own hands, which were about a week overdue for a manicure, and wished she had pockets she could stuff them into. She had never met a man who made her feel self-conscious about her looks before, and it was troubling.

But she had worse things to worry about than whether she looked all right. She needed to know if she was in time to sabotage another Miracle Chef meal and get rid of Daniel Rogers for good.

"Aunt Vivian, what are you doing here?" Georgia heard Emma Rose say and turned to see that her mother was also cozily ensconced in a chair on Callie's veranda.

Georgia clenched her teeth, wishing her mother would also go away. Having her here just reminded Georgia how critical it was to ensure that Callie's meal was a disaster.

"Shall I let Callie know she's got company?" Daniel offered, sounding amused. "She just went in to get us some dessert."

"No, thank you. I'll go tell her," Georgia said, stepping inside before anyone could stop her. She hurried down the hallway, headed toward the kitchen. Damn. They were already on dessert. Maybe if she could get there soon enough, she could mix something in Daniel's portion of whatever Callie had prepared to convince him once and for all that challenging the Miracle Chef wasn't worth his time.

She entered the kitchen at a dead run, nearly running right into Callie.

"Georgia, what are you doing here?" Callie asked, obviously surprised to see her.

"Did you cook Daniel supper using the Miracle Chef?" Georgia asked breathlessly.

"Yes, of course. He came all the way from California to see how it works. You didn't think I'd just let him leave without a demonstration, did you?"

Unfortunately, Georgia *had* thought that. Now she just had to figure out a way to send Daniel back to L.A. for good.

※

Six

$\mathcal{O}$ut on Callie's porch, Daniel found himself surrounded by women. Vivian Elliot had arrived and seated herself like royalty in a high-backed rocking chair, while Georgia's cousin—who Daniel now realized was the one who had slipped her phone number into his pocket that morning at the dress shop—remained standing near one of the white columns flanking the wide front steps. As Emma Rose peppered him with thinly veiled comments such as, "Oh, it's a shame your wife couldn't make it down to Ocean Sands with you," Daniel watched the screen door open just wide enough for white-shrouded Caroline to slip out. The toddler stealthily crept behind Vivian's rocker and climbed up onto a porch swing, then looked pleadingly at Daniel with her dark brown eyes. Obligingly, he reached out with one hand and set the swing in motion.

As he settled back in his seat, he looked up at Emma Rose, who had blond hair and brown eyes, and bore no small resemblance to her cousin. "I'm not married. Never have been. Not engaged, either. I've had two long-term relationships, both of which ended amicably when the lady in question and I simply realized we weren't cut out for a lifetime of togetherness. Oh, and, no, I am not involved with anyone at the moment."

Emma Rose's right hand fluttered to her throat. "I'm so sorry, I didn't mean to pry."

"It's perfectly all right. I just figured I'd get that all out of the way right up front. Save everyone the hassle of asking without asking, if you know what I mean."

"Don't you know that we Southerners thrive on thinking up ways to say something without actually saying it?" Georgia asked, pushing the screen door open with her hip as she balanced a heavily laden tray in both hands. Daniel stood up and grabbed the door, a gesture for which he was rewarded with a slight smile and a nod. As Georgia brushed past him, he got a whiff of apples and vanilla, and wondered if it was her or the dessert that smelled so good.

Georgia set the tray down on a white wicker footstool and started passing out bowls of apple cobbler topped with whipped cream. "Take the expression, 'bless your heart,' for example," she said, handing a bowl to Caroline. "Sometimes we use it as a form of sympathy. Like when something bad happens to someone you like, you say 'bless your heart' to let that person know that you feel for her. In other cases, it means that we think you're a frightful little troll, but we're just too polite to say so. Here, have some cobbler. I gave this recipe to Callie myself. I think you'll find it . . . unforgettable."

"Bless your heart," Daniel said, grinning as he held his hand out to take the bowl Georgia offered him.

Georgia chuckled despite herself, but stopped when her mother reached out and intercepted the dessert that had been intended for Daniel. "I'll take that. It's smaller than all the other servings. We girls have to watch our weight, you know." Vivian fluttered her eyelashes up at Daniel flirtatiously, then turned to frown at her daughter when Georgia refused to let go of the bowl.

"I made this one especially for our guest," Georgia protested. "It has more . . . whipping cream on it."

Daniel looked from the cobbler being fought over by Georgia and her mother to the tray of remaining bowls and knew immediately what Georgia had done. He would say this for her, she seemed as determined to get him to give up on the whole Miracle Chef challenge as he was to go through with it.

At some point during the flight down to Ocean Sands—somewhere over New Mexico, Daniel recalled—it had occurred to him why he was so set on winning this cook-off: because it had nothing to do with his famous parents and their influential connections. If he could win this thing in a town full of people who, he was certain, would be rooting for the local favorite, then maybe he'd feel as if he had finally accomplished something on his own.

Clasping his hands behind his back, Daniel rocked back on his heels. "Oh, no, let your mother have it. I'm certain one of these other pieces will do me just fine."

As Callie came out the front door with a coffeepot, Georgia speared Daniel with a murderous look and gave one last tug on the dessert her mother insisted on having. She was no match for her mama, however, who ended the battle by telling her daughter she was acting like an ill-bred Yankee, which Daniel assumed was the highest of insults when Georgia let out an audible sigh and let go of the bowl.

Daniel helped himself to what he hoped was an untainted dessert and turned to find his seat occupied by a whipping-cream-smeared child. Conceding his chair to Caroline, he went to sit on the porch swing, digging his fork into the soft apples as he sat down.

After last night's doomed dinner, he had expected tonight's meal to be only marginally acceptable. The beef Stroganoff that Callie had served as the main course was good. Not great or surprising or restaurant worthy, but definitely better than the bone-dry chicken he'd had last night. Even after Callie's dinner, he had a niggling doubt that this competition would be laughably easy to win, giving him nothing more than yet another hollow victory.

But as Daniel swallowed his first bite of dessert, he felt like a hunter who had been stalking a deer, only to turn and discover that a lion was stalking him.

It was delicious.

The apples were soft but not mushy, the biscuitlike crust flaky and moist. Daniel tasted mild cinnamon and the slight bite of cloves in the filling, the spices offset by the silky coolness of the whipping cream.

Daniel took another bite of cobbler, and then looked up when Vivian covered her mouth with her napkin in a discreet cough. He was fairly certain that she had used it as an excuse to spit out her own dessert, since he saw her eye the remainder of it distastefully as she pushed her bowl away.

Hiding a smile, Daniel forked the last bit of his own dessert into his mouth and savored the tastes on his tongue. He'd always loved good food and, as a teen, had dreamed of becoming a world-famous chef. That dream died a quick death when his parents, who seemed to know everyone, arranged for him to work with Wolfgang Puck one summer. The days were grueling, with the constant pressure of delivering one meal after another after another. It was nothing like Daniel had thought it would be—no room for creativity of any kind. Dishes were made exactly as described on the menu, and it was only the head chef and his trusted assistants who had any input into menu selections. Daniel found the work stressful and boring, and, at seventeen, he graduated from high school without knowing what it was that he wanted to do for the rest of his life.

Four years later, after graduating from Princeton, he still had no idea what sort of a career would interest him. Fortunately—or perhaps unfortunately—he had a trust fund that made it unnecessary for him to immediately enter the workforce. Instead, encouraged by his parents, he hooked up with some of his fraternity brothers and headed off to Europe.

It was a trip that had changed his life—not because of the grand churches or ornate palaces or priceless artwork that he saw, but because he realized after two months of meandering aimlessly from one place to the next and watching his friends party all night and sleep all day, that he needed his life to be about more than that. He needed to be *doing* something. And so, he combined his natural talent for writing with his love of food and wrote a book about being an American traveling and eating in a foreign country. When the book was done, Daniel sent a copy to his parents to show them that he had not wasted his time in Europe. Only, upon his return to Los Angeles, in addition to their glowing praise (he was their son, after all), they gave him something more—a literary agent and a publishing contract. Poof. Just like that. As if getting published were easy.

Of course, when you were the son of two of Hollywood's biggest names, getting published *was* easy. Just like going to work for one of the world's top chefs was easy. Or getting into an Ivy League college was easy.

"You're being awfully quiet," Callie said, settling into the porch swing next to him.

Daniel shook his head to clear the past. "Sorry about that. Your cobbler was delicious. You're a great cook."

Callie snorted. "No, I'm not. I can hardly make toast without burning the house down. Without the recipe cards Georgia gave me after experimenting with her Miracle Chef, tonight's meal would have been Campbell's tomato soup and grilled cheese sandwiches. Which I probably would have found some way to ruin," she added with a self-deprecating smile. "Georgia's the cook, not me."

"Mmm," Daniel said, looking at the woman in question. He had suspected that she'd sabotaged last night's dinner and now his suspicions had been confirmed. But what was he going to do now? Georgia may be the better cook, but she wanted nothing to do with taking the Miracle Chef challenge.

Daniel narrowed his eyes, considering his next move. Perhaps if her best friend's image was at stake, Georgia would step in and help to make this a real test—one they would all be proud to pass.

Tuning out the warm sound of Georgia's laughter at something Caroline had said, Daniel turned to Callie. "I'll bet it's expensive to maintain a house like this, especially with four children."

"Yes, these old homes have their charms, but their charming exteriors hide some pretty nasty secrets. Like leaky plumbing, for instance. Rotted floors. Nice, cozy places where mice like to nest. You learn to make do." Callie smiled and shrugged.

"Everyone does," Daniel agreed. "But a few thousand dollars might help fix some of those problems, wouldn't it?" he asked, as if it were a hypothetical question.

"Of course. There's no such thing as extra money in my bank account."

"If you come on the show and demonstrate the Miracle Chef, we'll pay you two thousand dollars." Daniel let that sink in for a minute, and then added, "That's not bad money for six to eight hours of work."

Georgia had stopped laughing and was halfway out of her seat when Callie responded with an incredulous, "Where do I sign?"

"No," Georgia said. "You can't do it. The Miracle Chef was just for you."

"Georgia Marie Elliot, you sit down and hush. You're making a scene," Vivian hissed, looking up and down the street to make sure the gathering on Callie's porch was not somehow under observation by the etiquette police.

"Why, Georgia, what do you mean that the Miracle Chef is just for me?" Callie asked with an odd sort of look in her eyes.

Daniel watched as Georgia sat back down in her chair and folded her hands in her lap. "I just meant it was something special I picked out for you," she said quietly.

Callie leaned forward and put a hand on her friend's arm, and the chains holding the porch swing groaned in protest. "I know, honey, and I appreciate it. But just think of how many other people there are like me in the world. They need to see what a great product this is." Then she sat back and shrugged. "Besides, you know I could use the money. Caroline's preschool tuition is going up at the end of the month and, let's face it, this wedding is costing Trey and I a lot more than we'd planned. With an extra two thousand dollars, I won't have to worry about cutting back on the flowers or the photographer in order to pay for Caroline's school."

Daniel saw Georgia toss a tortured glance toward her mother and wondered again just what the hell was going on here. It wasn't like Georgia was trying to hide a secret career as a porn star or a fortune made by selling drugs to schoolchildren. She'd simply invented a time-saving product that her best friend loved. She should be crowing about her talents instead of hiding behind her pretty face.

"I understand there's a football game Friday night that kicks off the Ocean Sands Shrimp Festival. How about we square off at a pregame barbecue that afternoon? We plan to do a best-of-five cook-off series, with each show highlighting some aspect of life here in Ocean Sands.

If possible, we'd like the final show to be held at the Shrimp Festival in two weeks. That is, if you can last that long," Daniel said with more than a hint of challenge in his voice.

"You're on." Callie grinned and held out a hand to shake on the deal, then gasped when her daughter, who had been behaving amazingly well so far, chose that moment to let out a blood-curdling scream.

Daniel nearly fell over the back of the porch swing as he jerked backward in surprise. In seconds, he was on his feet, looking out into the darkness for whatever it was that had frightened the child. Callie, on the other hand, had leaped up and clapped a hand over her daughter's mouth and, in the refrain of parents immemorial, said, "How many times do I have to tell you not to do that?"

Vivian looked on disapprovingly, as if to say, "No child of mine would ever do something like that," while Georgia and Emma Rose appeared to be stifling giggles.

"What?" Daniel asked, feeling as if he were the only one not in on the joke.

Georgia cleared her throat and demurely crossed her ankles, leaving an embarrassed-looking Callie to answer.

"She doesn't like it when I touch men other than her daddy," she said, rolling her eyes toward heaven as if hoping that God would take pity on her and miraculously tame her wild offspring.

Her plan had backfired.

Georgia eyed Daniel's rental car—a tan Mercedes convertible that had now been parked outside Mama's house for three days—and scowled. He was still here, and still determined to expose the Miracle Chef on the air. And with the first show set to tape tomorrow afternoon, Georgia was fresh out of ideas on how to stop it from happening. She supposed all she could do now was just sit back and hope that no one else was as determined to discover the true identity of the Miracle Chef's inventor as Daniel had been. It was too late now to change the name on the patent; it would take months to go through the process of getting that done.

As she passed the stop sign at the corner of Main Street and Oak, she tried reciting the Serenity Prayer—the one that told you to accept the things you couldn't change and all that—but it didn't really help. Instead, she was tempted to take out her frustration on Daniel by letting the air out of his tires. Not that it would make him stop being so damned stubborn about this challenge, but it might just make her feel better.

With a longing sideways glance at the car, Georgia walked past her mother's house without stopping. She knew she'd get caught if she even attempted to vandalize Daniel's vehicle. Some people could get away with the most heinous of crimes without ever being caught, but not Georgia. She hadn't even been able to skip a class in high school without Mama finding out. That's partly why her time in Oxford at Ole Miss had been so fun, although Georgia would be the first to admit that she'd gone a little wild surrounded by all that freedom. And that, of course, had led to her downfall. She should have known that her behavior would have disastrous and far-reaching consequences.

Georgia hated that word: consequences. It sounded so benign, so neutral, when in fact it could mean that your whole life had changed in an instant.

Georgia heard her phone ringing as she put her key in the front lock and pushed aside the thoughts of her time at Ole Miss and the events that had forced her to drop out of school. It was no use thinking about it now. Besides, what did she need an engineering degree for anyway? It wasn't like gift-wrapping deviled egg plates required much in the way of technical expertise.

She pushed open the front door and grabbed for the ringing phone. "Hello," she answered, letting her pocketbook slide to the floor.

"Hey Georgia. It's Callie," her best friend said unnecessarily.

"Hey. What's up?"

"I need help. Can you come over?"

"What? Is Caroline streaking again? Or did she flood the bathtub upstairs? Should I bring extra towels . . . or a bottle of tequila?" Georgia couldn't help but smile. Three-year-old Caroline made more trouble for her mother than the other three Mitchell children put together. The way Georgia figured it, Caroline was Callie's curse for continuing to have babies after the first three came out like perfect little angels. Callie had pressed her luck and lost, although Georgia secretly had to admit that Caroline was her favorite of Callie's kids. How could you not love a child who flaunted convention by peeing on the front lawn in full view of God and everybody?

"No, I'm pleased to report that my little brown-haired devil ate her supper and went straight to bed this evening. It's something else I'm struggling with, and I'm hoping that you might be able to help."

"Sure," Georgia said. "Just let me change out of these stockings and I'll be right over."

Panty hose were the bane of Georgia's existence. From the age of two, she'd been "encouraged" to wear tights, even around the house. ("That way, you won't fuss with them when you're onstage," Mama had said.) Now, they were the first thing Georgia took off when she got home every night. Well, after she toed her shoes off in the front entry-way, that is.

The night was warm, as late-September evenings in southern Mississippi often were, so Georgia decided to trade her dress for shorts, a T-shirt, and a pair of slip-on tennis shoes. Then she slipped out of her front door and made her way down the block to her best friend's house.

Seven

It wasn't that Daniel didn't believe people were entitled to their secrets. It was just that as the offspring of a famous couple, he had never been able to have any secrets of his own. His first real kiss, the open-mouth kind (at fourteen, after a junior high school dance, in the seconds before Renee Zachary's limo driver had arrived to pick her up) had been captured by the tabloid photographers who lurked around every corner. His first day of college, at a time when he was still naïve enough to believe that once he moved out of the family mansion, he could start living a normal life, he'd been ambushed by reporters from E!, who had already interviewed his mother about her impending empty-nest syndrome and wanted her first child's take on the situation. As if his growing up was some sort of national crisis that needed to be examined under the public microscope, every nuance picked apart and discussed ad naseam.

The thing was, though, it wasn't just *his* life that was under scrutiny. Everything his parents did and every move his sisters Kylie and Robyn made were deemed newsworthy, and Daniel had learned to hone his investigative abilities early so as not to be blindsided by seemingly well-meaning questions. Questions like the one he'd been hit with at fifteen when his then–best friend dropped a copy of the *National Enquirer* on his lap during lunch one day. With a well-aimed jab in the ribs, his friend jerked his head toward the magazine and said, "Looks like your dad got lucky. Man, please tell me he lets you go on his shoots. You gotta get yourself some of that."

Daniel looked down at the tabloid and, feeling sick, saw a picture of his father with his arms around two bikini-clad starlets. It took every ounce of his inherited acting ability to look back up and say, "What can I say? The old man is a babe magnet," without throwing up.

When he'd brought it up with his father, his dad had explained it was just a scene from an upcoming movie that the *Enquirer* had used to try to cause a scandal. With his mother sitting next to Dad on the couch, rolling her eyes at the ridiculous nature of their business, Daniel had no choice but to accept the explanation. And when, six months later, he sat in a movie theater and saw an exact replica of the *Enquirer* photo up there on the big screen, he knew that his father had been telling the truth.

Determined never to let himself be blindsided like that again, Daniel became somewhat of an expert on information retrieval, first by obsessively monitoring television and magazine coverage of his family, and later, using the Internet, by setting up automated Web searches that would let him know whenever they caught something of interest. This was why Daniel always knew where his baby sister, Robyn, was headed next on her singing tour or what latest disaster his younger sister, Kylie, had embroiled herself in up in Seattle. He'd even known about Kylie's pregnancy before she'd called to share the good news because his sweepers had picked up an on-line chat between one of the nurses at her doctor's office and a friend, where the nurse spilled the beans—and, at Daniel's insistence and without Kylie's knowledge, was later fired for divulging confidential information—about the results of Kylie's preg- nancy test. To find out his little sister was having triplets via an imper- sonal message on the Internet was not how Daniel preferred things to be. But, he figured, pretending to be surprised about the good stuff out- weighed being shocked by the bad.

Besides, if he ever lost his job as a host of *Epicurean Explorer*, he could always apply for a gig as an investigative journalist. He probably wouldn't have any trouble changing careers, since he was certain his parents knew Wolf Blitzer or Diane Sawyer or Ed Bradley or someone equally influential who wouldn't mind giving their son a job.

Daniel ruefully shook his head as the object of his latest investigation walked into his field of vision wearing white shorts and a bright yellow T-shirt. Georgia Elliot was determined to keep her secrets, and Daniel was equally determined to know why. He didn't care about exposing her or insisting that she admit to inventing the Miracle Chef, but he refused to be caught off guard if what she was hiding could be twisted to make him look like a fool. He didn't believe in leaving such things to chance.

That was why, as Georgia passed her mother's house on her way toward Main Street, Daniel decided it was time to pay a visit to the Ocean Sands library—a library that had not yet entered the twenty-first century by archiving copies of old editions of the *Ocean Sands Register* on the Internet where Daniel could search them at his leisure. Grabbing the extra set of house keys that Vivian had given him off the top of the dresser, Daniel sidestepped the substantial cedar chest at the foot of the bed and left the cozy guest room to make his way down the narrow U-shaped hallway.

He poked his head into the room directly opposite the one he was staying in, having learned that Vivian spent the majority of her considerable free time here in what Georgia had accurately dubbed the "trophy room." Vivian wasn't there, but Daniel spent a moment glancing around at the gold and silver awards littering the walls. Diamond-studded tiaras and silver trophies stood on Lucite shelves, looking like so many contestants in a pageant of their own. Vivian had arranged the trophies by size, the smaller ones leading up the wall to larger and larger ones. Next to the trophies were pictures of Vivian and her daughter in various costumes—evening gowns, bathing suits, and even glamorous-looking matching clown suits, which Daniel presumed had something to do with a talent competition. If he hadn't been raised in Hollywood, where pageantry was a way of life, he might have thought Vivian's preoccupation with beauty pageants was a little odd. But he'd met plenty of actors with nothing more going for them than their looks and an ironclad determination to succeed, who were paid a hell of lot more than even the most successful beauty queen for strutting around on-screen instead of onstage.

Backing out of the trophy room, Daniel turned to make his way downstairs. He found Vivian in her second-favorite spot—sipping iced tea on her front porch and watching the neighborhood go by.

"I'm off to the library to do some research. Do you have any plans for the evening?" he asked, propping one hip on the railing that separated the porch from the shrubbery below.

Vivian swallowed a sip of tea and daintily wiped her lips with a napkin before answering. "No. I'm afraid not. I thought I'd call Georgia to come over and visit, but I just saw her heading off to Callie Mitchell's house."

"Well, I'd invite you to come to the library with me, but it's not exactly a thrilling way to spend your evening. Isn't there anywhere else you could go for some company? Didn't somebody mention that your nephew owns a restaurant here in town?"

Vivian sniffled an unladylike "Hmph"—the least polite thing Daniel had yet to see her do. "Beau Conover does not own a *restaurant*," she said. "He runs a tavern; hardly the sort of establishment where ladies such as myself gather."

Daniel hid a smile. Sounded like a place he should visit. The local bar might be an even better place for him to ferret out information, but he'd at least give the library a chance to prove itself first. With a polite bow of his head, Daniel waved good-bye to Vivian and started across the street.

He didn't get far.

"Hey Daniel. Where you goin'?" a woman called out, halting his progress.

Daniel looked down the street to see Georgia's cousin leaning nonchalantly against her front gate, as if she had nothing better to do than lie in wait for passersby. This whole neighbor thing was definitely different from L.A. Daniel had lived in the same town house for six years. Five years ago, the ubiquitous Starbucks showed up around the corner and, for nearly every morning of those five years, Daniel had arrived at

8:00 A.M. for his daily shot of caffeine. Not once, in all that time, had any of the employees—many of whom had been on staff since the day the store opened—greeted him by name or even bothered to memorize his usual drink (double-tall Americano, no room for cream). Daniel often thought it was like that movie *Groundhog Day*, where Bill Murray was cursed to relive the same day over and over again, starting from scratch every morning at six.

Ocean Sands was not like that.

This seemed like the sort of place where if you didn't show up for your regular cup of morning coffee, the *barista* might call 911 and have the sheriff over at your house making sure you hadn't fallen in your tub and hit your head. Not that Daniel couldn't see where this might have its drawbacks, but in some ways, it was kind of quaint.

Without waiting for an answer from him as to his destination, Emma Rose had stepped through her front gate and was walking toward him. She wore a midthigh-length black skirt and a sheer white blouse with a white tank top underneath—not exactly the sort of outfit one wore for just hanging around on the porch, Daniel thought.

"I'm going to the library. I have to do some research. And you?"

"I'm working tonight. I'm a waitress down at the No Holds Bar. My brother's place," she added, just in case he didn't have all the background information he might need.

"Ah. The infamous tavern that's not a restaurant," Daniel said as Emma Rose fell into step beside him.

"You've been talkin' to Aunt Vivian, haven't you?" Emma Rose said with a shake of her head. "To hear her tell it, the No Holds Bar is on a par with a brothel or an opium den."

"I'm sorry. I didn't realize it was a sore spot," Daniel apologized.

Emma Rose laughed humorlessly. "It isn't. I just get . . . annoyed with my aunt sometimes, is all. She's got certain notions about what's what, and I suppose that's just the way she's always going to be. Makes me glad I'm not Georgia sometimes, though."

Hmm. Wasn't that interesting? Daniel mentally filed that information away for future investigation, but aloud he asked, "So, are your mother and your aunt very close?"

At that, Emma Rose genuinely laughed. "Oh, God, no. They detest each other. Have all their lives, to hear my mama tell it."

Even more interesting. Daniel wondered if the feud between Georgia's mother and her aunt had anything to do with why Georgia kept her invention a secret. It looked as if he now had a second mystery to solve.

Daniel steered the conversation to a more neutral topic and let Emma Rose guide him toward the library even though he had printed out a map of the area before he'd set off this evening. Not that it was too difficult to find anything in Ocean Sands. Most of the shopping and public buildings like the city hall and library were within two blocks of Main Street. At first, Daniel had thought about driving from Vivian's house to the library, but then he'd figured when in Rome, he should walk like the Romans did.

"Beau's place is just a block east of here," Emma Rose said as they arrived in front of the redbrick building that housed the Ocean Sands library. She smiled a half-smile up at him and pushed a lock of hair behind her ear with her left hand, a gesture that was eerily similar to that of her cousin. "If you get done with your research and want some company, you could drop by afterward. You know, to see for yourself that Aunt Vivian's exaggerating."

"I'll do that," Daniel said, figuring he might as well check out the place tonight as any night. He had a lot of work to do tomorrow morning to get the details of the show worked out with his film crew, who had arrived from L.A. that afternoon. Tonight, he might as well enjoy himself.

As Daniel started for the steps leading into the library, he saw a woman who looked vaguely familiar falter on the sidewalk when she caught sight of Emma Rose. Her hesitation was so slight that Daniel would bet that Emma Rose hadn't noticed it. She certainly didn't act as if she had, her smile widening when she caught sight of the pretty redhead.

"Sierra, honey, what are you doin' here?" Emma Rose asked.

Daniel knew this conversation was none of his business, but he remained where he was anyway, his senses on alert.

The redhead's smile seemed genuine as she gave Emma Rose one of those quick but friendly female greeting hugs. "Hi Emma Rose. I'm just . . . uh, going to the library to grade some papers. Tim's switched shifts down at the plant and he's sleeping in the evenings, so I come down here so I won't wake him up."

Emma Rose wrinkled her nose. "Grade papers? Since when do first-graders have homework?"

Sierra's light laugh seemed a bit forced to Daniel, who was watching the two women keenly. "Oh, you know, they have spelling tests and penmanship practice. You'd be surprised at all we try to teach them during their first year of school."

"I'm sure it's the same as when we were kids. It's just been so long, I've probably forgot. Not that I'm old, mind you," Emma Rose added with a coy batting of her lashes. "Oh, and where are my manners? Sierra, this is Daniel Rogers. He's the host of that food show that Callie watches all the time. He's here to do a show with her. And Daniel, this is Sierra Riley. She teaches first grade down at the elementary school on Second Avenue. Callie's twins are in her class this year."

"Nice to meet you," Daniel said, holding out his hand while Sierra awkwardly juggled her laptop from her right arm to her left. And wasn't that odd? She didn't seem to have any papers with her. Just her laptop and a notebook.

"I was at Callie's dress shop the morning you came by, but we didn't actually meet," Sierra said, explaining to Daniel why she looked so familiar. She smiled politely and Daniel decided that it was time to excuse himself. Before he'd set out this evening, he'd only had one mystery to solve—that of Georgia and her buried secrets—and now it seemed he had two more: Why were Georgia's mother and her aunt at odds . . . and why was Sierra Riley lying about what she was doing at the library?

Stepping into Callie's house was like stepping into a showroom at Robb & Stuckey. Georgia didn't know how she did it. Not with four children, and especially not when one of those children was Caroline. She supposed it was all those years of being president of the Junior League that did it. A woman who could not keep her house immaculate at all times would certainly crack under the pressure of heading up the Junior League.

Georgia shook her head as she pushed open the door leading to the kitchen, impressed by her friend's ability to maintain order amidst the chaos of her life. Then, as the scene before her unfolded, she started to laugh.

"I'm glad to see you're not perfect," she said, spying her friend through the cloud of flour that hung heavy in the humid air of Callie's kitchen.

"Oh, shut up. You know damn well I'm not perfect. It took me seven years to realize my husband was gay, my daughter uses the great outdoors as her own personal toilet, and tomorrow I'm going to go on national television and make a fool of myself." Callie reached out, clasped Georgia's hands, and wailed, "My life is a disaster."

Georgia squeezed her friend's hand. "I'm sorry I joked. I didn't realize you were so upset."

Callie blinked and a twin set of tears dribbled down her flour-coated cheeks. "It's not your fault. I'm just . . . tired, I guess. Normally these cooking mishaps don't even phase me. I must have a touch of Caroline's cold."

Pulling out one of the barstools that flanked the tile island in Callie's kitchen, Georgia sat down and rested her chin in her hands. It looked as if the abominable snowman had exploded. "Want to tell me what happened?" Georgia asked.

"I decided that I should practice for tomorrow and was making that coconut cake recipe you gave me. But for some reason, when I turned on the KitchenAid, flour went everywhere. It's never done that before. On top of that, I burned dinner for the kids earlier when I forgot to set the timer for the pork chops. I mean, how stupid is that? All I had to do was set the darn thing for seven minutes. Any idiot could do that. Any idiot but me, I guess."

With that, Callie started crying in earnest. Georgia hopped off her stool and threw her arms around her friend. "This isn't about coconut cake. What's wrong?"

Callie hiccupped and burrowed her face deeper into Georgia's T-shirt, so Georgia rocked her until her sobs quieted. Finally, Callie raised her head and sniffled. "I'm sorry. I think I got mascara on you. It's supposed to be waterproof." She sniffed again.

Georgia didn't even bother to look down at her shirt. "It'll wash out. God knows, my mama taught me how to get makeup out of everything. Now, do you want to tell me what's wrong, or shall I just get a washrag and start cleaning up this mess."

Callie laughed a watery laugh. "Can I pick both?"

Georgia grinned. "You got it. After all the Eagle brand you've helped me scrape off my ceiling, it's the least I can do."

The women wet rags and tackled the flour, cleaning in silence for several long minutes before Callie spoke. "I feel like I'm losing me," she said finally, but Georgia didn't know what that meant, so she stayed quiet, swiping at another smear of white powder that had settled on the counter.

"This morning, I was getting ready for work and I turned to my closet to decide what to wear when Jimmy came racing in to tell me that Caroline was sick. I ran out in my stockings to see what was wrong, and I slipped on a trail of vomit. Caroline tried to make it to the bathroom, but she missed."

"Bless her heart," Georgia said, feeling sorry for the girl.

"I know. But the thing is, it ended up in my hair and on my clothes, and when I went to pick her up out of bed, she got sick again all over me. Then the twins started crying and Jimmy stood in the doorway, looking at me as if I should just wave my magic mommy wand and make the chaos stop. It seems like all I do these days besides take care of wedding arrangements is feed and wipe and clean up after my children." Callie dashed away a tear that threatened to spill over. "There are times when I'm at the dress shop and I've closed up for the day and it's so . . . quiet." Callie said the word almost reverently, as if they were in church and she was saying the Lord's name. "And at times like that, I find myself lookin' at the clock and wishing . . ."

"Wishing what?" Georgia asked, speaking as softly as her friend.

"Wishing . . . wishing that time would just stop so I wouldn't have to go home. Wishing I could change out of clothes stained by throw up and dirt and . . . and finger paints, and put on one of the fancy dresses hanging on the racks and go out on the town like Jim and I used to do before he turned gay.

"And sometimes I wish I could turn gay, too, and walk away from my children and lead a completely different life from the one I lead now. Because I'm afraid that if I don't, Georgia, I'm going to lose myself forever. I'm going to wake up one day soon and there's going to be this robot where Callie Walker used to be. This robot that's too tired to care anymore about how she looks or what she wears or even what she thinks about anything besides what to put in the kids' school lunches. I'm just going to be gone."

Georgia furiously blinked back her own tears as she grabbed her friend's arms. "No, you're not, Callie. I won't let you disappear. You have too many people who care about you to let this happen. Now, where is Mother Mitchell? Is she in her room?"

"Yes," Callie answered woodenly.

"Fine. I'll go up and tell her we're going out. You get dressed in your sexiest dress—something that doesn't have throw up or dirt or finger-paint stains on it. I'm going to run home and change, but I'll be back in fifteen minutes." Georgia pushed Callie in front of her toward the stairs. As they reached the landing, she gently shoved Callie in the direction of her bedroom. Then she turned toward the set of rooms Callie's former mother-in-law inhabited and muttered, "And then I'm going to call an emergency meeting of the Tiara Club. Somethin' has got to be done about this."

Eight

Emergency meetings of the Tiara Club were only called in situations of extreme good or awful bad, and Georgia figured that Callie's near meltdown fell neatly into the latter category.

"Why the heck didn't she mention something sooner?" she wondered aloud as she hastily smoothed a pair of sheer stockings up her legs. She knew that Callie had her hands full with her children and trying to plan her wedding to Trey, but she hadn't realized things had gotten this bad.

Georgia slipped a sleeveless black dress over her head and watched in the mirror as the hem settled into place around midthigh. She checked her rear view—an instinctive behavior that came with the estrogen—and fluffed her hair one last time before figuring this was as good as she was going to get.

Grabbing her black evening bag off the bureau, Georgia stopped for just a moment to smooth a layer of muted pink lipstick across her lips. Then she dashed down the stairs, slid on the black pumps she'd left near the front door, and ran outside to meet her friend. She was halfway down the block, walking quickly down the sidewalk, when her mother's voice stopped her.

"Georgia Marie Elliot, you stop right now. Well-bred ladies do not run down public sidewalks. Would you have people think I raised you like that?"

"Do you have some sort of alarm system rigged to my front door?"

Georgia grumbled under her breath, slowing down nonetheless. There were times when this whole front-porch-sittin' thing was a damned nuisance.

"Did you say something?" Vivian asked from her perch on the porch.

"No, Mama. I've got to go. I'm not running anymore, so your reputation is safe." Georgia crossed her fingers behind her back to hope Mama wouldn't ask where she was going. She knew that would only garner her the "Back in my day, ladies did not hang out in bars" lecture.

"Where are you going at this time of night?" her mother asked, making Georgia cringe. It was only eight o'clock.

"I'm going to meet my girlfriends. Something's up with Callie. I left a message on Sierra's cell phone so I'm not sure if she's coming, but the rest of the gang's already waiting."

"Oh. Sierra? She's that Northern girl, isn't she?"

Georgia's teeth clenched together, and she had to force herself to take a deep breath before answering in her most polite voice, "Yes, Mama. Sierra has lived in Ocean Sands for three years now. I know that doesn't make her a Southerner, but you could stop calling her 'that Northern girl' anytime now."

"No need to take offense. I didn't mean anything by it."

Ri-i-ght. Georgia knew her mother better than that, but she wasn't going to stand out here on the street arguing with her. "I'll see you later, Mama," she said, turning to go.

"You're going to your cousin's tavern, aren't you?" Vivian asked suspiciously.

Georgia sighed and wrapped her arms around her waist. "Yes, I am going to the No Holds Bar. With my friends. Women do that nowadays, Mother. I promise that it doesn't reflect poorly on my upbringing for me to step foot in a bar in the twenty-first century. Now, if you'll kindly excuse me, it's rude to make Callie wait for me like this."

Georgia sensed rather than heard her mother's distasteful sniff, but she ignored it, giving Mama a backward wave as she set off—at a demure pace—toward Callie's house. When she got there, she was delighted to find Callie wearing a sparkly blue cocktail dress, although the hangdog expression on her face didn't quite match her friend's festive attire. She ignored that, however, as she led Callie out of the house and into the warm night.

Walking through town always took four times as long as driving, not because of the distance but because of the number of times you were stopped by neighbors and friends who wanted to say hello, check up on your relatives, or tell you about their latest medical malady. Georgia, who had lived in Ocean Sands nearly all her life, knew this, so she had called a cab to take them to the No Holds Bar that night. No use worrying about drinking and driving, she figured, even if they *were* only five blocks from home.

Georgia gave the cabdriver—who was also one of Deborah Lee's cousins—a generous tip as she stepped out onto the sidewalk in front of the No Holds Bar. The sidewalk itself seemed to pulsate along with the bass from the live band inside. Georgia couldn't hold back a grin as she pulled open the heavy front door and was slapped in the face with the music and the din of people shouting to be heard above the band.

"I love this place," she said, dragging Callie into the bar behind her.

From behind the bar, Beau shot her a wink and a wave that barely interrupted his expert filling of drink orders. Georgia noticed that Miranda Kingsley—bless her heart—was sitting down at the end of the bar all by herself, staring at Beau in that desperate "I'll wait for you forever, if I have to" way that all of the women her cousin loved and left seemed to do.

Georgia just didn't get it. Why did every girl Beau went out with think that *she* was going to be the one he wouldn't leave? It wasn't like they didn't know his track record before agreeing to go out with him.

Oh well, poor Miranda's heartbreak was none of her business. She saw Emma Rose pointing to a table near the back of the packed bar and threaded her way through the crowd.

"What a mob scene," Callie said—the first words she'd spoken since Georgia had single-handedly dragged her out of her house.

"I know. It's great, isn't it?"

"Don't these people have jobs? Or children?"

Georgia stopped and turned to her friend. "Yes. They do. They just make sure to take some time out for themselves sometimes. Which is exactly what you need to do, too. I mean, how long has it been since you and Trey went out on a date? And why didn't I realize that the highlight of your social calendar was our Tiara Club meetings?"

Callie studied the scratched and worn wooden floor for a moment before raising her head to meet Georgia's gaze. "I'm not the only one," she said quietly. "When was the last time *you* went out on a date? Correct me if I'm wrong, but I don't think you've slept with a man since you and Trey got divorced. If you have, you certainly haven't told me about it."

"Well, well, well, if it isn't my beautiful ex-wife and my even more beautiful fiancée."

Georgia felt the heavy weight of a man's arm being draped across her shoulders. "Hmm," she said, cocking one eyebrow at her ex-husband, "speak of the devil."

Yes, of course, Trey would have to be here tonight. Although, as Georgia recalled, there was nothing unusual in Trey being down at the bar most every night. Not that he was an alcoholic or anything. Trey just liked to be surrounded by people all the time, especially the adoring citizens of Ocean Sands, who thought their young, handsome mayor could do no wrong. That attitude came, of course, from the many years their current mayor had helped bring the state football championship trophy home to Ocean Sands.

Of course, it might have been nice if Trey had thought to invite Callie out with him every once in a while. Though, of course, that might mean he'd have to share the spotlight with someone else for a change—something Georgia had learned years ago that her ex-husband did not like to do.

"Oh, I don't know, honey. As I recall, you were pretty devilish your-self. At least in certain areas of your life." Trey winked at her and Georgia shot him a saccharine smile.

"I was worried that if I didn't do something occasionally to liven things up, we'd have to check each other's pulse just to make sure we were still alive."

"All right you two. Stop your teasing and make up," Callie scolded.

For the sake of her friendship, Georgia turned and let herself be enfolded in one of her ex-husband's overly friendly bear hugs. He nearly squeezed the breath out of her lungs before pushing her back a few feet and draping an arm over Callie's shoulders. "Honey, you look absolutely stunning tonight. Why didn't you tell me you wanted to go out?"

"It was a spur-of-the-moment thing," Callie murmured.

"Well, I'm glad to see you here. You look extra-special pretty tonight," he said, then nuzzled Callie's ear. Georgia cringed and turned away, feeling awkward.

Callie seemed to be perking up, which made Georgia feel a mixture of happiness that she'd been right to get her friend out of the house and annoyance that her best friend's fiancé hadn't been the one to suggest that maybe she needed a night off from her responsibilities.

"I need to stop at the ladies' room," Callie announced, pulling away from Trey. "I'll meet you back at the table, Georgia. Trey, I know you're hanging out with your cronies from the city council, but you'd better save me at least one dance tonight." Callie waved her fingers flirtatiously at her fiancé as she headed to the ladies' room.

Before Georgia could make a similar excuse, Trey said, "Oh, and speaking of pretty, Georgia honey, did you put in your application for the Shrimp Queen Pageant? Tomorrow noon's the deadline."

"Well, isn't that somethin'. I plum forgot all about it. Guess I'm just goin' to have to miss it this year," Georgia said, shaking her head and doing her best to appear earnest.

"Well, that's a darn shame. If you ask me, you're still one of Ocean Sands' finest." Trey rewarded her with a smile, and Georgia was almost surprised he didn't pat her on the head. The pompous ass. She was saved from trying to think up a suitable response when her ex-husband spotted someone more important across the bar and said, "I'd best be off." Then, after flashing her once more with his pearly whites, Trey turned his back on her and made his way to the entrance of the bar.

"For crying out loud, he sure lays it on thick," Emma Rose said from behind her, obviously having overheard Trey's speech.

"That he does," Georgia agreed. And when she'd first come back from Ole Miss, defeated and disheartened and looking to do anything to please her mother, she had embraced Trey and his charming ways.

All Mama ever wanted was for her to be pretty, to act pretty. And that was all Trey ever wanted from her, too. It seemed like the perfect match. Only, after a few years, Georgia found herself wanting more from herself. It stopped being enough that she looked good in an evening gown or knew how to make Christmas table decorations from the pine trees out back.

And as for sex, she had never discussed this with another living soul—not even Callie—but Trey wanted their lovemaking to be as pretty and understated as his wife. They never made love anywhere but in their bed (at night, with the door locked and the lights off), and once, in the beginning of their relationship, he had commented that she was probably the noisiest woman he had ever slept with. That, of course, had the effect of shutting her right up. Who wanted to be known as the loudest sex partner a man had ever had?

One night early on when Trey was working late, Georgia had driven over to his office wearing nothing but her overcoat, a pair of high heels, and a see-through teddy. Instead of being thrilled to see her, Trey had frowned disapprovingly and asked her what would have happened if Sheriff Mooney had stopped her for speeding or having her right rear brake light out.

"Word would get around that my wife likes to dress up like a hooker and drive around town, that's what would happen. Now go on home and put some clothes on. And, for God's sake, be careful not to get arrested," Trey had said.

Georgia was tempted to race past the sheriff's office with her horn blaring but, in the end, she hadn't needed to do that. She was so angry with Trey that she sped through a questionably yellow light and Sheriff Mooney pulled her over anyway. To this day, Georgia hadn't heard even the slightest whisper about her attire that evening, even though she had made certain to give the poor flustered sheriff an eyeful as she pretended to fumble around trying to find her license and registration.

"This place is rocking tonight," Kelly Bremer said, interrupting Georgia's wandering thoughts.

Sliding into a booth near the back of the bar, Georgia took a look around the crowded bar and agreed. "Beau must be delighted."

Emma Rose waded through the crowd to take their order. "Hey. Wish I could join you guys. I'm hoping it'll let up in an hour or so, but right now I'm too swamped to take a break." Then she put the tip of her pen on a pad of paper and asked, "So what can I get y'all?"

Deborah Lee ordered a fuzzy navel, which made Georgia smile. Who drank those things after college anyway? Kelly had a double martini with extra olives. Georgia ordered Callie a margarita, and then asked, "What's the hot new drink nowadays?" when Emma Rose got to her.

Emma Rose squinted as she pondered the question. "Well, cosmopolitans are definitely out. They're so . . . I don't know. So *Sex and the City.* Mojitos had their fifteen minutes of fame, but I think that's on the wane. I guess I'd have to say the lemon drop is probably what's on the way up now. It's a martini made with citrus vodka, orange liqueur, and sour mix. Beau coats the martini glass with a dash of lemon juice before pouring in the drink. That's his own special addition."

"That sounds great. Bring me one of those."

When their drinks and Callie arrived simultaneously, Georgia scooted over to let Callie in, raised her glass, and said, "To the Tiara Club. May beauty reign in our hearts forever."

"To hell with my heart. I want beauty to reign in my *thighs* forever," Kelly said, clinking her glass noisily with Deborah Lee's.

That drew laughter from everyone, including Callie, who seemed to be loosening up a bit now that she was nowhere near anyone who needed help wiping anything or was on the verge of projectile vomiting.

Just as Georgia put her martini glass back down on the heavy wooden table, Sierra rushed up to them, her cheeks flushed as if she'd been running. "What's wrong? Your message said it was an emergency. Is someone hurt? Was it Emma Rose?" she asked breathlessly.

Georgia scooted toward the middle of the booth to make room for the newcomer. "It's not that kind of emergency. Callie was fixin' to have an emotional meltdown and was in desperate need of a diversion, so I called an urgent meeting of the Tiara Club. I'm sorry if I scared you."

Sierra blew out a relieved breath and plunked down on the bench seat next to Callie. "Well, that's a relief. I mean, not that you're about to have a nervous breakdown, but that nobody's in the hospital," Sierra amended.

"I knew what you meant. Thank you for coming," Callie said, squeezing Sierra's shoulder and, for the first time, noticing that Sierra had a laptop under her arm. "Why'd you bring your computer?" she asked.

Sierra's gaze darted toward the ceiling for the briefest of seconds before she answered, "I was down at the library grading papers when I got Georgia's message and I rushed right over here without even thinking about stopping at home to drop off my laptop."

"Oh, that's so sweet of you," Callie said, giving Sierra's shoulder another squeeze as the band struck up a new song that set Deborah Lee to squealing.

When she recognized the familiar opening notes of the popular eighties hit "Footloose," Georgia grinned and nudged Callie out of the booth with her hip. "Come on, y'all. We've gotta cut loose!" she shouted.

Accompanied by enthusiastic whoops of delight from Kelly and Deborah Lee, they all filed out of the booth. Sierra stepped back to let them by, clutching her laptop to her chest. But Georgia was having none of that. Taking the computer by its edges, she tugged it out of Sierra's hands and set it down on the table before grabbing Sierra's hand and pulling her toward the dance floor.

"Wait a second," Sierra protested, trying to get her hand back from Georgia's grasp. "I can't dance."

"Don't worry about it. There's no one on God's green earth less co-ordinated than Kelly, and even she can manage to dance to this song," Georgia joked as she and Sierra stopped just behind the woman in question.

Kelly turned, her eyes alight with self-deprecating humor. "Yeah, thank God there were enough scholarship pageants out there that didn't judge us on talent. Otherwise, I never would have won enough money to pay for law school."

"Okay, just follow me," Georgia said excitedly to Sierra as the song got into full swing.

Sierra did her best to stumble along as Georgia, Kelly, Deborah Lee, and Callie went through a routine that they'd obviously practiced dozens of times before. The first time she tripped over her own feet she would have snuck off the dance floor rather than worry that people were laughing at her feeble attempt to appear coordinated, but Kelly—who actually did seem to be as lacking in rhythm as Georgia had said—saw her stumble and laughed as she shouted, "Come on, babe. If I can do it, you can do it." Then she put her hands on her hips and wiggled them in an exaggerated mockery of the same move Georgia, Callie, and Deborah Lee were executing. Soon, Sierra was having too much fun to even think about what onlookers might say about her dancing.

"Get ready for the big finish," Emma Rose shouted from the sidelines with a mocking roll of her eyes. Sierra jumped back out of the way just as Callie grabbed Georgia by the wrists and dragged her under her legs while Kelly and Deborah Lee slid from opposite sides of the dance floor toward the other two, their hands outstretched in a pose that would have made Bob Fosse proud.

Sierra laughed and turned toward Emma Rose, startled to see that Daniel Rogers was standing next to Georgia's cousin, clapping and wolf whistling along with the rest of the crowd who had gathered to watch the dancers. "Wow, that was something," she said, after she'd had a chance to catch her breath.

"Yeah, you can say that again," Emma Rose agreed, with just a trace of sarcasm.

"Where'd they learn to do that?" Sierra asked.

"We all learned it for the Shrimp Festival Princess Pageant one year. Of course, Georgia won the crown *again* that year. She always did love to hog the spotlight."

Taken aback at the resentment in Emma Rose's voice, Sierra glanced over at Georgia's cousin and saw that she was staring fixedly at Daniel, who in turn was staring fixedly at Georgia as she and Callie took their bows out on the dance floor. That was one thing about always being an outsider, Sierra thought. Since you were never really a part of things, you noticed things that other people might not. And what she noticed right then was that Emma Rose was more than a little peeved at the attention Daniel Rogers was paying to her cousin.

That got Sierra to thinking about what it would be like always to come in second place to someone whom you loved on the one hand but resented on the other hand. As far as Sierra knew, Emma Rose had never acted on her feelings, but what if, one day, she finally blew? What lengths would Emma Rose be willing to go to in order to prove to her cousin—and to herself—that she wasn't second best?

"Hello-o-o? Sierra? Are you in there?" Emma Rose asked, all traces of jealousy erased from her pretty face as she waved a hand in front of Sierra's nose.

Sierra blinked and came back to the real world with a start. "Uh, yes. Sorry," she said, shaking her head. Then, as she followed Emma Rose back to the table the Tiara Club had staked out, she said, "I heard someone mention that there's a pageant for older women at the Shrimp Festival. Are you planning to enter it?"

"Yes, although I don't know why I do it. I never win." Emma Rose wiped a rag across the tabletop and leaned a hip against the back of the booth. "Tradition, I guess," she said with a shrug.

"What's it like to be in a beauty pageant?" Sierra asked, putting her laptop across her knees as she slid into the booth.

Emma Rose squinted and tilted her head, as if she were considering the question for the first time. "I don't know," she answered with another shrug. "I guess you could say it's like acting. You're just there to give the judges what they expect to see. You smile like there's nowhere else that you'd rather be, and you answer their questions the way you know you should, not necessarily the way you'd answer them for real. It's like . . . a game, I guess."

"What are y'all talking about?" Deborah Lee asked, grabbing her fuzzy navel from off of the table and sipping it daintily through two thin straws.

"Sierra wants to know about beauty pageants," Emma Rose answered before Sierra could say it wasn't important.

"Oh, that's great!" Deborah Lee gushed. "Are you thinkin' of tryin' out for Shrimp Queen this year? That would be so fun!"

"Uh—" Sierra began.

"What's that? Who's trying out for Shrimp Queen?" Kelly asked, coming up behind Deborah Lee and snaking a hand out to snag her martini. She speared the olive in the bottom of the glass and sucked the pimento out before dropping the now-hollow olive back into the gin to let it soak up some more alcohol.

"Sierra is," Deborah Lee answered while Sierra sputtered.

"You're certainly in the right group if you want some pointers," Kelly said, waving her toothpick in the air like a baton.

"No, but—" Sierra tried to interject.

"Pointers about what?" Callie said, dropping into the booth and drinking down her margarita as if she'd just run a half-minute mile. "Whew, I'm hot. It's been ages since I danced like that," she said, fanning herself.

"Becoming a beauty queen," Deborah Lee answered. "Sierra's gonna enter the Shrimp Queen Pageant and we're gonna help her win. Isn't that exciting?"

As they all started tossing around statements like, "We're going to have to do *something* about that hair" and "Let's get together at Callie's after the cook-off tomorrow to see if she knows how to walk" and "Do you think Preparation H is going to take care of her eyes or should we call Dr. Andrews," Sierra slunk farther and farther down in her seat and wondered exactly how it was that she had managed to get herself in this mess.

An hour later, Georgia was enjoying herself immensely, having been asked to dance by Sheriff Mooney, whom she secretly suspected was wondering what she had on under her dress this evening. Callie, she noticed, seemed to be having an equally enjoyable time dancing with the Rydell's oldest son, Frank, since Trey was deep in discussion over zoning rights or the next election and didn't seem to have the time to spare to entertain his fiancée. Out on the dance floor, Georgia frowned and tried to catch Trey's attention and signal to him that he needed to be a bit more attentive, but he pointedly ignored her.

Well, she supposed she should just mind her own business. Besides, Callie certainly didn't seem upset to be dancing with Frank Rydell.

The band had just started playing The Georgia Satellites' eighties hit, "Keep Your Hands to Yourself"—one of Georgia's personal favorites, and not just because the band was named after her—when a familiar voice said, "Excuse me, do you mind if I cut in? You've had the pleasure of Miss Elliot's company for nearly half an hour. Isn't it time someone else got a turn?"

Sheriff Mooney smiled good-naturedly and raised his eyebrows at Georgia as if asking if she minded dancing with this stranger, and she had to force herself to stop gawking at Daniel Rogers like some starstruck groupie and nod her approval.

Damn, but he looked good.

Even in jeans and a dark blue polo shirt, he looked like a movie star. Georgia found it difficult to get her feet moving again, but Daniel helped by reaching out to take her hand. He danced as if he'd learned from a professional; as if he had been taught how to do this with a partner as opposed to most men of her age, who had learned to dance in junior high—a sort of trial by fire where thirteen-year-olds were forced to gyrate in front of one another while everyone stood on the sidelines and snickered if you looked funny. Which, of course, everyone did.

Georgia shivered as Daniel's hand skimmed down her arm, his fingers catching hold of hers to pull her toward him as the band played on. Her slightly flounced skirt flirted with her legs as she moved. Her breasts lightly brushed Daniel's chest as he pulled her closer, and Georgia found herself getting aroused at even that slight touch.

Wow. Her formerly dormant libido was surfacing with a vengeance.

She supposed her self-imposed celibacy had more to do with the fact that she knew sleeping with a man from Ocean Sands would just complicate her life, which she had spent considerable time and money trying to un-complicate. The thing was, most of the men she knew planned on living in Ocean Sands until the day they died. And since Georgia also planned to live in the same town until the day she died, the thought of walking down the street and running into men who knew her most intimate secrets was incredibly unappealing.

Of course, she could have driven to Biloxi or Jackson to find herself a one-night stand or two over the years, but the sad fact was that she was plenty satisfied with her own imagination and her vibrator. At least a vibrator couldn't give you a disease (although she supposed there might be a slight danger of electrocution) or go blabbing to the whole city council that you had a tendency to scream during sex.

But she had to be honest with herself and admit that her vibrator did not make her aware of her own body the way Daniel's touch was doing. And it didn't make her shiver when it touched her skin, or make her heart flutter like a hummingbird's wings, or make her mouth dry or her breathing slow or her knees weak. No, those were things only a man could do; things this particular man was doing quite well.

The last notes of the song died away, and Georgia joined the rest of the crowd by turning toward the band and applauding. They announced they were taking a short break, and Georgia had to admit she was glad for it. Dancing with Daniel Rogers was giving her entire body a workout.

"That's quite a lethal combination you have there," she commented as Daniel put a hand in the small of her back to escort her off the dance floor.

He leaned into her, presumably to hear better, and the instant his body made contact, Georgia felt goose bumps rise on her skin. "What's that?" he asked, his breath tickling her ear and making goose bumps rise on top of her goose bumps.

Georgia turned slightly to smile up at him. "Good looks and you're a great dancer, too. I can't believe you've managed to escape getting snagged by some adoring woman until now."

"In a town like Hollywood, I'm not as hot a commodity as you might expect."

"Well, in Ocean Sands, you're like pork bellies."

"Is that a good thing?" Daniel asked.

Georgia stopped at the edge of the table the Tiara Club had claimed and turned to face Daniel. "Well, of course it is. Just check out the commodities market sometime. Pork bellies are almost always a sure thing."

"Ah. Then thank you." Daniel inclined his head to accept the compliment.

When he looked back up at her, his blue eyes were shining with laughter and Georgia was suddenly struck by a crazy idea. Yes, Daniel had come to Ocean Sands and threatened to expose a secret she could not afford to have exposed, but wouldn't he be inclined to keep mum about it if they were sleeping together? Well, okay, that was really a lame rationalization for the fact that his touch had awakened a sleeping giant that was now clamoring to be fed. But, still, if they became lovers, he would have some incentive to keep quiet, wouldn't he?

"Tell me," Georgia began, laying a hand on his forearm (which was tan and hard and tempted Georgia to give it a squeeze), "you're not the type to settle down in a place like Ocean Sands, are you?"

Daniel frowned, as if unsure how best to respond. "Uh, I don't know. Why do you ask?"

"Well, the way I see it, there are big-city people and small-town people and when you put a small-town person in the big city, they can never be happy and vice versa. Not that Ocean Sands is a small town, but it isn't exactly New York City, now is it?"

"Um. No."

"Right. I mean, we're only a few hours from Jackson and New Orleans, and, of course, you can fly all over the world from almost anywhere these days, but still, Ocean Sands is pretty isolated, don't you think?"

"Uh . . ."

"No, no, that's all right," Georgia said with a wave of her hand. "It is. Heck, we don't even have a shopping mall here."

"But—"

"Well, we don't," Georgia interrupted. "A developer wanted to build one, but our zoning commission nixed the permits. But that doesn't matter. The fact remains that the nearest mall is thirty minutes away."

Daniel had rocked back on his heels and crossed his arms over his chest and was looking at her strangely, but he didn't say anything, so Georgia continued. "So there you have it. A big-city man like you would never be happy in a place that didn't even have a shopping mall. I mean, look at the way you dress. You've obviously got to be near a place that sells Cole Haan loafers and Ralph Lauren dress shirts. But that's good. Really good." Because if Daniel Rogers was going to leave

Ocean Sands after this silly Miracle Chef challenge was over, that meant Georgia could use him in her own personal sex experiment and never have to worry about running into him on Main Street two years from now and having to hide her head with shame because she'd asked him to let her cover his body in chocolate and whipped cream and lick it off as a prelude to sex.

"What's that look for?" Daniel asked, frowning.

Georgia blinked her eyes and smiled. "What look?"

"The one you were just giving me. Like you're the cat and I'm the canary and you just found the key to my cage."

Her laugh was light and feminine and didn't give away that he had just hit the proverbial nail on the head. "Oh, don't be silly. I—"

And then her cell phone rang.

And the rest of the Tiara Club returned from the dance floor.

And Trey came up and clapped Daniel on the back and said, "Well, howdy, stranger. It looks like you're gettin' awfully familiar with my wife."

And Georgia sighed because sometimes, in a small town, you never seemed to be alone when you most wanted some privacy.

Nine

"Mama, I can't come over tonight. Callie needs me." Georgia put a hand over her left ear and pressed her cell phone tighter to her right ear in an attempt to hear over the din. Even back here in the hallway leading to the restrooms, it was loud.

"But I think I just saw someone outside," her mother whispered.

"Do you want me to send Sheriff Mooney over? He's right here." Georgia craned her neck to find the off-duty sheriff in the crowd surrounding the bar. She spotted him talking to a morose-looking Miranda Kingsley.

"No, that's all right. I wouldn't want to bother the poor man on his night off."

Georgia bit back a sigh. Right. Mama didn't want to bother the sheriff, but calling an end to her daughter's evening was another matter. If Georgia suspected there was any truth at all to Mama's so-called intruder, she'd be outside her mother's door with the sheriff himself in ten seconds flat. The problem was, she didn't believe a word of it, and Mama's next words just cemented that belief.

"It's probably nothing," Vivian said with a long-suffering sigh. "You know how it is when you're alone all the time. You start seeing bogeymen hiding behind every shrub."

Georgia knew it was no use in telling Mama that if she was so tired of being alone, she was welcome to meet them here at the bar. That would only earn her another lecture. Still, she was having fun and wasn't ready to leave yet, so she tried another tactic.

"I'm sorry that something scared you, Mama. Hey, listen, I have tomorrow off from the store. We could spend the day together. Wouldn't that be fun? And tomorrow night's the Ocean Sands High homecoming game. Everyone in town will be there. Why don't I pick you up at noon and we can make a day of it?"

"That sounds nice, dear. But . . ." Mama paused and Georgia knew what was coming next. With the phone still attached to her ear, she started back toward their table to find her pocketbook. She might just as well give in now. "But I'm just feeling so down right now. You know how having you around helps cheer me up. You've always been my best baby girl. You know that, don't you?"

Georgia closed her eyes for a moment. "Yes, Mama. I know. I'll be there in about fifteen minutes. Why don't you make some popcorn? We can watch one of those old movies you like so much."

"Oh, honey. You don't have to leave your friends on account of me. I'll be all right here by myself."

Uh huh. "No, it's okay, Mama. Callie should be fine now."

"That's so sweet of you. You're the best daughter I could have ever hoped for."

You can say that again, Georgia thought, but didn't say the words aloud. Instead, she hung up and turned to her friends and said, "Mama has struck again. I'm sorry, but would y'all mind if I had to go? Callie, you all right with that? You havin' fun?"

The sparkle that Georgia had seen in her best friend's eyes just moments before dimmed when Callie frowned. "Yes, I'm having a great time. And so were you. I don't understand why you can't just tell your mother that you'll see her tomorrow morning."

"You do jump whenever your mother crooks her little finger at you," Kelly agreed, taking a sip of the fresh martini Emma Rose had just deposited in front of her.

Georgia shuffled her feet on the scarred hardwood floor as she answered, "It's one of those family things. You know, like how when you're around your daddy, you pretend you have no idea how to fix a leaky pipe. That's just the way it is."

"I guess so," Kelly grumbled, obviously not convinced.

"It's not like that at all," Callie said, her voice laced with anger. "Kelly's daddy doesn't make her do things she doesn't want to do like your mama does. Why don't you stand up for yourself?"

"I—" Georgia stopped, took a deep breath, and started again. "I just can't, is all. You don't understand."

Callie stepped closer and Georgia could feel the emotion radiating from her best friend as Callie grabbed her upper arm in a tight hold and said, "Then help me to understand, because I don't like to watch you being manipulated like this."

Georgia looked down at Callie's hand on her arm, the skin turning pink from the grip Callie had on her. When she looked up into her friend's eyes, her own gaze pleaded for understanding—an understanding that would have to come from faith, because Georgia couldn't tell even her best friend why it was that she had put up with her mother's machinations for so long.

Callie held her gaze steady for a moment before dropping her hand and giving an unladylike snort of disgust. "That's what I thought," she muttered, stalking her way to the bar like a sleek jaguar hunting its next supper.

"Well, I think it's sweet that you're so nice to your mama," Deborah Lee said into the awkward silence that had descended over the table.

Georgia patted her friend's hand appreciatively as she reached across the table for her black evening bag. "Will one of you give Callie a ride home tonight? I was going to get Trey to drive us home but he left about half an hour ago." He'd pled exhaustion, as if sitting around for hours drinking beers with his buddies on the city council was taxing. She was going to love seeing how exhausted Trey was after he and Callie got married and he had four children to deal with on a daily basis.

"I'll do it," came a deep voice from behind her, making her jump.

Georgia turned to see her dark-as-sin cousin Beau leaning nonchalantly against the table behind her.

"Y'all live in the opposite direction. I'm happy to give Miz Walker a ride home tonight. It's on my way."

Georgia's gaze shifted from Beau to Callie and then back to her cousin, and all she could think was, *Oh no, not less than three weeks from her wedding, you don't.* But then again, maybe what Callie had said the night of their Tiara Club meeting was true. Maybe she *was* the one woman in Ocean Sands not related to Beau Conover who was immune to his charms.

But what if she wasn't?

Now, wouldn't that be interesting?

Georgia shot her cousin a measured look from beneath her lashes. "Well, that's mighty neighborly of you, Beau."

And she could have sworn she heard Beau mutter, "Neighborly, my ass," as she turned to leave, only to find Daniel in her path.

"Why are there men lurking behind me at every turn?" she mumbled under her breath.

"Pardon me?" Daniel asked, frowning.

Georgia waved one hand dismissively. "Nothing."

"Are you leaving? I was just coming to see if I could claim another dance now that your watchdog of an ex-husband has gone home."

When he smiled at her, Georgia felt her desire to be a good daughter start to crumble. Why couldn't Mama just let her be for one night? It wasn't as if Georgia hung out in bars every night of the week, being squired around the dance floor by movie-star-handsome men. Maybe she could get away with just one more dance. The band was playing something slow and moody, and Georgia shivered in anticipation of her body so close to Daniel's that—

Her handbag vibrated.

Georgia's vision of her and Daniel slow-dancing dissipated like soft mist in the morning sun. "Excuse me," she apologized, fishing in her pocketbook for her cell phone.

"Could you pick up some Co-cola on your way home? I'm all out," her mother said even before Georgia had said hello.

"Yes, Mama. I'll be right over. With a six-pack of Coke." Georgia sighed as she hung up the phone and dropped it into her purse, then looked up to find Daniel watching her. "I'm sorry. I've got to go. Mama needs me."

Daniel seemed to be studying her as if she were some sort of puzzle he was trying to figure out, but Georgia wasn't certain if she wanted to be solved or not so she turned on her heel and walked away, her skirt swishing around her thighs. Daniel caught up with her at the door, pulling it open and holding it for her as she stepped out into the warm night.

"So what is it your mother wants?" Daniel asked as he fell into step beside her.

My life. Georgia stumbled on the smooth sidewalk when the words popped into her head.

"Are you all right?" Daniel asked, putting one strong hand beneath her elbow to steady her.

"Yes. I'm fine. I just stumbled on a crack, I guess."

Daniel glanced back at the unmarred surface of the concrete sidewalk, but didn't question her further.

My life. The words kept repeating themselves in Georgia's head, but she shook them away. That was ridiculous. Mama didn't want her life. She just wanted her undivided attention. And what was so wrong about that? Her daughter—and her memories—was all Vivian Elliot had.

"My mother just gets lonely sometimes," Georgia answered finally. "But just because I had to leave doesn't mean you should. I can guarantee you'll have more fun back at the bar than watching old movies with Mama and me until midnight. Mama usually falls asleep halfway through the movie. She really just doesn't want to be alone."

Daniel shrugged and his arm brushed against hers, making Georgia shiver despite the warm breeze. "I was tired anyway. Besides, tomorrow's going to be a long day. The *Epicurean Explorer* film crew got in today and we'll be setting up for the show at Callie's house first thing tomorrow."

Georgia didn't want to be reminded of anything to do with the Miracle Chef right now. It just made her even more frustrated about her relationship with her mother. Her entire life, it seemed, was ruled by secrets and suppressed longings.

"How long have you been the host of the show?" she asked, trying to get him to talk about anything but tomorrow's challenge.

"Only about a year. I started out as a food and travel writer, and the network came to me with the idea for the show. I was looking to do something different at the time, so I figured I'd give it a try."

"Do you like it?"

"Mmm." One corner of Daniel's mouth drew up in a half-smile. "I'm successful at it."

"That's not what I asked," Georgia said.

"Yeah, I suppose I like it. What about you? Do you enjoy being an inventor?"

Georgia frowned at the sudden change in topics. "I—" She started to deny it and then stopped. What was the use? She halted in the middle of the sidewalk and Daniel turned to face her, his eyebrows raised mockingly, as if he knew his question would irritate her. "I love it," she said fiercely. "I love that a product I invented helps my friend have quality time with her family. I love that I developed that product from scratch and that I was able to fix all the initial design flaws and make it work. I won beauty pageants because of my parents' genes. I got into the sorority at Ole Miss because of my mother's social connections. I was only considered marriageable by my first husband because his father was impressed by my family tree. But inventing the Miracle Chef was something I did myself. Nobody will ever be able to take that away from me."

Georgia expected Daniel to be annoyed by her belligerent response, but he wasn't. Instead, he watched her with those amazingly clear blue eyes of his and said, "You're lucky. At least you have that."

Blinking with surprise at his mild reaction to her outburst, Georgia slowly asked, "What do you mean?"

"I mean, I know what it's like to have things come too easy. My whole life, things have been that way. I write a book at twenty-three years old and send a copy to my parents and—boom!—I'm published.

And not just published, but hitting all the bestseller lists because of who my family is. It was as if the part that I had done, the writing, meant nothing at all. As if I could have sent my folks a collection of grocery lists and the outcome would have been the same." Daniel laughed a humorless laugh and ran his left hand through the hair at his temple. "I guess you could say that I'm still searching for my Miracle Chef. . . ."

With that Daniel started walking again, leaving Georgia standing in the middle of the sidewalk, staring at his retreating back.

"Louis, I think this is the beginning of a beautiful friendship."

Beside Daniel on the couch, Georgia was doing a terrible job of trying to hold back her tears as Humphrey Bogart and Claude Rains walked across the tarmac in the heavy fog. As she had predicted, Mama had fallen asleep somewhere between the scene where Bogey sipped champagne and said, "Here's looking at you, kid" to a lovesick Ingrid Bergman in Paris and the one where Ingrid shows up at Bogey's bar looking for forgiveness. Now Mama was snoozing graciously—no snoring or drooling for this former Miss Mississippi hopeful—in one of the high-backed chairs facing the television screen while her daughter tried not to wake her with her sniffling.

Daniel couldn't help but grin at Georgia's splotchy cheeks and red-rimmed eyes. He'd never met a woman yet who could make it through *Casablanca* without shedding a tear or two. Frankly, he liked women who cried at chick flicks. It just showed that they had hearts.

With a glance over at her sleeping mother, Daniel put a finger to his lips and motioned for Georgia to follow him. Then he grabbed the popcorn bowl and empty Coke cans from the coffee table and led the way back to Vivian's kitchen.

Georgia walked down the hall in her stocking feet, having discarded her shoes near the front door earlier. The floor creaked under her feet, like the floors of most old houses did. Georgia liked to think of the noise as echoes of the past, as if by walking where previous inhabitants of the house had walked, you allowed them to live again.

A silly notion, she knew, but she doubted there were many true Southerners who didn't believe in at least the *possibility* of ghosts.

She let the kitchen door swing shut behind her on silent hinges— probably the only part of her mother's house that didn't creak, squeak, or groan when it moved.

Dropping her own empty soda can into the recycle bin, Georgia turned to find Daniel behind her. *Close* behind her. So close that she could see the way his eyelashes curled slightly upward at their tips and could smell the faintest hint of the cologne he had put on that morning.

She seemed unable to move, mesmerized by the unfathomable look in those gorgeous eyes of his.

He reached out with one hand and traced a line down her cheek with the pad of his thumb. Georgia swayed, leaning into his touch while he dried her tears.

"Good movie, huh?" he said, his voice low and husky in a near whisper.

"I cry every time Ingrid Bergman leaves. You'd think I'd be immune to it by now."

Daniel smiled down at her and took a step even closer. Their bodies were separated by a space no wider than a sheet of paper, their heat mingling as if they were already one.

Georgia closed her eyes, enjoying the anticipation of the touch of his skin against hers. She opened them again when she felt his hands slide through her hair, his fingers caressing her scalp.

"I've wanted to do that since the day we met," he said.

Georgia slid her arms around Daniel's waist and pressed herself against him from thigh to chest. "And I've wanted to do this," she said, standing up on her tiptoes to bring her lips closer to his.

Daniel's mouth touched hers and, in an instant, it was as if all the passion she had pent-up inside herself all these years decided it was time to get un-pent. She felt heat pool between her thighs and pressed herself even closer to him, nearly gasping in delight at Daniel's unmistakable arousal. Resting against the edge of the counter behind her, Georgia drew one leg up and wrapped it around Daniel's hips. Her dress slid up her nylon-clad thighs and when Daniel pulsed against her, the roughness of his jeans rubbed against her most sensitive parts, making her squirm in an attempt to feel him even closer.

Daniel groaned and broke their kiss. "We can't do this," he said.

Georgia nearly screamed with frustration. Yes, she could definitely do this. And, from the hardness of Daniel's erection, Georgia guessed that he could do it, too. "Yes, we can. I picked up some condoms from Broussard's when I went in to get Coke for my mother."

Daniel grinned and laid his forehead on hers, his breathing labored. "No, that's not what I meant. I—"

"You what?" Georgia interrupted. "You think I'm a nice girl but you don't want to get involved right now? Well, guess what? I don't want to get involved, either. Frankly, I was just hoping I could use you for sex until you went back to L.A."

"You what?" Daniel took a step back, shooting her an incredulous look.

Georgia shoved a lock of hair behind her ear and took a step forward. "I'm not interested in a relationship. Isn't that what all guys are afraid of? That they'll sleep with a woman and she'll start getting all dreamy eyed and trying his last name on for size? Well, not me. I've already been to the circus, as they say. You don't have to worry. I'm only interested in you for sex."

Daniel coughed.

Georgia took that as a good sign and wrapped her arms around Daniel's waist, this time letting her hands wander to his firm buttocks.

"So, when were you planning to start . . . uh, using me?" Daniel asked.

"Well, I'd hoped it would be tonight. Of course, that was before Mama called and dragged me away from the bar. But just now I thought that maybe we could get started tonight anyway. I mean, we'll have to be quiet with Mama in the other room and all, but I think I can manage that. I've had a lot of practice," she added dryly.

"You have?" Daniel asked, seeming more amused and less turned on by the second.

"I didn't mean practice with having sex. I meant being quiet."

"What if I don't want you to?"

"What? Have sex?" Georgia asked, confused and frustrated that this was not turning out the way she had hoped.

Daniel laughed softly, then reached down to put his fingers under her chin. Slowly, he tilted her head up until their gazes locked. "No. I most definitely want you to have sex. With me," he added, just in case she needed clarification. "It's the quiet part I don't want. As a matter of fact, the first time I make you come, I'd like the neighbors to hear you scream."

Then he lowered his head, inch by infinitesimal inch, savoring the way Georgia's brown eyes got darker and darker as his mouth got closer to hers. And then, at the last possible moment, she let her breath out on a soft sigh, moistened her lips with the tip of her tongue, and fluttered her eyelids closed just as their mouths met.

Ten

Daniel had never been used just for sex before and he hoped he could live up to Georgia's expectations of what an ideal boy toy should be. She was certainly doing a good job of helping him give a star performance, with those little purring noises she was making, her hands on his ass, and her hips rubbing against his erection.

He broke their kiss again, but didn't make the same mistake he had made earlier when he'd said they couldn't do this. What he'd meant was, they couldn't do this *here*. Not in Vivian's kitchen with her napping in the other room. When he and Georgia had sex for the first time, Daniel wanted it to be, if not perfect, at least not some quickie slam up against the kitchen counter, with his hand over her mouth so her mother wouldn't hear it if she got loud.

"Come on. We're going to your place," he ordered, reaching around to take one of the hands Georgia had buried in his back pocket.

"My place?" Georgia asked dumbly, making Daniel have to force back a self-satisfied grin. Yeah, he was definitely up to the task of being her sexual plaything.

"Your place," he agreed, pulling her behind him out the back door. No way was he going to chance going through the front hall and awakening Vivian. "You know, where your mother does not live. Where we can get naked and be as loud as we want without worrying about what your mother might think."

Georgia stopped in the middle of the pathway leading around the front of the house and Daniel, holding her hand, had no choice but to quit walking. Damn. What was wrong now?

"The condoms. They're in my purse," she whispered, as if admitting to some sort of crime.

Daniel grinned. "I stopped at Broussard's the day after we met. I've got a supply in my wallet."

This time, it was Georgia's turn to take the lead, tiptoeing quietly under the living-room window and then picking up the pace to a near run as she crossed the street with Daniel in tow. They dashed up her front steps, their way brightly lit by the porch light she had turned on when she'd left earlier that evening. Since she'd left her purse over at Mama's, Georgia reached up and slid her hand along the top of the doorframe, her fingers closing around her spare key.

Laughing with the sheer joy of doing something so impulsive and so . . . well, so unladylike, Georgia turned and collapsed against her front door as the doorknob slipped in her hand. Daniel reached out to get the door, then stopped, his body pressing Georgia's back up against the warm wood. He put his left palm on the door, trapping her between his arms.

Georgia reveled in the feel of his body pressing against hers, his tongue warm and seeking. It had been a long time since she'd felt so desired, as if Daniel couldn't wait until they got in the house to have her.

He ran a hand from her waist to her breast and Georgia shivered with anticipation. His fingers brushed the side of her breast, but his touch was fleeting, teasing. She wanted more, so she arched her back, pressing her sensitive nipples against the fabric of her dress, delighting in the sensation.

Daniel pulled her closer as he fumbled with the doorknob behind her back. The door stuck in its frame and he gave it a push, sending them both stumbling inside when it gave under his touch.

Georgia laughed as they righted themselves, but stopped laughing as he pushed the door shut, came up behind her, and pressed her against the wall in her hallway. Pushing her thick hair to one side, he lightly bit her neck, sucking, licking at the soft skin at her nape.

She nearly purred with delight when his hands came around to rest just under her breasts, caressing her through the thin fabric of her dress. She'd gone braless tonight, her dress cut just low enough in the back to make wearing a bra impossible. His fingers teased the undersides of her breasts, coming closer and closer to her nipples with every pass.

"I can't wait to be inside you, Georgia," he whispered, his breath hot in her ear as he finally, finally ran the pads of his thumbs over her sensitive nipples.

Georgia moaned with pleasure and pushed into him, flattening her palms against the wall and closing her eyes as Daniel caressed her breasts, making her hips pulse forward as she felt an answering pull between her thighs.

She could feel every inch of her own skin, from the way her panty hose stretched tight across her toes, to the draft on the front of her thighs and the heat of Daniel's body where his erection pressed into the small of her back. She went up on her tiptoes and spread her legs wider, rubbing herself against Daniel, who groaned with pleasure.

Georgia tried to turn around but Daniel kept her pressed there, against the wall, facing the fading burgundy paint. It drove her wild to be so . . . not in charge of the situation, as if it were she and not Daniel who was the sexual plaything.

Daniel reached up under her dress and slid both her stockings and her panties off in one smooth movement, lifting up each of her feet in turn to slide them off her feet. Then she heard a zipper being tugged down, but she didn't turn, enjoying the feeling of not knowing what was going to happen next, or when. The air in the hallway was cool, and Georgia could feel every draft on the sensitive skin between her legs that Daniel had laid bare. And then he was back, his hips pressing into hers from behind. His penis teased her, but he didn't push into her as she'd expected. Instead, he taunted her, letting just the tip of him slide into her and then pulling out again.

Slowly, he reached around and slid his hands up her thighs, coming closer and closer to the spot she most wanted him to touch. Georgia was torn between the desire to push back toward him, to feel him fully inside her, or to pulse forward into his fingers. The anticipation driving her mad with want, Georgia nearly screamed when Daniel thrust into her at the same time his searching fingers found her, wet and ready for his touch.

Georgia pressed her aching breasts up against the wall, delighting in the way each thrust of Daniel's hips made her move against the rough surface, teasing her nipples until Georgia let out an involuntary moan of delight.

"Oh, God," she groaned. "I can't last much longer."

With that, he pulled all the way out of her and then, in one powerful movement, pushed himself inside her until Georgia felt so filled with him that she couldn't take any more. But then he thrust again and again, filling her even more and Georgia, suddenly feeling as if she would explode if she didn't move, shoved against the wall to take every inch of him inside her.

And then she screamed as her world went black.

Vaguely, she heard Daniel groan her name as he stiffened and then collapsed against her, pressing her cheek to the wall, his hands on top of hers where she'd planted them to keep herself upright.

"See, I told you I wanted the neighbors to hear you scream when I made you come for the first time," Daniel whispered into her ear.

Georgia was too spent to do anything more than grunt in a most unladylike manner.

Georgia stepped out of the steamy bathroom and stood in the doorway, studying the rumpled sheets on her bed where she and Daniel had last had sex. He'd slept for a while afterward, lying on his stomach with his face turned toward her. He looked the same sleeping as he did awake—gorgeous. Guys like that weren't supposed to be good lovers, but Daniel sure as heck broke that rule. Georgia couldn't remember the last time she'd had such great sex. With a wry smile, she wondered if she had enjoyed it more because it hadn't carried with it any obligations. They'd had a great time, but there was no reason they had to see each other again after he left Ocean Sands. And even for the next two weeks, she should be able to avoid him for the most part. For someone who had seen the same faces over and over again her entire life, knowing she

wouldn't have to sit across the aisle from Daniel at church and be reminded of the intimacies they had shared in the early hours of the
morning was really very freeing. With Daniel, she'd never have a "remember the time when you did that" experience.

Yawning, Georgia tightened the belt of her robe and left the bedroom. She wasn't exactly certain what time it had been when Daniel
had dropped a light kiss on her cheek and stolen out of her bedroom,
presumably to return to her mother's house. In the heat of the moment,
she hadn't given much thought to Daniel's exit strategy—hadn't even
cared if Mama knew she and Daniel had slept together. Now she realized that this was for the best. After all, what did one more secret between her and her mother matter?

Georgia padded to the kitchen on bare feet, the planks of her pine
floor smooth beneath her toes. It was a bit chilly in the room, so Georgia turned up the thermostat on the baseboard heater some previous
owner of the house had installed. The new homes that were being built
on the north side of town came with central heat and air conditioning,
but most of the houses on Oak Street relied on less modern forms of
heat. In the next month, Georgia would make her yearly call to Mr.
Broussard who, aside from running the corner grocery store and apparently keeping the whole town in condoms, supplied them with the
small amount of firewood they used in the winter.

Curling her toes into the rug in front of the kitchen sink, Georgia
pulled the carafe out of the coffee machine and filled it with the usual
six cups of water. Then she frowned. Did Daniel like coffee in the
morning or was he one of those soda people? Strange to think that
she'd shared one of the most intimate acts two people could share and
not know something as mundane as that.

She turned to pour the water into the coffeemaker, but gasped when
she saw Daniel leaning against the doorjamb, looking at her with an
unreadable expression in his eyes.

"Good morning," Georgia said evenly, trying to keep color from
flooding her cheeks. So much for not having to face the memories of
what they'd done last night.

"Would you like some coffee? Or tea? I've got iced tea in the icebox or I could put a pot of water on to boil if you prefer it hot. Or do you like Coke instead? There's one of those in the fridge, too, if you'd like."

Wordlessly, Daniel stepped toward her and slid a hand around to the back of her neck. His fingers were cool against her warm skin and Georgia, who was getting a little tired of her body's instantaneous response to his every touch, fought back a shiver. Then he nuzzled her hair away from her ear with his chin and kissed the sensitive skin just below her earlobe.

Georgia leaned into him, her back against his broad chest, and enjoyed the feel of him behind her, his arousal prodding her at the base of her spine.

"Good morning," he said softly, his breath tickling her ear.

"I thought you'd left."

"I did. I didn't think it was right to stay out all night without letting your mother know where I was."

"So you told her you were over here?" Georgia felt slightly ill at the thought.

"Yes. There's no reason to keep it a secret. We're both adults. I offered to move to a hotel if that would make her more comfortable, but she said that wasn't necessary."

"How did she seem? I mean, did she get quiet all of a sudden?"

Daniel frowned and took a step backward. "I don't think so," he said with a slight shrug of his shoulders. "Why?"

"No reason. She just gets that way sometimes," Georgia evaded. She had to get over to Mama's as soon as she had a cup of coffee and got dressed.

She poured the water into the reservoir of her coffeemaker and busied herself finding a mug in the cupboard. "You never said if you drink coffee," she said, hesitating over bringing down a second cup.

"I do. Black. No sugar. But I had my fill over at your mother's. Is anything wrong? Something doesn't feel right here."

"No, it's fine. Look, didn't you say you had a busy day ahead of you today? You'd better get going."

Georgia went to walk past him, but Daniel put his hands out to stop her. "I didn't tell your mother anything that would embarrass you. I said you and I are getting to know each other better, and that I respected you—and her—and didn't want her to think we were sneaking around behind her back. That's all."

"That's . . . fine. Nothing else you could have said." *Except nothing at all.*

Daniel seemed to be getting annoyed, the tiny lines around his eyes deepening as he frowned. "Listen, you may not have a problem trying to keep secrets from your mother, but I just don't believe in that."

Georgia felt all the blood drain from her face. "Oh, God. You didn't tell her about the Miracle Chef, did you?" she asked, raising one hand to her neck.

Daniel frowned. "No. I can't say that the topic came up."

She released her breath in a relieved gasp as she turned and put a hand on Daniel's arm. "Please promise you won't tell her. Ever."

"Why? I just don't understand your insistence on keeping this a secret."

Georgia shook her head, then pushed a lock of hair behind her right ear. "It doesn't matter why. Just promise me you won't say anything about it."

Daniel cocked his head and considered her for a long moment. As the silence lengthened, Georgia clenched her fists at her sides, her fingernails digging into her palms. What would she do if he wouldn't agree to keep quiet? What had she thought last night, that perhaps sleeping with Daniel would make him more amenable to doing as she asked? She forced her fingers to relax, took a step forward, and ran her fingernails lightly from Daniel's taut stomach up to his chest.

Rubbing her hips against his, Georgia looked up into Daniel's eyes and blinked up at him. "Please?" she whispered.

Daniel sighed and slid his arms around her waist. "All right, I'll keep quiet. But I want you to know that I think you're making a mistake. When something is out in the open, nobody can use it against you. It's the secrets that have the power to destroy you."

And looking up at him, Georgia thought, *You don't understand anything at all.* In her life, it had been the truth that had come close to destroying her, not the secrets she worked so hard to keep buried.

Eleven

Georgia pounded once more on her mother's locked front door. "Come on, Mama, answer the door," she said as loud as she could without shouting. She'd already tried the back door—also locked—and the spare keys Mama kept under various potted plants and welcome mats had been removed. She was about to run back to her own house to get her emergency set of keys from her cookie jar when the front door handle turned.

The door swung open with its customary protesting groan, and there Mama stood in all her regal splendor. Her blond hair was caught up in a turban, her body encased in a silk lavender dressing gown. Her fingernails and toenails were painted the same shade of pearly pink—anything but red or pink was simply too tacky—and she was looking at Georgia as if she were some pauper here to beg forgiveness from the queen.

"Mama, where have you been? And what did you do with all your spare keys? They're gone."

Vivian did not step back to let her daughter in. "I was in the shower, which is why I didn't come out here immediately to tell you to stop your unseemly hollering. I swear sometimes, Georgia, you've never listened to one word I've said about proper behavior. And my keys are not missing. I moved them. What if some thief discovered where I hid them? It would be silly of me to leave them in the same place all the time."

Georgia closed her eyes, inhaled a deep breath, and counted to ten.

Chetco Community Public Library

Slowly. Mama had left her spare keys in the same place since she'd moved into the house on North Oak over twenty-five years ago. But of course she had chosen this morning to figure out that might not be the smartest thing to do. Ri-i-ght.

"Can I come in? I need to talk to you and I'm sure this is something you'd rather we not discuss out here on your front porch."

"I suppose so, but I don't know what's so all-fired important that you needed to rush over here and drag me out of the shower. I barely had time to get all the crème rinse out of my hair."

Georgia stepped over the threshold of her mother's house and closed the door behind her. She needed more coffee to get through this ordeal, so she headed directly to the back of the house toward the kitchen. As she'd expected, Mama already had a pot brewed, so she got two cups and saucers down from the cupboard and poured them each a cup. She added a splash of cream to her mother's, but left her own black. Like Daniel, she liked her caffeine undiluted by milk or sugar.

She handed her mother her cup and said, "So, Daniel and I plan to, uh . . . see each other until he goes back to Los Angeles."

Vivian took a sip of coffee and eyed her daughter over the rim of her cup. "I expect you want me to say that it's none of my business."

Georgia gripped the handle of her own cup of coffee. Her hands were cold and she was tempted to wrap them around the cup, but knew it was still too hot and she'd just end up getting burned.

She glanced at her mother. "No. Believe me, I know better than to expect that. But I would like you to at least acknowledge that I'm an adult who is aware of the repercussions of her actions. I have no intention of embarrassing you—or myself—by flaunting my relationship with Daniel. What we do will remain private."

Mama was shaking her head sadly and Georgia wondered irritably how she managed to keep that damn towel from unraveling and flopping in her face.

"There's no such thing as private in a town like this," her mother said.

Georgia narrowed her eyes at the woman standing across from her.

"That's not true and you and I both know it. We all have some secrets we've managed to keep, haven't we, Mama?"

Her mother's face turned hard, the muscles in her jaw clenched tight, as if holding back words she knew she wouldn't say. Vivian set her saucer down hard on the tile countertop and coffee sloshed over the edge of her cup. Then, without a word, she turned on her heel and marched upstairs, leaving Georgia alone with her anger.

Callie watched the television crew walk her dining-room table out the set of French doors and set it down in the backyard near the old swing set that had been around since before she was born. Soon, her dining room would be set up with row after row of folding chairs in preparation for their "live studio audience" to come watch Callie either emerge victorious or be humiliated on national TV. Her stomach did a double backflip at the thought.

She was going to be on television.

Only, that wasn't the part that had her scared. She'd been in front of the cameras at too many televised pageants to be nervous about that. No, what worried her was that she couldn't cook.

Really.

She was just about the world's worst cook. Without the recipe cards Georgia had made up for her, she'd be at a loss to fry an egg, much less make an entire dinner. When she'd been married to Jim, they had a maid who came every day and took care of the cooking. And growing up, she'd been the adored only child of elderly parents who practically waited on her hand and foot. If she wanted so much as a piece of toast, her mother not only toasted the bread, but also cut off the crusts and sliced each piece into four little triangles like she preferred.

Before last night's disaster, she had meant to ask Georgia to help her plan for today's show. Unfortunately, her near nervous breakdown had interfered with her intent to be prepared and Georgia was nowhere to be found this morning.

She was going to have to do this herself.

Callie squared her shoulders and added the last ingredient to the grocery list that Shana Goldberg, the show's producer, had asked her to provide. She had decided to go with a tailgate party theme in honor of tonight's homecoming football game. Barbecued chicken with roasted potatoes, corn on the cob, and coconut cake for dessert. She was determined not to make the same mistake with the cake that she had made last night while she was practicing for today. The recipe card clearly said to add butter and ice water to the flour in the mixer before turning it on. And it probably hadn't helped that she'd turned the KitchenAid on to its highest speed with all that flour in there all by itself. No wonder she'd had an eruption.

"Are you ready?" Daniel asked, looking up from his own completed grocery list.

Callie took a deep breath and then let it out. "No," she said, squinting until her eyes shut.

Daniel patted her back comfortingly. "You'll do fine. The purpose of this show isn't to make you look bad. It's to demonstrate to people that they can cook a meal in under thirty minutes—with or without the help of some so-called miracle machine."

"You still think the Miracle Chef is a fraud, don't you?" Callie asked, leaning back against the granite-topped island in her kitchen.

"No, not a fraud. Just . . . unnecessary, I guess."

"Maybe unnecessary for you. You know how to cook. And you have thirty uninterrupted minutes to prepare a nice meal. Me, I'm lucky to get three minutes without one of the kids running into the kitchen asking me where the Aegean Sea is located or warning me that Caroline's about to set fire to the drapes. That's what's so great about the Miracle Chef. I do about ten minutes of prep work and get things started and then I can deal with the latest crisis until the timer beeps at me to let me know that it's time for the next step."

Daniel raised his hands in surrender. "Okay, okay, I know how much you love this gadget. Now I think it's time to let our judges show America whether they agree that this product lives up to its name."

"Who are the judges, by the way?" Callie asked.

"We didn't want to be accused of being elitist, so instead of gathering a panel of chefs or other cooking experts, we decided to pick five people at random out of the show's audience."

Callie raised her eyebrows. "Didn't you consider that the audience might be biased toward picking my meal? I mean, as the hometown favorite and all."

"That just makes me even more determined to cook a meal that will earn the judges' votes. If they pick me over you, then there will be no doubt in anyone's mind that I deserved to win."

"But what if I win?" Callie asked.

Daniel looked away for a moment before turning back to her with a grin. "You won't," he said.

"Well, you certainly don't lack for confidence, do you?"

"I've been told it's one of my most charming qualities," Daniel agreed.

Callie rolled her eyes, then turned to find the producer to give her the completed grocery lists. "Someone created a monster," she muttered, grinning to herself when she heard Daniel start to chuckle as she walked away.

Two hours later, she was wishing she had a bit more of Daniel's self-confidence. The groceries had been delivered and neatly separated into two piles—one for her and one for Daniel. The one-hour show (minus twenty-one minutes for commercials) would be taped right here in her kitchen.

The *Epicurean Explorer* show aired Mondays and Fridays at 8:00 P.M. Most shows were taped in front of an audience to be aired later, and Daniel had explained that they broke for commercials during taping in order to make certain both that the show didn't run over and require a lot of editing to get it to fit in its time slot, but also to make it appear to the TV viewing audience that the show was actually airing live. Callie had asked if any of the cook-offs would actually be aired live, and Daniel said that if the timing was right, they'd do so, since there was an excitement that came from a live show that just wasn't there with taped segments.

Daniel told her he'd start off by explaining the set of challenges to the audience, letting them know that he and the Miracle Chef would go head-to-head in the best out of five competitions. The loser of to-day's cook-off would get to choose the venue for the next event, which would need to be taped over the weekend in order to air on Monday. Then he'd introduce Callie as a businesswoman, mother, former con-tender for the Miss Mississippi crown, and the Miracle Chef's number-one fan. And then the challenge would begin. They'd each have thirty minutes to magically transform their respective piles of groceries into appetizing meals. Shana Goldberg would warn them when they hit the twenty-minute mark, and then every five minutes after that.

Callie swallowed the lump in her throat. God, she wished Georgia were here. While Daniel had made it clear that neither of them would have help getting their meals on the table, Callie would have liked to run through the process with her friend before the show started taping.

The last two hours had done nothing to soothe her nerves. While Daniel had been busy handling details of the show's taping, she had stood around watching the crew set up cameras and lighting, getting more and more nervous as each second passed. Fifteen minutes before, she'd been fitted for a microphone, the bulky transmitter clipped to her waistband at the small of her back.

She nearly jumped when her phone rang. *Please let this be Georgia,* she silently prayed. She'd left messages at her friend's house, on her cell, and down at the gift shop, all to no avail.

"Hello," she said into the phone's receiver.

"Callie? This is Roberta down at the day care. I'm sorry to call. I know you're busy with that TV show and all, but it's kind of an emergency."

Callie's stomach dropped to the floor. Caroline had seemed all bet-ter this morning after a good night's sleep. Her temperature was nor-mal, and she said her tummy felt fine. Had she got sick again? Or worse?

"What's wrong?" she asked, trying not to panic. "Day care" and "emergency" were not words any parent ever wanted to hear uttered in the same breath.

Before Roberta could answer, Callie's doorbell rang.

"Are we ready to let the audience in?" Shana yelled.

Callie stifled a groan.

"What's wrong?" she repeated into the phone while Daniel agreed that it was time to let in the crowd.

Roberta lowered her voice, as if afraid she might be overheard. "Caroline won't stop kissing Sam Broussard. Her teacher has tried everything, including giving her a time-out. I'm really sorry, but you're going to have to come down and get her. On the news the other day I heard about some parents from South Carolina who filed a sexual harassment suit against a day care for letting their little boy get kissed by one of the girls in his class. We just can't risk something like that. I'm sure you understand."

Callie dropped her head into her hands and closed her eyes.

This child was surely her punishment for having a happy, easy childhood herself. She'd been well liked, was on the cheerleading squad, was voted homecoming queen, and went on to compete for the title of Miss Mississippi. She'd graduated from college, married a handsome, successful businessman, moved to Jackson and had three beautiful children.

And then Jim had asked for a divorce and she'd gotten pregnant with Caroline.

From the first week of that pregnancy, her life had gone down the toilet. She had twenty-four-hour-a-day morning sickness, but still managed to gain a whopping sixty pounds. Her husband had announced that the real reason he wanted a divorce was that he'd figured out that he preferred men. Then she'd discovered that for the previous two years, when Jim had left for work every morning, he'd been lying to her. Instead of putting in time at the office, he'd been attending "lifequest" workshops led by Guru Ramu—workshops that uncomplicated attendees' lives by uncomplicating their financial portfolios. By the time the divorce was final, Jim was wearing orange diapers and had donated their last mortgage check to help Guru Ramu renovate an old plantation just outside of Natchez to use as a retreat center for those of his followers who could still afford the $2,200 a night he charged to help them "discover the purpose within."

"Um, Callie? Are you okay?" the day-care worker asked, sounding worried.

Callie sighed and lifted her head, startled to find Beau Conover leaning against her refrigerator, watching her with those dark eyes of his. She gave him a weak smile. "Yes, Roberta. I'm fine. I'll be over there in a minute."

She hung up and Beau leaned toward her, blocking out the activity around them with his large, warm body. "How are you feeling?" he asked, alluding to her tipsy state when he'd led her back to her front door last night. Callie wasn't 100 percent certain, but she was pretty sure she may have kissed him out there under the porch light. And she could swear that he was the one who had pulled back first.

Which was good, since she was getting married in two weeks to someone other than bad boy Beau Conover.

"I'm fine. Just a little flustered with all this." She waved her hand to indicate the chaos around them. "Of course, Caroline picked this moment to go boy-crazy. She's apparently decided Sam Broussard is going to kiss her whether he likes it or not. And if you say, 'like mother, like daughter,' I warn you I won't be responsible for the consequences."

Beau's laughter sounded rusty, as if it was something he didn't do very often. When he tilted his head toward her, Callie was afraid he intended to kiss her, but he didn't. Instead, he just looked at her, studied her, as if she were some sort of alien life-form he had never seen before.

"Would you like me to go get her? It looks like you're kind of busy here, and, if I recall correctly, today's the day your former mother-in-law drives to visit her gay Buddhist-in-training son."

It was Callie's turn to laugh. "Guru Ramu isn't a Buddhist. He's some sort of new age shaman who believes the holy spirit lies at the bottom of others' bank accounts," she said dryly.

"Well, whatever. Seems to me you might be in need of a little logistical assistance."

Callie's mouth twisted a bit skeptically. Was ladies' man Beau Conover really volunteering to pick up her three-year-old? Did the man know what he was getting into?

"We start taping in ten," the show's producer shouted to anyone who happened to be listening.

Beau was right. She needed some help. There was no way she could get to the day care and back in ten minutes. Of course, the next problem was, what was she going to do with Caroline during the show?

Callie shook her head. She'd figure that out when Beau got back.

"You sure you don't mind?" she asked.

Beau shrugged and straightened up, breaking the illusion of intimacy. "Not at all. I'm always happy to help out a friend."

Callie tilted her head up at him. Was that what this was? A friendship? Seemed more like a wary dance to her, circling each other cautiously every time they happened to meet. She only hoped that after she and Trey got married, this awkwardness between them would disappear.

"I really appreciate it," she said. "I'll call ahead and let Roberta know it's okay for you to pick up Caroline. Don't be alarmed if she doesn't want to come with you at first. She's like that with people she doesn't know too well."

Beau smiled that devilish smile of his and ran his hand down her cheek, making her shiver. "Oh, don't worry about Caroline and me. We get along just fine."

Twelve

"This'll be fun, Mama," Georgia said as she and her mother turned down the sidewalk leading to Callie's house. She'd been doing her best to cheer Mama up all day, to no avail. Her mother refused to utter more than monosyllabic answers to anything Georgia said.

"Hmm."

Georgia bit back a sigh and wondered if she was crazy for bringing Mama here. Daniel had, of course, invited them both to the taping of the *Epicurean Explorer* show. Georgia would have been happy to skip it—after all, disassociating herself from the Miracle Chef was her number-two priority. Unfortunately, her number-one priority was to take care of her mother, and, no matter how moody Mama was being right now, she'd never forgive Georgia if they missed an event that would have the whole town talking for years. Vivian liked to be included in such things, even though she often pretended to attend them only under duress. Georgia had never understood it, but she supposed it was Mama's way of manipulating the situation so that she felt she was doing you a favor.

Amazing the crap you put up with from family.

Vivian straightened her hat as Georgia rang the doorbell. "You look pretty enough for the society pages," Georgia told her mother as they waited for the door to be answered. And she wasn't embellishing the truth. Mama had on a seafoam green dress with a matching pastel pink-and-green-dotted belt. The pretty pillbox hat she wore was the same shade of green and was decorated with a pale pink ribbon. Mama's shoes and pocketbook, of course, perfectly matched her dress. Georgia couldn't remember a time her mother left the house without matching shoes and purse.

"Is that the dress you bought last week for Trey and Callie's wedding?" she asked, suspicious all of a sudden.

Her mother looked like she'd just swallowed a cockroach. "Heavens, no. Of course not," she sputtered. "That's an evening wedding. These colors would just not do at all. You know that."

Georgia sighed. "Did you buy this outfit just for the show today? I told you that you're running low on funds, Mama."

Vivian straightened her shoulders and refused to look her daughter in the eye. "I don't know why you have to be so mean and stingy. I'm doing the best I can to keep up appearances and not let everyone in town know that we're destitute. I would think you'd appreciate that."

One.

Two.

Three.

Oh, hell. What did one more dress matter?

And a hat. And a pair of custom-dyed shoes. And a matching handbag.

Callie's door was flung open from the inside and a harried-looking woman with spiky, unnaturally red hair said, "Taping in three," as if expecting them to understand what that meant.

Georgia saw Callie poke her head out of the kitchen and then come hurrying down the hall. "Oh, thank God you're here. I was afraid you wouldn't make it. Hello, Miz Elliot. How are you, you look lovely, please come on back. The taping starts in three minutes and I'm a nervous wreck. The day care called to tell me my toddler is a nymphomaniac and I'm nowhere near the cook you are and why in the world did I agree to do this?"

Callie stopped to take a breath and Georgia took the opportunity to hug her friend. "You're going to do fine. Daniel won't let you make a fool of yourself," she whispered, patting Callie comfortingly on the back and praying that what she said was true. After all, if his victory came easily, it would just make him look like a show-off, right?

"Taping in two," the red-haired woman shouted.

"Come on," Callie urged. "I saved you seats in the front row. Please send me a signal if you see me doing something I shouldn't."

"I will. Now, remember our pageant training. Breasts out and perky, chin up. It's sparkle time!" she said, giving her best pageant coordinator imitation. "Oh, and did you put some Vaseline on your teeth to keep your lips from sticking when you smile? I have some here in my pocketbook." Georgia immediately started riffling through her purse.

"Thanks, I already did that," Callie said, leading them into the bustling kitchen.

Georgia immediately picked Daniel's voice out of the crowd, but she refused to turn and look at him. *You're here for Callie,* she reminded herself. Which was true. But . . . well, that didn't mean she could turn off her attraction to Daniel Rogers like turning off hot water dripping from a spigot.

She and Mama took their seats, right up front as Callie had promised. Georgia kept her eyes focused on Callie, who looked darling in a pair of chocolate brown slacks and tan sweater that Georgia hadn't seen before.

Callie's sales must have doubled since Daniel came to town, Georgia thought wryly.

And then the spiky-haired show's producer shushed them all, counting down the seconds until the cameras started rolling. She did the last five seconds silently, ticking the time off on the fingers of one hand. When she dropped the last finger, there was a pause and then the *Epicurean Explorer* theme song began.

Shana Goldberg raised her hands and mimicked clapping and the audience took the hint and started applauding. Then Daniel leaned his hands on Callie's kitchen island, smiled at the camera, and welcomed them to the show.

Georgia couldn't help but look at him now—he was standing barely ten feet away and looking directly at her. And as she feared, in the cool light of day, the memories of what they had done last night came flooding back, making her cheeks go pink with embarrassment.

Maybe she'd been better off with Trey than she'd thought. All that talk about wanting to be wild in bed and totally uninhibited was all well and good during that hot rush of passion, but thinking of how close she'd come to not even caring about having sex in her own mother's kitchen last night made her cringe. She didn't want to be a prude or think that she had sexual hang-ups, but the truth was, she did. Mama thought all her talk about "proper" behavior had gone in one ear and out the other, but, unfortunately, that was not the case.

She and Daniel had shared steamy sex and she'd enjoyed every second of it, and now she felt guilty for enjoying it.

Maybe she should take up being Catholic.

Georgia snorted under her breath at her own joke. No, she wasn't about to convert from being a good ol' Southern Baptist—that would cause Mama even more upset than knowing that her unwed daughter was sleeping with a man and didn't care if everyone in town knew about it.

She glanced at Daniel, wondering if any of the women he'd slept with back in L.A. worried about what their mamas thought about their sex lives. She doubted it.

Briefly, she considered the cost of moving to California to escape her guilt. Then she noticed Emma Rose waving at her out of the corner of her eye and waved back. And old Miss Beall gave her a friendly smile. And even the boy who had played the part of the Union soldier at the last reenactment nodded his head in greeting.

Who was she kidding? She was never going to move. She didn't really even want to. She liked it here in Ocean Sands. They had a theater and a symphony, and the Gulf of Mexico was only a few minutes away. They may not have a mall, but they had great little shops along Main Street and several restaurants that rivaled those Georgia had eaten at in cities such as Atlanta, where she'd gone to visit some of Daddy's relatives a year or so back.

Unfortunately, that meant she was going to have to do something to deal with Mama's disapproval about her and Daniel. She just didn't know what, exactly.

Georgia leaned over and squeezed the hands Mama had clasped primly in her lap. "Doesn't Callie look wonderful?" she whispered.

"Mmm."

Well, that didn't work. Georgia decided she might as well leave Mama alone for a while. Maybe she'd cool off without any interference. God knew, Georgia had done everything she could to ease her mother's fears that her daughter was about to ruin their reputations . . . everything, that is, except agree to stop seeing Daniel.

Georgia watched Callie pour two cups of Hunt's ketchup into a mixing bowl to make the barbecue sauce for her chicken and gave her friend an almost imperceptible thumbs-up. Callie smiled shakily as Daniel asked her to explain to the audience what she was doing. She seemed nervous at first, but Daniel put her at ease, asking easy questions and making jokes until Callie felt confident enough to start bantering back and forth with him.

As he talked, he deftly worked with his own ingredients, reducing a small mountain of vegetables to a neatly chopped pile that he then threw under the broiler for a few minutes. He turned and caught Georgia staring and gave her a look that nearly melted her in her seat.

The easy thing, she knew, would be to tell Daniel that she couldn't see him again. But she couldn't, even knowing how much it upset her mother.

She'd felt the same when she and Trey got divorced and Mama insisted that she move back home. Georgia still remembered the awful weeklong silences she'd endured when she refused and made arrangements to buy the old Grainger place a few doors down the street instead. Yes, it was impractical from a financial perspective. Yes, they could live cheaper with only one mortgage instead of two. She just couldn't do it, though. When Trey had left, it had been because Georgia couldn't live that life anymore—Trey had treated her like the Swarovski crystal butterflies that were on display down at the gift shop, put high up on a shelf to be looked at and admired, but not to be touched . . . and certainly not expected to flap their wings and try to fly.

The night he'd walked out on her, she'd been in the middle of studying for the final exam for a class she was taking down at the community college. It was a class on the invention process, from filing a patent and building a prototype to finding a manufacturer and getting your product to market. At first, Georgia told herself that she was taking the class just because the subject matter interested her. Which it did. But the truth was, she had always loved tinkering with things, even as a kid, and she knew that someday, she wanted to become an inventor.

Which was why when Trey came home the night before her final exam and announced that he'd decided to run for mayor and was going to have several people who he hoped would be his key supporters over for a cocktail party the next night to make his announcement, Georgia asked if they could postpone it for one night.

"No, I can't," Trey had said, looking at her as if she'd just asked him to help her rob the First Trust Bank. "I've taken out an ad in the paper that's going to run the day after tomorrow. The whole purpose of tomorrow night's party is to show these people how special—and important—they are to my campaign by letting them in on the secret before anyone else knows."

Georgia looked up from her copy of *The Inventor's Notebook*. "I have a test tomorrow from seven to nine, so I may be a bit late. But I'll find a caterer in the morning. It's a Thursday night, so hopefully I won't have any trouble getting anyone on such short notice. Last time we had a party, I was able to hire a couple of the Broussards' grandkids to help out with serving. I'll see if they're available, too." She made notes on a clean sheet of paper as she talked, trying not to let the stress of all she had to do from now until tomorrow night creep into her voice. She knew running for mayor was important to Trey. He'd been talking about it since they first started dating.

Trey put a hand over her notes. "You have to be there. What sort of impression will it give to everyone if my wife isn't even there to show her support of my candidacy?"

"What sort of impression will it give to them if I drop out of this class on the last day? Do you want people to think your wife is a quitter?"

"Honey, all people think of you is that you're beautiful. That's not going to change, whether you miss some exam or not." Trey laughed and Georgia shoved back the dining-room chair she had been sitting in. She had to get up, had to move around, before the pressure building in her head caused her scalp to blow off.

"I'm not missing this test," she said, pulling back the drapes to look out into the darkness of their backyard. This was her second attempt at going back to school, and for the second time, it seemed that she had to fight her husband every step of the way to succeed.

"Georgia, don't be ridiculous." Trey flipped her book closed and snorted. "I mean, what the hell are you ever going to do with this crap anyway? You're no more an inventor than I'm a . . . well, than I'm a beauty queen. We both know you're just taking these classes to fill your nights since I've been working so much. That will end once I'm elected mayor. You'll have all sorts of social functions to fill your calendar then. As my wife, all the ladies' groups in town will want to have you come talk to them about what it's like to be married to a political leader. Pretty soon, you won't have time to miss me anymore."

"Miss you?" Georgia asked, her eyes narrowing. "You only work until eight or nine at the very latest, and I don't get home from the gift shop until seven-thirty. I see you every night. How in the world could I possibly have time to miss you?"

"Now, you're just saying that. All the other guys' wives complain that their husbands aren't home enough."

"Well, I can't speak for them. I can only speak for myself, and I can assure you that I am perfectly capable of entertaining myself during the time that we're apart." As a matter of fact, ever since she'd started taking this inventing class, her brain had been buzzing with ideas, only whenever she started getting into the details of one of them, it seemed like Trey came home, demanding her full attention like some sort of lapdog.

She stared out into the black night, clutching the drapes as she labored to suck air into her lungs. She felt as if someone were sitting on her chest, preventing her from taking a deep breath. As if she were being smothered.

Georgia started to cry silently, watching tears slide down her cheeks in the reflection in the window. "I'm going to take that test tomorrow night, Trey. If you can't accept that, then we're through," she said, not turning around.

She saw him frown at her back, and she jumped when he swiped a hand across the dining-room table, knocking her textbook, pad of paper, and cup of tea to the floor. She winced as the fragile teacup splintered into pieces. It had been her grandmother's.

And then he'd left—gone to his father's house, she had learned later, to work late into the night drawing up their divorce papers. Trey gave her the silent treatment the next night after she'd come home from her final exam and joined the party, but Georgia made sure to play her role as the charming hostess to his friends. Then, on Friday, Trey had come home from work and slapped the divorce papers on the kitchen counter, as if daring her to sign them. Georgia had looked up from the piecrust she'd been experimenting with and the look in his eyes made her feel like taking every dish out of the cupboards and smashing it at his feet. He was mocking her, one eyebrow raised, with a smirk playing across his lips.

In that moment, Georgia realized that she had to get out. He didn't believe that she'd go through with it, didn't think she had the courage to walk away from him. What Trey didn't understand was that she was tired of being looked upon as some sort of trophy. She wanted him to be proud of her for her accomplishments, not for how she looked in an evening gown.

She left the rolling pin right where it was, the piecrust in a lump on the counter, as she signed the papers with a flourish. Then, with a nod and a smile to acknowledge Trey's flabbergasted gasp that she had actually gone through with it, Georgia had gone upstairs, packed a suitcase, and left.

Looking back now, Georgia realized that her grandmother's teacup had been a small price to pay for her dreams. After her divorce, she had been determined to prove to herself that she was more than what

Trey—and her own mother—wanted to believe. She was an inventor. Even if the Miracle Chef never did more than make her best friend's life better, Georgia had made a difference in someone's life. That made this whole struggle with her mother worthwhile.

Looking from her mother's straight-backed, stubborn form to Daniel as he joked with the audience, Georgia could only hope that she'd feel the same way about sticking up for herself where Daniel was concerned when it was all over and he'd gone back to L.A.

In the twenty minutes it had taken Beau Conover to drive the five miles from Caroline Mitchell's day care back to Oak Street, he had had to stop seven times to get the toddler (whom he had started referring to as Houdini) back into her car seat and then had to make an emergency pit stop less than a mile from Callie's house when Caroline started shouting "pee-pee" over and over again at the top of her amazingly well-formed lungs.

Fortunately, the Broussards were happy to let him use the restroom at the back of their grocery store and—thank God—Mrs. Broussard, a grandmother to several granddaughters, even volunteered to take care of the dirty details that Beau hadn't realized would come with the job. After Caroline was safely buckled up again (only after Beau agreed to buy her a pack of Cat in the Hat gummy candies so he could get her out of the store in the first place), Beau had a new respect for the mothers of the world.

How did anyone accomplish anything with children around? Then he thought of Callie, with a full-time job, no husband, and four children under the age of eight.

Beau shuddered.

No wonder she had needed a night out to blow off some steam.

He looked in the rearview mirror to find Caroline smiling at him, looking like a brown-haired little angel. "It's a good thing God makes kids cute. Otherwise, y'all might not make it to adulthood," he muttered under his breath.

Caroline's grin widened.

Beau stopped at the intersection of Oak and Main and looked down the block to Callie's house. Cars lined the street, making it seem as if half the town had shown up to witness the cook-off between Callie and that Hollywood movie star he'd seen in the No Holds Bar last night. The guy was too concerned with his own appearance, if you asked him. Beau preferred T-shirts and jeans—old ones that had plenty of washings behind them to break them in—to the fancy slacks and designer shirt he'd seen the TV show host wearing this afternoon. But the guy was from L.A., after all. Besides, as long as he stayed away from Callie, what did Beau care what the guy wore?

Therein lay the secret Beau Conover had dragged around for over a decade. He'd fallen in love with Callie Walker when she was a senior in high school. All of a sudden, the girl who had been his cousin's best friend seemed more woman than girl. And Beau, who worked nights at Broussard's while putting himself through college during the day, had been the first to tell Callie "no way" when she tried to sweet-talk him into selling her a six-pack of beer. She'd turned all that beauty queen charm on him and Beau had decided then and there that he was going to make something of himself one day and, when he did, he was going to ask Callie Walker to be his wife.

Only life had different plans for him, as it so often does.

While Beau was busy working and going to school, Callie went off to college. He'd expected her to do what almost all the Ocean Sands' girls did after college—come home. But she hadn't. Instead, she'd gone and married some rich jackass up in Jackson and when she'd finally come back where she belonged, she'd brought a broken heart back with her.

The broken heart he could have handled. It was her kids that were the problem.

Behind him, somebody honked, reminding Beau that he'd been sitting at the stop sign for way too long. With an apologetic wave in his mirror, he turned right, away from Callie's house.

"Beep beep beep beep," Caroline sing-songed from the backseat.

Beau sighed. What was he going to do with her? If he took Caroline back home now while her mother was getting her big break on TV, he'd look like he couldn't handle one small child. But if he kept Caroline out of Callie's hair for an hour or two, he'd come off like a hero.

What to do?

He thought about seeing if Emma Rose was home to help him baby-sit, but figured there was no way she wouldn't be at the taping. And he knew his mother wasn't home. She was working the swing shift—

Oh, yeah. That was it. He'd take Caroline to the bar, which, contrary to its name, was actually fairly family-friendly. At least, before ten P.M. it was.

He pulled into the driveway of his mother's house where he, his mother, and Emma Rose had managed to cohabit relatively peacefully for quite some time, and turned the car around. He figured he'd wait until after the show was over to call Callie to let her know where he'd taken Caroline, just in case they'd forgotten to turn off the ringers.

In no time at all, he pulled up in front of the bar—little Houdini in the backseat had apparently become tired of her game of trying to escape from the car seat so no more unscheduled stops were necessary—and parked his sporty, two-door BMW on the street. Trying to get Caroline out of the backseat wasn't easy, especially now that she seemed to want to stay in the safety of her car seat forever.

Why'd the kid have to be so damn contrary?

Beau wrapped his arm around Caroline's middle and hauled her from the car, slamming the door shut with his foot.

He pushed open the door to the bar and was greeted with the familiar scents of fried food and draft beer, and the sound of loud music on the jukebox. He prided himself on keeping the place clean and the hardwood floors, though scuffed, gleamed and the chrome lining the bar sparkled.

Beau spotted his mother taking an order across the bar and heaved a sigh of relief. He didn't mind keeping an eye on the toddler, but he had underestimated the amount of work it would be. He had also underestimated how protective he would feel toward the kid. The first time he'd seen her crawl out of her car seat, he'd hurriedly turned off into a parking lot, afraid some car would come out of nowhere and hit him before he could get Caroline properly restrained again. He'd given her a lecture about car safety and crash statistics before getting back on the road, but she hadn't seemed to absorb the gravity of the situation because in less than two minutes, she had escaped again.

Now she was giggling, apparently enjoying the "game" of being dragged around like a sack of dog food.

"Mom, I need your help," Beau said desperately as his mother turned from taking her latest order.

"Oh, hello Beau," she said, her eyes widening when she saw what—or, rather, who—he was carrying. "Well, what do we have here? Is this Miss Caroline Mitchell or a twenty-pound bag of potatoes?"

His mother's voice did that high-pitched-girl thing that seemed to happen whenever a woman got within ten feet of a child under the age of five. He just didn't get it. How'd they all know how to do that?

Caroline was screeching with laughter as Beau's mother tickled her and then swung her up in her arms, shoving her order pad at Beau as she took the child from him.

"A little out of your league, huh?" she asked, looking at him over Caroline's shoulder.

Beau grinned sheepishly. "I'm not even playing the same game," he agreed. "But I told Callie I'd pick this little flirt up from day care where she was doin' her best to get young Samuel Broussard to return her affections, much to the dismay of her teacher, who is trying to run a strictly G-rated operation. Callie's in the middle of taping that food show that's got the town all abuzz, so I thought I'd do her a favor and keep Caroline out of her hair for another hour. Do you mind helping?"

His mother smiled at the little girl, who seemed delighted to be the center of so much adult attention. "Not at all. I miss having little ones around."

Beau sent up a silent prayer of thanks. "Great. I'll take your tables if you'll keep her occupied."

Rose Conover didn't seem to be paying any more attention to him, captivated as she was by her new charge. And when Beau came out of the kitchen ten minutes later, his mother was sitting at a booth with a young couple who had a little girl Caroline's age. As the children colored, the adults seemed deep in conversation—about potty training or the latest childhood illness or what, Beau had no idea. He was just glad to have the burden of watching the toddler off his hands . . . and he couldn't help but wonder how Caroline's mother might choose to show her appreciation for his trouble.

Daniel was accustomed to winning. Whether it be writing contests, publishing contracts, TV show hosting, he had never had to truly face defeat.

He had a feeling that today was not going to be the exception, only his victory was going to be even more hollow than usual. When Callie Walker Mitchell said she couldn't cook, she was not kidding. During the cook-off, she'd confused her recipe cards twice and put ketchup in the cake and baking soda in her barbecue sauce.

This was going to be a disaster. He wanted to win, but not this way.

He saw Georgia cringe from the front row as the fourth judge suspiciously eyed the brown dessert on his fork before putting it into his mouth, chewing it twice, and then naming Daniel as the winning chef.

Shana Goldberg turned to the fifth judge who had been randomly selected from the audience. "And the winner of the first man-versus-Miracle Chef challenge is . . ." she paused, waiting for the woman to cast the deciding vote

Astoundingly, two out of the first four judges had voted for Callie Mitchell's bizarre hodgepodge of dishes. Daniel was convinced that these were merely sympathy votes. They had to be.

He surreptitiously took a bite of her ketchup coconut cake and found, much to his surprise, that it wasn't nearly as bad as he'd thought it would be.

Hmm. Maybe those hadn't been sympathy votes after all.

"Daniel Rogers," the fifth judge announced.

Daniel first looked at Georgia, who seemed relieved by the outcome of the cook-off. Then he turned to Callie, who was taking her defeat in stride and graciously thanking all of the judges, even the three who had voted against her.

Shana turned the show back over to him, and he announced, "Thank you for tuning in to the first of our five challenges. Miss Mitchell, we told you earlier that whichever of us was not the winner of today's cook-off could pick the second event. Would you care to choose the next venue?"

Callie turned toward the camera. "Yes, Daniel, I would. I'm getting married in two weeks and my bridal shower is on Sunday. I'd love it if the next cook-off could happen there . . . and if my best friend, Georgia Elliot, would take over for me and cook for us using the Miracle Chef." Callie held her hand out to Georgia, who sat in the front row suddenly looking as if she wanted to either bolt or throw up. "Come on, Georgia. Will you do it? For me?"

Daniel watched Georgia squirm in her seat. He saw Vivian nudge her daughter and whisper something that he imagined had to do with being polite or having the manners of a Yankee or some such thing. Georgia briefly closed her eyes before opening them again and standing up to take Callie's hand.

"I'll do it," she announced morosely, as if she were agreeing to dance at her own funeral.

As Callie hugged her friend excitedly, Daniel heard Georgia add, "Once again, it looks like I don't have a choice."

Thirteen

It's important that you use the right technique here, Sierra," Deborah Lee lectured as the rest of the Tiara Club looked on and nodded in unison like devoted followers of a beloved sage.

"But—" Sierra began, her third attempt since the film crew had departed to tell Deborah Lee that she wasn't really interested in becoming a beauty queen. Once Georgia had called the meeting to order, however, each woman had noisily unloaded her own stack of beauty supplies onto Callie's kitchen table and the group had taken seats, looking upon their collective offering with a reverent, almost cultlike devotion. To be perfectly honest, this whole thing was starting to creep Sierra out.

Deborah Lee ignored Sierra's attempted protest as she stood up and started unbuttoning her blouse.

"What are you doing?" Sierra all but squeaked, shielding her eyes.

Deborah Lee looked puzzled as she tossed her shirt onto the back of one chair and tugged off her slacks in one smooth movement.

Sierra peeked out from between her fingers to find that underneath her clothing Deborah Lee had worn a pale yellow one-piece swimsuit and was now standing with her back to the group, holding the rear of her suit away from her body. She turned to look at Sierra over her shoulder as she pulled a spray can seemingly from out of nowhere and started squirting something on her butt.

"See, you have to put the suit on first, and then spray the glue on your fanny. If you spray yourself first, the suit won't stick properly."

Sierra's eyes widened as Kelly grabbed a pad of paper off the table and started fanning Deborah Lee's "fanny," as she called it.

"You've got to let the Firm Grip get tacky before you put the suit against your skin," Callie explained as Kelly continued fanning.

"If you don't, the glue just soaks into your suit," Georgia added.

"And make sure to bring a wet washcloth in a Baggie in order to wipe yourself down after the swimsuit competition. Otherwise, your evening gown will stick to your hiney," Emma Rose tossed in.

"But—" Sierra tried again as Deborah Lee let go of her swimsuit and wiggled her butt to show off how well the demonstrated no-skid technique worked.

"What? Would you like me to show you again?" Deborah Lee asked, looking hopeful.

Sierra dropped her hands from her face. "No. Please. I've got it. It's just that . . . Uh . . ."

"What? Are you nervous about being up onstage with just a swimsuit on?" Kelly asked, patting her arm sympathetically.

"Every girl up there feels the same way," Deborah Lee said, stretching her arms above her head and twisting from side to side in her continued effort to prove to Sierra that, once glued in place, her swimsuit would not ride up.

"What I do is to visualize the tiara," Callie said. "As I walk toward the judges, I imagine that they're placing that crown on my head. That helps me keep smiling and takes my mind off everything else."

"It's all about the crown," Emma Rose agreed, the look in her eyes so serious that Sierra felt a shiver climb up her spine.

"I don't think I'm beauty queen material," she said.

Georgia tsked and shook her head. "Of course you are."

"Yes, self-confidence is the most important thing," Deborah Lee said as she pulled out one of Callie's dining-room chairs and sat down, presumably to show Sierra that her swimsuit wouldn't budge, even when she was sitting. "You have to believe in yourself even when others don't."

As Kelly started talking about proper temporary breast-enhancing techniques, Sierra thought about what Deborah Lee had said. Was that her problem? Was that why she couldn't confess the truth to the women who had befriended her? Why she'd rather go along with their crazy scheme to try to shape her into a beauty queen rather than tell them the real reason she had asked about pageants in the first place?

Sierra's musings were interrupted when the front door of Callie's house slammed open with a bang accompanied by a high-pitched voice squealing, "Mom-eeee." Caroline Mitchell streaked down the hall—literally—and joyfully threw herself into Georgia's lap.

"I'm not Mommy, you silly goose," Georgia said, hugging the child anyway.

"I couldn't keep this on her," Beau Conover said as he stepped into the dining room, his dark presence seeming to take up all the extra oxygen in the place.

Sierra, like every other woman in the room not directly related to Beau, watched mesmerized as he crossed the floor toward Callie. From the first time she had met him, Sierra had thought that Beau would make the perfect tortured hero in a romance novel. She had no idea what secrets he hid behind his nearly black eyes, but she had imagined several alternatives involving betrayal, greed, loss, and alienation. When her curiosity had finally gotten the better of her and she'd asked Emma Rose about her brother's past, she'd discovered that his life to date had been fairly ordinary. Yes, he'd raised some hell as a teenager and struggled with what to do with his life until he'd hit thirty, but other than that, he was just a regular guy.

Which is why Sierra liked fiction better than fact. It was often so much more interesting than the truth.

Beau handed Callie her daughter's dress and stooped down to drop a light kiss on her cheek just as Daniel Rogers stepped into the dining room, followed by Sierra's boyfriend, Tim.

"Sorry for just walking in, the door was open," Daniel said.

Sierra looked at her watch, surprised to find that it was already seven o'clock—the appointed time for the Tiara Club meeting to break up so everyone could go to the Ocean Sands High homecoming game. What surprised her most was not the lateness of the hour, but that they had managed to pass nearly two hours discussing makeup, hair, swimsuit choices, and shoes. Who knew that so much time and effort went into making a beauty queen?

Sierra stood up and stretched, smiling at Tim as he stood off to the side of the dining room, shifting uncomfortably from foot to foot. She didn't know if it was the Tiara Club that made Tim nervous or what, but he always acted a bit awkward around them, keeping his distance as if he were almost afraid they would all start rubbing up against him like hungry cats if he got too close. Which, of course, was ridiculous. She loved Tim, but he was hardly the irresistible stud-muffin type.

"What's all this stuff?" Daniel asked, waving toward the table laden with the accoutrements of the pageant circuit.

Sierra felt a blush creep up her neck. She hadn't told Tim about the club's mission to prep her for the runway. Frankly, she had hoped he wouldn't find out about it. After all, she didn't even *want* to be a beauty queen. And what with the deadline for the Shrimp Queen Pageant passing at noon today—without her putting in a application—there was no reason Tim needed to know about this.

"Oh, the gals were just showing me what all it takes to win a pageant," Sierra answered hurriedly, hoping that would be the end of that.

"Didn't Sierra tell you?" Deborah Lee asked excitedly, obviously misinterpreting Sierra's frantically waving hands as a "go right ahead and keep talking" gesture as she blurted, "Sierra's gonna try out for this year's Shrimp Queen."

Tim snorted and shot her an incredulous look. Even though disbelief was exactly the response she had expected, Sierra didn't exactly find Tim's reaction flattering. Before he could say anything, however, Trey Hunter showed up and all the beauty pageant paraphernalia was forgotten when Trey took one look at Beau Conover's arm draped over Callie's shoulder and asked, "So, Beau, rumor has it that you did Callie a favor by taking Caroline off her hands this afternoon."

And Beau, his eyes narrowed as if he suspected a trap was about to spring shut on his leg, shrugged and replied, "Yeah. What of it?"

Then the room went quiet as Trey, mimicking Beau's shrug, shot a pointed look toward his intended and said, "Oh, nothing. I just thought that even *you* would know better than to bring a toddler to a tavern."

Southerners take their football very seriously.

That was Daniel's first thought as he pulled his rented convertible into a neighborhood right next to Ocean Sands High. Vehicles were parked literally everywhere, blocking driveways and in front of fire hydrants, their trunks open and tailgates down as people wandered from car to truck to see what sort of food or libation someone else may have brought for this pregame free-for-all. As he got out of his car, Daniel saw a few familiar faces in the crowd and waved.

"This is a madhouse," he said to Georgia, walking around the hood of the car to open her door.

She smiled and took the hand he offered to help her out of her seat. "Yeah. Homecoming always is."

Daniel didn't know how it was that she managed to get him hot with just that smile of hers, but she did. Although she was beautiful, that wasn't it. He'd been surrounded by beautiful women all his life and, sort of like being surrounded by money, you either became obsessed with it or you became immune to its charms after awhile. Daniel had chosen immunity over obsession.

Not that he thought pretty women had nothing going for them but their looks, but Georgia had something special, something different than he'd ever seen before. He just wasn't quite sure how to put that special something into words. So he didn't, putting his feelings into an up-against-the-car, I-could-do-this-all-night kiss instead. She didn't seem to mind, wrapping her arms around his waist and her tongue around his as the noise of the crowd faded away until the only thing left was the sound of their breathing.

When Daniel lifted his mouth, he was fairly certain his eyes were just as glazed over as Georgia's were.

"You sure you don't want to skip this game and go back to your place?" he asked.

Georgia laughed weakly. "If you kiss me like that again, we might not even make it *that* far."

Daniel grinned. "Glad we feel the same way."

Georgia looped her arm through his and pushed herself away from the car. "I'd never be forgiven if I skipped the homecoming game. I've only missed one game my whole life." She seemed to stumble for just a second, but then grimaced and kept moving across the lawn toward the entrance to the high school stadium where her friends were gathered.

Kelly Bremer was the first to greet them with a friendly hug. "We're all here," she yelled, and the group started moving.

Georgia looked around and frowned, her forehead crinkling as she asked, "Where's Callie?"

Kelly shook her head and snorted with disgust. "I think she's still back at the house, taking a layer off Beau Conover's hide for bringing her baby into his restaurant this afternoon. I think she's overreacting, but that seems to be the dissenting opinion among the group. What do you think, Georgia? Was Beau wrong to take Caroline into his bar? I think Callie might as well get used to seeing that child in honky-tonks. Even at three, she's got a wild streak half a mile wider than my own." With that, Kelly reached forward and squeezed the butt cheek of a man who looked to be at least ten years younger than herself. The man grinned back at Kelly before grabbing her hand and tugging her forward to walk beside him.

"Well, I don't think Beau's bar classifies as a honky-tonk. Plenty of people take their kids there for supper, so I do think Callie may be blowing things out of proportion. Besides, Beau *was* doing her a favor. That should count for something," Georgia said, and then, with barely a pause, she introduced the man Kelly had been fondling, "Daniel, this is Stuart Grainger, Kelly's fiancé. His grandparents used to own the house I live in now, but they moved to a retirement community in Fort Myers, Florida, a few years back. They had to sell the place for the down payment on their new condo, but I've promised Stuart that if I ever decide to sell the house, he'll be the first one I call."

"Yeah, you could say she's just taking care of the place until the Graingers buy it back," Stuart said good-naturedly, dropping Kelly's hand so he could give Daniel a proper welcome.

"Daniel Rogers," Daniel introduced himself, surprised at the younger man's firm grip. "I'm sorry, but I don't come with any sort of a story."

Georgia gave him a mock glare from under her lashes. "Are you making fun of me?"

Daniel put his arm around her shoulders and gave her a tight squeeze, feeling a corresponding tightness in his chest.

Good God, what is this woman doing to me?

He dropped a light kiss on her temple. "Of course not. I think it's charming the way it takes you ten minutes to get to the point."

She poked him in the ribs. "It does not. I'm just trying to give you information in some sort of context. If I just said, 'Daniel, meet Stuart,' you wouldn't know anything about him or how it is that we're connected."

She kept talking, but Daniel had stopped listening.

Wasn't that odd? Georgia introduced people in terms of their connection to her. What would happen if he were to try to do the same? Aside from his parents and sisters, what could he say?

"This is our cook, Tony. He's been with us a year or two longer than most, but he'll quit someday when a better offer comes along. They all do."

"These are our neighbors, Ben and Jennifer. They won't be married more than eighteen more months. They'll both move out during their bitter breakup and the house will stand vacant for at least two years while the divorce is going through court."

"Meet my producer, Shana Goldberg. She and I get along really well now, but as soon as my ratings start to slip, she'll set up meetings with the network execs to make sure it's my head on the chopping block and not hers."

"Here's my old high school pal Rob Mortensen. His parents gave him a Porsche on his sixteenth birthday and he went a little wild that night celebrating. Five minutes after he dropped me off for the night, he ran into the fence surrounding Lucille Ball's old house and killed two of my best friends, who were sitting in the backseat without their seat belts on. His parents' money paid the high-priced attorney who managed to get the involuntary manslaughter charges dropped, but Rob never forgave himself. He dropped out of high school and spends his days getting wasted and wandering the empty rooms of his folks' mansion. The money they left him will last forever, but, unfortunately, his guilt will last even longer."

Daniel suddenly realized that this was why he'd felt so out of sorts when he'd first read Callie's letter and decided to come to Ocean Sands—he had been feeling disconnected, even from his own family. His parents had each other, his sister Kylie had her husband and children, his self-centered youngest sister Robyn had herself (which seemed to be all she ever needed), and Daniel was alone. Unconnected to those around him.

"Are you all right?" Georgia asked, nudging Daniel's arm.

Startled, he blinked himself back to Ocean Sands and Georgia's side. "Yeah, I'm fine. When does the game start?"

"We should get settled just in time for kickoff."

Georgia's eyes shone with excitement and Daniel felt that odd tightness in his chest again; that feeling that made him want to press his lips to hers and keep kissing her until he had absorbed some of that wide-eyed enthusiasm for himself. He had to step away from her to keep from doing just that because he was afraid that with the emptiness he felt inside just now, he'd drain her of everything she had.

But she wouldn't let him go, reaching out with one hand to stop his retreat. Her fingers were small and warm as they grasped for his, and when she touched him, Daniel couldn't help but hold her tighter than he had intended. He felt as if he were standing in a jar of honey, slowly being sucked into its sweetness until he drowned in it.

The worst of it was, he wasn't sure if Georgia's hold on him was saving him . . . or pulling him down with her.

And right now, he didn't much care, not when she nuzzled close to his side, her wild curls tickling his chin and her scent invading his nostrils. Daniel couldn't believe this. He was horny, and she wanted to watch football. Talk about your role reversals.

As the Tiara Club and their various significant others filed through the turnstiles, Daniel found he and Georgia were in the center of the chaos, with people talking all at once and shouting things like, "Remember that year when . . ."

Someone handed him a beer, which he offered to Georgia, who refused it with a snort and a, "Mama would kill me if she caught me drinking that straight from the bottle." Daniel grinned and took a swig of the brew for himself. His own mother would have no such misgivings, even if she weren't two thousand miles away.

They crowded into the stadium, which was large enough to make an NFL team proud. Already, the stands were packed, the lights from the field brightly illuminating not only the emerald green lawn below but the enthusiastic fans as well.

Georgia started up the steep stairs, the tightly packed group keeping him close behind her as she went. Daniel nearly groaned aloud when she stopped suddenly, the nicely rounded ass he'd been admiring rubbing against his groin. She turned her head and shot him a sultry look over her shoulder.

"Is that a goalpost in your pocket or are you just happy to see me?" she asked, her voice low and husky.

Daniel wrapped an arm around her waist and pulled her even closer into him. "I was even happier to see you last night, lying naked under me as I made you come for the third time," he whispered into her ear and grinned delightedly as her cheeks turned bright red.

It seemed to take an hour to get to the section that had been roped off for them, mostly because they stopped every few feet for Georgia to talk with someone she knew. Which was most everyone in town, it seemed. Of course, she also introduced him to everyone she chatted with—which meant that by the time they reached the top row of seats, Daniel knew the entire history of every family that had ever set foot in Ocean Sands.

As he sat down next to Georgia, his head was swimming with who owned what business or lived in which house, which used to be owned by someone else's family, but that was before they moved up North during the Depression, so now someone new lived in the house or ran that business, but it still rightfully belonged to that other family.

And that didn't even cover the "who used to be married to whom" conversations.

Whew.

Speaking of which, Daniel spotted Georgia's ex-husband—who had acted decidedly territorial the night before at the No Holds Bar—a few rows down. Trey Hunter turned just then and sent up a phony friendly smile and a wave.

Daniel took another drink of the beer that he'd been handed earlier, surprised to find it was almost empty. He typically wasn't much of a beer drinker. "When is Callie's wedding, by the way?" he asked.

"Two weeks from now, the same day as the Shrimp Queen Pageant."

He waited for Georgia to ask if he'd like to come as her date. And waited. And waited.

Daniel looked at her out of the corner of his eye, finished off his beer, and waved to Stuart Grainger to pass him another.

She was blushing again, clearly able to interpret his signals. "I already have a date. Mama set me up."

"Oh?" Daniel twisted off the cap of his Budweiser.

"It was before we started, uh . . . you know."

Daniel fought to keep his voice neutral when all he really wanted to do was pound his own chest and tell Georgia he didn't want her going out with anyone but him. But that was silly. He'd known her less than a week, and in another two weeks he'd be gone, and she'd be nothing but a pleasant memory of the time he'd spent in a sleepy Southern town. And what would he be to her? Some slick Hollywood type who came into town wearing expensive clothes, determined to get what he wanted and to hell with her reputation?

Feeling sick all of a sudden, Daniel set his beer down on the concrete next to his feet. Was that how Georgia's mother saw it? Was that why Georgia had been so worried about what Vivian might think about them sleeping together?

In a way, of course, that impression was right. When the Miracle Chef cook-off was over, Daniel would pack up and leave town. Only the impact he'd made on the residents of town would remain.

But Georgia had insisted that she wasn't interested in anything long-term, that all she wanted was no-strings-attached sex. The thing was, though, it couldn't be no-strings-attached for her—not because she wanted a commitment from him, but because every pebble she threw into the pond of her life created ripples that impacted those around her. For Daniel, who lived in a world where the strangest and most sexually promiscuous behavior barely even caused a stir, there weren't the same repercussions for his actions.

Daniel saw Vivian making her way up the stairs and it suddenly occurred to him to wonder why such a beautiful, seemingly vibrant woman spent so much of her time alone. Where were the men her age who should be swarming all over her? Was there something in her past that had made the men of Ocean Sands wary of her? Had she, like her daughter, taken up with a man and, at the end of the affair, been left with nothing but a reputation in tatters?

His research at the library hadn't turned up much in the way of Elliot family history. He'd found the obituary for Georgia's father—a man struck dead long before his time, but not from suspicious circumstances. He'd died peacefully in his sleep from a heart attack. Nothing scandalous there. And no further mention of Georgia or Vivian except their string of pageant wins through the years.

What he really needed was to get into Vivian's attic. After all, didn't people store all manner of secrets up there, from faded old love letters to secret newspaper clippings?

Daniel stood up and waved to encourage Vivian to come sit next to him. She looked as if she wanted to refuse, but noticed that people were watching her, so she batted her eyes coquettishly and took his hand so he could help her to her seat.

"Why, thank you, Daniel. I don't know where I'd have found a place to sit in this crush." Vivian smiled, pulled a handkerchief out of her pocketbook, and dusted off the bleachers before sitting down.

"Hello, Mama. You look lovely in that outfit," Georgia said, leaning across Daniel and offering her mother a verbal olive branch.

"Thank you," Vivian responded shortly, letting Georgia know that she was not yet forgiven for potentially bringing scandal down on the Elliot name.

Daniel could feel the tension from both sides, but didn't know what to do to ease it, aside from getting on the next plane to L.A.

"Well, look who decided to grace us with her presence."

Daniel winced. No matter who the middle-aged blonde was directing her comment to, both Georgia and her mother stiffened.

"Auntie Rose," Georgia said, the tone of her voice saying "please, don't do this."

"What honey? I'm just so surprised to see my big sister out of that ol' house of hers. Seems like it's been years since she left her front porch."

"Maybe that's because there's nobody around worth visiting," Vivian said, smoothing one sleeve of her dark green sweater.

"Georgia doesn't think so, do you honey? Why just the other night she came over and we had ourselves a wonderful supper, didn't we?"

Beside him, Georgia squirmed uncomfortably, so he stood up, blocking her from the view of her aunt.

"Hello," he said, sticking out his right hand. "I'm Daniel Rogers, the host of the *Epicurean Explorer* cooking show. You must be the aunt Georgia talks about all the time. I've met your lovely daughter, Emma Rose, but I don't believe I've yet had the pleasure of making your acquaintance." And if that long-winded speech didn't distract her, Daniel didn't know what else to try.

"Ah, so you're the one who's causing such a stir around town," Aunt Rose said, taking his hand in her own cool, smooth one. "Yes, I'm Georgia's aunt. Rose Conover. Pleased to meet you."

"Oh, excuse me. There's someone I need to go say hello to," Georgia said, shooting Daniel an apologetic look for deserting him as she jumped off the bench and started down the stairs.

Daniel grimaced when Rose took Georgia's newly vacated seat on his left.

"I can see now why Emma Rose is so jealous of the attention you're paying her cousin. You're mighty good-looking, if you don't mind me saying so."

Daniel nearly choked on the beer he'd just swallowed. "Uh." He coughed. "Thank you. Of course, I can't take any credit for that. I was just the recipient of good genes."

Rose leaned forward and speared her older sister with a glare. "See. Some people know better than to get all full of themselves because of how they look."

Vivian's spine straightened even further, a feat which Daniel would not have thought possible. "There's nothing wrong with being proud of one's appearance."

Rolling her eyes, Rose leaned back and said loudly, as if to annoy her sister, "Fortunately, Georgia got her daddy's smarts as well as her mama's good looks. Did you know that just last week, Mrs. Broussard was raving about how Georgia made her this new contraption out of a cane and an old set of Rollerblades that makes it so that she can continue going on her daily walks even when her arthritis is acting up. Georgia called it the Rollercane. Isn't that clever?"

Daniel saw the muscles in Vivian's jaw clench and wondered just what in the hell was going on here. Why would Vivian be upset by Rose's praise of her daughter?

Next to him, Vivian seemed to tense every muscle in her body as Daniel attempted to change the subject. "It seems like your son has a pretty good business going," he said to Rose.

"Yep, Beau's a smart one, too. But he's more street-smart. Georgia, on the other hand, is smart about figuring things out. She always has been. Isn't that right, Viv?"

Vivian stood up, refusing to even look at her younger sister. Daniel was astonished when she pushed past him without so much as a "beg your pardon." That was not like her at all. He watched as she hurried down the still-crowded steps and disappeared from view.

With a frown, he turned to Rose, who, rather than looking pleased that she'd upset her sister, seemed a bit green around the edges. "What in the hell was that all about?" he asked, past caring that he was being impolite.

Rose sighed. "I don't know. I just get so tired of the way my sister manipulates everyone around her. I can't seem to stop myself from needling her."

"Why does it upset her that you think Georgia's smart?"

Rose sighed again. "I think she's jealous. Vivian was never a good student, never excelled at anything but being pretty. I guess it bothers her that her daughter is smarter than she is."

Rose's explanation sounded logical, but Daniel was still puzzled. Although Vivian didn't strike him as being ready to debate the pros and cons of nuclear proliferation, she certainly wasn't stupid. Something about the whole episode made him feel that there was a lot more to Vivian Elliot than he or Georgia or even Rose knew.

Vivian, he thought, was hiding something. And he intended to find out just what her secret was.

Fourteen

Vivian Elliot poured herself a Scotch with trembling hands, and then brought the drink into the darkened living room. Curling her feet under her, she sat in an overstuffed chair covered with a faded floral print and contemplated the bottle of sleeping pills on the table next to her.

The whiskey burned all the way down her throat as she swallowed nearly half the glass in one swallow. Tonight, she couldn't seem to drink enough to drown the memories.

The hand on her thigh, sliding up toward the white cotton panties she wore under her school uniform.

The voice, whispering, "You're so smart, Vivvie. That's why I chose you instead of Rose."

Vivian shivered violently and golden brown whiskey sloshed over the rim of her glass and onto her slacks, but she didn't care. She could still hear the voice, whispering in her ear, the hot breath against her skin making her stomach heave.

She drained her glass and put it down on the table next to the pills. If she took a handful, peaceful darkness would come and the voice reminding her of her worst fear would be silenced. Didn't Georgia realize that being smart made her a target? That men saw intelligence as something they needed to dominate, to defeat? They weren't threatened by pretty women, only smart ones. That was why it was so important for

Georgia to hide her intelligence, so she wouldn't be hurt the way her mother had been.

Vivian closed her eyes and leaned back in the chair, resting her head against a pillow. She felt the tears hot on her face, felt her hair sticking to her wet cheeks as she thrashed her head from side to side, trying to get the voice to stop, trying to erase the feel of those hands on her body.

She couldn't stand thinking that her daughter, her baby, was risking the same fate. Why couldn't she just be happy winning beauty pageants? The only way Vivian had known to keep her headstrong daughter from standing out academically had been to use her only child's love for her mother to make her do what Vivian knew was best for her. But even now, Georgia didn't seem to understand the danger she put herself in by letting people know she was smart.

Vivian opened her eyes and gasped for breath in the stiflingly hot room. She grabbed her glass from the table and got up to pour herself another drink, stumbling over the edge of the carpet that marked the boundaries of her living room. The Scotch went down easier this time as she stood and drained her glass once more. Refilling it one more time, she didn't bother going back to her chair, sliding down onto the hardwood floor instead. She set her glass down and lay down, resting her cheek on one warm plank. Staring at the liquid in the glass, Vivian took small, panting breaths and tried to slow her racing heart.

She lifted her head and took another long drink.

Finally, the voice quieted, the whispers so low she almost couldn't hear them.

Her eyelids were getting heavy, the edges of the room hazy. She was so tired. Tired of secrets. Tired of memories. Tired of loneliness and fear.

Tired of everything.

That was her last thought as Vivian closed her eyes and let the darkness take her.

———

The Ocean Sands High Mighty Tides football team botched another touchdown when Deborah Lee's cousin's son, Scott Fitzgerald, fumbled the ball at the five-yard line. A groan went up among the Ocean Sands fans. They were approaching halftime and the score was 14–0 against the home team.

"That boy's nothing like my Trey," Georgia's ex-father-in-law Rock-well Hunter said, shaking his head sorrowfully. His voice sounded so much like his son's that Georgia had often—before Rock got them a new phone that came with caller ID one year for Christmas—mistakenly answered her father-in-law's greeting with, "Hey, honey." Fortunately, Rock managed the local office of the telephone company, so the then-expensive new technology had come at a reasonable price.

"Yes, seemed like Trey could catch anything anyone ever threw him," Georgia agreed.

"He had golden hands," Rock said with a nostalgic sigh.

Georgia clamped her mouth shut in the effort to not add, "On the field." Her former father-in-law certainly didn't need to know *that* about his son.

After she'd escaped the feud between Mama and Aunt Rose in such a cowardly manner, Georgia had spent the next half hour visiting just about everyone she knew in order to avoid having to go back. Mama, she knew, would be in her usual snit. For whatever reason, Aunt Rose got on Mama's nerves faster than ice dissolved in sweet tea on a summer day. It had been like that as long as Georgia could remember and it just seemed to get worse the more they tried to stay out of each other's way. When Grandma Ella Rose was alive, Mama and her sister were cautiously polite to each other. But after Grandma died, back when Georgia was barely ten years old, the family get-togethers seemed to get more and more strained. Now, they almost never got together, except for holidays like Thanksgiving or Christmas where Georgia insisted that Mama and Aunt Rose call a temporary truce.

Georgia had ceased trying to make peace between her mother and Aunt Rose. Whenever she'd broached the subject with Mama, Mama started slamming things and saying, "Your aunt is an ungrateful brat who has no idea the sacrifices I made for her." And when Georgia confronted Aunt Rose with her mother's comments, Rose had nearly fallen to the floor with mocking laughter and said, "Sacrifices? You have got to be kidding. Vivian was Mother and Daddy's favorite since the day she was born. I see how she manipulates people to get what she wants and I refuse to fall for it like everyone else does. That's why we don't get along. I'd like to know just what the hell it is she thinks she ever sacrificed for *me*. I'm the one who got all her hand-me-downs all my life. She got everything first and whatever was left got passed down to me. Sacrifices, indeed."

When Georgia tried to ask Mama what she meant by her comment, Vivian's skin had taken on a deathly pall. "Don't you ever ask me that again," she'd said and shut herself up in her bedroom for three days.

Georgia was eighteen when that happened, the summer before she'd gone off to Ole Miss, and she'd never broached the subject again. Instead, she did her best to soothe Mama's moods whenever Aunt Rose upset her, but still tried to stay close to her aunt and cousins because Georgia, of all people, knew the truth in Aunt Rose's accusation. Mama *was* manipulative and when she turned on the charm, most everyone leaped into action to do her bidding. And when that didn't work, Georgia had seen the depths her mother would sink to in order to get what she wanted.

"Hey, it looks like that Hollywood fella is trying to get your attention," Trey's father said, nudging her back to the present.

Georgia winced. She knew it hadn't been right of her to flee the scene of the battle and leave Daniel trapped there between Mama and Aunt Rose, but she'd had to get away from them before they tore one another apart. Unlike Daniel, who could shrug off the ugliness the minute he stepped on the plane to L.A., she had to live with the wounds her family inflicted upon each other.

"Thanks," she mumbled, getting up off the bleacher. But before she could head up the stairs to rescue Daniel from her mother, Rock stopped her.

"Hey, I need your help in trying to find the perfect gift for Callie and Trey. After all, she is your best friend."

And he's your ex-husband. That's what Rock—or anyone else in town—wouldn't say, at least not to her face. They came into the gift shop, asking for her to help them find just the right wedding present for Trey and Callie, always saying the same thing: *After all, she is your best friend.* Of course, they were right, so Georgia knew she was being petty and small for not being more enthusiastic about the whole thing, but no matter how often she reminded herself that Trey and Callie getting married didn't bother her, the truth was, somewhere deep down inside, it did.

But it was too late to be airing her misgivings about that now. The wedding would happen, and she'd stand up next to her best friend while it did, so she might as well make sure Callie got some nice things. It seemed the least she could do.

"Come on down to the shop next week, and I'll help you pick something out," Georgia said to her ex-father-in-law before heading up the stairs.

She'd gone halfway up to where Daniel was sitting when the crowd got to its feet and roared. Georgia turned around to see Scott Fitzgerald in the end zone, staring at the ball in his hands as if he wasn't quite sure how it had gotten there.

"And that's a touchdown for the Mighty Tides," the announcer said over the loudspeaker, making the crowd clap even louder. Georgia couldn't believe she had missed it.

"Story of my life with Mama," she muttered under her breath, continuing to climb the stairs.

Only, when she got up to their seats, Mama wasn't even there. Aunt Rose had moved up a few seats to sit next to Emma Rose. They both waved to her as she approached and she waved back.

Daniel patted the empty bench beside him. "I saved this for you," he said.

Georgia ducked her head as she sat down. "Sorry about that. I guess I lost track of time."

"Uh-huh." Daniel reached out and pushed the curtain of hair separating them away from her face. "I'm glad you're back."

"I love my mother, but sometimes I just have to get away from her," Georgia said without rancor. She had long ago accepted Mama's idiosyncrasies. To have tried fighting them would surely have driven her mad by now.

His eyes were warm and full of an understanding she'd never felt from anyone else before. "She's family," he said.

Georgia leaned her head into the hand he had buried in her hair and closed her eyes. "Thank you," she whispered. She basked in the comfort Daniel offered for just a moment, but straightened when the crowd let out a collective groan. With one minute remaining in the first half, the Mighty Tides had missed the field goal.

"Where is my mother, by the way? Did she go get something to eat?" Georgia asked.

"I think she went home," Daniel said, putting an arm around her shoulders and pulling her closer. "Your aunt was giving your mother a detailed list of your recent accomplishments, which seemed to upset your mother for some reason. She left a few minutes after you did."

Georgia's breath caught in her throat. "She left? Oh, God, I thought she just went to the concession stand or something."

Daniel's arm tightened on her shoulders. "Why are you so upset that your mother went home?"

Georgia pasted a wobbly smile on her face. "I'm not upset," she said, trying to calm her uneven breathing. Clenching her fingers into fists, Georgia scanned the crowd. Her mother had been gone over half an hour. She had to get back home to check on her, but Mama would be angry if she caused a scene. Unless . . . Georgia swallowed past the lump in her throat.

Unless it was already too late.

"Will you excuse me? I have to go to the ladies' room."

Without waiting for Daniel's response, Georgia leaped up off the bench and flew down the stairs. She was prepared to run all the way back to Oak Street in order to keep this to herself, but Daniel had other plans. Georgia didn't even realize that he'd followed her until she was almost at the gate that marked the stadium's exit.

"I believe the ladies' room is back there," he said dryly.

Startled, Georgia tripped over a hole in the pavement and would have fallen if Daniel hadn't caught her.

"Come on. We can take my car," he said when she couldn't manage to think of a way to explain her odd behavior.

Wordlessly, Georgia nodded and hurried ahead of Daniel to his rental car. If something had happened . . . Georgia slid into the passenger seat of the car and buckled her seat belt. If something had happened, then she'd deal with it like she always had.

She was grateful for Daniel's silence as they sped across town. With nearly everyone at the game, there was very little traffic, but it still seemed to take forever to get to the intersection of Main and Oak. Georgia was out of the car and had vaulted up the stairs to her mother's house before Daniel had even put the car in park.

She stood on the porch, watching the drapes sway in the gentle breeze of the ceiling fan inside Mama's living room.

Please, God, let her be okay, she prayed as she raised her hand and knocked tentatively on the door.

Georgia nearly collapsed against the warm wood in relief when she saw a shadowy figure in the living room.

Thank you, thank you, thank you, she mouthed silently.

Daniel came to stand behind her just as Mama opened the door. Georgia felt the warmth of his body seeping into her taut shoulders and she was oh so tempted to take a small step back and lean into him, to let him cradle her in his strong arms and feel the solid sturdiness of him against her.

"What are you two doing here?" her mother asked, her eyes red as if she'd been crying.

"Daniel told me you'd left the game and I was worried about you being lonely," Georgia said, reaching out to press her mother's smooth hand between her own. With surprising insight, Daniel had summed up her feelings about her mother perfectly when he'd said, "She's family." Yes, Mama had a controlling, manipulative streak that made her daughter's hair stand on end. But Georgia loved her anyway, because that's how it was with family. If you only cared about the ones who didn't drive you nuts . . . well, you'd end up with a pretty small table set for holiday suppers.

Mama's face crumpled then, and Georgia put her arms around her mother's shoulders and comforted her while she cried. She didn't know what Aunt Rose had said to Mama to upset her like this, but Georgia was determined to have a talk with her aunt when she saw her next.

The smell of alcohol was unmistakable, but her mother's feet were steady as Georgia led her down the hall toward the living room.

"I'll go make some tea," Daniel said, slipping past Georgia and giving her arm a comforting squeeze.

By the time he returned with the tea, she had settled her mother back on the sofa with the blanket that Grandma Ella Rose had crocheted a few years before she died. Daniel deftly poured the tea, adding a little cream to Mama's before handing her the delicate cup and saucer.

Georgia sat next to her mother and watched him, marveling at how comfortable he seemed with such a homey task, and it struck her suddenly that she was glad he was here. She had always had to deal with Mama by herself and it made it much nicer to have someone else to lean on.

Daniel handed her a cup and then settled into the wingback chair her mother usually preferred. They sipped their tea in silence, a silence that went on just a bit too long to be considered comfortable, but Georgia didn't know what to say to end it. She didn't want to talk about the football game in case that got Mama upset again. And the Miracle Chef cook-off was another touchy subject. Since that was Daniel's entire reason for being here, that pretty much killed that topic.

Hmm. What did that leave?

"Nice weather we're having," she said brightly, taking a sip of her tea.

Daniel raised his eyebrows. "Uh-huh."

"I don't mean to be rude, but would you two mind if I retired to my room? I would like to be alone right now."

Georgia nearly dropped her teacup. Mama actually *wanted* to be by herself? That was a first.

"You don't have to go anywhere," Daniel said, standing up and taking the cup and saucer out of Georgia's hand. "We'll go. If you need us, we'll be over at Georgia's. All right?"

Vivian barely seemed to hear him as she nodded vaguely and waved them off. Daniel wasted no time getting them across the street. As he pushed open the door to Georgia's house, he took her by the arm and said, "Okay, what in the hell was that all about?"

Georgia turned on him, the look in her brown eyes intense, and Daniel frowned, expecting her to tell him to mind his own business or kick him out of her house. Instead, she grabbed his hand and dragged him into the kitchen and said, "Have you ever seen the movie *9½ Weeks*?"

If he'd been wearing a tight collar, Daniel would have loosened it just then. "Uh, yeah."

"Then you know that one scene . . . you know, the food scene?"

Daniel cleared his throat. "Yes."

"I want to do that."

"What? Why now?"

Georgia looked at him solemnly for a moment, and then a sly smile spread across her face as she put a hand on his chest and pushed him backward. "Because," she said, "I don't want to talk about it and I thought I'd distract you with sex."

Daniel swallowed and stepped over the threshold to the kitchen. "Oh. Well, that sounds like a pretty good reason."

She pulled open the refrigerator door and surveyed the lighted interior. Then she looked at him, her gaze sweeping assessingly from his dark brown boots to the top of his head and back. She rubbed the index finger of her left hand over her bottom lip, then touched her tongue to her fingernail, making Daniel groan.

"You're not allergic to chocolate, are you?" she asked.

Daniel silently shook his head.

Georgia reached into the fridge, grabbed a bottle of Hershey's syrup, and handed it to him. "Here, why don't you take this up to the bedroom. I'll be up in minute." With that, she turned and busied herself with gathering other foodstuffs. Daniel started out of the kitchen with his bottle of liquid pleasure, raising his eyebrows when he heard her mutter something about deviled eggs.

He went up the stairs and walked into her bedroom, looking from Georgia's neatly made bed to the bottle of chocolate in his hand and back. Hmm. From what he could remember of *9½ Weeks*, neither Kim Basinger nor Mickey Rourke seemed particularly concerned about the mess they were making. However, this wasn't the movies, so Daniel grabbed one corner of Georgia's pretty floral bedspread and yanked it off the bed. Cleaning just the sheets would be much easier.

"I expected you to be all dressed up as my very own chocolate bar by now," Georgia said huskily, coming up behind him and wrapping her refrigerator-chilled hands around his waist.

Daniel turned in her arms and grinned down at her. "Sorry. They make this look so much easier in the movies. I was worrying about the mess."

Georgia frowned, her forehead crinkling. "Hmm. And me without a tarp."

"We'll just have to make do," Daniel said, as if they were about to make the ultimate sacrifice.

"Yes, we will," Georgia agreed, taking the Hershey's syrup from him and setting it down on the nightstand next to her bed. Then she reached up and unbuttoned the blue-and-white-striped oxford shirt she was wearing. It hung open, revealing the white lacy bra she wore underneath. Slowly, she pulled one sleeve down and then the other.

Daniel watched as the tops of her breasts rose and fell with each breath she took. When her shirt was unbuttoned to her waist, she turned away from him, bending down to pick something up off the floor. Then she reached around and, with a sultry look, unhooked her bra and let it fall to the carpet.

She turned back around, the creamy mounds of her breasts exposed to his gaze. Her rosy nipples puckered and Daniel was tempted to take her in his arms, but held back. For some reason, he felt that she needed to take the initiative this time—to prove to him, to herself, that she could be outrageous without him encouraging her. So he stood, unmoving, watching as she raised a can of whipped cream to her mouth and stuck out her tongue. With their eyes locked together, she depressed the tab until a dollop of frothy cream came out. She pulled her tongue back into her mouth, then licked her lips like a cat.

Daniel was finding it difficult to stand, so he walked over to Georgia's bed and sat down on the edge, his eyes never leaving hers. He was glad he was sitting down when she squirted a generous amount of whipped cream into her right hand, set the can down, lightly rubbed her hands together, and then cupped her hands around her breasts. He reached out then, tugging her toward him until she was standing between his knees.

The whipped cream was nearly tasteless, an airy, lightly sweet mixture. Daniel licked a circle of it off Georgia's left breast, exposing one erect nipple. She arched her back, pushing herself inside his mouth, and Daniel sucked, then pulled back. Georgia rubbed her jeans-clad thigh against his crotch as Daniel licked more cream off her other breast, exposing her taut nipples to his warm breath.

"Here, let's get you out of these clothes," Georgia said, her voice thick like an aged Kentucky bourbon. Daniel raised his arms and let her slide his shirt over his head. Then he unzipped her jeans, slid his hands around her waist, and slowly inched the material past her hips and down her legs.

Georgia kicked the puddle of material at her feet out of the way, and then pulled Daniel off the bed. No way was she going to let him sit there half-dressed with her completely naked. She grabbed her can of whipped cream and stood back, her arms folded across her chest.

"Okay, lover boy," she said, "off with your pants."

Daniel grinned, his hands already at the fly of his jeans. "Yes, ma'am," he said obligingly.

Georgia nodded with satisfaction as he shucked the rest of his clothes. Then, with a wicked smile, she reached out with one hand and caressed his already erect penis with one hand while, with the other, she sprayed a thick line of whipped cream along its length.

She looked up at him and started laughing. "You know what they say. Life is short, eat dessert first." Then she crouched down and licked the tip of his penis as if it were a particularly tasty ice-cream cone. Daniel groaned when she took him all the way in her mouth, her tongue flicking along his sensitive skin.

He closed his eyes and buried his hands in her wildly curly hair. "That feels so good."

She let him slide out slowly, her hands gently kneading his thighs as she pushed him back on the bed.

Daniel pulled her down on top of him, the whipping cream still on her chest smearing into his. Reaching out, he grabbed the plastic bottle of Hershey's syrup and squirted a cold line along Georgia's spine, ending in a puddle right where her lower back met her buttocks. She squealed and laughed at the same time, saying, "That's cold."

Daniel dropped the bottle at their side and ran his fingers through the sticky line he'd drawn down her back. He felt her shiver as his hands passed over her skin, warming the chocolate as they went.

Georgia put her legs out to either side of him and sat up, straddling him. She pulled his hands from behind her and laced their fingers together as she wiggled backward until he felt the heat of her teasing him. She rubbed herself against him and his hips pulsed upward, seeking her tight wetness.

God, she was dangerous. This smart, beautiful woman with her life full of friends, family, and secrets. Whenever he was around her, he felt fulfilled in a way he never had before. He felt like a part of something bigger, more important, than himself.

Daniel pushed her off of him before he could do something stupid—like bury himself in her without a condom and to hell with the consequences. Panting with the effort it took to control himself, he forced himself not to touch her, watching her instead as she lay there looking back at him with half-lidded eyes.

"Is something wrong?" she asked, frowning.

Forgetting that his hands were covered with chocolate, Daniel ran his fingers through his hair. Realizing what he'd just done, he grimaced, then shrugged his shoulders. What did it matter? They were both going to need a shower after this anyway. "Yes, something's wrong," he said, then grinned wolfishly. "Lying there like that, you look good enough to eat."

"Thank you," Georgia said, the look in her eyes so serious that Daniel wondered what was going on in that mind of hers.

He decided it was best to keep her brain otherwise occupied, so he looked through the cans and bottles she'd brought up from the kitchen. His eyes narrowed on a jar of maraschino cherries. Oh, yeah, this was definitely going to blow her mind.

Daniel leaned across Georgia, picked up the glass jar, and unscrewed the lid. He took one chilled cherry out of the jar and dangled it over her stomach until a fat drop of syrup dripped onto her skin. Then, holding it by the stem, he dangled it over one of her breasts, bringing it closer and closer to her erect nipple.

"What are you going to do, tie a knot in the stem?" she asked huskily.

Daniel shook his head. "No. I have something more interesting in mind."

Her eyes went nearly black with wanting. She inhaled a lungful of air, then gasped when the cool smooth skin of the fruit touched her sensitive nipple. Daniel swirled it around her breast, taunting her. Then he pushed her legs apart with one knee, making her open herself to him. Slowly, he inched down until he was lying between her legs. He licked his way up the inside of her thighs, and Georgia felt as if she would explode at any second. She watched him, barely able to keep her eyelids from fluttering closed.

She moaned when his tongue touched her, then nearly came up off the bed when he ran the cherry stem across her sensitive flesh. Then he did something she had never imagined, even in her wildest fantasies: He slid the cold cherry inside her. As he pulled it out with his tongue, Georgia came with a force she'd never experienced before, her mind going blank for what seemed like hours. Every muscle in her body tensed just before she collapsed in a boneless heap on the bed.

When she finally came back to her senses, she opened her eyes to find Daniel watching her with a satisfied grin on his face. He was lying next to her on his side, his head propped up in his right hand. He held the stem of that wicked cherry between the thumb and index finger of his left hand, dangling it between them.

Then, with a grin that would have made Pastor Jackson faint, Daniel stuck out his tongue and sucked the cherry into his mouth. Then he popped off the stem, tossed it away, and said around a mouthful of candied fruit, "So, are you ready for seconds?"

Fifteen

Callie Walker Mitchell was up to her elbows in filmy peignoir sets that Georgia could have told her friend she'd never get to use. Could have, that is, but didn't. It was too late now. In two weeks, Callie would become Mrs. Trey Hunter, and Georgia figured her input regarding Callie's night wear would not be appreciated. Especially not here, in Callie's living room, on the morning of her bridal shower.

Georgia sighed and rested her chin in her hand as Callie pulled a lavender nightie from the tissue paper at the bottom of yet another silver gift box. The fabric of the gown was hardly more substantial than the tissue paper, which made Georgia think of the silly game they'd played earlier when they'd been instructed to break up into groups of five by a surprisingly bossy Mrs. Mitchell and forced to construct wedding dresses for one member of their group using nothing but rolls of toilet paper. Despite her protests that Francie Rydell would make a much better mock bride than herself, Georgia, of course, had been elected to be the guinea pig of her group. She was still picking scraps of tissue out of her hair.

She shivered slightly at the memory of being attacked by four women wielding t.p., their determination to win the prize for most fashionable dress glittering in their eyes like the shine coming off of Callie's marquis-cut diamond engagement ring. A wisp of toilet paper wafted to the carpet like snow falling to the ground. As Georgia reached down to pick up the errant tissue, the crowd gathered around Callie oohed. She looked up to see a gorgeous white satin nightgown being lifted from the gift box in Callie's lap.

"Too bad it'll be wasted on Trey," she muttered under her breath.

"Pardon me?" Emma Rose said from the couch beside her.

Georgia shook her head and another white toilet paper snowflake drifted to the floor. "Um, I said, 'That will look beautiful on Callie's special day,'" she lied.

Emma Rose frowned as if she didn't believe her, but let the topic drop, whispering instead, "So, guess who I saw skulking out of your house early this morning?"

Georgia rolled her eyes heavenward. "Oh, gee. Let me guess. The milkman?"

"I don't know why I should be surprised," Emma Rose groused. "You always get the guy."

Shoving the fingers of her right hand into her hair, Georgia leaned her elbow on the arm of the couch and eyed her cousin irritably. "Yeah, lucky me. I get great sex for a couple of weeks and then Daniel goes back to L.A. What do you want me to do? Be noble and step aside so that you can have him? Because I will if that's what you want."

Emma Rose's frown turned to a scowl. "Get real, Georgia. I don't want your hand-me-downs. I've had enough of that to last my entire life."

It was Georgia's turn to scowl as the crowd hooted at a crotchless red panty and camisole set that Deborah Lee, of all people, had bought for Callie. She heard Kelly ask how long the bride had to stay married in order to keep the gifts and everyone laughed as Georgia sat up straighter on the couch and fixed her cousin with a hard-eyed stare. "Well, then, Emma Rose, why don't you tell me what it is you *do* want? Because you seem to think that I have everything my heart desires and I can assure you that nothing could be further from the truth. If you'd like to trade lives, you just say the word. You can have Daniel, but you're going to get my mother in the bargain. And not only does she disapprove of my illicit love affair, she doesn't much care for my friends, my job, or my wardrobe, either."

Emma Rose opened her mouth, then closed it again without saying a word. A faint blush crept up her neck as she lowered her gaze to Callie's carpet.

Georgia nodded once and muttered, "That's what I thought." Then she rose from the couch, shook yet another scrap of toilet paper from the folds of her skirt, and headed to the kitchen to kill any hope she might have of winning the next Miracle Chef cook-off.

"This is terrible. It's supposed to be dessert, but it's . . . I don't know. Salty."

Georgia watched Francie Rydell pucker up her face as she poked at the remains of the sour cream pound cake on her plate. It was salty because Georgia substituted salt for the two cups of sugar she was supposed to add. And the Velveeta chicken (which had been nearly impossible to ruin until Georgia hit on the idea of mixing in some undiluted cornstarch) was lumpy, and the rice was watery. She'd even overcooked the broccoli until it was that sickly yellow color it got when it turned mushy.

It had worked. Her meal was a disgusting disaster, and she should be pleased with her success.

But she wasn't.

Callie looked as if she were about to cry. Kelly and Deborah Lee, who had volunteered to be judges, wouldn't meet her eyes. Mrs. Broussard had surreptitiously spit every bite of Georgia's food into her napkin, and even old Miss Beall, who thought Jell-O was gourmet eating, was eyeing her plate distastefully.

And Daniel? Daniel was royally pissed, if she read his narrowed eyes and clenched jaw correctly.

The smile he turned on the cameras definitely looked forced. Georgia fiddled with the ends of her apron strings as he finished the show, saying, "Well, it looks as if the Miracle Chef is oh-for-two. Seems like my philosophy is holding true, folks. Whenever something appears too good to be true"—Daniel turned and speared her with those blue Hollywood-star eyes—"it usually is."

Ouch.

"Okay, and that's a wrap," Shana, the spiky-haired producer, yelled.

Georgia blinked and twisted her finger around the apron string, trying to stem the tears that had gathered in her eyes. She hadn't expected her failure to be quite so . . . spectacular. Or so painful.

She spun around when a chair scraped loudly across the tile floor of her best friend's kitchen. Callie stood glaring at her, her shoulders shaking with rage.

"Georgia Elliot, I can not believe you just humiliated us on national television. If you're upset about me marrying Trey, you should have had the courage to come right out and say so. This disgraceful display is about the tackiest thing I've ever seen. You've ruined my bridal shower and now I want you to get out of my house. I never thought you could be this mean."

Georgia held out a hand beseechingly. "No, Callie. It wasn't like that. I'm not—uh, I mean, I didn't . . . Ah hell. I'm really sorry. This is not how I planned for this to turn out at all."

Callie started sobbing, turning to Deborah Lee for comfort. And Deborah Lee, who would rather pluck herself hairless than hurt another living being, shot Georgia such a look of reproach over Callie's shoulder that Georgia felt as if she'd been slapped.

Daniel crossed his arms across his chest and leaned back against the counter, eyeing her coldly. "I should have known you'd do this," he said. "I thought maybe you cared enough about your friends not to do it, but it's clear that I was wrong. I don't even want to think about what this says about how you feel about me. You obviously don't care about making a mockery of me on my own show."

Georgia tugged on her apron strings until the bow came undone. Slowly, she lifted the still-neat garment from around her neck and laid it on the counter.

How had this become so complicated? When she'd invented the Miracle Chef, all she had wanted to do was make her best friend's life easier. How had it snowballed into this mess, where everyone in town seemed to be mad at her?

"I'm sorry," she mumbled. Then, without knowing what else she could do to make it better, she slunk out of Callie's kitchen and made her way back home, suddenly feeling very much alone.

Sixteen

Do you have any ideas for the final show?" Shana Goldberg, *Epicurean Explorer*'s producer asked, gulping down the hot, black coffee the waitress had just poured for her. "We want it to be something big, something showy."

Daniel glanced at a neighboring table and watched as a large, flannel-clad man mooshed his over-easy eggs together with his grits, salted and peppered the mess, and then scooped it up with a triangle of toast. Daniel wasn't quite sure he understood the appeal of grits. To him, they were this sort of tasteless goo, but one thing he'd always been firm about was eating the way the locals did wherever he went. He detested people who traveled all the way to Rome, got off the bus at the Spanish Steps, and hightailed it to the nearest McDonald's. People like that, he figured, should just stay at home. He was seeing it more and more, especially in the States. You could go to Boston or Seattle or Miami and shop at J.Crew or the Gap and eat at Outback Steakhouse.

It was a troubling trend, this homogenization of the nation, which was why Daniel made it his personal mission to avoid chain restaurants whenever he could. Hence the fact that he was now sitting in the Tidepool Diner, contemplating his own breakfast of grits and eggs and pretending to himself that he wouldn't have preferred an Egg McMuffin and Starbucks coffee to this local fare.

"Yes," Daniel answered his producer's question. "Before coming to Ocean Sands, I researched the perfect venue for our last show. At the end of the Shrimp Festival the Saturday after next, there's this giant shrimp feed that culminates with the serving of the world's largest sweet potato pie. It would be a great place to add in some local color in addition to taping the cook-off, but I doubt we're going to make it that long. When we started this whole thing, I figured we'd get to do all five, or at least four, of the cook-off challenges, but it looks like our next show might be our last."

"Yeah," Shana said glumly, taking another swig of coffee.

Daniel loaded his fork with another bite full of dripping grits and eggs. This was really unappealing.

"Excuse me," an elderly woman said from beside him.

Daniel gratefully put down his fork without taking a bite and turned toward the woman, who looked to be somewhere between seventy and ninety, with her deeply wrinkled skin and unnaturally dyed blond hair. "Yes?"

"You're that TV man, aren't you? The one who's here to do some sort of cook-off?"

"Yes, I am." Daniel slid out of the booth and held a hand out to the woman. "Daniel Rogers, at your service."

The woman smiled at him with teeth that looked like she'd overdosed on the Crest Whitestrips. "Velma May Boleen."

"Well, Miss Boleen, it's a pleasure to meet you. I hope you're a fan of the show."

She continued to hold his hand, stroking it as if he were a favored family pet. "I'm sorry to say that I don't have much time for television, what with my canasta group on Mondays, dance lessons on Tuesdays, church on Wednesday. Oh, and Sunday, too, of course. Thursday is the night I go out to the home and visit Mother. No, I really don't have much time for television these days."

Daniel smiled down at the woman. "What about Friday and Saturday? Do you leave those two days for knitting or catching up on your rest?"

Miss Boleen laughed. "Heavens, no. I'm not one of the knitting and napping crowd, I'm happy to say. I keep my Fridays and Saturdays open for the boys."

"Oh. Do you have grandchildren, then?"

Velma Boleen dropped his hand and took a step back, shaking her head. "Well, I do, but that's not what I meant. You young people think you're the only ones who like a little romance. I keep my weekends open for dates, my boy."

Daniel grinned at the elderly woman. "Good for you."

She grinned back. "Yes, as a matter of fact, it is."

"So, what can I do for you then? You're not a fan of the show, so I assume you aren't here for an autograph."

"No. It's actually not anything I want for myself. It's my sister, June. She must have written you three dozen fan letters over the past year. I was wondering if you couldn't somehow include her in one of the shows you're taping here in Ocean Sands."

Daniel looked at Shana, who looked back at him and shrugged.

They needed a place to host the next cook-off, so why not kill two birds with one stone, as the saying went? He'd be doing a favor for a fan and her delightful sister, and they'd have a place to tape the next show.

"It looks like today is your sister's lucky day, Miss Boleen," Daniel said. "How do you think she'd like it if we taped this week's show at her house?"

The elderly woman clutched her hands to her chest, and Daniel saw the glint of tears in her eyes as she said, "Oh, that would be wonderful. Junie always wanted to be on TV."

As Georgia neatly taped gift wrap smattered with silver foil wedding bells around a set of Francis I silverware, she winced as she recalled the debacle at Callie's house for the thousandth time in—she glanced at her watch—twenty-eight hours and thirteen minutes. Georgia had tried calling Callie several times since the Miracle Chef disaster yesterday afternoon, but Callie refused to pick up the phone.

"Damn caller ID anyway," Georgia muttered, folding an edge of the gift wrap down before taping it in place.

"What's that, dear?" Mrs. Broussard asked, looking up from the porcelain cocker spaniel she'd been inspecting while she waited for Georgia to finish wrapping Callie and Trey's wedding gift.

"Oh, I'm sorry. I was just talking to myself," Georgia answered, then held out the prettily wrapped package.

"That's lovely, dear. Thank you," Mrs. Broussard said as she took the present.

Both Georgia and Mrs. Broussard looked up as the warning bells on the gift shop doors tinkled. As Callie stepped in, Mrs. Broussard gasped and shoved the package she was holding behind her back, as if Callie had X ray vision and could divine the contents of the box merely by looking at it.

"Well, I'll be going. Thank you again, Georgia. Callie," Mrs. Broussard said, tipping her head as she sidled past, still holding the present behind her back.

Callie shot Mrs. Broussard a puzzled frown, then shrugged and turned to Georgia, who nervously twined her fingers in the white ribbon that she'd just used to wrap Callie's wedding silverware. Although she'd wanted to talk to Callie about what had happened at the cook-off, she hadn't wanted to be face-to-face with her best friend when she did. Direct confrontation wasn't exactly her strong suit.

"Hey, Callie," she said, giving her friend a half-hearted wave.

Callie stopped in front of the cash register and stood looking at her, her arms folded across her chest, and Georgia had to fight the urge not to squirm.

"Why did you lose that cook-off yesterday?" Callie asked, dispensing with the pleasantries in a decidedly non-Southern manner. "Is it because of Trey . . . or is it something else?"

Georgia clenched the ribbon in her fist as her stomach knotted. Callie was the last person Georgia could talk to about her mother. Georgia had discovered that years ago, when she'd been forced to drop out of Ole Miss and Callie, without knowing exactly why Georgia was leaving, had correctly assumed that it had something to do with Georgia's mother. Although the ensuing fifteen years had dimmed Georgia's memory of their argument, she clearly recalled the general gist of it—

Callie was disgusted by Mama's machinations and even more furious with Georgia for sacrificing her education at the whim of her mother. And Georgia had hurled back some pretty ugly accusations of her own, something to the effect that Callie had no way of understanding what Georgia was going through since her own parents had spoiled her since the second she took her first breath.

They'd made up the very next day, but that one argument had made Georgia realize how fragile even the strongest bonds of friendship were. After that, Callie still occasionally voiced her frustration with the way Vivian got in the way of Georgia's plans, but never again had they really talked about all that Georgia had given up for her mother.

And Georgia wasn't going to open that old wound again now.

She shook her head slightly, then pushed a lock of hair behind her ear and finally met Callie's gaze full-on. "I'm not jealous that you're marrying Trey, if that's what you think."

Callie looked at her for a long moment, unmoving. When she spoke, she sounded less angry—but just as determined to hear the truth—as before. "Then what is it? You never talk to me about Trey, not like girlfriends usually do. Whenever his name comes up, you get this look on your face like someone's put vinegar on your grits. I never really believed that you wanted him back, and I sure hope this . . . this *thing* that you're doing with Daniel Rogers isn't to take your mind off of me and Trey, but how am I supposed to know if you won't even talk to me about it?"

Georgia swallowed. Then she took a deep breath and swallowed again. "I, uh, I can assure you I'm not with Daniel because of Trey. Trey and I getting a divorce was the right thing for both of us. I'm just . . ." She paused, trying to think of a way to say what she wanted to say without actually saying it, but unable to think of how to do it. In the end, she blurted, "I'm scared for you."

Callie uncrossed her arms and took a step toward her, her eyebrows drawn together as she frowned. "What do you mean? What are you scared about? Trey would never hurt me."

"No, I didn't mean that. Of course Trey would never lay a hand on you. Or the kids. It's just—" Georgia stopped, the enormity of what she wanted to say crushing down on her. How could she do this? What if she was wrong, and Callie was still alone, five or ten years from now, blaming Georgia for making her second-guess one of the most important decisions of her life?

She couldn't do it.

"Forget it," Georgia said, dropping the ribbon she'd been clutching like a lifeline. "Maybe you're right. Maybe I am just upset because Trey and I were once married. I'm sorry for being so petty. It won't happen again." Then, because she didn't want to talk about anything upsetting anymore, she forced herself to smile and asked, "So, hey, are you going to come to the Tiara Club meeting tonight? Deborah Lee said she has a big surprise in store for Sierra. Do you know what it might be?"

Unfortunately, it appeared that Callie was not going to play this one by Georgia's rules. Instead of letting the matter drop, she closed in on Georgia, placing her hands on the counter and leaning across it, nearly pinning Georgia to the back wall. "All right, Georgia Elliot, I have had it. It's obvious that you don't want a real friendship. That's why the Tiara Club is so important to you—you get the illusion of having friends without really letting us into your life. Well, I've had enough. If superficial relationships are all you want in your life, that's fine. But I want more than that. I want friends who trust me enough to talk to me about their fears and their dreams. That obviously rules you out. Good-bye."

With that, Callie turned on her heel and stalked out of the gift shop, leaving Georgia to wonder if her entire world was falling apart.

"Aren't you going to try making caramel again tonight?" Kelly asked, pouring herself a vodka martini and forgoing the banana daiquiris Georgia had dispiritedly blended a few minutes before.

"No. I'm giving up," Georgia said as she muted the television in the sitting room with the remote control, wincing as the *Epicurean Explorer* show that had been taped yesterday came on the air.

"But it's something you've wanted to do for months. You can't give up now," Kelly protested.

And Georgia had to turn away, busying herself with the dishes in the sink because all she wanted to do was scream, "Yes, I can give up. Don't you know that's what I am—a goddamn quitter!" Her fight with Callie had left her angry and depressed. How could Callie just throw away a near-lifetime friendship like that? Okay, so maybe Georgia hadn't exactly told her everything about her mother or Trey or why she'd lost the cook-off, but was that really so awful?

"Boy, you really screwed that up," Kelly said, pointing to the TV screen as she lounged in the doorway of Georgia's kitchen.

Georgia rubbed her pounding temples with a wet hand and sighed. "I know," she mumbled.

As Tiara Club meetings went, this one was pretty depressing.

From across the kitchen, Deborah Lee sent Georgia a hurt look, as if she had caught Georgia kicking somebody's puppy. "I think you owe Callie an apology," she said.

Georgia grabbed a dish towel and wiped her hands off before answering, "I tried. She's still too upset with me to let it go."

"Well, I don't blame her. You ruined her bridal shower," Kelly said, matter-of-factly.

"Don't bother sugarcoating it," Georgia muttered.

Kelly grimaced as she took another sip of her martini. "Sorry. I'm in a foul mood tonight."

"What's wrong?" Deborah Lee asked, obviously somewhat placated by knowing that Georgia had at least attempted to make peace with Callie since her back lost some of its previous ramrod stiffness.

Kelly waved a hand dismissively and spoke around the olive she was chewing, "Stuart and I had a fight. I tried to pin him down to a wedding date but he refuses to cut short our engagement."

"Well, can you blame him? I mean, you married your two previous husbands within a few months of meeting them and look how those turned out," Emma Rose said, coming in from the parlor to refill her drink.

"Whose side are you on anyway?" Kelly asked, only half in jest.

"I just think y'all take your relationships with men too much for granted," Emma Rose said, pulling up a stool to join the pity party.

"The way I figure it, the sooner Stuart and I get married, the sooner we can start working on the divorce," Kelly said dryly, draining her martini in one gulp.

Deborah Lee gasped and looked like she was going to say something, but Georgia's back door opened just then and Sierra came in, carefully shaking the rain from her jacket before stepping into the house. She looked like she'd been crying and had tried to cover it up, without much success.

"Hey, Sierra," Georgia said, and Sierra immediately burst into tears.

Great. Was no one in Ocean Sands happy tonight?

"Honey, what's wrong?" Deborah Lee asked, jumping up off her chair and rushing to comfort Sierra while Kelly poured her a drink.

Sierra's shoulders were shaking, her acres of rich red hair for once not clipped back in a ponytail. She cried noisily for a few moments, but the sobs soon subsided, no match for the pampering ministrations of the members of the Tiara Club.

"Here, drink this," Kelly said, forcing a banana daiquiri into Sierra's shaking hands.

Sierra looked up and smiled through the last of her tears. "Thanks. And I'm sorry. I didn't mean to come here and rain on everyone's evening."

Emma Rose snorted and handed Sierra a box of tissues. "Honey, the mood here tonight is as heavy as my mama's baking powder biscuits. There's nothing you could do to make it worse."

"So, what's gone and upset you? Did one of your students tape tacks to the other kids' chairs again?" Kelly asked, mixing herself another martini.

"You tryin' to drown yourself in those?" Deborah Lee asked with a frown.

"Don't you worry. I know where Georgia keeps her life jackets," Kelly answered, favoring Deborah Lee with a mocking wink.

"No, my students are fine," Sierra answered Kelly's earlier question. "It's . . ." She paused and took a quick glance around the kitchen, looking awkward. With a deep breath, she continued, "It's Tim. When I told him that I was coming here tonight, he made fun of me. You know, about the beauty pageant stuff."

Georgia watched in surprise as Deborah Lee's hands clenched into fists.

"Why would he do a thing like that?" she asked.

Sierra shrugged with a half smile curving her lips. "I don't know. I guess I can't blame him. It *is* kind of silly for me to think that I could really do it. I mean, look at me. I'm no more a beauty queen than . . . than . . ." She waved her hands helplessly in the air. "I can't even think of an example absurd enough to use. That's how ridiculous this whole idea is."

Georgia hated for Sierra to think that she wasn't good enough to at least give it a try. Throughout her pageant career, she'd seen girls she never thought had even the slightest chance of making it to the finals end up wowing the judges and winning the crown. In her opinion, it wasn't so much a matter of being beautiful as it was of really believing that you could win. And she started to tell Sierra that, but Deborah Lee interrupted, surprising them all when she nearly shouted, "What is it with people nowadays? If Tim loves you, he should believe that you can do anything you put your mind to."

"Hear, hear," Kelly said, toasting her friend with her martini glass.

Apparently, that was a mistake, because Deborah Lee whirled on her next. "And you," she growled. "All your talk about divorcing Stuart when you're not even married yet. How do you think that makes him feel? Stuart is a wonderful man and he loves you and you act like he's disposable—as if he's human Kleenex or something. You make me so mad sometimes."

If Georgia hadn't been so worried that sweet Deborah Lee's head was about to start spinning around on her neck, she might have laughed. Instead, she instinctively ducked behind the kitchen island when Deborah Lee whirled on her, one accusing finger outstretched, which would have horrified Georgia's mother who believed that "Thou Shalt Not Point" was one of the Ten Commandments. "Then there's Georgia, who jeopardizes lifelong relationships because she keeps everyone at arm's length and doesn't get personal, even with her very best friends. And Emma Rose, who blames Georgia for the fact that she isn't getting what she wants out of life because it's easier to do that than to acknowledge that it's her own damn fault for not trying hard enough."

Georgia blinked up at her cousin, who blinked right back. She hoped that Deborah Lee was about through, because her legs were starting to ache from crouching down behind the island. Besides, who else was left for Deborah Lee to castigate?

It turned out, however, that just because Callie was absent this evening, that wasn't going to stop Deborah Lee from taking a turn at scolding her. "Finally, we come to Callie, who never asks for help because she thinks that if people care enough about her, they'll just tend to her needs without her even asking, like she's some goddamn princess or something. Well, I am sick of all of you. Our relationships with other people are too important to treat with such casual disregard and it's going to stop, right this minute."

Georgia's legs were about to give out so she reached out and grabbed the countertop and slowly pulled herself up from behind the island. She risked a peek in Deborah Lee's direction as soon as her head cleared the top of the counter. Deborah Lee's face was nearly glowing with righteous indignation and Georgia found herself holding her breath, waiting for what she might say next.

"We are all going to help Sierra win this beauty pageant and prove to her that she has what it takes to be a queen. There will be an emergency meeting of the Tiara Club on Friday night, and you will all be here, do you understand?" She glared at each one of them in turn and they were all too frightened to do anything but nod like obedient sheep. "Good. Kelly, you make up flash cards so we can drill Sierra on questions the judges might ask. Emma Rose, you're going to be in charge of the talent portion. Callie can take hair and makeup and I'll be responsible for the evening gown competition."

Georgia licked her lips and hesitantly raised her hand, waiting until Deborah Lee nodded sternly in her direction and said, "Yes, what is it?" before asking, "Um, what do you want me to do?"

"You're job is to find the perfect swimsuit, one that will flatter both Sierra's figure and her coloring," Deborah Lee answered before sweeping the room with her gaze again. "Is everyone clear?"

"Yes, ma'am," they all said in unison, even Sierra, who had not been given an assignment.

Deborah Lee nodded sharply in approval. "Good. Then I'm going to bed. I'll see you all back here on Friday. Seven-fifteen, sharp."

Nobody moved, even after the front door slammed. Afraid Deborah Lee might come back for a second helping of their hides, Georgia figured.

She nearly jumped to the ceiling like a startled cat when her doorbell rang. Georgia desperately looked to the other women in the kitchen for help, but Kelly, Sierra, and Emma Rose were already backing away from the door.

"It's your house," Kelly said, at least having the grace to blush.

Georgia tiptoed down the hallway, telling herself not to be afraid. If Deborah Lee had come back, surely she would have just let herself in.

"Who could it be, the grim reaper?" she muttered under her breath.

Georgia pulled open the door and a blast of cold air slapped her in the face. It was neither Deborah Lee nor the grim reaper. It was the UPS guy. Miranda Kingsley's brother, Michael, to be exact.

"Hey, Georgia," he greeted her cheerfully.

Well, at least somebody was happy tonight. "Hey, Michael," she replied, trying to shake off the sense of doom engulfing her.

"I've got a delivery for you," Michael said.

Georgia blinked several times, trying to hold back the sarcastic comment that was trying to escape from her lips. Finally, she could keep it in no longer. "Really? A delivery? From UPS? Who would have thought?"

Michael grinned good-naturedly. "Don't be a wiseass. I was going to deliver it earlier, but I know you were working down at the gift shop today and I didn't think it would have been right just to leave it on your porch. I didn't want to take the chance of it getting stolen."

"What is it? A block of gold from Fort Knox?" Georgia couldn't remember ordering anything lately. Maybe Mama had bought something from a catalog and had it shipped to Georgia's house, although why she'd do that, Georgia had no idea.

"Well, I don't exactly know what it is. I just know there's a lot of it and I didn't want to leave it here all day."

"Oh. Well. Thank you."

"No problem," Michael said, making Georgia wince. Mama had drummed it into her head over and over again that the only proper response to "thank you" was "you're welcome."

"I'll just start bringing them in. You let me know where you want 'em."

Georgia nodded, but thought it was pretty hard to know where you wanted something when you didn't even know what it was. She stood in the doorway and waited for Michael to return, which he did almost immediately, pushing a hand truck and whistling. As soon as Georgia saw the boxes, she realized what was in them.

It was the extra Miracle Chefs she'd had manufactured for her friends and family. Only, they couldn't see her with them now. She hadn't thought up a reasonable story to tell them about where she'd found them. She needed more time.

Michael was halfway up the stairs when Georgia started down. "No, wait. I can't accept these right now. I . . . I don't have any room."

Her UPS man frowned. Apparently, she'd said something to destroy his chipper mood. "We're not a storage facility, you know."

"I know. I know. It's just that, well, maybe you could come back tomorrow night? I'll have time to clear out some space for them by then."

"I made a special trip out here tonight. I don't usually work this late," Michael protested.

"You could deliver them to the shop first thing tomorrow," she wheedled. Yes, that was perfect. She could just store them in the stockroom until tomorrow night, and then bring them back here and hide them in her hall closet until the excitement about the cook-off died down.

"Well . . ." Michael hedged.

"Georgia, who is that at the door?" Kelly called from the front room.

"Nobody," Georgia hollered back, earning herself an insulted look from Michael Kingsley, who obviously took offense to being called a nobody.

"What's in the boxes?" Emma Rose asked, ambling outside to stand on Georgia's porch now that the coast was clear and Deborah Lee was gone.

"Hey, Emma Rose," Michael said, two curious red spots appearing on his cheeks as if he were embarrassed.

"Uh. Nothing. Just . . . stuff for the gift shop," Georgia answered.

"Oh, you guys get the cutest things," Sierra said, joining Emma Rose on the porch.

"Thank you. I do the ordering," Georgia said proudly.

"What's in these, then? Let us see," Sierra begged.

Kelly wandered out with her martini. "Yeah, give us a preview of this fall's hottest merchandise. Hey, Michael," she added.

Michael nodded and rested his hands on the handle of his hand truck. "Hey y'all."

Then, before Georgia could do anything to stop this disaster from unfolding, Emma Rose stepped forward, grabbed the top box off Michael's stack, and pulled back the packing tape.

Georgia's brain seemed frozen. Why couldn't she think of something to say? Most likely because she knew she wasn't a good liar. Telling tales was something she'd always had to practice. She'd only been able to play hooky from school when she'd thought out a plan ahead of time. She had to think about it, to write out every possible question someone might ask and what her response would be. Most of the time, it wasn't worth it. She spent more time practicing her lies than if she'd just gone to school.

By the time she thought to tell everyone that these were just boring old supplies—nothing they'd be interested in seeing—it was too late. Emma Rose had pulled a gleaming new Miracle Chef from the box and was holding it aloft as if it were the product of the second virgin birth.

"Surprise," Georgia said glumly. "I bought these for y'all."

Seventeen

What an awful day.

Georgia pushed open the door of the gift ship and grimaced as the cheery bells jangled their warning. She popped open her umbrella and held it over her head. There was an overhang on the building that should have kept her dry, but the wind blowing in from the north was driving the rain against the front windows of the store and down the collar of her lightweight coat.

Georgia shivered.

All day today, people coming into the shop talked about nothing but the cold front that had swept through Ocean Sands, pushing their normally mild autumn temperatures down into the fifties. This was, of course, still mild by other states' standards, but the residents of Ocean Sands were more accustomed to warm weather than cold and, thus, any deviation from the expected became the subject of endless discussion.

Georgia turned the key in the lock and tugged on the door just to be certain it was locked, even though she could clearly see that the dead bolt had latched. An automatic gesture, she supposed, like checking the mail chute to be sure it was empty after you'd dropped in an envelope.

As she checked the door again, she looked down Main Street to Callie's dress shop. The lights were off, so Georgia assumed that Callie had gone for the day. Not that it mattered. Callie still wasn't speaking to her.

Georgia sighed. She hadn't expected to feel this badly about doing what she knew was the right thing. Nor had she expected Callie to get so angry about it. Sometimes, friendship really sucked.

Georgia took a step back from the door of the gift shop . . . and then screamed when someone tapped her on the shoulder. She spun around, instinctively holding her umbrella out as a weapon.

Daniel stood watching her with a dubious look on his face. "You'd never survive a week in L.A."

Putting a hand to her racing heart, Georgia put the umbrella back over her head. "Am I supposed to apologize for living in a place where your life is *not* threatened on a daily basis?"

"Touché." He raised his hands, palms up in mock surrender, and Georgia found herself feeling even grumpier than before. She had no idea how he managed to look so perfect, even in the dripping rain. He had on a chocolate brown leather coat, a pair of worn blue jeans, and a lightweight fisherman's sweater, and he looked better in the standard male attire than any man Georgia had ever seen.

"What are you doing here?" she asked, wishing he'd just go away.

"Could we go inside? It's cold out here."

"Yes, of course," Georgia said politely, although what she really wanted to say was, "It's probably warm and sunny back in California."

She unlocked the door she had just finished locking and turned to her left to flick on the fluorescent lights overhead. The lights blinked on in that way they had, as if someone were jabbing them with a cattle prod to make them come on. She set her pocketbook on the counter and leaned her umbrella on the floor to let the rain drip off.

Daniel looked around the gift shop. Assessing the merchandise, Georgia figured. She felt her spine stiffen defensively, even though she knew it was silly to get her back up. "We carry Waterford and Swarovski," she felt the need to point out.

"Looks like you've got some nice stuff," Daniel said, taking a step toward her.

Georgia pressed her back against the counter. His body seemed to take up all the extra space in the room and she hadn't realized before how small the gift shop was. Now, with Daniel standing there watching her, she felt crowded all of a sudden.

"Why are you here?" she asked.

"To see you."

Surprised, Georgia lifted her gaze to his. "Why?"

"I figured you'd be trying to avoid me after what happened on Sunday, and there's something I want to discuss. You have a habit of trying to get me into bed every time I want to talk, so I figured I'd have to confront you someplace where that wouldn't happen." One corner of his mouth drew up in a cockeyed grin. "Well, at least someplace where the chance of it happening would be diminished."

Georgia shot him a narrow-eyed glare. "I thought men liked women who didn't want to talk all the time."

"There's a difference between talking all the time and refusing to discuss any topic at all."

"I don't refuse to talk about everything," Georgia protested.

"What were you afraid was going to happen to your mother on Friday night?"

Daniel had gone from teasing to serious in the space of a heartbeat, as if he had flipped a switch inside himself. Georgia glanced down at the puddle of water that had pooled beneath her umbrella. She tried to keep her own voice calm and free of emotion as she answered, "I wasn't afraid that anything would happen to her. I just worried that she might be lonely."

He reached out and, with one strong hand, lifted her chin until their eyes met. "That's bullshit."

Georgia blinked, her gaze sliding to the case of crystal figurines she'd dusted that morning. "You've seen how she gets. I figured she'd be calling me on my cell phone before the game was over anyway, so why not just be proactive and go over there without her having to ask? That way, I get points for being a good daughter."

"You are a good daughter." Daniel stepped closer, the toes of his boots nearly touching hers. "But you're not a good liar," he added softly.

Georgia's gaze darted back to him. "What does it matter? You're going to be gone in—what?—a week and a half? Why can't you just leave it alone?"

"Because I want to know what motivates a smart, beautiful woman to spend her days selling crystal unicorns and deviled egg plates when she's capable of so much more."

Daniel's grip on her chin softened, his thumb brushing over her bottom lip.

"I want to know why you dropped out of college. I want to know why you don't stand up to your mother. I want to know why you're not proud of being an inventor. I want to know *you*."

He said the last so softly that Georgia almost didn't catch the words as he lowered his mouth to hers in a kiss that was unlike any they'd previously shared. It was soft and strong, and lacking in passion, but not promise.

Georgia felt tears well up behind her closed eyelids. How easy it would be to tell him that the answer to all of his questions lay in one moment in time that had changed her life forever. She'd said it herself—he would be gone in a matter of days. What difference would it make if he knew the secret she'd kept inside her for so long?

But what if he didn't keep that secret? What if he told someone? What if he told her mother that he knew? What would Mama do then?

And there it was. The question that always gave her pause, that made her evaluate whether or not she was willing to take that risk.

Daniel pulled back and searched her face, and it was obvious from the disappointed way he looked at her that he knew she had decided not to take a chance on telling him her darkest secrets.

He took a step back and, in one smooth movement, unzipped the front of his jacket and pulled out a sheaf of papers. "I thought you might be interested in seeing these," he said quietly, laying the pile down on the counter right next to her elbow.

It took her a moment to switch gears. "What—" She shook her head and rain dripped from her hair onto the papers. "What's this?"

"Fan letters," Daniel answered, rocking back on his heels and sliding his hands into the back pockets of his jeans.

"Fan letters for the Miracle Chef?" Georgia asked incredulously. How in the world could people like the cursed machine? After all she'd done to make sure that it would flop?

"No," Daniel corrected, the chill in his voice sending a shiver down

Georgia's spine. "They're fan letters to me. Thanking me for exposing the so-called Miracle Chef as a fraud, a way to separate people from their hard-earned cash. Without exception, the author of every letter we've received wants to see your invention fail. I guess I should thank you for making it so easy for me to win this cook-off."

Then, with a curt nod, he was gone, leaving Georgia standing in a puddle of rainwater, staring at the crystal figurines whose eyes seemed to be winking at her mockingly in the glow of the overhead lights.

✕

Eighteen

Velma Boleen's sister June did not look well when Daniel and the rest of the *Epicurean Explorer* crew showed up at her house on Wednesday at noon. It wasn't that she didn't have on makeup or hadn't just had her hair done, because she had. It wasn't even that she was wearing the wrong clothes, because she was dressed impeccably.

It was that she was dead.

And she had been dead for five days.

Today, however, she was going to her final resting place. After the viewing, and the potluck . . . and the televised cook-off.

"Oh, somebody just kill me now," Shana groaned.

"Don't say that too loudly. These people obviously love a good wake," Daniel said, looking around at the happy mourners gathered in "Aunt Junie's" living room.

"Oh, you made it. We're all so excited." All five feet of Velma Boleen seemed packed with energy as she gripped Daniel's hand and pulled him into the kitchen. "June would have been so thrilled. Did I tell you that we're going to film this and bury her with the tape? Mr. Broussard has one of those fancy home cameras that he bought when his first great-grandson was born. The tape is only this big." She put her thumb and forefinger about two inches apart and said, "Can you imagine?"

What Daniel couldn't imagine was how he had fallen right into Velma's trap.

"We can't air this," Shana hissed. "It's a funeral."

Daniel closed his eyes and slapped his forehead with his palm. "I know."

"Now, wait. You can't leave. Junie would be so disappointed."

Daniel looked down at the elderly woman who didn't seem to realize that his audience really wasn't going to appreciate watching a cook-off over a dead body.

"Your sister is dead," Shana pointed out.

"Well, dear, here in the South we like to say she's gone to her eternal rest. Now doesn't that sound much nicer?" Velma patted Shana's hand as if trying to reason with a recalcitrant child.

"However you say it, it's not like she's really going to care whether or not we're here."

"Oh, you don't believe in heaven then, dear? I'm so sorry." Velma marched over to the refrigerator and scribbled something on a notepad. "Do you spell your name with one 'n' or two?"

Daniel saw his producer's brow furrow with consternation. "One. But why do you need to know that?"

Velma finished writing and turned, bestowing an angelic smile on them. "I'm adding you to our prayer list."

"Wh-what?" Shana sputtered.

"Yes, we'll all get together and pray against the damnation of your eternal soul. Would you like a deviled egg?" Velma held out a platter of eggs topped with whipped yolks and garnished with alternating dashes of paprika and sliced green olives. Her smile was so beatific that Daniel wasn't certain if she had meant the offer as a dig or not.

He shook his head. Surely not.

"All right, look, we're already here, so maybe we can just try to make the best of it. I mean, June's out in the living room—"

"Yes, and doesn't she look lovely?" Velma asked.

Daniel cleared his throat. "Yes, she does. I'm sure she's, ah, looking down from heaven right now and thinking about what a nice send-off you all are giving her today."

Velma laid a hand on his arm, her skin cool and thin. "Oh, aren't you a nice boy?"

Behind the older woman's back, Shana rolled her eyes and Daniel gave her a little shrug. One of Vivian's sayings flashed through his mind. *Easier to catch flies with honey than vinegar*, she said.

"So anyway," he continued, "I don't see why we can't just set up in here and pretend this is a regular old potluck. It's not like the viewers at home need to get a glimpse of Aunt Junie all laid to rest, right?"

Shana pursed her lips, considering his plan. Then she waved her hands in the air and said, "Okay. Let's do it."

Velma squeezed Daniel's arm. "Oh, thank you. You'll never know how much this means to us."

"No," Daniel said. "I don't suppose I will."

"You ready to go to Miss Harris's viewing?" Vivian asked, breezing into the gift shop on the jangle of warning bells and a cloud of Chanel perfume.

Georgia glanced up from the cash register, where she had been banding together one-dollar bills. Her mother was dressed in her best funeral finery, from the tips of her black pumps to the dark netting attached to the brim of her hat.

"You are one of the only women I know who can pull off wearing a hat," Georgia said.

"Thank you, dear." Mama ducked her head to acknowledge the compliment.

Georgia slid the drawer of the till closed and leaned down to pick up her pocketbook. Unlike Mama, she wasn't religious about matching her purse to her shoes, but today she had moved her driver's license, cell phone, and keys to a black handbag that would be appropriate for a funeral.

Georgia followed Mama out into the sunshine, glad that the rain was gone today, even if the cold had remained. It didn't take her long to lock up and slide into the front seat of her mother's enormous burgundy Mercury Marquis.

June Harris was a spinster who had lived with her older sister and brother-in-law since she graduated high school and moved out of her parents' house. Georgia saw the appeal of the situation—June's sister

Velma was a hoot. Rumor had it that Aunt Junie, as everyone called her, had fallen hard for a handsome young army medic who got temporarily stationed in Biloxi after World War II broke out. Of course, as happened with so many love affairs at the time, this one died a tragic death when Aunt Junie's beau shipped out and was returned home three months later in a pine box.

As far as Georgia knew, June had never so much as dated another man since.

Velma, on the other hand, had been faithfully married to her high-school sweetheart for nearly sixty years when he died. She gave herself a year to mourn and then had to "get back out amongst the living," as she put it.

As much as she admired Velma's joie de vivre, Georgia knew in her heart that she was more like June. Getting intimate with another person—deeply, emotionally intimate where you shared each other's secrets—was something Georgia was afraid to do. Yes, she had good friends who she could talk to . . . but not that she could confide *everything* to. Even Callie, who had been her best friend for nearly thirty years, didn't know everything about Georgia's life.

When June had fallen in love with her soldier, she had most likely laid her own heart bare. And he had betrayed her by dying, teaching her that giving too much of yourself to another person only left you open to pain.

"Georgia, honey, where are you? We're here."

Georgia's eyelids fluttered when her mother snapped her fingers in front of her eyes. She gave a small laugh. "Oh, I'm sorry. I guess I was a million miles away."

"Would you mind getting the casserole out of the backseat? I've got my hands full with this coffee urn Velma asked to borrow."

Georgia opened the back door of her mother's car and spied the covered glass dish nestled on a towel on the floor. No Southern wake would be complete without turkey tetrazzini. "Got it," she called to her mother, who was already halfway up the walk.

The front door was open and the house inside crowded with people here to see Aunt Junie off on her final journey. Georgia nodded to the people she knew who were still talking to her after Sunday's fiasco as she carried the casserole through the house to the kitchen, where she nearly dropped it in surprise.

What was Daniel doing here? Even more important, what was his film crew doing here?

Georgia set the heavy dish on a table nearly groaning under the weight of food people had brought for the viewing.

"Is there anyone in this town you don't know?" Daniel asked, eyeing her as warily as she was eyeing him.

Georgia pondered the question for a moment before answering, "I don't think so. Why are you filming June Harris's funeral?"

Daniel shot a sideways glance at June's sister, Velma. "I was hoodwinked. But we're not going to be filming the funeral. We're going to shoot a cook-off segment here in the kitchen."

"Oh. Is, uh, is Callie going to be today's chef?" Georgia asked.

"No. She refused to be a part of it. She said she'd been humiliated enough, so I decided that I'd have one of my staff members man the Miracle Chef. How hard can it be?"

"Well, it's not difficult, but you do have to keep track of time. Food cooks faster in the Miracle Chef, you see. The secret is the combination of pressure and—" Georgia stopped as she caught Daniel's amused eyebrow-raise. She looked across the room to make certain that her mother wasn't paying her any attention before continuing, "—the patented dry-steam process."

"Uh-huh."

"What is your staff going to cook in the Miracle Chef?" Georgia asked.

"Chateaubriand, potatoes *dauphinoise,* steamed carrots with dill, and trifle for dessert."

Georgia grimaced. "That's not funeral food."

"So what?" Daniel shrugged. "That just means the Miracle Chef will lose and this will all be over. Isn't that what you wanted?"

"Yes, of course," Georgia said as Daniel retreated to Miss Boleen's kitchen to begin preparations for the cook-off, but she wasn't so sure anymore. When Daniel had handed her those letters accusing the Miracle Chef of being a fraud, she had been upset—not because the letters were right, but because they were so very wrong. The Miracle Chef worked. And she, as the inventor, had done something remarkable.

Georgia thought back to the letter Callie had written that had set off this whole chain of events. In her letter, Callie had told Daniel why the Miracle Chef was important, and it wasn't as simple as just being able to spend less time in the kitchen every day. It was about her family, about spending time with them every night as they grew up and encountered joy and challenges and sorrow, about giving them the chance to share in one another's hectic lives when for the rest of the day they were all running in opposite directions.

A product she—Georgia Elliot—invented had done that.

But nobody else would ever know her product was a success, and, all of a sudden, that hurt. If the cook-off went the way Daniel planned, the Miracle Chef would be soundly trounced one final time and it would all be over. Everyone would be convinced that her invention was useless.

Unfortunately, there was nothing she could—

"Excuse me. This dish is hot and I need to set it down."

Georgia instinctively moved out of the way even before recognizing that it was Callie who had come up behind her. Callie set the casserole she was carrying down on the already overloaded table and then turned, looking right through Georgia as if she were made of glass. Georgia cringed at the icy look in her friend's eyes. Callie had never stayed mad at her this long before and, for the first time, Georgia considered that Callie might actually make good on her threat to end their friendship. She couldn't imagine what life would be like without her best friend. No more invitations to Callie's children's birthday parties, no watching Caroline grow up, no one to laugh with over beauty pageant rituals she was forced to endure, no one she could really talk to about her love life or her dead-end job. Maybe she didn't always share her most private thoughts with Callie, but Georgia would feel Callie's absence like a giant hole that had been punched out of her life.

She couldn't just stand here and not do anything to try to stop that from happening.

"Hey, Callie," she said, trying to stop her voice from shaking.

"Georgia." Callie coolly inclined her head to acknowledge the greeting before she started to walk away.

Georgia laid a hand on Callie's shoulder to stop her. "Please," she said softly. "Please don't give up on me." Suddenly, Georgia found her eyes filling with tears. She couldn't lose her best friend. Callie was too important to her. "I'll do anything to fix things. Just . . . just tell me what you want me to do."

For a long moment, Callie stood silent and still and Georgia didn't think that she was going to respond. Slowly, Callie turned around, an assessing look in her eyes. "You'll do anything?" she repeated.

Georgia swallowed. Was Callie going to make her eat a goldfish on TV or something equally humiliating? She squared her shoulders, determined to make things right between them, no matter the cost. "Yes. Anything."

Callie stared at her, unblinking, but Georgia's gaze didn't falter. Finally, Callie nodded, her eyes softening. "All right then. Here's what I want you to do." She paused, and Georgia took a deep breath, praying for strength. Whatever Callie asked of her, she would do. No matter how embarrassing or silly or—

"I want you to stop being who your mother wants you to be and have the courage to be yourself instead."

Startled, Georgia frowned. "What?"

Callie crossed her arms across her chest and looked at Georgia skeptically. "You said you'd do anything to fix our friendship. That's what I want you to do."

"I didn't say I wouldn't do it. I'm just not sure what it is exactly that you want from me."

"I want you to stop tiptoeing around life, worried about doing or saying something that might upset your mother." Callie reached up and grabbed Georgia's hand, crushing her fingers so tightly that Georgia winced. "Can you do that for me?"

Georgia still didn't understand what it was that Callie wanted from her, but the one thing she did know was that she didn't want to ruin this opportunity to fix things with Callie. And since their friendship had blown up because she'd sabotaged the last cook-off, maybe one way she could get things back to the way they had been was to see if Daniel would give her a second chance to win this one. After all, what could it hurt?

She squeezed Callie's hand back before letting it drop. "I'll do the best I can," she said.

"Well," Callie said, "for both our sakes, I hope that's good enough."

Proper funeral food could be categorized into four basic food groups: fried chicken, anything made with Campbell's cream of mushroom soup, deviled eggs, and dessert. Since Georgia saw no fewer than half a dozen plates filled with deviled eggs on the table Miss Velma had set out for the food, she figured she'd concentrate her efforts on the other three categories.

"I need a fryer—cut up if you can get the butcher to do it for you right then. If not, I can just as easily do it myself," she told *Epicurean Explorer's* producer. Hell, she'd been making fried chicken since she was twelve years old. She could probably cut up a fryer faster than Joe Quinn down at the Piggly Wiggly could. "A can of French-cut green beans, cream of mushroom soup, some Velveeta . . . Oh, wait a minute. Miss Velma most likely has everything I need right here."

Georgia tugged open the door of the pantry and saw that, indeed, there was no need for an emergency trip to the grocery store.

"What? Is no Southern home complete without Velveeta?" Shana Goldberg muttered, making Georgia laugh.

She pulled what she needed off the shelves and busied herself arranging the ingredients she'd need for each dish. Once Daniel had agreed to let her square off against him in this cook-off, she'd quickly decided on a menu of fried chicken, the ubiquitous green bean casserole, cornbread, and pineapple upside-down cake. Daniel, not realizing that funerals in the South had strict—yet unspoken—guidelines about what was proper to eat at a viewing, was preparing a fancier spread of steamed trout, roasted peppers, rice pilaf, and lime sorbet with raspberry sauce.

Wining this cook-off was going to be like taking the Junior Miss Sweet Potato crown from that bratty Debbi Lynn Macpherson back when she was ten. Debbi Lynn thought she could win by batting her big ol' black eyelashes at the judges, but it was Georgia who had taken home the title that day by tap-dancing her way into their hearts. Oh, and the homemade chocolate chip cookies she brought probably hadn't hurt, either.

She could only hope that by winning the cook-off, she could also redeem herself in Callie's eyes as well.

"Now, Georgia, didn't you tell me the other day that you like to soak your chicken overnight in buttermilk before you fry it?" Daniel asked in his TV-show-host voice.

Georgia grinned into the cameras. "Yes, typically I do. But if you forget, you can always brine your chicken for a few minutes in a mixture of salt and water. Rinse the chicken thoroughly and pat it dry before you dip it in the egg wash, and this will help lock in some extra moisture. Of course, the most important thing to do is not overcook it. There's nothing worse than dry fried chicken."

Daniel shot her a pointed look. "Isn't that the truth," he muttered, putting his hand over his microphone so the viewing audience couldn't hear.

Georgia kept an angelic expression pasted on her face as if she had no idea what he was talking about. Daniel went back to his own preparations, commenting on a certain technique he'd used or explaining something about the ingredients he'd chosen. He asked her opinion on several things and drew her into a conversation about the locally grown fruits and vegetables, and it became obvious to Georgia that he had done his research about the area.

When Shana announced that they had one minute left to plate their meals for the judges, Georgia took a deep breath and looked out into the audience who had moved in from the living room to watch the cook-off.

People she'd known nearly all her life were there—Callie, Trey and his dad, Kelly Bremer, Francie Rydell and her parents, the Broussards, her own mother. She wondered what they'd all say if she blurted out that she was the inventor of the Miracle Chef. She wondered if they'd even believe her. She doubted Trey would, but what about the rest of them? Most of all, she wondered how her mother would react. Would she be proud of the time, the hard work—the intelligence—it had taken her daughter to invent such a thing? Or would she, as Georgia feared, slip into that awful cold, deep depression that had nearly killed her the last time her daughter had proven that she was much smarter than anyone had thought?

"It looks as if my cohost is frozen with fear now that the final judging is about to begin," Daniel joked, jolting her back to the moment.

Georgia gave him a weak smile and hurried to get her meal dished up, but his words stuck in her mind. Frozen with fear. That's exactly what she was. Frozen with fear of what her revelation might cause her mother to do. That was why she spent her days selling crystal unicorns and deviled egg plates instead of tinkering with her latest invention. That was why, no matter how proud she was of inventing the Miracle Chef, she couldn't tell the people she cared about the most what she had done.

It was also why, she thought, watching Daniel charm the cook-off judges, she didn't want a real relationship with a man. She knew what a burden it was to be responsible for someone else's life. Georgia already had to act in a way that was acceptable to her mother. She couldn't do the same with somebody else, too.

"So, judges, what do you think?" Daniel said, giving Georgia her cue to step out from behind the counter and come stand next to him.

As the cameras moved to focus on the five seated judges, Daniel reached out and squeezed Georgia's hand. She squeezed back, not realizing until that moment how very much she wanted the Miracle Chef to win.

The judges had been randomly selected by the age-old, toss-your-name-into-a-hat method. When the first four names had been drawn—Joe Broussard, Velma Boleen, Mrs. Rydell, and Miranda Kingsley—Georgia had figured she had a fairly even chance of winning. And then came the name of the fifth judge. Debbi Lynn Macpherson. Her archenemy from the age of ten.

Georgia prayed there wouldn't be a tie.

Joe Broussard, who owned the grocery store just up the street from them, surprised Georgia by voting for Daniel. "I'm sorry," he said, dipping his head sheepishly. "I'm a fisherman. I love trout."

The cameras panned back to her and Daniel surreptitiously let go of her hand. Georgia pasted a weak smile on her lips. "That's all right, Mr. Broussard. Don't worry, I won't start shopping at the Piggly Wiggly."

Everyone laughed and Georgia felt as if her heart was being squeezed when the cameras turned on Velma Boleen. She voted for Daniel, too.

Georgia fought the sick feeling welling up in her stomach. Even if both Mrs. Rydell and Miranda Kingsley voted for her, Debbi Lynn would vote for Daniel just to pay her back for stealing the crown from her all those years ago.

She leaned back against the counter and listened as both Mrs. Rydell and Miranda Kingsley raved about her fried chicken. Fat lot of good it would do, but at least she hadn't been completely trounced.

Daniel nudged her shoulder as he stepped in front of the cameras. "Miss Macpherson, before you cast the deciding vote, I want you to remember that this challenge was always meant to be about the food. When I came here to Ocean Sands to pit my skills against the Miracle Chef, it was because I didn't want people wasting their money on a gadget that didn't deliver on its promises. Now, I want you to tell me, do you think the meal prepared using the Miracle Chef is one you'd serve to your own family?"

Debbi Lynn seemed to consider this very seriously. "Yes," she answered, frowning at Georgia.

"Is it as good as the meal I made?" Daniel asked.

"Yes," Debbi Lynn answered again.

Then he asked his final question. "Is my meal better than the one that Georgia prepared using the Miracle Chef?"

Georgia waited for Debbi Lynn to parrot another "yes." Instead, her gaze flicked to Georgia's face for the briefest of moments.

"No," Debbi Lynn admitted. "I like Georgia's better."

Georgia sagged against the counter and the entire audience seemed to let out its breath. From the front row, Callie smiled at her, and Georgia hoped that meant she had been forgiven.

Daniel turned and looked into the camera. "Well, folks, it looks like the Miracle Chef may be able to give me a run for my money after all." Then, without sparing Georgia a glance, he added, "It's a shame we still can't locate a store that's stocking this product. I'm certain that after today's show, many of our viewers would like to get their hands on one of these timesaving gadgets for themselves."

Georgia sucked in a breath.

The bastard.

She saw Kelly wave frantically in Shana Goldberg's direction, trying to get her attention. Georgia watched as the producer leaned forward, as if in slow motion.

What was Kelly doing?

"Daniel, it appears that we've finally managed to locate the manufacturer of the Miracle Chef. This young woman got her hands on one last night and she's got the packing slip right here." Shana held aloft a bright pink piece of paper. "The number viewers can call to order their very own Miracle Chef is 1-800-555-4646."

Georgia groaned, burying her head in her hands as Daniel closed up the show and Shana yelled her usual, "It's a wrap."

When the cameras stopped rolling, Daniel turned to her and pulled her hands away from her face. The look in his eyes was serious, watchful. "It looks like your secret is out," he said softly.

Georgia shook her head, her blond curls tickling her chin. "But don't you see, Daniel, it can't be."

He reached out and brushed a lock of hair away from her face. "It's too late," he said.

"No," Georgia whispered.

"Yes," Daniel said.

And then, as if it were agreeing with him, her cell phone rang.

Nineteen

Thursday. 8:34 A.M. Temperature: 68 degrees. Fifty Miracle Chefs arrive. Moved luggage out of hall closet and had Michael Kingsley put boxes there. Covered with hot air balloon blanket Gma. Ella Rose made for twelfth b-day.

This was like an experiment gone horribly wrong. In her bathrobe and a towel wrapped turbanlike on her head, Georgia peeked out her front door and looked to see if any of her neighbors were watching the UPS guy cart his third and final load of Miracle Chefs into her house.

"That's all of 'em," Michael said cheerfully after unloading his cargo into her closet.

"Thanks," Georgia muttered.

The phone calls had started immediately—the phone number on the packing receipt was one Georgia had set up to make it seem as if her dream of becoming a successful inventor had a chance of becoming a reality. When she'd moved after her divorce, the phone company was offering a special on a second number for $4.95 a month. Georgia, feeling rebellious after all she'd gone through, had purchased the number, set up automated voice mail for GME Industries, the company she'd registered in her name after she'd aced her final in the inventing class, and used it for all calls relating to her inventions—including the Miracle Chef. She had the calls forwarded to her cell phone, but if she didn't answer, a machinelike voice would take messages for her—or, rather, for GME Industries. And it seemed as if everyone in Ocean Sands who had attended Miss Harris's viewing yesterday had called to place an order.

Now, their friends and relatives had begun calling. Georgia had been jolted out of a restless sleep at five in the morning by Kathy Clarkston in Greenville, North Carolina, who was Francie Rydell's second cousin and, after Francie told her about the Miracle Chef yesterday afternoon and given her the number to call to place her order, couldn't wait to get a Miracle Chef of her own.

Georgia, who'd had more than three dozen such calls since the cook-off, turned off her cell phone's ringer and hoped that Kathy Clarkston would be her last caller. After all, she'd thought as her eyelids drooped, how many people really needed a product like this?

Yesterday, right after Junie Harris's wake, she'd asked the manufacturing plant to rush her fifty more Miracle Chefs. Surely, that would be enough.

Georgia yawned and rubbed her eyes as she made her way back upstairs to her bathroom. She had to get a move on if she was going to open the gift shop on time. Not that people were typically standing in line when she unlocked the front doors, but with Trey and Callie's nuptials just over a week away, there was sure to be a rush on last-minute wedding gifts.

It didn't take her long to do the usual hair and makeup routine, pull on a pink sweater and a long green skirt that had strawberries and tiny white and pink blossoms scattered throughout the fabric, and tug on a pair of low-heeled tan sandals that made a clomping sound when she walked.

She made it to the gift shop with one minute to spare, juggling her travel mug of coffee, notebook, purse, keys, and umbrella (just in case the weather turned fickle again) as she unlocked the door. As she turned on the lights, it occurred to her that she had better turn the ringer of her cell phone back on. She reached into her pocketbook and pulled out the small silver phone, noticing as she did that the voice mail icon had been activated, indicating that she had new messages.

Hoping it wasn't going to be a dozen more people asking about the

Miracle Chef, Georgia pushed the key combination that would put her into GME's voice mail just as the bells on the front door jangled.

Her mother stepped into the shop carrying a sack of what Georgia guessed—by the smell—to be her nearly world-famous beignets. She set the bag down in front of Georgia on the counter and the scent of warm, slightly greasy, deep-fried heaven wafted out.

"I was feeling energetic this morning so I made a batch of these," Mama said, but Georgia barely heard her over the oddly automated voice-mail operator that announced, "You have—" short electronic pause "—one hundred and sixty—" another pause "five messages."

A cloud of powdered sugar puffed up into her face as Georgia's cell phone slid from her suddenly nerveless hand and into the sack of freshly made doughnuts.

When Daniel heard Vivian's front door click shut, he pressed his back against the wall and flicked open the curtains of his room with one finger as he tried to remain out of sight. He watched as Vivian cleared the walkway, looked both ways down the empty street, crossed to the other side, and continued down the sidewalk toward Main Street.

He felt a rush of anticipation.

Georgia's mother had finally left him alone in her house.

Now he could go poke around in her attic and see if he could find any clues as to why Vivian and her sister didn't get along. Had their rift been created over a boy they both fancied? Was Vivian jealous because her little sister had been a better student or more popular? Or was it just your typical sibling rivalry?

Daniel dragged a sturdy chair out into the hall where, a few days ago, he had noticed what he presumed to be an entrance to the attic. Standing up on the chair, he tugged on a circular piece of metal that turned out to be attached to a piece of string. When he pulled the string, a set of stairs swung down, nearly toppling him over the balustrade and onto the first-floor entryway.

Holding the steps to keep the chair from tipping over, Daniel did his best to regain his balance.

"Jeez, that was close," he muttered.

He hopped down from the chair and moved it out of the way so the stairs could extend all the way down, nearly to the floor. Tentatively, he tested the first step, holding on to the ropes that served as makeshift railings as he put his weight on the stairs. They seemed to be capable of holding his weight, so he took another step and was soon at eye level to the attic floor.

Like most attics, this one smelled warm and musty from being closed off for too long. The sunlight peeking in through the gaps between where the walls met the roof was heavy and sluggish with dust. Daniel reached up and pulled the metal chain of a bare bulb hanging from the rafters and a weak glow illuminated the sparse room.

The neatly stacked boxes seemed innocuous, ordinary. As he hauled himself up onto the plywood floor, Daniel began to doubt he'd find much up here in the way of clues as to why Rose and Vivian were at each other's throats. Still, he had to look.

The first box he opened contained baby clothes, mostly dresses— pink ones with little white flowers sewn into the hem, sunny yellow ones with butterflies or bees appliquéd on the front, green ones the color of mint chocolate chip ice cream—and those girly panties with rows of lace sewn across the rear.

"Poor kid was doomed from the start," Daniel muttered, thinking of Georgia as a baby, dressed up like a miniature beauty queen. The clothes were worn but clean, with none of the typical stains from baby food dribbled on the front or spit up or other various baby-related messes—things he'd known nothing about until his sister had triplets six months ago.

Daniel moved the baby clothes box out of the way and opened the next one down, only to find more neatly folded clothes, these just slightly larger than the ones in the first box.

"No wonder nothing's dirty. She probably never wore any outfit more than once," he said to himself in the silence of the attic.

After looking through a dozen more boxes that contained nothing but clothing, Daniel figured this sleuthing mission was a bust. Straightening up, he rolled his shoulders and looked around to see if there was anything he'd missed, but there was nothing more up here besides a few old lamps and a baby carriage loaded with porcelain-faced dolls.

Daniel turned off the light as he backed down the stairs.

So much for people hiding secrets in their attics.

He gave the stairs a push and they retracted neatly back where they came from. Then he dragged the heavy chair back into the guest room, stubbing his toe against the corner of the heavy wooden chest at the foot of the bed as he repositioned the chair in front of the desk where he'd set up his laptop and the other paraphernalia he needed to plan the *Epicurean Explorer* shows. He sat down on the chest and pondered what to do next.

The next cook-off wasn't scheduled for a week hence. After June Harris's funeral, Georgia had asked him if they could do the fourth cook-off at Callie's bachelorette party. Figuring that it would help heal the breach between the two friends by giving Georgia another chance—and hoping they'd make it to the final cook-off the Saturday after that at the Shrimp Festival—Daniel agreed.

In order to make the show more interesting to his viewers, Daniel figured he needed to dig up some information about the history of Ocean Sands, which should be fairly easy. He'd found most towns like this had a museum manned by a flock of elderly ladies just dying to get their hands on anyone who showed even the tiniest inkling of interest in their city.

Daniel stood up and the chest creaked, relieved of his weight. Absently, he swiped a hand over the smooth surface of the rectangular cedar box. At least, he assumed it was cedar. Most of these old chests were constructed of cedar, which kept their contents dry and fresh-smelling. Curious to see if he was right, Daniel lifted the lid.

Then he stepped back and slapped his forehead with the palm of one hand.

He'd been sitting on the evidence he'd been looking for this whole time.

Georgia couldn't recall anything about her mother's visit aside from fishing her cell phone out of the beignets. That number just kept flashing in her head like a neon "hotel" sign that dominated an entire city block. One hundred and sixty-five. In the four hours since she'd turned off her phone, she had 165 calls. All of them, she assumed, were like the first twenty she'd managed to get through before Trey walked into the gift shop and, without noticing (or caring) that she was on the phone, announced that he needed a gift for his lovely bride and asked Georgia for a suggestion.

What she'd suggest is that Trey buy his wife-to-be something a little more personal than the scented soaps or iced tea pitchers they carried here at the gift shop, Georgia thought as she hung up in the middle of a message.

She stepped out from behind the counter. "Well, I bought her a full place setting of Francis I silverware, but that's not exactly the sort of gift a woman expects from her groom. We have some, uh, lovely figurines," she said, waving her hands at the display case like Vanna White showing off letters on *Wheel of Fortune.*

Trey barely spared the assorted shepherdesses, ballerinas, and courtesans a glance. "Naw. Those don't seem right. Come on, what would you want if it were you?" He leaned close to her and put a heavy arm across her shoulders. "That shouldn't be so hard to imagine."

"I'd want a nice honeymoon," Georgia said dryly, shrugging to get out from under his grasp. "Somewhere other than the Holiday Inn out on Route Sixty-three like where you took me."

"Well, howdy. It looks like you're gettin' awfully familiar with my girlfriend," Daniel drawled from the front of the store, throwing back nearly the same accusation Trey had leveled at him the night they'd met at the No Holds Bar.

Georgia nearly choked on her surprise. Why hadn't the bells rung when Daniel opened the door?

Trey stepped back and crossed his arms across his chest, looking mighty pleased with himself, but Georgia had no idea what he had to be happy about. "Aw, that was nothing. Me and Georgia, we go way back."

Then Daniel shocked her by striding purposefully across the store, turning her to face him, and laying a claiming, possessive kiss on her lips. At first she resisted, knowing that this was just male posturing. But as he buried one hand in her hair, cradling her scalp with his strong fingers and brushing his tongue against hers, she relaxed. After all, it wasn't as if she didn't enjoy kissing him.

When he finally raised his mouth from hers, Georgia felt a little dazed. He swiped his thumb across her lips, smiled, and gave her another, lighter kiss as if finding it impossible to resist. Then he turned to Trey, who looked somewhat bemused by this public display of affection. "And that," he said, "was *something*. Me and Georgia, we may not go way back, but we do just fine."

Georgia coughed. Okay, she knew she should get annoyed and tell Daniel and Trey that she wasn't some slab of . . . of prime rib or something that they could fight over, but the truth was, it was nice that Daniel was just a teensy bit jealous. No, that didn't mean she wanted them to go flying through the plate-glass window of the gift shop like Colin Firth and Hugh Grant in the *Bridget Jones's Diary* movie she and the rest of the Tiara Club had watched about a million times, but . . .

Well, on second thought, that sort of grand gesture might not be unwelcome after all.

Not that she wanted either Trey or Daniel to get hurt, mind you. It was just that the notion that someone would care enough to fight for her was so romantic.

"Georgia, honey, did you hear me?" Trey asked.

"Huh?" she answered, the movie clip in her head of Trey and Daniel bursting through the window, kicking at each other like, well, like two guys who hadn't been in a fistfight since their playground days, still running in her head. Everyone within a two-block radius would come outside to watch and, within an hour, the whole town would be abuzz.

"Did you hear what that movie star did? He actually punched out Georgia's ex-husband!"

God, Mama would just die from the shame of the scandal—especially after Daniel got on a plane to L.A. and never came back.

So much for romance.

"What did you say, Trey?" she asked, resolutely stepping away from Daniel.

"I said, if you think of anything Callie might like, you give me a call down at the city hall, okay?"

"What? Oh, yes. Sure I will," she said.

The warning bells, she noticed, didn't have any problem ringing as Trey left.

"What are you doing here?" she asked, once she and Daniel were alone.

"I tried calling you on your cell, but just got voice mail," Daniel replied, not really answering her question.

At the mention of her voice mail, Georgia groaned. "Don't even say that word. Do you realize I've had nearly two hundred calls since yesterday's cook-off and the show hasn't even aired yet? What am I supposed to do now?"

Daniel leaned back against the counter and slid his hands into the front pockets of his jeans. "Order more Miracle Chefs," he said calmly.

"Well, I . . . that's . . ." Georgia let out a frustrated breath. "That's not the point. How am I supposed to keep people from knowing I invented the—"

"I'm back, dear. Did you get a chance to wrap up that copper casserole holder I bought for Callie?"

Georgia sucked in a breath and raised a hand to her heart. "Mama," she gasped, praying her mother hadn't heard what she'd just said and wondering at the same time what the hell was wrong with those damn bells.

"Ah, just the woman I wanted to see," Daniel said.

Vivian smiled and fluttered her lashes at her guest. "Well, isn't that nice of you to say?"

Daniel pulled a slip of paper out of the pocket of his jacket and slid it across the counter to Vivian. "Why does your sister say you were never a good student? According to this report card, you got straight A's."

Vivian's smile remained pasted on her face, but Daniel could almost see the wheels turning in her mind as she tried to think of a plausible lie to tell. When she looked up at him, she gave him her patented, "Aw, shucks, I'm just a pretty blond airhead" look—the same one her daughter had used on him the first time they met—and said, "I'm sure it's just a mistake. Since I was the first to go through Ocean Sands Junior High, I'll bet they accidentally switched my name for Rose's. She was the good student, not me."

Daniel kept his eyes locked on Vivian's. "Then why," he asked, flipping over the faded brown piece of paper, "does it say nineteen sixty-one? This couldn't possibly be Rose's report card. She was eight years behind you. She'd have had to be six years old in the eighth grade for this to be hers."

Vivian didn't even look at the report card. "I assure you, I don't know. I was not a particularly good student. If you don't believe me, you can check my high-school records. I was barely even able to graduate."

Daniel pulled out a white piece of paper that had curled at the edges. "Yes, I saw that. This is your high-school transcript, which does, indeed, show you as a D student. What I'd like to know is what happened between junior high and high school to turn a bright young woman into a student who could barely pass home ec?"

Beside him, Georgia picked up the documents he'd discovered and studied them with a frown.

Vivian, however, had gone on the defensive. "Where did you get those?" she asked.

"The chest in my room," Daniel answered truthfully. "I stubbed my toe on it this morning and that got me to wondering if it was made of cedar, so I opened it. I found these, too." He laid two photos down, watching as Vivian's expression turned guarded. The top photo showed a delighted-looking Vivian sitting spread-eagled on the floor with her little sister between her legs. Rose, who looked to be about three in the picture, was smiling up at her sister, and Vivian held her in a tight grasp that suggested the typical protective manner with which an older child might treat her younger sibling. When Vivian pushed that photo out of the way and saw the one underneath, all the color drained from her face.

Georgia, who was also watching Vivian's reaction, came around the counter, alarmed. "Mother, are you all right?" she asked, grabbing her mother's arm.

Vivian recovered her composure, further puzzling Daniel when she patted her daughter's hand and laughed lightly as if nothing had just happened. "I'm fine, dear. I just thought I saw a ghost." She turned to Daniel, the look in her eyes surprisingly assessing. "You know how that is, don't you? All of these old Southern towns have their ghosts. It adds to our charm."

Daniel narrowed his eyes and put his hands back in his pockets. "Yeah," he said. "I'm beginning to see that."

Twenty

"I don't see what it is about those pictures that's so important," Georgia said, sliding into the booth opposite Daniel at the No Holds Bar and putting her purse on the end of the table next to the Durkee sauce.

Daniel slid the photos in question across the table as Georgia unrolled the paper napkin from her utensils and neatly arranged her flatware. Salad and entrée fork to the left. Knife on the right, blade facing inward (a tradition supposedly dating back to the Middle Ages when pointing the blade of your knife toward anyone's heart but your own could get a man killed—amazing the wealth of useless knowledge Daniel had acquired while researching his books and, later, his TV show). Spoon next to the knife, the bottom edges of the handles all neatly aligned.

Daniel was tempted to push her salad fork out of alignment just to see how she'd react.

"Well, the first picture—the one with your mother holding your Aunt Rose and looking pretty delighted with her baby sister—goes against everything you've told me about them. It's obvious from this photo that Vivian and Rose *did* get along at some point. As a matter of fact, they did more than just get along, they adored each other. So, why did that change? *When* did it change?"

Georgia traced the smile on her mother's lips in the photograph. "I don't know. I've never seen this picture. I just assumed that what my mother and Aunt Rose said about their relationship all my life was true. Why would they lie to me?"

Daniel leaned forward, resting his arms on the heavy table. "It seems like there's a lot of that going around in this town."

Georgia looked at him then, her brown eyes troubled. "I've never lied to you."

"No. But you haven't exactly told me the truth, have you?"

Their gazes locked for a long moment, his demanding and hers uncertain. Daniel heard the clanging sound as her knee knocked against the metal pole supporting the table when Rose Conover appeared as if out of nowhere, pad in her hand, and said, "Hey, Georgia. Hey, Daniel. What can I get you today?"

Daniel didn't move, refusing to be the first to look away.

Georgia cleared her throat and straightened her already neat silverware before turning to her aunt. "Hey, Aunt Rose. I think I'm going to have the fried catfish. And sweet tea."

Rose scribbled a note on her pad. "And what can I get for you?" she asked, glancing at Daniel.

"I'll have a beer. Whatever you've got on draft is fine. And go ahead and make it two of the catfish platters. I wouldn't want to be the only one in Ocean Sands without clogged arteries."

Rose grinned at that and started to leave, but Daniel stopped her by holding out the second photo he had shown Vivian, the one that had made her look as if she really had seen a ghost. "Have you ever seen this before?" he asked.

She took the photo and studied it, frowning. Then, with a shake of her head, she handed it back to him. "No, I don't think so. I was— what?—six years old in that picture."

"So you don't remember the day this was taken? At the nineteen sixty-one Shrimp Festival?" Daniel pointed out the banner behind the two girls who were holding hands and, unlike the first picture, looking rather unhappy.

Rose shook her head. "No. I'm sorry, I don't. Why's it important?"

She seemed to be telling the truth, so Daniel put the photo down on the table and pointed to the right edge, where Vivian's hand was outstretched.

"See, here," he said, his finger right below the hand in the picture. "Vivian's holding someone's hand. A man's hand, by the look of the shirtsleeve and heavy watch."

Both Georgia and Rose peered closer to see what Daniel was indicating. Georgia was the first to pull back. "So what?" she asked with a shrug. "So Mama and Aunt Rose went to the Shrimp Festival with a man. Probably their daddy. What's wrong with that?"

Daniel picked up the picture and pointed again to the edge. "Because if this was just a picture of a happy family going to the fair, why did someone cut out the man holding Vivian's hand?"

Georgia had noticed earlier that the left edge of the photo was ragged, as if someone had taken a pair of dull scissors to it, and the white rim that ran around the other three sides of the picture was missing. It appeared that Daniel was right. Someone had destroyed the man standing next to her mother. But why?

"Yes, that's right. I need another two hundred Miracle Chefs. By Saturday? That should be fine." Her cell phone's call waiting beeped and Georgia sighed silently. "No, wait. Make it two hundred and fifty. Okay. Yes, by ten A.M. would be great. Thank you."

Just as she hung up from her call to the manufacturer's rep, her cell rang again. Then the gift shop's phone rang. And the front door's warning bells jingled as Beau walked in.

Holding up a finger to indicate that she'd be right with him, Georgia answered the store's phone. Rock Hunter, like half the residents of Ocean Sands who all seemed to have called while she was out having lunch with Daniel, had apparently forgotten the gift shop's hours— hours that had remained the same during the entire decade Georgia had worked there.

"Yes, Rock, that's right. Ten A.M. to seven P.M. Monday through

Saturday with my lunch break from noon to one. Closed on Sunday like always."

Trey's father seemed surprised.

"No, we're not closed on Saturdays. I work most weekends, but the day of Callie and Trey's wedding, Mr. Talmadge will be here with his daughter."

Rock expressed more confusion.

"No, Mr. Talmadge didn't seem to mind switching my day off from Friday to Saturday this one time."

Georgia rolled her eyes. Did everyone in town pay this much attention to her comings and goings?

"Well, if you need my help picking out a wedding gift for Trey and Callie, I'll be here today and Saturday this week, then all next week through Friday night at seven."

Rock sounded like he was taking notes now.

"Yes, that's right. From ten till seven." Georgia paused. "Uh-huh. I'll see you then."

"Looks like you're in demand," Beau commented, reaching out to stroke a black glass cat with eerie green eyes that had arrived in the morning's shipment. It was one of Georgia's favorite new items, one she wouldn't mind owning herself, although she was fairly certain it wouldn't last a week in her house without getting broken.

Georgia rested her elbows on the counter and put her chin in her hands. "Nobody's said this, but I think everyone believes I can steer them toward the perfect gift for Trey and Callie. Seeing as how I was married to Trey for three years and all, you know."

Beau snorted. "Well, yeah, that and because you're Callie's best friend."

Georgia sighed, hoping that Beau was right and that she'd been restored to best friend status since the cook-off at Miss Boleen's. "Yes. That, too."

"Isn't it strange to have your best friend engaged to your ex-husband?" Beau asked.

"Of course it is, but what am I supposed to do?"

"Tell Callie what an asshole Trey is?" Beau suggested, leaning up against a shelf and leveling her a dark look from under his lashes.

Georgia laughed without humor. "It's a little late for that. Besides, maybe Trey just wasn't the right man for me."

Beau looked at her for a long, silent moment. "Do you think he's the right man for Callie?" he asked finally, surprising her with the serious note in his voice.

Georgia glanced away from those dark, knowing eyes. What was she supposed to say? That Trey was right for Callie because she believed he was the only man who would accept that she and her kids were a package deal? That if someone else—say, Beau, for example—told Callie that Trey wasn't the only man in this town who had feelings for her, Georgia suspected that Callie might consider calling off the wedding? And what if that didn't work out? What if that someone else—again, using Beau as a purely hypothetical example—only *thought* he could accept the added responsibility of a ready-made (and fairly large) family in addition to the woman he was so obviously attracted to?

Chewing on the inside of her bottom lip, Georgia blew out a breath that lifted the curl that had settled over her right eye. "I think you'd have to ask Callie that," she answered, taking the coward's way out of this conversation.

When the gift shop's phone rang again, Georgia hastened to answer it, glad for the interruption.

"Hello," she said into the receiver.

"Hey, Georgia. It's Callie."

Georgia beamed into the phone. Callie sounded like her old self again, with no hint of the awkwardness that had clouded her voice yesterday. Georgia glanced up at Beau. Maybe it was time she stopped being a martyr where Callie and Trey were concerned and—if not come right out and ask Callie if she really knew what the hell she was getting into—at least stir up a little doubt on Callie's part. "Hey, Callie. How are you? Beau's over here. He said to say 'hello.'"

Beau's dark eyes narrowed dangerously and Georgia shot him an apologetic shrug. What could she say? She was through trying not to meddle, and perhaps reminding Callie of Beau's existence wouldn't hurt.

"Oh, well . . . uh, tell him I said 'hey' back," Callie answered, sounding a bit flustered. "No, wait, don't tell him that. Instead, ask him if he'd like to take the twins to Hooters. Or maybe to a strip joint?"

Georgia coughed to cover a laugh. So, although Callie seemed to have forgiven Georgia, it looked like she was still upset that Beau had taken Caroline into his bar. Or maybe it wasn't that that had her so annoyed. Maybe she was blowing the whole thing out of proportion just to prove to herself that, while she might find Beau attractive, he was not cut out to help her raise her children.

"Callie wants to know if you want to take the twins to Hooters," Georgia said without covering the mouthpiece of the phone. She heard Callie's gasp on the other end of the line and smothered an amused grin.

"Georgia Marie Elliot, you know I was just kidding. How could you tell him I said that?"

"All right, that's it," Beau said, storming out the door, the warning bells jangling furiously.

Georgia's eyes widened as she sucked in her own breath. She had expected Beau to drawl something like "Very funny," and leave it at that. "He's on his way over there," she squeaked in a rush, then hung up the phone to race after her cousin.

Beau was yanking the door of Callie's dress shop open when Georgia caught up with him. She wasn't certain what Beau intended to do, but she didn't want to be responsible for her best friend's murder . . . or her cousin's.

Callie stood in the middle of the room, a pincushion around her wrist and a voluminous pastel green dress spread out on the worktable behind her. She crossed her arms across her chest and looked as cool and calm as the waters of the Gulf on a still day.

Georgia admired her friend's composure in the face of Beau's wrath.

Her cousin stalked—there was no other word for the predatory way Beau walked over to Callie, planting his feet in their sturdy black boots on either side of Callie's white canvas tennis shoes. He dwarfed her, and Georgia could barely see the top of her friend's head peeking out from behind Beau's broad shoulder. The air was filled with an odd sort of tension and, suddenly, Georgia felt very much of an intruder on this scene because she knew exactly what was in the air here . . . and it wasn't murder. Georgia recognized the feeling very well, having experienced the same thing herself with Daniel last week in her mother's kitchen. It was I-don't-care-that-we're-not-alone, do-me-right-now sexual tension.

Which, since Callie was going to be married in nine days to a man who was *not* Beau Conover, was even more dangerous than murder.

Georgia cleared her throat. "Callie was just making a joke," she said lamely.

"Go away, Georgia," Beau said without taking his eyes off Callie.

Georgia wrung her hands, unsure what to do. She didn't want to leave Callie alone, not with the heat that was flying around this room, but she also didn't want to interfere if it meant that Callie might finally get it through her thick skull that Trey Hunter was not the only man who found her attractive—children or not.

"Callie?" she asked uncertainly.

Callie's head appeared over Beau's shoulder as her friend stood up on her tiptoes. "Call me in fifteen minutes," she said. "Beau and I have something to, ah, discuss."

Georgia backed out of the dress shop and was tempted to stand at the window to make sure they didn't kill each other, but wasn't quite certain she actually wanted to know what was going on in there. If Beau kissed Callie, did that obligate Georgia to remind her best friend about that pesky other man—her fiancée? But what if Georgia *wanted* to see Callie and Trey break up?

Aargh. This was just too complicated. Georgia decided it was better for Callie to have her secrets and resolutely spun around so her back was to the dress shop as she walked back to her own store.

She took two more calls about the gift shop's hours, assuring both Francie Rydell and Miss Boleen that she'd be here to help them pick out wedding gifts for Trey and Callie through next Friday night at seven as she watched the clock tick away the minutes until she could call the dress shop. The second fifteen minutes was up, she pressed #2 on the speed dial.

Callie answered on the second ring. "Can you come down here for a minute?" she asked, sounding bemused.

Georgia looked outside to make sure no shoppers were hovering about. "Sure, be there in a sec," she said, after determining that the parking lot was empty.

"Okay, spill," Georgia said, raising her voice over the electronic buzz that sounded as she entered the dress shop.

Callie was standing in the same place Georgia had left her, but her arms were at her sides instead of crossed defensively. "He offered to baby-sit," she said with a stunned look on her face. Callie reached out and picked up a white marking pencil from the worktable and absently twirled it between her fingers.

"What?"

"Yeah, that's what I said. I thought he was going to—" Callie stopped. Looked down at her tennis shoes. Cleared her throat and started again. "I thought he was going to kiss me." She laughed dryly and looked back up at Georgia. "That or strangle me. But he didn't. He just watched me with those eyes of his and then offered to watch the kids next Friday night during my bachelorette party."

"All of them?" Georgia asked incredulously. She couldn't imagine Beau being able to handle four children all by himself, especially not when one of those four was Caroline.

"Yes." Callie shook her head in disbelief. "Why do you think he'd do a thing like that?"

And suddenly it struck Georgia exactly why her cousin would offer to watch Callie's kids—he wanted to prove to her (and maybe to himself) that he could do it. Then something else struck Georgia and before she could think of the implications of what she was about to ask, she blurted, "Has Trey ever watched the kids? By himself, I mean."

She and Callie's gazes locked then, Callie seemingly dumbfounded by this turn of events.

"No," she said. "He's never been alone with more than two kids at once. And I've *never* left him alone with Caroline," she added, as if that were completely unthinkable.

"Beau seemed to handle her okay," Georgia said, keeping her features schooled in an impassive mask.

"He took her to a tavern. Miranda Kingsley told me she saw him put Caroline right on top of the bar, right next to the olives and lemon twists. What sort of message does that send to an impressionable three-year-old?"

"Eat your fruits and veggies?" Georgia suggested with a smile tugging at the corners of her mouth.

Callie pursed her lips with annoyance. "Very funny. Besides, Miranda said your Aunt Rose was the one who was really watching Caroline. Beau was waiting tables, leaving his mother to take care of my child."

Georgia considered her friend and wondered if she should just keep her mouth shut. After all, Callie had already made her decision by accepting Trey's proposal six months ago, by agreeing to marry the only man she had dated since her divorce became final. The problem was, Georgia knew what it was going to be like for Callie to be married to Trey. He was going to expect the children always to be clean, always be well-behaved and quiet, just as he would expect his wife to be.

Georgia realized that she couldn't just say nothing anymore and watch her friend get trapped in a passionless relationship, whether it turned out that Beau was the right man for her or not.

"What's wrong with that?" she asked, trying to make Callie see Beau's motives in another light.

Callie had turned and was absentmindedly making white markings on the yards of green fabric on her worktable. "Huh?"

"What's wrong with Beau asking for help from his mother? I mean, he could have brought Caroline back to your house and disrupted the taping of the show. Would that have been better?"

Callie frowned at her over her shoulder. "No, of course not."

"Then what was it he was supposed to do? Take her to his house, which is not child-proofed, and try to entertain her by himself? When he has absolutely no experience with children? I mean, it seems to me that Beau did exactly what a parent would want him to do. He thought about what was best for Caroline and then he did it. There's no way Caroline could get into any trouble down at the bar, there's always too many people around for that. And his mother's raised two children, so I guess he figured she knows what she's doing. So, why don't you cut him some slack? Plenty of people bring their kids down there to eat. It's not like the No Holds Bar is some sleazy strip joint or something." Wow, this speaking your mind stuff wasn't so bad once you got started, Georgia thought, finally stopping to take a breath.

Callie opened her mouth and then closed it again. She turned to the fabric and made another mark. Then she set down her marking pencil, blew out a breath, and ran an agitated hand through her auburn hair. "I know," she mumbled.

"You do?" Georgia asked, taken aback by her friend's sudden capitulation.

Callie sighed. "Yeah. I do. I'm just . . . Your cousin's got me thinking things I shouldn't be thinking a week before my wedding," she confessed, propping her hip up on the worktable and letting one tennis-shoe-clad foot swing in the air. "I suppose it's easier for me to tell myself that Beau Conover would make the worst father in history rather than having to face the fact that I'm attracted to your cousin in the worst way," she admitted sheepishly, toying with the pencil at her side and refusing to meet Georgia's gaze.

"Well, duh," Georgia said, rolling her eyes heavenward.

Callie laughed. "That obvious, huh?"

"'Fraid so." Georgia scooted up onto the worktable next to her friend. "The question is, what are you going to do about it?"

Callie flicked the pencil and they both watched it roll across the surface of the table, coming to a rest against the soft fabric of the skirt she was working on. "Nothing. I'm a parent now, and I can't think in terms of what I want. I have to think about the kids and put their needs first. The truth is, Trey's willing to take over the role of their father, and they need that. I need that. You saw the other night how difficult this is for me, trying to raise them myself. Jim's mother is a big help, but she's getting older, and even just watching the kids after school for a few hours is getting to be too much for her."

Georgia put an arm over her friend's shoulders and squeezed. "I know it's hard."

Callie rested her head on her friend's shoulder for a moment, taking the comfort Georgia offered. Then she laughed and raised her head, wiping her eyes. "I guess I just wasn't prepared for this. Not for having to raise four children on my own *or* for suddenly being confronted with the choice of selfishly pursuing something I want instead of doing what I know is the right thing for my kids. Because, believe me, when Beau Conover looks at me with those bedroom eyes of his, I am temped to say to hell with trying to find the best father for my children and find the nearest motel room and have my way with your cousin, instead."

Georgia's heart ached for the woman who had been her best friend for over twenty years. Why did the choices life throw at them have to be so hard, anyway? Why couldn't Callie have a man she felt passionate about *and* who'd be a good father for her children? Why couldn't she, herself, have the man *she* felt passionate about and not worry about the secrets he kept threatening to expose? Daniel believed that having everything out in the open neutralized the power these secrets had over you, but, in her case at least, she knew he was wrong.

"I guess we've both sacrificed in order to do what's best for our loved ones," Georgia said, thinking of how much it hurt her to keep pretending that she hadn't invented the Miracle Chef.

Callie frowned and Georgia realized that her friend had no idea what Georgia had given up in order to keep her mother safe all these years. Georgia wasn't about to tell her now, so instead, she hopped down off the table and laughed, the noise sounding forced to her own ears. "So, what did you call me about in the first place?" she asked, changing the subject.

Tapping her marker on the table, Callie glanced at the dress laid out on her table and then looked back at Georgia. "I wanted to let you know your dress is done," she said.

"Oh, that's great. I'll bet you were getting nervous, what with the wedding only nine days away."

"What are you talking about?" Callie asked.

"My bridesmaid's dress, silly." Georgia's laugh was genuine this time. It was true that brides tended to get a little cuckoo as the wedding approached, but this was ridiculous.

Callie shot her a strange look and then walked over to one of the racks and pulled out a frothy white-and-pink concoction that looked to contain more than half a dozen yards of fabric. "I'm not talking about your bridesmaid's dress. I'll be finishing those up on Sunday."

She handed the plastic-covered dress to Georgia, who nearly staggered under the weight of it.

"What's this then?" Georgia asked, perplexed. She knew she hadn't ordered such a thing. It looked like the sort of dress one would wear to a reenactment or something, and Georgia had no intention of—

"No," she muttered. "Tell me this isn't what I think it is."

Callie took a step backward. "You mean, you didn't know?"

Georgia was tempted to throw the dress down on the ground and stomp her foot and scream that she was not, not, not going to do this.

"Oh, honey. I'm so sorry. I wouldn't have ordered the dress if I'd known."

"It's not your fault," Georgia said, wishing her mother were here so she could strangle her. Who else would have ordered her a dress for the Shrimp Queen Pageant? Georgia hadn't entered this year, hoping her mother wouldn't ask about it. Indeed, the deadline had passed without a word from Mama, lulling Georgia into a false sense of security. She should have known her mother wouldn't let her escape so easily.

It looked like she was going to have to don this ridiculous outfit and tape her breasts one more time, after all.

✠

Twenty~one

First-grade teacher Sierra Riley jumped when Daniel came up behind her and tapped her on the shoulder. Since the Ocean Sands History Museum was closed on Thursdays, he had come to the library to get some information to use on his next show, instead. He also figured he might as well do some more research about the mysterious picture he'd found in Vivian's cedar chest. As with the last time he'd come here, Sierra was holed up in a dark corner of the library, hovering protectively over her laptop.

"Hey," he said, having absorbed enough of the local lingo to notice a slight drawl in his voice.

"Hey," Sierra said back, surreptitiously closing the lid on her laptop. She was definitely trying to hide something, Daniel thought as he slipped into the chair next to her. "So, what are you working on?" he asked nonchalantly.

"Oh, you know. The usual. Grading papers. That sort of thing."

"That's interesting." Daniel leaned back in his chair and stretched out his legs, crossing his ankles. He was becoming accustomed to wearing jeans more and more and, despite the fact that he could spot the difference between Hilfiger and Ralph Lauren at twenty paces, he was finding it a bit of a relief to not have to care. Unlike L.A., where he felt as if his every move was watched, here in Ocean Sands, he was starting to relax. "Why don't you actually have any papers, then?" he asked.

Sierra blinked her blue eyes at him owlishly. "Pardon me?"

"If you're grading papers, where are they?" Daniel waved at the table in front of them, which held only a green, spiral-bound notebook and a matching pen. But there was not one neatly lettered or messily erased homework assignment in sight.

Sierra's neck turned bright red, a color that clashed with her equally bright red hair. Nervously, her gaze shifted to the stacks of books beside him. Probably hoping they'd magically come crashing down on his head, Daniel guessed.

Finally, she sighed and raised her hands in surrender. "Okay, you caught me. I'm not grading papers," she admitted.

Daniel noticed she didn't volunteer any further information, but that had never stopped him. The key in getting to the truth, he'd found, was in being tenacious in one's pursuit of information. "Then what are you doing?" he asked.

She blew out a loud breath. "Why do you care?" she asked, rather grumpily he thought.

Daniel shrugged. "I guess you could say that I like to know the truth about people."

"And what if they tell you to mind your own business!" Sierra asked, her voice dripping with saccharine.

"Then I figure I'd best leave them alone," Daniel said, grinning as he got to his feet. No use pressing the issue. It was Georgia and Vivian's secrets that he was really interested in uncovering.

She laughed sheepishly. "Sorry, I didn't mean to be rude."

"That's all right. You're entitled to keep your skeletons firmly locked up in their closets."

Sierra waved her hand in the direction of the chair he'd just vacated. "All right. Sit back down. I suppose my so-called skeletons are something you of all people might understand."

Hmm. Curiouser and curiouser, Daniel thought as he took his seat again and waited for Sierra to confess whatever deep dark secret lurked in her soul.

"I'm writing a novel." She paused and cleared her throat, the blush creeping back up her neck. "A romance novel. That's why I asked Georgia and her friends about what it's like to be a beauty queen—the heroine in my book is going to be one. It just seemed . . . I don't know. Right, I guess."

It was Daniel's turn to blink owlishly at her. "Oh," he said.

Sierra gave a little laugh. "Yeah, I know. Silly, isn't it?"

"I didn't say that," Daniel protested.

"You didn't have to." She straightened the laptop across her knees. "That's why I haven't told anyone, they'll just think it's ridiculous. It would be different if I were trying to be the next John Grisham or Stephen King. But romance?"

Daniel leaned forward earnestly. "There's nothing wrong with that. I write nonfiction myself, but that doesn't mean I haven't seen the statistics on other genres. Romance is big business."

Sierra ducked her head. "Yeah, I know. It's just . . . well, not everybody sees it that way."

"Everybody, who?" Daniel asked, trying to keep the frown out of his voice. It was stuff like this that really pissed him off—and made him even more aware of how lucky he was to have such a supportive family. He could have come home from Europe after college and announced that he was going to make a career out of painting replicas of the Sistine Chapel on the ceilings of Volkswagen Beetles and his parents would have clapped him on the back and told him they were proud of him. In some ways, it was frustrating because no matter what he did, no matter how insignificant the accomplishment or how easily success came to him, his folks encouraged him in his endeavors.

But Sierra just shrugged and refused to meet his eyes, telling Daniel without saying a word that someone very close to her had come close to crushing her dreams.

"Does your boyfriend know that you want to be a writer?" Daniel asked, wondering what he'd say if she told him that it was Tim who thought her desire to write was ridiculous.

He'd probably tell her she deserved a better man.

And then he'd get on the phone and try to find one for her.

"No," Sierra admitted quietly, making his grand gesture unnecessary. "Tim doesn't know. He thinks I come down here every night so I won't wake him up while he's sleeping. He works the graveyard shift and sleeps until seven or eight at night," she explained.

"Ah," Daniel said. "But that doesn't explain why you haven't told him what you're doing."

Sierra bit her bottom lip. "I guess it's just too . . . precious to me, I guess you'd say. I'm afraid that if I told him and he thought it was stupid, it would hurt too much. He already sort of made fun of the beauty pageant stuff. I can't tell him about the writing."

"But if you can't tell your loved ones your deepest secrets, what does that say about your relationship?" Daniel asked, thinking about Georgia and the secrets she was keeping from her mother. And the ones she was keeping from him.

A sudden tension seemed to hover over them, a tension that dissipated when Sierra laughed lightly and said, "It says it's time for me to get home and get started on dinner."

Daniel laughed with her, even though he had this niggling sense that something was suddenly very wrong. Only, he couldn't decide whether it was because he was worried about Sierra and what might happen to her fledgling dream if her boyfriend quashed it, or if it was what Georgia's continued silence said about their relationship that was bothering him the most.

Of course, according to Georgia, they didn't have a relationship. They had sex, and nothing more.

And, hell, he was a guy. Sex should be enough, right?

But that had never been enough for him. Growing up in a world where everyone was rich and beautiful, where people who professed to love one another were apart for months at a time, he'd seen what "just sex" could do. It ruined marriages, it broke hearts, it wrecked self-esteem, it humiliated people's children when evidence of their parents' indiscretions ended up as tabloid fodder.

"Just sex" almost never turned out to be just sex.

It wasn't just sex with him and Georgia, no matter what she might tell herself. There was no way she could open herself to him so absolutely and still believe that. The trouble was, until he could convince her to stop tiptoeing around her mother, she would never be free to live her own life, at least not the way she wanted.

And Daniel suddenly realized that he cared very much about Georgia's happiness. He had never experienced such a connection with another person. Around Georgia, Daniel felt that he was a part of something bigger than himself, something important.

She made him feel as if he belonged.

Somehow, he wanted to give her that same sense of fulfillment he had been given since meeting her. He'd seen the way it upset Georgia when people thought the Miracle Chef was a fraud. She was proud of her invention, but until she could announce to the world that she was more than just an aging beauty queen, she'd always be hiding away that part of herself that made her, her. And since she wouldn't tell him why she pretended to be someone she wasn't, he was determined to figure it out for himself.

Daniel always liked to know what he was up against.

Which is why, after he waved good-bye to Sierra, he took the photo of Rose and Vivian and the missing man back to the microfiche machine and started looking at newspapers from the first week in October 1961. It wasn't difficult to go through a week's worth of papers. Even now, the *Ocean Sands Register* wasn't more than twenty pages long. On Sunday.

Back in 1961, it had been even shorter.

Daniel wasn't certain what he was searching for. He knew it would be an enormous stroke of luck to find the exact same picture he held in his hand neatly laid out on the front page of the paper with a caption identifying everyone in the photo. Nobody got that lucky.

Not even in fiction.

The Ocean Sands Shrimp Festival dated back to the late 1930s when, at the height of the Great Depression when the residents of many cities across the country were standing in bread lines, the residents of Ocean Sands celebrated their own good fortune to live on the Gulf of Mexico, which provided a bounty of seafood—including enough shrimp to sustain them during the rough years ahead. Back then, the festival was about escaping the crushing worry of impending war and financial ruin for just one day. The Ocean Sands Shrimp Festival Princess reminded townspeople that beauty still existed in a world full of ugliness. The shrimp feed was a treat for families who came from as far away as Oxford to feast on something different than potatoes and bread. The crowning glory, however, was the homemade sweet potato pie—twenty-two feet wide by twenty-eight feet long—baked in a special brick oven built by Ocean Sands' then-mayor whose full-time job was as a bricklayer.

By now, the festival's roots had been pretty much forgotten; the celebration more a weeklong reason to party and suck their fair share of tourist dollars into the local economy. Still, the shrimp feed and serving of the sweet potato pie by the town's volunteers marked the official end of the festivities, the same as they had since the fair began nearly seventy years ago.

All of this Daniel learned as he read the Saturday paper from back in 1961. The front page that day was dominated by a picture of the enormous pie being pulled from the custom-made oven by a bevy of women in high heels and dresses covered with neat white aprons.

"Speaking of beauty queens," Daniel murmured. These women, indeed, looked as if they had just stepped off a runway to whip up a 616 square-foot pie. He read the caption:

From l. to r.: Mrs. Borden Jeffries, Mrs. Rex Broussard, Mrs. Bobby Kingsley, Miss Genevieve Conover, and Mrs. Jackson Hughes remove another perfectly baked sweet-potato pie from the oven. Could this year's Shrimp Festival pie princesses be any sweeter?

Daniel studied the women, but none of their faces seemed familiar, except in that vague way where you suspected you'd perhaps met one of their children or seen some semblance of their former beauty in a flash of an eighty-year-old smile.

He skimmed the rest of the paper, coming back to the front page when it became obvious that he wasn't going to find anything amidst the ads for hi-fis for sale at Conover and Son's electronics store or a reminder from the police that the ten-mile-an-hour speed limit on Main

Street was going to be strictly enforced throughout the remainder of the fair.

Daniel's eye suddenly caught on a headline. ALABAMA MAN MISSING SINCE THURSDAY. Well, that wasn't your typical church potluck or rotary club meeting reminder.

He read on.

> Local resident and city council member Jackson Hughes reported his brother Carter missing today after the Birmingham native failed to show up for a fishing trip the men had arranged last week. The Alabama man had been visiting his brother for about a month when he disappeared last Thursday. Mr. Hughes said he and his brother were not close, and he wasn't suspicious of his brother's absence at first.
>
> "I thought Carter may have gone to Biloxi for a few days," Mr. Hughes said when asked about his brother's disappearance. There has been no answer at Carter Hughes's apartment in Birmingham and police in Alabama are cooperating with the local investigators, according to County Sheriff Robert Boleen. Foul play is suspected.

Well, Daniel thought, it looked like the Hugheses were dominating the front page. Still, that had nothing to do with Vivian Elliot and her sister, so it wasn't of much use in his investigation.

At least he'd gotten some information about the Shrimp Festival to use on the next show.

He checked his watch and saw that it was nearly seven o'clock. He'd promised Vivian a home-cooked meal after winking at her and telling her the one condition: that she had to get her daughter to come over if she wanted to indulge in his nearly world-famous cannelloni stuffed with ricotta and spinach and topped with a combination of béchamel and marinara sauces. She had laughingly told him she'd do her best, and Daniel had no doubt that meant he'd see Georgia this evening whether she wanted to come over or not.

"Guess this whole manipulation thing might not be so bad after all," he said to himself, as he turned off the microfiche machine and headed outside into the warm late-September evening.

"I can't believe you entered me in the Shrimp Queen Pageant without asking first."

"But, honey, you know I love to show you off. You're so pretty." Vivian poured about a tablespoon of Coca-Cola into a highball glass and then filled the rest with Scotch.

Georgia closed her eyes and counted to twenty, then gave up and poured herself a drink, too. "I told you that I was finished after last year," she said, adding a handful of ice to her own glass.

"I wanted Daniel to see you as you really are. I know you two are carrying on like you have no future, but once he sees how beautiful you are when you make an effort with yourself, he won't be able to leave."

Her mother brought her glass to her pink-lipsticked lips and took a sip, while Georgia stared at her in open-mouthed horror. "You have got to be kidding, Mother."

Vivian dabbed at her mouth with a cocktail napkin. "No, dear, I'm not. I like Daniel. He's smart, he comes from a good family, he's nice to us both. Plus, he's rich," she added with a small smile. "The only fault I've been able to find with him is that he's perhaps a bit too nosy, but then, he's a Yankee. He probably doesn't know any better."

"Mama—" Georgia began warningly. Great, this was just what she needed, her mother playing matchmaker.

Vivian held up a hand to stop her. "No, hear me out. For years I prayed that you and Trey would get back together. You two made such a handsome couple, and your children would have been adorable. But I can see now that will just never work."

"Yeah, he's marrying my best friend in nine days," Georgia interjected.

"Ladies do not say, 'yeah.' We say 'yes.'"

"Whatever," Georgia muttered under her breath, raising her own glass to her lips as her mother shot her a sharp look.

"In any event, I've come to terms with the fact that it's time for you to move on. It's my duty as your mother to help ensure that you find a proper husband. It's obvious from the way you and Daniel act when you're together that you enjoy a mutual attraction. I think once he sees you up there on that stage, looking your best, he'll realize that he can't get on that plane to Los Angeles and leave you. He'll see that you'll make him the perfect wife. You're beautiful, you can cook, you have poise and grace—"

"Yeah, and I can twirl a baton like no one else he knows," Georgia interrupted sarcastically, unable to keep her mouth shut any longer. Her mother was just so . . . so clueless about this. It was as if she were living in some time warp when women were valued for nothing more than their physical appearance and ability to get a hot meal on the table when their husbands came home from a hard day's work. The thing was, Georgia suspected this fantasy world had never even existed at all, except in her mother's own mind. And, suddenly, all her years of frustration from trying to live up (or down, as the case may be) to her mother's expectations seemed to crush in on her. She was sick of living this way, of hiding her true self under this veneer of politeness and charm. She felt like a chick who had been pecking and pecking little by little at the shell trying to hold her in and, finally, she had made enough of a hole in her white prison to smell freedom.

And it smelled good—it smelled of happiness, of success, or promise and excitement. While inside her shell, the air was stifling and stale.

Georgia carefully put her glass down on the counter, reining in the impulse that told her to slam her glass down on the tile countertop until it shattered. "I'm done with this Mama. I love you, but I can't be who you want me to be anymore. You say you want Daniel to see me as I really am, but I don't. Do you know why? Because all he'd see is a woman trapped under her mother's thumb, a woman who is afraid to live her own life for fear of how others will perceive her, a woman who is only free when she's with someone she knows is going to leave and take her secrets with him."

She paused and took a deep breath, feeling as if her lungs had shrunk to half their normal capacity. Her mother looked shocked, so Georgia held out a hand to her beseechingly. "Can't you understand, Mama? I don't want Daniel to see that woman. I want him to see the woman I *could* be, instead."

"Oh, I think he does," Daniel said, stepping into the kitchen from the hallway beyond.

Georgia gasped and turned to see him looking gorgeous as ever in a pair of blue jeans and a plain green polo shirt that seemed to make his eyes even bluer than usual. He put a hand on her shoulder, his fingers solid and warm through the fabric of her shirt.

Vivian started shaking, the ice cubes in her glass clinking together as she raised it to her lips and took a long, steadying drink. When she was finished, she put the glass on the counter and smiled a plastic smile. "Well, then, I guess I've fulfilled my obligation as a mother. If you two will excuse me, I feel a migraine coming on and am going up to my room to lie down." She wafted past them on a cloud of pride and perfume.

The minute she was gone, Georgia felt herself deflate, as if her desperation to break free of her mother's expectations was all that had been keeping her from collapsing into a puddle on the floor. If Daniel hadn't enfolded her in his arms just then, she feared she might have done just that.

Resting his chin on top of her head, Daniel held her quietly for a moment. Then he said, "Come on, let's get out of here," his warm breath tickling her scalp.

Georgia nodded, figuring they'd go back to her house for the night. Instead, once they were outside, Daniel steered her toward his rented convertible. She didn't ask where they were going, even after Daniel stopped at Broussard's and left her in the car while he ran in and came out five minutes later with a sack full of groceries.

He turned the car away from Oak Street and headed through town, the warm night air blowing Georgia's curls across her face.

"Want me to put the top up?" Daniel asked, as Georgia attempted to gather her hair up in one hand and hold it behind her head.

"No, the wind feels wonderful."

In no time at all, they were out of the downtown area and headed south toward the Gulf of Mexico. Georgia smelled the heavy salt air and heard the never-ending wash of waves against the shore as they pulled into the deserted parking lot that the city maintained for the public.

Georgia took off her shoes and left them in the car as she carefully picked her way across the sidewalk and onto the beach, making sure not to step on any errant shards of glass left by irresponsible tourists or local teens.

The sand was still warm from the sun and Georgia buried her feet in it, enjoying the silky, slippery feel of it between her toes. She turned toward the breeze and drew the salty, humid air into her lungs. She sensed that Daniel had come up behind her, although he didn't say anything or touch her. Instead, he just stood at her back, his presence solid and comforting.

"I love it out here," she said.

Daniel twisted a lock of her hair around a finger and tugged and Georgia took a step back toward him.

"One of these days, we're going to have to talk about your mother," he said, looking out over the calm, dark waters of the Gulf of Mexico.

Georgia turned and laid her head on his shoulder. "Not tonight, okay?"

Daniel sighed. It was always, "not tonight." Every time something traumatic happened with her mother, Georgia wanted to have sex, as if the intimacy of sharing her body with him could make up for the lack of what they shared emotionally. Unfortunately, with her rubbing up against him like a cat after a can of tuna, his body kept telling his brain that it didn't matter. Still, he tried to stop rewarding her—and himself—for her refusal to talk to him.

"I bought some things for a picnic. Wine, cheese, bread," he said.

Georgia smiled up at him, batting her eyelashes flirtatiously. "I've never done it on the beach. Want to give it a try?"

Daniel's gaze swept the shoreline. There seemed to be no one around for miles. "Uh, what about the wine?" he asked.

Georgia slowly unzipped her dress and let it slide off her shoulders to pool at her feet. She stood in the gathering twilight wearing only her matching pale pink bra and panties, her smooth skin almost glowing. "I think it'll keep for later, don't you?" she asked huskily, taking a step toward him on the sandy beach.

"I'm sure it will," Daniel agreed, reaching out to pull her close and letting his libido win this argument once again.

The skin of her back was smooth and warm beneath his fingers as he slid his hands up and down, stopping at the waistband of her panties to rub his thumbs over the dimples where her buttocks began. She tugged his shirt free of his jeans and trailed her hands up his back, her fingernails lightly scratching his skin as Daniel lowered his mouth to hers. In seconds, he had forgotten why he'd been protesting. Their mouths, their bodies, fit too well together.

Georgia pulled back just long enough to slide Daniel's shirt over his head. She tossed it on top of her dress and shook out her hair, letting the light evening breeze grab at her curls. The soft lapping of the Gulf against the shore calmed her, as if her worries were grains of sand being cleansed by the warm water washing over the beach.

Briefly, she considered tugging Daniel out into the surf, but then she reconsidered. Sharks were known to feed at dusk, and she figured it wouldn't be very arousing for either of them to be mistaken for some hungry predator's supper.

"What are you thinking about?" Daniel asked, smoothing a strand of hair away from her face.

Georgia chuckled. "Sharks," she answered truthfully.

Daniel looked toward the water, then back at her. "Maybe we should find ourselves a nice, safe hotel room," he suggested.

With a grin, Georgia reached behind her back, unsnapped her bra, and let it fall to the ground. Then she stepped out of her panties, kicking them toward him with her toe. She raised her arms above her head, stretching and feeling freer than she could ever recall being before. "I don't think so," she said.

Daniel looked up and down the deserted beach again just to make certain they were alone. "You know, when you said you wanted to use me for sex, I didn't realize you'd require my services quite so often."

Georgia grinned and reached out to hook her thumbs in the belt loops of his jeans. She tugged him closer until her breasts were touching the hair on his chest. She twisted ever so slightly, running her nipples back and forth against him until they became erect. Then she looked up at him and asked huskily, "Are you complaining?"

Daniel's blue eyes gazed intently into hers. He remained silent just long enough to give Georgia pause, then answered almost angrily, "No. The sex is enough for now."

Before Georgia could consider just what he meant by that, Daniel picked her up, his palms resting under her rear end as Georgia was forced to straddle him. "What are you doing?" she asked.

"Well, I didn't bring a blanket, not having planned for sex on the beach and all, and I didn't figure either one of us wanted to try getting sand out of places where sand should never go. Sorry to disappoint you, but I think I'll opt for sex on the car instead." With that, Daniel set her down on the trunk of the car and, in one smooth movement, tugged off his jeans.

Georgia braced her heels on the bumper of the Mercedes and then gasped when Daniel sheathed himself with a condom, put a hand on the back of her neck and, with no more seduction than that, plunged himself inside her. She felt herself stretching, accommodating him as he pulsed into her again and again, making her take more and more of him. Their gazes locked together, but Daniel didn't lower his mouth to kiss her, and Georgia found this almost primal mating incredibly arousing. She scooted her hips forward on the warm metal of the trunk to get even closer to him. He pulled out and then pushed back into her, grinding against her most sensitive spot and making her squirm.

"Tell me you like it," Daniel ordered, tightening his hold on her neck.

Georgia threw her head back, reveling in the rawness of their lovemaking, in knowing that Daniel didn't want her to be quiet or demure or decorous when it came to sex.

"I fucking love it," she said with a note of desperation in her voice, nearly sliding off the car in an effort to get him to rub against her again. All it would take is one more time, one more touch, and she'd fly apart.

But Daniel held back, making her beg. "Come on, tell me you want it," he said.

Georgia looked at him then, at the man who had pushed her and prodded her, who tempted her to want more from her life than she ever had, who frustrated and pleased her in equal measures. And she wondered if he believed that she would have been satisfied just having sex with any stranger who had showed up in Ocean Sands, wondered if that's what was making him drive into her with what seemed a desperation to mark her.

She wove her fingers into his hair, holding his head steady as she gazed at him intently. "I want *you,* Daniel," she whispered.

With a groan, Daniel pushed into her one last time, his back stiffening as he came. Georgia felt her own eyelids start to close with the force of her orgasm, but strained to keep her eyes open, watching him. He shuddered and rested his weight on his arms, his palms on the warm trunk of the car at either side of Georgia's hips.

Georgia let him remain like that for a long moment, then tugged on his hair to make him look at her. When their eyes met, she saw that whatever anger he may have felt earlier had dissipated, leaving behind a strange sort of sadness instead.

She smoothed back a lock of hair that had fallen forward onto his brow. "Thank you," she said softly.

Daniel regarded her coolly with those ocean-colored eyes of his. "For what?"

"For letting me be me," she answered, then dropped a light kiss on his forehead and hopped down off the car to retrieve the clothes they'd left lying on the beach.

Twenty~two

Friday. 7:15 P.M. Miracle Chef orders too numerous to count and show hasn't even aired yet. Situation becoming desperate. Experiment in trying to maintain secret life quickly disintegrating into disaster.

Georgia morosely stared down at the notes she'd scribbled in her notebook. The rest of the Tiara Club—with the exception of Callie, who had called a few minutes ago in near meltdown mode because the restaurant that was supposed to host her rehearsal dinner next Thursday had caught fire that afternoon and now she had to find another place that could accommodate forty people with less than a weeks' notice—were scheduled to arrive any moment, but Georgia's phone would not stop ringing. She would have turned off the ringer, but her electronic mailbox was full and wouldn't allow anyone to leave any more messages. And she could barely keep up with the calls coming in, much less have time to go through the hundreds of messages still left on her voice-mail system.

And it was only going to get worse after *Epicurean Explorer* aired at eight o'clock.

Georgia put her head in her hands and groaned. What was she going to do?

"Hey, Georgia. Did you get Sierra's swimsuit?" Deborah Lee asked as she came through Georgia's back door carrying a large cardboard box.

Despite the ever-increasing phone calls over the past two days, Georgia had not been willing to incur the wrath of Deborah Lee by not successfully completing her assigned task of finding just the right swimsuit for Sierra to wear. "Of course," Georgia answered, just as her phone rang again. Not wanting Deborah Lee to hear her taking yet another Miracle Chef order, Georgia grabbed the phone and said, "I'll just run upstairs and get that suit. Be right back."

Ten minutes—and two more orders—later, Georgia returned to find that everyone except Sierra had arrived. Her kitchen looked like the dressing room backstage at the Miss Universe Pageant, with beauty supplies, hair extenders, high-heeled shoes, gowns, and several batons covering every surface.

"So, what's tonight's drink?" Kelly asked, tackling the most important topic first.

"I figured everyone was sick of the banana drinks, so I moved on to one called 'Banging the Captain Three Ways on the Comforter,'" Georgia answered glumly, her mind still occupied with her Miracle Chef troubles.

"Ooh, I like the sound of that," Kelly all but purred. "What's in it?"

"Rum, Southern Comfort, and a mixture of orange, pineapple, and cranberry juice," Georgia said. She'd mixed up a batch before everyone arrived and proceeded to take the pitcher out of the icebox and pour drinks for everyone except herself. She filled her own glass with Southern Comfort. Straight up.

Emma Rose raised her eyebrows as Georgia slugged back her drink. "Bad day?" she asked.

"You don't know the half of it," Georgia muttered, doing her best not to choke as the fiery booze slid down her throat.

"Sierra's here," Deborah Lee squealed excitedly from the parlor, obviously having taken up watch for Sierra's car. "Y'all come here. I want you to see the look on her face when I give her her surprise."

"What the hell's she talking about?" Kelly whispered to Georgia as they obediently followed Deborah Lee's order.

Georgia shrugged and knocked back another mouthful of Southern Comfort. "I have no idea. She's obsessed with this whole beauty queen thing if you ask me. She's startin' to scare me."

"Tell me about it. She called me a dozen times at work today to make sure I had all the questions Sierra could possibly be asked on my flash cards. The last one was, 'If you could be any kind of fruit at all, what would you be?' Now, what kind of asinine judge would ask a stupid question like that?"

"I had one ask me why I thought putting an end to global starvation would be a good thing. He marked me down because I hadn't weighed the positive side of children not starving to death with the negative of the increased costs of health care were they to survive long enough to have heart attacks or get cancer." Georgia rolled her eyes and snorted. "Like I'm supposed to solve all the world's complex problems during a five-minute interview at a beauty pageant."

"Well, don't tell Deborah Lee that. She's convinced that Sierra's got to have an answer for everything, from how to reverse the effects of global warming to how to bring democracy and lasting peace to the Middle East," Kelly muttered under her breath as they gathered in the foyer to await Sierra's arrival.

"Did you say something?" Deborah Lee asked, shooting Kelly a look that told her that her answer had better be "no."

"No, ma'am," Kelly said with an innocent smile and two fingers crossed behind her back.

Georgia started to laugh but quelled her mirth when Deborah Lee turned her puckered-lip face on her. She held up a hand to ward off the evil thoughts being sent her way. "Sorry."

"Hmph," Deborah Lee said.

Sierra knocked hesitantly on Georgia's front door before opening it and poking her head inside. "Oh. Were you all waiting for me?" she asked, surprised to see the whole group gathered in the hall.

Deborah Lee clapped her hands together—rather like a mad scientist who was about to unleash her latest potion on the world, Georgia thought—and then reached out to drag Sierra into the house. The porch door squeaked shut on rusty hinges, banging against the door frame as Deborah Lee pulled Sierra along behind her to the sitting room.

"What's going on?" Sierra asked when Deborah Lee finally released her.

"I got you a present," Deborah Lee said. She bent down and retrieved a brightly colored bag that seemed large enough to fit a small Volkswagen.

Sierra looked at the bag for a moment, wondering what exactly it was for. Then her manners returned and she took it with a polite, "Thank you. It's very nice."

Deborah Lee beamed. "Look inside."

Sierra did as instructed, stunned to find it packed full of stuff. She reached into the bag and drew out a handful of things—Q-Tips, Preparation II, hair gel, underarm pads, packing tape, more hair gel, a curling iron, Baggies, even more hair gel. Confused, she looked up at Deborah Lee. "Did you knock off a drugstore?" she asked.

Deborah Lee's laugh tinkled like the pleasant sound of wind chimes on a soft breeze as she leaned forward and squeezed Sierra's arm. "No, honey. Of course not. This is your very own pageant survival kit. We all have one."

Sierra looked around to see Emma Rose, Kelly, and Georgia all nodding. Unlike her, they didn't seem surprised at the sheer volume of products Deborah Lee had stuffed in the bag. She felt guilty that Deborah Lee had gone to the trouble and expense of procuring all these supplies for her when she had no intention of actually going through with the beauty pageant. As she'd told Daniel Rogers the other night at the library, the only reason she'd even asked about pageant life was because the lead character in her novel had that same self-confident air that the women in the Tiara Club exhibited, and Sierra wanted to know more about how pageants had helped them to develop that trait. There was no way she was going to strut around on a runway in front of half a dozen judges and a quarter of the town. Just like Tim had said, the idea of her trying to be a beauty queen was ridiculous. Although it had hurt to have him say it, she knew he was right.

But when she opened her mouth to tell Deborah Lee that she appreciated the thought but wasn't going to have any need for all these things, Deborah Lee surprised her into silence by announcing gleefully, "But, wait! I have another surprise for you."

Sierra's smile felt a bit wobbly. She could end this all right now if only she'd confess her true reason for asking about pageants, but what if her new friends thought that the idea of her writing a book was as silly as Tim had thought entering the Shrimp Queen Pageant was? The women of the Tiara Club were the best friends she had. Was she willing to risk that friendship by telling them the truth? What if she hurt their feelings by telling them she didn't want to go along with their plan?

"This was the surprise I was going to tell y'all about on Monday before all that ugliness happened," Deborah Lee said. "I called Tessa Broussard down at the festival office last week and she told me you'd forgotten to put in your application for the pageant. So . . . Guess what?"

Sierra didn't need even a tenth of the imagination she'd been blessed—or some might say cursed—with to know what was coming next. Her mouth went dry when she thought about her choice: keep quiet about her writing dream and don't risk her friendships or humiliate herself in front of the entire town. Hmm.

Deborah Lee was squirming like a puppy who had done its business outside for the first time and was awaiting praise from its master as she squealed, "I put in your application for Shrimp Queen! Isn't that exciting? Now you'll be one of the Tiara Club for real."

And that was what made up Sierra's mind. If she went through with this, for the first time in her life, she might actually find somewhere that she belonged.

"They're gonna take points off if you hit 'em in the head with your baton," Emma Rose said patiently, taking a sip of her Banging the Captain Three Ways on the Comforter rum drink.

Sierra exhaled loudly and went to retrieve the baton in question from where it had landed in Georgia's sink. "I'm never going to get the hang of this," she whined, sounding very much like one of her students.

"You just have to be good enough to not let it go flying and hit anyone," Emma Rose said.

"Yeah, the talent portion only accounts for five percent of your score in this pageant," Kelly agreed. "You'll get two points just for showing up, and that can be enough for you to take the crown."

"Okay, try it again. From the top." Emma Rose hit the play button on Georgia's CD player and started humming along to a rousing John Philip Sousa marching tune as Sierra bumbled through the routine Emma Rose had shown her earlier.

The baton went flying again when Georgia's phone rang for what seemed like the hundredth time that evening. This time, it hit a frying pan that was hanging on Georgia's pot rack and ricocheted back toward Sierra, Kelly, and Emma Rose, who hit the floor as the baton whizzed past their heads.

"Georgia Marie Elliot, would you unplug that dang thing already?" Emma Rose shouted once it was safe for her to get up off the floor.

"Sorry. I got it," Georgia shouted back from upstairs.

"What's going on with all these phone calls?" Sierra asked, dusting off her jeans as she rose from the linoleum.

"One way to find out," Kelly said breezily, picking up the kitchen extension, covering the mouthpiece with her hand, and slowly pressing her thumb over the on button.

Stunned at this invasion of Georgia's privacy, but impressed by Kelly's quick thinking, Emma Rose and Sierra leaned close to listen in.

"That's right. I'd like two Miracle Chefs. One for me and one for my sister Eileen. You ready for the addresses?"

"Um, no. Wait just a second. I'm out of paper. Hold on, I'll be right back," Georgia said, sounding frazzled.

They heard her rustling around, then heard hurried footsteps on the stairs.

"Hurry, hang it up," Sierra hissed, her eyes wide with fright.

Kelly clutched the mouthpiece even tighter. "No way. It's just getting good. Emma Rose, grab that pad of sticky notes off the counter there and hand them to your cousin."

Emma Rose did as instructed, stopping in the doorway of the kitchen and holding out the Post-its just as Georgia reached the bottom of the stairs.

"Thank you," Georgia muttered absentmindedly as she grabbed the pad, turned around, and went back upstairs. A few seconds later, they heard her voice on the other end of the line again. "Okay, I'm ready now. Go ahead."

The woman reeled off two shipping addresses and a credit card number while Emma Rose, Kelly, and Sierra listened in. Then Georgia promised the Miracle Chefs would be shipped out within the next two weeks, thanked the woman for calling, and hung up. When the call ended, Kelly hit the off button and the three women in Georgia's kitchen took turns blinking at each other.

"I've got the flash cards all in order. Are y'all ready for the mock interview?" Deborah Lee asked, padding into the kitchen.

Before anyone could answer, there was a low creak from out in the hallway, as if someone were trying to step on a loose floorboard in just the right place to dampen the sound. A blond mop of curls appeared in the doorway, followed by a forehead and one brown eye. The eye blinked, but the face it was attached to didn't come any closer, instead keeping the wall safely between it and the rest of the Tiara Club.

Kelly leaned back against the counter and crossed her arms across her chest. "Well, well, well. Is there something you'd like to tell us, Georgia?"

The blond curls shook vigorously.

"Why are you taking orders for the Miracle Chef?" Sierra asked with a puzzled frown.

"What? She's taking orders for the Miracle Chef?" Deborah Lee parroted.

"I know you ordered some for us, but why would people call you to get them?" Emma Rose asked.

The one brown eye they could see closed for a moment, then opened again. Then Georgia inched sideways until she was no longer hiding behind the wall. She took a long, slow deep breath, as if it might be her last, and said, "All right. You guys are my friends, right?"

All four women nodded, but Georgia wasn't satisfied. "I can trust you with anything?" she asked, an oddly pleading note in her voice.

"Of course you can, honey," Deborah Lee said, reaching out to take Georgia's hand in hers.

Georgia nodded. Licked her lips. Took another deep breath. "I invented the Miracle Chef," she announced, looking from one friend to the other to gauge their reactions. "The phone number from that packing slip you had, Kelly? That's registered to me. Or rather, to my company, GME Industries. And in about . . ." She paused and glanced at her watch. It was three minutes to nine. Right about the time when Kelly would read that phone number aloud on the *Epicurean Explorer* show that was airing now. ". . . two and a half minutes, I suspect my phone is going to start ringing off the hook with people wanting to place orders, if the reaction from the people of Ocean Sands who already saw the show is any indication."

She stopped talking for a moment to let her news sink in. Sierra appeared to be the only one who was truly shocked. Deborah Lee and Emma Rose seemed only mildly surprised, and Kelly looked as if she had suspected the truth all along.

Georgia wrapped her arms around her waist and studied the pattern of the linoleum on the kitchen floor. "I couldn't tell y'all the truth before and I can't tell you why. I know it's a lot to ask that you keep my secret for me, but I'm desperate. I need your help. I can't do this on my own."

Fighting back tears, she raised her head and looked up at her friends. "Will you help me?"

Deborah Lee stepped forward and Georgia relaxed, expecting a hug. Instead, Deborah Lee hauled off and smacked her—hard—on her right arm. "You idiot. Of course we'll help you. Why did you wait so long to ask? What do you think we are, a bunch of low-life snitches?"

"Yeah, what kind of friends do you take us for?" Kelly asked, giving Georgia's shoulder a shove.

"Well, I think it's wonderful," Sierra said, surprising Georgia by pushing the other women away to give her a big hug. "I'd be happy to help you fulfill your dreams. Just tell me what to do."

And Emma Rose surprised her most of all when she grabbed a pen and legal pad out of Georgia's junk drawer, scraped a stool across the kitchen floor, and said, "Okay, the first thing we need to do is to create an order-entry system. You can't go on collecting information on Post-it notes. I'll need you all to sign up for shifts to answer the phone. It's a shame I didn't know about this sooner or I could have had someone create a website. Of course, we're going to need a secure server."

Emma Rose went on mumbling to herself, scribbling down notes as fast as she could write, and Georgia looked around at her friends and felt some hard part inside herself start to crumble, as if a wall had just fallen away from around her heart. She blinked and two fat tears rolled down her face. Sniffling, she wiped them away.

"Thank you all so much," she whispered.

And Deborah Lee smacked her again and said, "Isn't that what friends are for?"

Twenty~three

"Hey, Georgia. I'm sorry to wake you, but I've got the opening shift down at the restaurant and I wanted to fill you in on my progress before I left," Emma Rose said, shaking her cousin out of deep, dreamless sleep.

Georgia groaned and cracked one eye open. She'd been up all night taking Miracle Chef orders, finally getting to sleep at seven A.M. when Emma Rose had come over to relieve her. She glared at the alarm clock on her nightstand as if it were its fault that she'd only gotten two hours of sleep this morning, then was forced to sit up when Emma Rose sat down at the foot of her bed.

"I created a very simple order-entry database that we can use to not only capture our sales information but also to track when orders are received and when they're shipped. The program I created also automatically logs the order-taker's initials, so we'll be able to calculate data entry error rates. I wrote up a brief set of instructions on how to use the program and e-mailed it to everyone this morning. It's Web-enabled, so now we can forward calls to whoever's shift it is and she can take orders at home or wherever she has Internet access."

Georgia slapped her forehead with her palm and shook her head as if that might help to clear it. "What?" she asked groggily, having understood less than 10 percent of what Emma Rose had just said.

Emma Rose sighed and repeated it all again. Very slowly. Then she continued, in that same come-on-try-to-keep-up-with-me-here voice,

"I didn't think you'd want to have a round-the-clock business set up downstairs in your dining room, so I figured out a way for us to take orders over the Web. The orders get collected in a central database that we can use to print shipping labels, track order history, and so on. This way, once your shift is over, all you have to do is forward the calls on to the next person."

Georgia knew that her mouth was hanging open in shock, but couldn't seem to close it. "Where did you learn all this?" she asked.

"You're not the only one who took classes down at the community college, you know," Emma Rose answered dryly, then patted her cousin's feet under the blanket before standing up. "I called in an order for a thousand more Miracle Chefs based on our orders to date. They should arrive Monday morning. I'll work on setting up a Web site next, but first I have to go open the bar for the early lunch crowd. I've already forwarded calls to Deborah Lee, who said she didn't mind taking the eight to four shift. I've got Kelly lined up from four to midnight, and then Sierra from midnight to eight so you can get some sleep tonight. I was going to see if Callie would take the early morning shift tomorrow. I know she gets up early with the kids anyway."

Georgia was already shaking her head. "Let's not tell Callie about this until the wedding's over with. She's got enough to deal with right now, and I know if we ask her to help, she'll do it, no matter how exhausted or overwhelmed she is already. I can pull a double shift tomorrow. It's my day off from the gift shop and it seems only fair since this whole mess is my fault."

"You don't have plans with Mr. Hollywood?" Emma Rose asked, raising her eyebrows. "If it were me, I'd be keeping him plenty occupied until he went back to California."

Georgia pulled her knees up to her chest and wrapped her arms around her legs. "Well, I'm seeing him tonight, but he's been pretty busy with doing research for his show." *And meddling in Mama's affairs,* she added silently. "Besides, he and I both know this is just a fling. He'll forget about me as soon as he steps foot on the plane for home, so it would be stupid of me to try to make him too much a part of my life while he's here."

If anything, Emma Rose's eyebrows only went higher. "Uh-huh. You just go on trying to push him away. Who knows, you may succeed. God knows you've had plenty of experience doin' it."

Emma Rose turned to leave and Georgia felt the sudden urge to stick her tongue out at her cousin. What did Emma Rose know about it, anyway? This was the third time this week that she'd been accused of isolating herself when the truth was, she was surrounded by people. Just because she didn't choose to blabber on and on about every single aspect of her life, that didn't mean she pushed people away or kept them at arm's length. Really, she figured they should be glad about the fact that she didn't burden them with all her problems.

By the time she'd showered, put on her makeup, gotten dressed, and left for work, Georgia had worked herself up into a state of self-righteous indignation at the way her so-called friends kept nagging at her.

"Ungrateful and judgmental. That's what y'all are," she muttered darkly to herself as she unlocked the door of the gift shop and yanked open the door.

An hour later, when the brown UPS truck pulled into the parking lot, Georgia was still mumbling under her breath about friends who hid their true wolf selves under sheep's clothing.

"Hey, Georgia," the ever-cheerful Michael Kingsley said as he entered the gift shop with a loaded down hand truck.

"Hey, Michael," Georgia grumbled. "I didn't expect a delivery for the shop today."

"This isn't for the gift shop. It's for you. I went by your house earlier but you weren't there and this shipment is way too large for me to haul around until tonight, so I thought I'd come by here and see what you wanted me to do with it."

Georgia frowned and then looked at the box on the top of Michael's stack. When she saw the return address, she squinched her eyes closed and groaned. It was the Miracle Chefs she'd ordered after the cook-off at Miss Junie's funeral. How many had she ordered? Two hundred? Two-fifty? Ugh. Where was she going to put them all? Even if she could risk Mr. Talmadge not noticing all the boxes when the octogenarian owner of the gift shop and his daughter came in on Saturday to cover her shift, the stockroom wasn't big enough to hold that much. And she couldn't store them at her house. What if Mama took it in her head to drop by for a visit?

"Look, Michael, I can't take delivery of these here. You're going to have to hold on to them until I figure out—" Just then, the gift shop's phone rang. Georgia held up her hand and said, "Just a second."

"Hey, Georgia. It's me," Callie whispered when Georgia picked up the receiver.

"Hey," Georgia whispered back, without knowing why they were whispering.

"Your mama's out front and I don't want her to hear me," Callie explained. "She's picked out two new dresses, a pair of shoes, and a pocketbook and wants me to put it on her account. I know you told me not to let her buy anything more on credit, but she told me that was nonsense. What do you want me to do? You know I can't tell her no. She gives me that look of hers like I'm still five years old and it scares me to death."

Georgia sighed. So much for giving her mother the "We're going to the poorhouse if you don't stop spending money we don't have" lecture. Still, she couldn't fault Callie for not standing up to Mama. She knew exactly how Callie felt. "Go ahead and charge her purchases. I'll take care of it like I always do," Georgia said.

She heard the relief in Callie's voice when she said, "Great. Thank you. I'll talk to you later." Then Callie hung up, presumably so she could go ring Mama up and get her out of the store.

Georgia turned back to deal with Michael, but he wasn't there. She rubbed her neck with one hand and felt more than a little relieved herself. Good. Michael must be taking the Miracle Chefs back to the UPS warehouse and—

"Sorry, Georgia, but I've got to get rid of these things. I can't get to anything else in my truck until I do," Michael said, bringing in another stack of boxes from the truck outside and leaving them sitting in the middle of the gift-shop floor as he went out to fetch another load.

Georgia followed him out and up the ramp leading into the truck.

She had to convince him to take these darn things back until she could figure out what to do with them.

Michael slipped the bottom of his hand truck under another stack of boxes and effortlessly tilted them up. When he turned and saw that Georgia was in the truck, he lost his previously cheerful demeanor. "You can't be in here. It's against company policy."

Georgia stepped in front of the hand truck and folded her arms across her chest. "I'm sorry, Michael, but I can't let you unload these."

Michael looked like he was about to argue when Georgia heard her mother's voice trill, "Georgia, honey, where are you?"

Georgia gasped. Her mother couldn't see her with all these Miracle Chefs. A dozen or two she could explain away. But not two hundred and fifty.

"Shoot," she cursed, racing toward Michael. "Get back."

If the situation weren't so dire, she might have laughed at the stunned look on Michael's face when she put her hands to his chest and pushed him toward the front of the idling truck. She pulled him behind a set of boxes and hissed, "Don't let her see you."

"Georgia—" Michael protested, but she cut him off with a murderous look.

All was quiet for a second, and Georgia prayed that her mother would just go home. She peered out from around the corner of a box, only to see Mama approaching the ramp of the truck. She had to do something, and fast.

Georgia turned to look behind her, but—crouched down as she was—couldn't see over the dashboard of the UPS truck. From her vantage point, all she could see was that Michael had a full tank of gas, that the transmission was in park, and that the key was in the ignition.

Hmm. The key was in the ignition. She chewed the inside of her cheek and asked herself what other choices she had. When she realized the answer was, "None," she made her decision, sprinting from her crouched position and leaping into the driver's seat of the truck.

"Hold on," she warned, shoving the transmission into drive and flooring the accelerator.

The truck lurched from its parking space, the still-extended ramp clattering behind like tin cans tied to a cat's tail.

"Hey, you can't drive this thing," Michael yelled, standing up just as Georgia took a turn too wide and bumped over a curb. Michael flew up into the air and came back down again, landing on his rear end with his brown shorts bunched up around his thighs.

"You don't have to tell *me* that," Georgia muttered as she stood on the gas pedal to get up enough speed to make it through the yellow light at the intersection ahead. She had no idea where she was going, her only goal being to get away from Mama and her prying eyes. But when the neon sign outside the No Holds Bar flashed on two blocks away, she got an idea. Beau had a banquet room at the back of the restaurant that he only opened up when the VFW had their annual banquet or during the holidays when all the businesses in town had their Christmas lunches. The chances that he'd be needing that room in the next week, before her newly formed workforce got organized enough to start shipping the Miracle Chefs out, were pretty slim, so Georgia figured she could store the Miracle Chefs there.

It was the perfect plan. Emma Rose didn't need help to open the restaurant in the morning, so neither Beau or Aunt Rose would be there. They could unload the Miracle Chefs into the banquet room, lock the door behind them, and nobody would be the wiser.

Satisfied that this could work, Georgia focused her gaze on an empty parking spot right outside the front door of the bar. She sped up, only to see Mrs. Rydell's powder blue Lincoln Continental start to pass her out of her side view mirror. Mrs. Rydell was a regular for lunch at the No Holds Bar, meeting her former boss down at the paper company there every Saturday at 11:15 A.M. sharp for chef salads and fries. The whole town knew that wasn't the only thing they met for—after all, it was easy enough to do the math when lunch was eaten by noon but Mrs. Rydell and Mr. McKinnon didn't make it back to their respective homes until three—but Georgia figured that if Mr. Rydell didn't mind his wife getting a little something extra on the side, then it wasn't any skin off her nose. Still, that didn't mean Georgia was just going to give Mrs. Rydell the prime parking spot that *she* had spotted first.

She swerved into Mrs. Rydell's lane just the tiniest bit and the blue Continental fishtailed as Mrs. Rydell slammed on her brakes. Georgia stuck her hand out the window and waved as if to say she was sorry—which, of course, she wasn't—when the other car's horn sounded.

Slowing the truck down was just as difficult as getting it to speed up, Georgia discovered as she overshot the parking space by a good car length and then attempted to parallel park the beast. Fortunately, Michael had weaved his way up to the front of the van by then and said, "Move over. I've got it from here."

Georgia threw it into park and obediently slid out of the driver's seat to let him take over. He expertly maneuvered the truck into the tight-fitting spot and then, with an annoyed glance in her direction, twisted the key in the ignition and pocketed the keys.

With an apologetic shrug, Georgia said, "I'm sorry. You can unload those boxes here. Just let me go in and get Emma Rose to open the alley door. It'll be faster to get them through that way."

She trotted down the ramp, guessing that if Michael didn't need to get the Miracle Chefs off his hands—and out of his truck—he might be tempted to just drive away and leave her there. As a matter of fact . . . She looked back over her shoulder to see him loading up his hand truck, muttering under his breath.

Great, she thought as she pulled open the door to the No Holds Bar. It looked like she had managed to cheat disaster once again.

Daniel had spent Friday preparing for the fourth cook-off challenge. He figured that for Callie's bachelorette party next week, an array of hors d'oeuvres would be better than an actual meal, so he'd experimented with some of his favorites in Vivian's kitchen to make sure he could get them to the table in under thirty minutes. Vivian had stayed in her room all day, but Daniel had made a point of taking her up coffee and sliced fruit for breakfast and a chicken salad sandwich and iced tea for lunch. He didn't know if she'd eaten any of it, but he'd left trays on the table outside her room and let her know there was food outside. Both trays had disappeared, so Daniel assumed she was eating, even though she refused to put in an appearance. Georgia had said she couldn't see him that evening since she had plans with her friends, so he had a quiet dinner down at the No Holds Bar and woke on Saturday to bright sunshine and temperatures back in the low seventies.

Once he was satisfied that he was ready for the next show, Daniel decided to make another stop at the Ocean Sands History Museum, which was two blocks south of Main Street on Post, across from city hall. As he parked on the street, he saw another man getting out of a car in front of a building with a sign proclaiming "Wright, Bremer & Grainger, Attorneys at Law." Absently, he wondered if Kelly Bremer and Stuart Grainger made up the Bremer and Grainger part of the firm. The man getting out of the car looked remarkably like Trey Hunter, so Daniel assumed he was most likely some sort of relation— not unusual since most everyone in this town seemed to be related to everyone else by blood, marriage, or commerce.

The Ocean Sands History Museum was housed in a single-story brick building with white columns out front. Daniel pushed open the front door and was greeted immediately by Miss Beall, of stolen fork fame. She was dressed in a starched blue taffeta dress that barely had an inch unadorned by flounces, bows, or lace, and had a matching blue hat with a white ostrich plume balanced jauntily atop her white hair.

"Miss Beall, I don't believe we've formally met. I'm Daniel Rogers, of the Los Angeles Rogerses," Daniel said, extending his hand. He had, over the course of his time in Ocean Sands, learned that a proper introduction in these parts included at least some indication of your bloodlines—or "your people," as he'd heard Georgia say.

"Oh, yes. You're that movie star everyone in town's been talking about. Pleased to meet you." Miss Beall gave his hand a surprisingly firm shake for a woman of her age.

"Miss Elliot brought me over to see your reenactment last week. It was quite impressive."

Miss Beall tilted her head coquettishly. "Well, now, you know we do try to entertain the tourists. And, of course, I strive for historical accuracy in the retelling of that story. I feel that's very important."

"I'm sure you do a wonderful job," Daniel said, pulling out his picture of Vivian and Rose at the Shrimp Festival as Miss Beall stepped out from behind the welcome desk.

"Let me show you how we authenticated the costumes," she said.

Daniel looked down at the photo in his hand and then shrugged, following the rustling mass of taffeta that was Miss Beall into the bowels of the museum. He'd learned that one of the best ways to get a source to give you the information you wanted was to be willing to listen to what they wanted to tell you first. He figured it was a form of auditory payola.

An hour later, he wasn't feeling quite so charitable. Not that Miss Beall's recounting of the entire saga of the stolen fork wasn't fascinating but . . . well, it wasn't fascinating. Especially since Daniel had seen the story acted out live a week and a half ago.

"That's very interesting," he said, looking at yet another yellowing picture that Miss Beall had dug out for his perusal. "But I'm actually interested in history that's a little more recent. Nineteen sixty-one to be exact."

"Oh." Miss Beall sounded disappointed as she stored the scrapbook back in its temperature-controlled drawer.

"Yes, you see I have this photo here but, as you can see, the man on the right is missing. I'd like to know if you happen to have copies of this? Perhaps it was an official Shrimp Festival photographer who took it?"

"Hmm." Miss Beall studied the picture Daniel handed her for a moment before giving it back. "The Shrimp Festival room is back here. Let's see what we can find out."

She led him to a room filled with various paraphernalia relating to the town's annual fair. While Miss Beall rummaged around in a series of drawers, Daniel scrutinized the pictures on the walls, hoping to find a replica of the one he held in his hand. He stopped in front of one that, according to the placard below it, was from the same year. He didn't have much time to study it however, as Miss Beall had found what she'd been looking for and plunked a stuffed file of photos down in front of him with a satisfied, "Here we are. These are the official photos from that year."

It took him half an hour of sorting through pictures to determine that he was nearing a dead end.

Vivian refused to admit that she knew the identity of the man in the picture. Rose seemed to honestly not recall that photo, and he hadn't found anything here in the museum to give him another clue.

Daniel frowned at the photo. The two girls in it didn't appear to be much happier than he was at the moment. Why would that be? Typically, going to a fair was something children enjoyed. There would be games and cotton candy and rides. So why did Rose and Vivian look as if they were being dragged to the dentist?

He turned the picture over and noticed, for the first time, that someone had written the number 4113 in pencil along the side. Hmm. What did that mean?

Daniel returned to the photos Miss Beall had handed him. This time, he turned them over, trying to find another one that might have been numbered similarly.

To his astonishment, he found several.

He took the pictures up to the front of the museum, where Miss Beall was rearranging the items for sale, putting the ceramic ashtrays shaped like giant Gulf prawns in front of a selection of coffee-table books featuring the town's antebellum homes.

"Do you have any way of knowing where these photos came from?" Daniel asked, sliding them across the counter toward the elderly woman.

She squinted at them through the thick lenses of her glasses, and Daniel waited for her to say, "Of course not." Instead, she pulled a laptop out from under the counter and clicked a few keys. Then she nodded and turned the computer toward him, her index finger pointing to one spot on the screen. "We catalog everything that comes into the museum," she said. "It looks like these were donated by June Harris back in nineteen eighty-two."

Great. Too bad Miss Harris was no longer alive to give him any insights into what her numbering scheme might mean.

Daniel rubbed his forehead in frustration as his investigation slammed into yet another brick wall. "Well, good thing I brought a ladder," he muttered, taking the photos to the back room and neatly filing them away.

If he couldn't go through that brick wall, he'd go over it.

Twenty-four

She'd run out of condoms and, since she and Daniel were seeing each other again in about an hour and Georgia fully intended to continue using him for sex, she'd decided to stop at the grocery store after work to stock up on necessary supplies.

Georgia looked up and down the aisle in Broussard's grocery store to make sure she was alone, then furtively snagged a box of extra large ribbed Trojans. Then she tossed another box into her basket just in case.

Georgia turned to dash from the health and beauty aisle . . . and ran straight into Trey, who, she noticed, was perusing the contents of her basket with avid curiosity as he held out a hand to steady her. She tilted the red basket and the bag of limes she'd bought rolled over the boxes of condoms that were each brightly decorated with a romantic sunset scene of a couple on the beach. Which just reminded her of what she and Daniel had done Thursday night on the beach, causing a blush to creep up her cheeks.

She coughed and tried to think of anything besides the condoms lying in the bottom of her basket.

"Hey, Trey," she mumbled.

"Georgia," Trey acknowledged, sounding somewhat distant.

They stood looking at each other awkwardly for a long moment, with the voice inside Georgia's head repeating, "Think of something to say." Finally, she said, "Uh, so what do you and your friends have planned for Friday night when we're throwing Callie her bachelorette party? They takin' you into Biloxi for a wild night on the town?"

Georgia knew better, but it was the only thing she could think of to ask. Knowing Trey, he and his friends would spend the night watching various sports games on television, have a few beers, and turn in early. He didn't exactly run with a wild crowd, which, she supposed, was as it should be for the town's mayor.

"Naw. We're meeting down at the No Holds Bar for a few beers, but I don't want to make it a late night. I've got a busy day planned for the next day, what with the Shrimp Festival and all."

"Um, yes. And your wedding that night."

"Yes, of course. That, too," Trey agreed offhandedly, making Georgia want to thwack him in the head with a juicy lime.

But she couldn't do that, so instead she asked, "How's Callie doing? I haven't had a chance to talk to her since this morning."

"She's got a headache. That's why I'm here. She ran out of aspirin. I told her she should stock up on the industrial-sized bottles with those kids of hers." Trey laughed as if he'd just made a joke, and Georgia put her basket behind her back so she wouldn't reach in and pull out the heaviest piece of fruit to lob at his head.

Trey reached beside her and grabbed a bottle of aspirin, shaking it as if it were a maraca. Then he grabbed another, grinned and said, "His and hers."

Georgia was really glad he took the medicine and left, as she wasn't certain she could restrain herself much longer. "Pompous ass," she muttered, dithering around near the shampoo to give Trey time to make his purchase and leave.

"Georgia, what are you doing here?" Sierra Riley asked, coming around the panty hose display at the end of the aisle.

Georgia felt as if she'd just been caught pawing through the triple-X-rated movies that Rudy Jeffries kept in the back room of his video rental store rather than stocking up on citrus fruits—and condoms—at Broussard's. "Uh," Georgia said, making sure said condoms were safely tucked away from prying eyes, "I was just picking up a few things."

Sierra sniffled at that and Georgia suddenly noticed that her friend's eyes were red. She pulled a tissue out of her pocketbook and handed it to Sierra. "Oh, honey, what's wrong?" she asked, setting her basket down on the linoleum floor of the market so she could put her arm around Sierra.

As with most women, the very act of being comforted seemed to be the cue Sierra was waiting for to start crying in earnest. Georgia patted her shoulder, murmured soothing words of comfort, and, with her free hand, grabbed a box of Kleenex off the shelf behind her and ripped open a fresh supply of tissues.

After awhile, Sierra's tears subsided and she stepped back out of Georgia's embrace, taking the tissues with her. "I'm sorry," she said, swiping at her leaky nose and eyes. "I didn't mean to cry all over you like that."

Georgia reached out and squeezed Sierra's arm. "That's what friends are for."

Sierra sniffled again and picked up a three-pack of Kleenex. "This is what I came for. I picked a bad time to run out." She gave Georgia a watery smile and started crying again.

Georgia scooted a giant package of diapers out of the way and sat down on the bottom shelf, patting the seat next to her to indicate that Sierra should sit down. "Do you want to talk about it?" she asked.

Sierra dabbed at her eyes as she took a seat. "I made the mistake of taking someone's advice when I should have known better. Although, I suppose I should tell you that you're partly to blame, too."

"What?" Georgia asked, incredulous. What had she done to make Sierra cry?

Twisting a tissue between her fingers, Sierra drew in a shaky breath. Then she turned to Georgia and said, "I have a secret."

Georgia blinked, somewhat taken aback by the hasty change of subjects. "You do?"

Sierra nodded and wiped away the last of her tears. "Yes, I do. I've always wanted to write a novel. That's why I wanted to know about the pageant stuff—because the heroine of my book was a beauty queen, too, just like you and the rest of the Tiara Club."

"But that's wonderful," Georgia said, putting an arm around Sierra's shoulder. "If you want to write a book, you've certainly come to the right place. Mississippi has produced more writers per square mile than any other state. We've got claim to William Faulkner, Eudora Welty, and John Grisham, just to name a few."

"No," Sierra interrupted before Georgia could continue. "I want to write romance novels."

"Oh." Georgia paused, considering that news. Then she shrugged. "Well, there's nothing wrong with that."

"You wouldn't think so, would you?" Sierra murmured.

Georgia didn't know what to say to that, so she remained silent.

"For the past six months, I've gone to the library every night after work and worked on my book. I never told Tim what I was doing. I just let him believe that I went there to grade papers and stay out of his hair so he could sleep."

"What made you tell him now?" Georgia asked.

Sierra laughed shortly. "I was going to tell him soon anyway because the book's almost finished. I figured once I had written 'the end' on it, it wouldn't matter how Tim reacted. You know, because he couldn't take that sense of accomplishment away from me once the book was done. But then you told the rest of the Tiara Club that you're an inventor and I saw how much help and support you got when you told us about your dream, and so I thought . . . Well, I thought maybe that would happen for me, too."

"But why would Tim want to take your dream away from you?"

Sierra dabbed at her eyes since they'd started leaking tears again. "I don't know. Daniel said—"

"Daniel? You mean, *my* Daniel?" Georgia asked, not realizing the implication of referring to him as hers.

Sierra nodded, temporarily unable to go on as her shoulders shook with sobs. Finally, she managed to get herself under control again. "I'm sorry," she said weakly.

"Nonsense. Now what did Daniel say that's got you so upset?" Georgia was ready to leap up and find the awful rat who had taken her friend's dreams and ripped them all to shreds. How could Daniel do such a thing? Especially since he was a writer himself.

Sierra drew in a hiccupping breath. "He asked me what it says about my relationship with Tim if I can't tell him my deepest secret."

"Huh?" Georgia said, confused.

"I know. I'd never thought about it that way, either. I mean, here I am, following this guy around from town to town for what seems like forever, and it suddenly occurs to me that Daniel's right. If I can't tell Tim about my dream of becoming an author and trust that he won't use it against me, why would I even consider staying with him?"

"What did Tim say when you told him?" Georgia asked, fearing she already had her answer in the form of a half-used box of Kleenex.

Sierra turned away at first, but then swung her gaze back to Georgia's. "He laughed."

Georgia felt pain stab her in the chest. Without thinking, she raised a hand to rub the aching spot. "No."

Sierra breathed in and out deeply before answering, "Yes, and it was even worse than when I told him about the beauty pageant stuff. He laughed and said that he hoped I planned to keep my book hidden under the bed. 'Not the sort of thing you want your students' parents to discover,' he said. As if I had just announced that I was starring in a porn flick or something."

Georgia blinked at the woman she'd met a year ago. She'd never known this about her friend. As far as she knew, nobody else in the Tiara Club had known it, either.

But—was Daniel right?—did keeping secrets make their friendship weaker? Or had it, instead, enabled them all to remain friends for so long? After all, what if Georgia told Callie what she really thought of Trey? Callie truly seemed to be looking forward to getting married, to having some help raising her children. What if Georgia was wrong? Just because she and Trey hadn't been right for each other, did that mean that Callie was making a mistake? If she did say something, was she putting Callie in the position of having to choose between her best friend and her fiancé? That was the last thing Georgia wanted to do.

And what if Georgia told the Tiara Club her deepest secret—that her mother had tried to commit suicide on two separate occasions because she was so disappointed by her only child's behavior? What if they thought she was exaggerating? Or, worse, what if they spread it around town and it got back to her mother that everyone knew?

Daniel, for all his lofty ideals, had no idea the damage he was doing by urging people to take these sometimes ugly truths and bring them out into the light. What if that's what the ugliness needed to grow and become strong, destroying people's lives like kudzu strangling everything else in its path? No, Daniel was wrong. It was better if people just kept their secrets hidden in the darkness. That was the only way that they would wither and die.

Georgia cleared her throat. "Are you and Tim, uh . . ." she began awkwardly.

"We've broken up," Sierra answered sadly, confirming Georgia's worst fears. "I told him that I didn't want to be with someone who thought my dreams were something to be ridiculed and he told me I sounded about as mature as one of my students. That's when I left. Deborah Lee told me I could stay over at her house until I figured out what I was going to do next. I stopped here because I ran out of Kleenex on the drive over."

She picked up the three-pack of tissues and stood up, then surprised Georgia by sliding them back on the shelf. "But, you know what? I don't think I'll be needing these, after all," she said. Then she gave Georgia a quick hug and continued, "By the way, please don't tell Deborah Lee about this. I told her that Tim and I broke up because we just didn't want the same things out of life anymore. It seems so important to her to make me into a beauty queen, I don't want her to know that it's not really what I want. I'll tell her after the pageant is over."

Still too stunned to do much more than hug Sierra back, Georgia muttered, "Uh, okay."

With one final sniffle, Sierra released her and stepped back. "Thank you for being such a good friend," she said, then grabbed the half-empty box of tissues she'd left lying at Georgia's feet, and waved goodbye, leaving Georgia staring after her, perplexed.

Didn't Sierra realize that Daniel had given her bad advice? If he had minded his own business, Sierra and Tim would still be together, Georgia and her mother would still be speaking to each other, and Mama and Aunt Rose wouldn't be at each other's throats. Well, not any more than usual, that is.

Georgia frowned. Daniel Rogers had come to town with his self-righteous air and insistence on having this cook-off, no matter the cost to her, and the entire town had danced like puppets whenever he jerked their strings.

Well, that was about to end. She was going to tell him to keep his nose out of where it didn't belong.

If he didn't . . . well, if he didn't, she just might be the one to bite it off.

"Hmph," Georgia snorted, grabbing her basket and rooting around in it until she felt the slim boxes of condoms that had settled at the bottom. She yanked them out of the basket and shoved them back on the metal hangers just as sixteen-year-old Jason Broussard walked past.

"Uh, do you need some help there?" Jason asked.

"No, thank you. I was just putting back something I will *not* be needing," Georgia announced, refusing to be embarrassed when the teen recognized the product she was restocking and turned a shade of red Georgia had never seen before.

Daniel was feeling pretty good as he left the library and headed toward his rental car. He was all ready for tomorrow's show and after his visit to the Ocean Sands History Museum earlier that day, he had another lead to follow up on with the mysterious photograph. And besides that, he felt as if his relationship with Georgia had shifted after they'd had sex at the beach two nights ago. Something had changed in her at that last moment. Daniel hoped that perhaps she had realized she wanted more from him than just sex.

His good mood took an abrupt turn for the worse, however, when something whacked him in the chest. Hard.

"Ouch," he said, rubbing the sore spot and looking around to see what had hit him.

Something whacked him again, this time on his right shoulder.

"What the—?" He jerked around, only to see Georgia standing

about fifteen feet away, her arm cocked back as if she were about to throw something.

Which is exactly what she was about to do. The something—something round and green—whizzed past his ear and thumped against the passenger-side door of the Mercedes. "Hey, knock that off," he said, striding purposefully toward Georgia.

"Why don't you just mind your own business?" Georgia shouted, taking something out of a plastic bag and getting ready to lob another missile at him.

He ducked and another shot hit the door of his rental car. Before she could reach into the sack for another lime (Daniel was close enough now to identify the weapon she was using against him), he lunged and grabbed the bag out of her hand. "What the hell do you think you're doing?" he asked, scowling at her.

"I'm . . . I'm . . . I'm losing my temper," Georgia sputtered.

"Gosh, I would never have figured that out on my own," Daniel said sarcastically, crossing his arms across his chest and keeping a tight hold on the bag of limes.

"You can't go around telling people to bare their souls to everyone. Don't you realize they could get hurt?"

Daniel noticed just then that they had an audience. A small crowd had gathered inside the grocery store, their noses pressed up against the glass like puppies at a pet shop. He grabbed Georgia's arm and hauled her behind him to his car, pushing her down into the passenger seat with enough force to let her know she wouldn't be wise to fight him.

He waved to the Broussards as he and Georgia drove past the shop, eliciting half-hearted answering waves from them before they disappeared back into the store. Daniel could just imagine how quickly the story of Georgia's lime tossing would get around town.

Daniel headed out of the downtown area and stopped on one of the quiet streets leading up to Velma Boleen's house. He wanted to talk to the elderly woman, but needed to find out what the hell was wrong with Georgia first.

"So," he said, turning off the engine and twisting in his seat so that he would have a clear view of the blonde sitting next to him. "What do you mean by lobbing limes at me?"

"You can't come around here and meddle in everyone's lives. You may think it's best for people to reveal their darkest secrets, but that doesn't mean you're right. What makes you the expert anyway?"

Daniel slammed his palm against the steering wheel of his rental car, startling Georgia. "What makes me the expert is a lifetime of watching people's lives destroyed by the secrets they try to hide. Don't you get it? Someone *always* finds out. No matter how long a secret's been buried, the truth always comes out eventually. I've seen marriages torn apart when affairs are revealed in the tabloids, children devastated to learn that their parents aren't who they thought they were, people ruined financially when they've paid off blackmailers who knew something they shouldn't. In all of these instances, disaster could have been avoided if people admitted their mistakes and dealt with their problems head-on, instead of trying to sweep things under the rug. It never works."

"That's not for you to decide," Georgia protested.

"You're right, it's not. Fate takes care of that." He paused, searching her brown eyes for some measure of understanding. "I care about you and I don't want to see you destroyed by whatever it is you're trying to hide. Why won't you tell me what you're so afraid of?"

And Georgia, who had carried this burden around in her heart for so long, couldn't seem to stop the words from pouring out. "I'm afraid that if I don't behave in the manner my mother expects she'll try to kill herself. Again."

Daniel's head snapped back as if she had slapped him. "What?"

"You wanted to know what I've been hiding. That's it. My mother tried to commit suicide once when I was eight and then again when I was twenty. Both times it was because I chose to excel in academics over taking part in something Mama thought was more important. And both times, I watched my mother nearly die because of it. That's why, no matter how much I may want to be an inventor, I spend my days selling deviled egg plates and crystal unicorns instead. No matter how wrong it is that my mother has this hold on me, I can't change it. And I couldn't live with myself if she finally succeeded in killing herself because of me."

Georgia watched Daniel's reaction, surprised at how calm she felt. She had never confessed this secret to anyone, and she would have expected to feel . . . something. Instead, it was as if her emotions were frozen inside a thick block of ice.

"My God," Daniel whispered.

Georgia found that now that she'd started talking about it, she couldn't seem to stop. "No one besides her doctor and I know that my mother has tried to commit suicide. The first time it happened was because of a school science fair. I was a finalist and the judging was going to be the next afternoon. Mama had entered me in a pageant that day, but the night before I told her I was more interested in science than in swimsuit competitions. Mama got angry and told me that I should be happy just being pretty and to stop trying to be such a show-off about how smart I was. I didn't understand why she was angry, but I got mad, too, and told her that I was sick of spending every weekend parading around shopping malls smiling at a bunch of strangers. I told her I was never going to step foot on a runway again. That's when she got all quiet on me, like she did whenever she was disappointed in something I had done. Like most times when she got upset, she shut herself up in her room and wouldn't talk to me. I figured she'd at least come down and make me supper, though, so I just stomped off to my own room and pouted, too."

"Where was your father?" Daniel asked.

"Daddy had passed away two years before, so it was just me and Mama," Georgia answered, reaching out to fiddle with the latch on the glove compartment.

Daniel noticed her hands were shaking and he was tempted to tell her to stop, that he didn't need to know her secrets after all. But he didn't.

Georgia lowered her hands to her lap. "When supper time came and went, I started to worry. Mama had been mad at me before, but she wasn't neglectful. Besides, I was getting hungry and I wanted her to feed me, so I pushed open the door to her bedroom, expecting to find her sleeping or staring out the window in her sitting room, like she did when she wanted to be left alone."

Georgia laced her fingers together and Daniel watched her knuckles turn white. He put a hand over hers and squeezed, but he doubted she even felt his touch.

"She was in the bathroom. On the floor. There was an empty bottle of pills lying next to her. I didn't know what to do, but it turns out that she had called her doctor before she passed out, because he showed up just as I was on my way out the door to get Aunt Rose. He put Mama in the backseat of his car and told me to sit next to her and talk to her while he drove us out of Ocean Sands. I realized later that he knew if he had taken her to the hospital here, word would get out that my mother had tried to kill herself. So you see, I'm not the only one who believes in keeping secrets."

Daniel leaned forward and pushed a lock of thick hair behind Georgia's ear. "What happened the second time?" he asked softly.

"The second time, I had just started my junior year at Ole Miss. I'd been, uh, runnin' around with a boy I knew my mother would not approve of," Georgia admitted sheepishly. "But I figured college was my time to go a little wild. So, I was. Only a friend of a friend of my mother's found out and you know how it goes. Word got back to Mama that I was cutting loose. The thing was, she called me about it. Told me that she understood that I was just having a bit of fun, but that I should try in the future to be a bit more discreet. Then she said the oddest thing."

"What?"

Georgia bit the inside of her lip. "She said it was okay. That my grades didn't much matter anyway. I shouldn't have said anything, but I was so surprised that I just blurted it out."

"Blurted what out?" Daniel asked, expecting Georgia to tell him she was flunking out.

"That I was a straight-A student."

"I'd think that's something any parent would love to hear."

"But it wasn't. I knew when I hung up the phone that something was wrong. I got in my car and drove to Ocean Sands as fast as I could but couldn't find Mama anywhere. That's when I started calling hospitals in the area. A few hours later, I found her. She had driven out of town to a motel and swallowed a bottle of pills again. This time, she'd called and ordered room service before taking the pills just to make certain someone would find her. I don't think she really wants to kill herself, but she gets to this place in her head where she feels it's the only thing she can do to keep me in line."

"I don't understand," Daniel said, shoving a hand through his hair. "It's not like you were doing anything horrible."

She looked at him then, her eyes beseeching. "Don't you get it? My mother wants me to be just like her—pretty and charming, but not too bright."

"That's just it," Daniel interrupted before Georgia could say anything more. "Your mother *is* bright. She, herself, was a straight-A student right up through her eighth-grade year. Then suddenly, she went from being an honors student to barely getting by. Something happened that year. Something that changed everything and that's still impacting her—and you—today. Did you ever ask your mother why she gets upset when people tell her how smart you are?"

Georgia glanced down at the floor mats under her feet. "No," she mumbled. "I knew it upset her and I didn't want to do or say anything that might throw her back into one of her moods."

Daniel rubbed his forehead with frustration. "It just keeps coming back to all these secrets. If you knew why your mother gets so freaked out every time she's faced with proof of your intelligence, you could deal with whatever it is that's frightening her. Instead, you've spent the better part of your life hiding from it—and you don't even know what it is."

Georgia squinted at him as the last rays of sunshine disappeared from the sky. He could tell she was considering what he had said and he wished he had something more compelling to say than, "Trust me and it will all work out."

Unfortunately, that was all the assurance he could offer.

"Come in, my boy. Come in. Did you bring your television crew with you?" Velma Boleen held her door wide open and peeked out at the porch, trying to hide her disappointment when the only other person she saw outside was Georgia.

"Not today," Daniel answered, pulling Georgia inside the house behind him. The air inside the elderly woman's home seemed warm and just a bit stale, as if it had been a bit too long since she'd opened a window.

"How are you, Miss Boleen?" Georgia asked politely.

"Very well, thank you. I can't stay and visit long this evening. I've still got to get out to the home and visit Mother. After that, I told Mr. Talmadge that I'd meet him down at your cousin's bar for a drink. I think he might have a crush on me."

Georgia smiled at the elderly woman's back as she led them into her parlor. "That wouldn't surprise me at all," she said, sitting down on the uncomfortable, straight-backed sofa that Miss Boleen indicated.

Daniel sat down next to her, his knee touching hers. He laid an arm on the back of the couch, and Georgia shivered when he lightly rubbed her arm with his fingers.

"I wonder if you might be able to tell me anything about this photograph," he said, holding out the picture of Vivian and Rose at the Shrimp Festival for the elderly woman to take.

She looked at it for a moment, frowning. "Well, it looks like Georgia's mother and Aunt Rose back when they were growing up. Is that right?"

"Yes, that much we knew. What I was really hoping you might be able to tell me about is the man who was in the photo beside the two girls. See, it looks like he was cut out of the picture."

Daniel pulled his arm from behind Georgia and leaned forward, and she missed the warmth of his body next to hers. She leaned forward, more to get back that comforting heat than to look at the photo she had nearly memorized by now.

Miss Boleen tilted her head and stared at the picture. Then she turned it around and, in an instant, her face brightened. "Oh, this is one of Junie's pictures," she said. "She was quite the photographer in her day. She even freelanced for the *Register* for quite a few years, and she always numbered her photos like this. Junie was very meticulous that way. I'm not certain that all photographers are like that, but, well, I guess it was just her way."

"What good would numbering the pictures do?" Georgia asked, confused as to why anyone would go to the trouble of doing that. What good would it do you to know that you'd taken a thousand pictures in your life or ten thousand?

"The number corresponds to an entry in her logbook. That's how she kept track of the names of the people in her photos. That way, if the *Register* wanted to use, say, picture number seven thousand twenty-four, June could go back in her notebook and find out who was in the picture to make sure she got the proper permissions for the photo to be run. It also came in handy when someone saw a photo in the paper that they liked. She could find which roll of film the picture was on and take the negative in to the photo lab for reprints. You can't imagine how many parents would call over here after seeing their children's pictures in the paper. You'd think they didn't have cameras of their own." Miss Boleen shook her head and laughed.

"Negatives? You have negatives?" Daniel asked. Beside him, Georgia felt his every muscle tense, as if he were forcing himself not to leap up off the couch.

"I'm afraid not. After June died, I went through her things and threw out box after box of old negatives," Miss Boleen said, making Daniel swear softly under his breath.

"Well, it looks like I've just run up against another brick wall," Daniel said, starting to get up off the couch.

Then Miss Boleen stood, handed back the photo, and said, "But I did keep all of Junie's logbooks, if you'd like to take a look at those."

Daniel favored the elderly woman with one of his movie star grins. "Oh, yes. I'd like that very much," he said.

Georgia noticed that Daniel's smile had much the same effect on

Miss Boleen that it did on every other female in Ocean Sands. Her feet seemed rooted to the carpet as she stared, mesmerized. Georgia knew exactly how Miss Boleen felt, so she cleared her throat to try to restart the elderly woman's heart. And, indeed, Velma clutched at her chest when she finally came out of her trance.

"I'll just go up and get those logbooks," she said, nearly tripping over her own feet as she turned and left the room.

For his part, Daniel seemed oblivious to the effect he had on women, for which Georgia was grateful. There was nothing worse than a man who knew he had every woman within a ten-mile radius drooling over him.

"Why are you looking at me like that?" Daniel asked, wiping his chin as if expecting to find something there.

Georgia gave him a slight smile. "I was just wondering why you're not more egotistical about your looks," she said, figuring there was no point in lying.

Daniel laughed. "Because I grew up in Hollywood. Hell, even the waiters there look like models. By L.A. standards, I'm ugly."

Georgia slipped her hand in his, although what she really wanted to do was to push him back on the couch and kiss him until they were both senseless. She liked that he didn't take his looks too seriously because she, of all people, knew how little that really meant. Yes, being good-looking was better than the alternative. But the truth was, you didn't get much say in it. It was genes and luck and God only knew what else that determined what you saw when you looked in the mirror. And Georgia, who had spent the majority of her formative years with some damn pretty people, had learned early that all the trite sayings were true—beauty really is only skin deep and pretty really is as pretty does.

Of course, that didn't prevent her from appreciating Daniel's appearance. . . .

"Here we are," Miss Boleen said as she came back into the parlor and interrupted Georgia's thoughts.

Velma set a heavy green-fabric-bound book down on the coffee table and flipped it open to the page she had marked. "This is it, photo number four thousand one hundred thirteen."

Georgia read the neat entry. The date: October 10, 1961. Time: 1:37 P.M. Subject(s): Rose, Vivian, and Carter Hughes. Location: Shrimp Festival, Ocean Sands, Miss. Her eyes narrowed again on the names, just as Daniel asked, "Your mother's maiden name was Hughes?"

"Yes," Georgia answered, then swung around to meet Daniel's similarly puzzled gaze. "But who the hell was Carter?"

"Well, I can tell you that," Velma said. "He was your mother's uncle."

Twenty~five

$\mathcal{G}$eorgia yawned at her computer screen as she opened the latest e-mail from Emma Rose. She looked at the figures her cousin had provided and was impressed once again by Emma Rose's business acumen. While Georgia had spent the weekend taking Miracle Chef orders and hanging around the house with Daniel, Emma Rose had created a forecast P&L, set up reports for sales by state and by day and time so they could predict future staffing needs, and modified the order-entry program to automatically print shipping labels.

"I think I've just found myself a CEO," Georgia mumbled to herself.

"See, I knew people kept their secrets stashed away in their attics," Daniel said, startling her so much that she jerked forward, missed putting her foot on the rung of her chair, and slipped off the seat and onto the floor.

Daniel hurried up the steps and came to her rescue, reaching out one hand to help her up off the hardwood floor.

"Sorry," he said. "I didn't mean to startle you."

Georgia didn't bother to lie and tell him he hadn't because, of course, he had. No one but she had ever been up to her attic. "What are you doing up so early?" she asked instead.

Daniel put his hands on top of her shoulders and bent down to give her what started out as a light kiss, but soon turned into a tongues-tangling, hearts-racing sort of affair. Finally, he pulled back, nearly as out of breath as she, Georgia noticed with some satisfaction. He rested his forehead on hers. "It's not early," he said.

"Huh?" Georgia said, her mind still occupied with the way his mouth felt on hers.

"It's not early," Daniel repeated. "It's almost nine."

"What?" Georgia gasped, glancing back at her computer's clock to see that the hours had indeed slipped by without her realizing it. "Damn. This always happens when I'm up here. It's like I get stuck in some sort of time warp or something."

Georgia shut down her laptop as Daniel wandered around the room, inspecting the items lying around in various stages of development. "What's this?" he asked, holding up a Rubbermaid container with a pump attached to the lid.

"Something I was working on to get meat to marinate faster. You put it into the container with the marinade, put the top on, and then suck out all the air."

"Does it work?" Daniel asked.

"Of course it does," Georgia answered, affronted.

Laughing, Daniel raised his hands in surrender. "I should have known." He reached out to touch a square of fabric she'd left drying on her workbench. When he tried to let it go, it stuck to his hand.

Georgia leaned back against her desk and crossed her arms across her chest. "You know that saying about curiosity killing the cat?"

Daniel looked at her, horrified. "This isn't going to kill me, is it?"

She rolled her eyes. "No, of course not. It's just a saying about people minding their own business."

He grinned at her, waving his hand in the air to try to get the fabric to let him go. "Has it ever occurred to you that in order to be a good inventor, you've got to be even more curious than I am?"

Georgia grimaced. "Well, no. I guess it didn't." She took pity on him then and picked up a spray bottle and spritzed his hand with water. As if by magic, the fabric drifted to the floor and Daniel stood over it, frowning as if he expected it to leap up and start doing the hula or something equally ludicrous. Georgia picked up a set of wooden chopsticks and used them to move the fabric back to her workbench. "It's something I'm developing for the beauty pageant industry," she said, heading toward the attic stairs. "A swimsuit material that will stay put."

Daniel clicked off the light and followed her downstairs. "I didn't realize that was a big problem."

Georgia threw a "you wouldn't believe me if I told you" look over her shoulder at him.

"What?" Daniel asked.

"Girls spray glue on their rear ends to keep their suits from riding up during competition. You wouldn't believe some of the stuff we do for pageants."

"Yes, I would. You seem to forget that I live in a place where people routinely have the fat sucked out of them by giant vacuum cleaners. They have botulism injected into their foreheads and collagen into their lips. They have saline-filled pillows inserted under their breasts. Spraying glue on your ass is minor league, if you ask me."

Georgia stopped in the hallway and threw her arms around Daniel's neck. "See, that's what I love about you. You don't find any of this stuff weird." Then she laughed and kissed him, meaning for it to be just a light peck on the lips.

Daniel, it seemed, had other ideas. He pushed her back against the wall, buried his hands in her hair, and nudged her legs apart with his knee. Georgia had thrown on his polo shirt when she'd sneaked out of bed an hour ago and the smell of him was even more potent as he crushed his shirt to her chest. Daniel had on jeans and nothing else, and the feel of the rough denim on the inside of her naked thigh sent a frisson of pleasure right to her core.

Georgia put her hands on Daniel's muscled backside and pressed him even closer. He groaned and broke their kiss in order to trail a line of hot fire down her neck. She shivered when he licked that sensitive spot just under her ear at the same time he rubbed his denim-clad thigh between her legs.

"Do you know what I love about you?" he asked softly, his hot breath tickling her ear.

"Mmm," Georgia purred, too caught up in what he was doing to pay much attention to what Daniel was saying.

"Everything," he said, his voice suddenly serious, the word echoing in the quiet hall.

Too stunned to think, Georgia just stood there and blinked up at him stupidly. Neither of them moved, neither of them spoke.

Then, suddenly, her doorbell rang, breaking the spell. They could see the telltale brown uniform of a UPS deliveryman through the leaded glass of Georgia's front door. Daniel grinned down at her, tapped her lightly on the nose, and said, "I'd have to kill the UPS guy if he saw you like that. Why don't you go take a shower and I'll get the door?"

Without waiting for her to sputter out an answer, he padded down the stairs in his bare feet, acting as if he didn't care that the entire town would soon know that a half-naked Daniel Rogers was spotted answering Georgia Elliot's door at nine o'clock in the morning.

Georgia would be surprised if her mother didn't insist on a wedding by noon.

"These Miracle Chefs are multiplying like rabbits," Michael, the UPS guy, said.

Daniel scratched an itch on his side and watched as the young man brought another load of boxes in and stacked them neatly in Georgia's dining room. "It sure looks like it," he agreed. He thought about offering to help bring the boxes in, but figured he'd make himself useful in the kitchen instead.

"You want a cup of coffee?" he yelled from the kitchen when he heard footsteps in the dining room, thinking it was Michael back with another load.

"I'd love one," Rose Conover drawled, leaning against the doorjamb, and eyeing him with interest.

"Good morning, Rose," Daniel said, unperturbed about being caught in Georgia's kitchen wearing nothing but his jeans. He grabbed another mug from the cupboard and held it out to her. "Should be done brewing in a minute."

"If it wasn't still early, I'd probably be able to come up with somethin' clever to say back. Somethin' about it being more than just coffee brewing over here this morning."

"Good thing it's still early then." Daniel winked at Georgia's aunt and propped his hip against the counter.

She laughed and Daniel realized that when she smiled, she was nearly as pretty as her older sister.

The coffee finished brewing just then, and Daniel poured the dark liquid into cups for himself and Rose, and then put the pot back on the burner to keep warm.

"So, what's all of this?" Rose asked, just as Georgia burst out of the bedroom door upstairs and flew down the stairs.

"Aunt Rose, I thought I heard your voice," Georgia said, trying to act as if it were perfectly normal for her to come racing out of the shower, her hair still soapy from the shampoo, and clutching her bathrobe tightly around her dripping body just to greet the aunt she saw nearly every day. A puddle of water formed at her feet and Daniel raised an eyebrow at her as he went back into the kitchen for a dish towel.

"Yes, I saw the UPS truck pull up and figured you must be awake. I wanted to ask you about a gift for Trey and Callie."

Daniel tossed Georgia the dish towel he'd pulled off the handle of her fridge and set a cup of coffee down in front of her, but didn't ask why she'd shot out of the shower as if a pack of paparazzi had suddenly jumped out from behind the bathroom door.

Georgia grabbed her aunt's elbow, momentarily letting go of the bathrobe she had clutched at her breasts. Daniel got an eyeful of creamy white flesh and just the merest hint of a nipple and found himself instantly getting hard.

"You can't go wrong with a deviled egg tray," he heard Georgia say as she all but pushed her aunt down the hall to the front door.

"That seems so trite," Rose said.

"Well, why don't you come on down to the gift shop later today and we'll find something perfect?"

"Okay, dear. I'll do that. Here's your cup back." Rose turned her head and resisted Georgia's not-so-gentle urging for a moment. "Thank you for the coffee, Daniel," she said just as Georgia shoved her out the door.

"You're welcome," Daniel called.

Daniel heard Rose say something, but couldn't make out the words. He did, however, make out the loud crash that followed, and hurried down the hallway to see what had happened.

He stepped outside to see Rose standing on the top step of Georgia's porch with a self-satisfied look on her face. Michael was at the bottom of the steps, eyeing Georgia warily. He gave her a wide berth as he brought in yet another load of Miracle Chefs, making Daniel think of that Disney cartoon where Mickey defies the wizard and turns one broom into two to help him bring in some water—only to have the two brooms turn into four, and the four into eight, and on and on until the whole castle was underwater.

Georgia's white bathrobe had been splattered with coffee when the cup Rose had handed her fell from her nerveless hand. She stood on the porch in her bare feet, surrounded by broken glass.

"Don't move. I'll get the broom," Daniel said, even though he had no idea where Georgia actually stored her broom.

He checked the hall closet first, but found the broom back in the utility room along with the washer and dryer. It only took him a moment to sweep up the mess, and then he ushered Georgia and her aunt back inside.

"Okay," he said, sitting them both down at the dining room table. "What's going on here?"

"She knows," Georgia said, breathing rapidly as if she were about to hyperventilate.

"Well, that explains everything," Daniel said dryly.

"She means, I know about the Miracle Chef," Rose said.

That managed to surprise even Daniel, who was glad he wasn't holding a coffee cup when Rose dropped her bomb.

"How?" Georgia croaked, her eyes glazed and staring. Daniel pushed his coffee at her, figuring she could use the jolt.

Rose shrugged and looked around at the room, which was rapidly filling up with boxes. "Beau told me."

"Your cousin knows you're an inventor?" Daniel asked, surprised that Georgia hadn't told him that at least one member of her family was in on the secret.

But Georgia was shaking her head. "No. Nobody knows but the Tiara Club," she whispered.

"Beau did," Daniel pointed out.

"I can't believe Emma Rose would have told him. I asked her to keep it a secret," Georgia said, angry and disappointed that Emma Rose had betrayed her.

"Emma Rose didn't tell him," Michael Kingsley, who was unloading yet another stack of Miracle Chefs in her dining room, surprised Georgia by saying.

"What? How do you know that?" Georgia asked.

"Because I'm the one responsible for Beau finding out, not Emma Rose," he said, having the grace at least to look embarrassed. "You probably don't remember this, Georgia, but about a year ago you scheduled a pickup but when I got here you told me you were out of envelopes. I always keep a handful with me, so I took what you handed me and brought it out to my truck. Before I put it in the envelope I . . . Well, I guess I glanced at it. You know, it's hard not to be curious about the packages you deliver for people. You wouldn't believe the stuff your very own neighbors order from those on-line places. They think it's all anonymous, but you know, lots of people see those packages before they make it to your door." Michael leaned toward them and lowered his voice, as if about to divulge the secret plans for the latest nuclear weapon. "Just last week," he whispered, "I delivered a giant box from the Love Pantry to Miss Beall's house. Can you imagine? She's nearly a hundred years old!"

Georgia screwed up her face and waved her hands in front of her. "I don't want to know things like that," she said.

"Definitely TMI," Rose agreed.

"TMI?" Daniel asked.

"Too much information," Rose explained.

"Ah," Daniel said.

"Anyway, what does that have to do with me?" Georgia asked.

"The stuff you handed me? It was your patent application for the Miracle Chef. I guess I kind of looked through it. I mean, it's cool that you're an inventor. I'd never seen plans like that before. I'm sorry I snooped, but I couldn't seem to help myself."

Georgia blew out a breath. "That still doesn't explain how Beau knows about it. How did it get from you to Beau? You two aren't friends, at least not that I know of."

"No. Uh,"—here Michael's face went red, the blush reaching all the way up to the tips of his ears—"I may have said something to my sister, Miranda. And, you know how she's always trying to catch Beau's attention. I think she may have used what I told her to finally get your cousin to ask her out."

"Well," Daniel said, looking around the room. "There's certainly no problem with the information system in this town."

Georgia turned to her aunt, her face pale. "Does Mama know?" she asked.

Rose shook her head. "I don't think so. That is, unless Miranda told somebody other than my son."

Twenty~six

Monday. 7:18 P.M. Miracle Chefs in every conceivable area of the house, including bathtub, spare bedroom, and beneath dining-room table. Shipping to commence this evening.

Georgia closed her notebook and looked around the kitchen at the boxes stacked ceiling-high on the counters and floor. She'd managed to make a path through them from the icebox to the sink, but it hadn't been easy. Fortunately, help was on the way. Emma Rose—bless her heart—had nearly run Ocean Sands' two office-supply stores dry of ink and shipping labels in her quest to print labels and postage for the 843 Miracle Chefs that had been ordered so far. They were still receiving about a hundred calls a day, and Georgia expected another spike after the fourth cook-off on Friday.

There was no way she could have handled this without the help of her friends and she suddenly wished that she hadn't kept her secret from them for so long.

"Hey, Georgia," Kelly said, pushing her way into the kitchen through the back door and into a mudroom full of Miracle Chefs. "Gawd, it's crowded in here," she complained.

"Tell me about it. I nearly lost Daniel this morning," Georgia joked.

"Well, now that would have been a cryin' shame. He's much too hunky to get buried beneath a bunch of kitchen appliances. I'd have made sure he was safely tucked away in the bedroom instead. Maybe even tied him to a bedpost just to be sure he didn't go missing," Kelly said with a wink.

Georgia felt the blush creeping up her cheeks and turned toward the blender full of frozen drinks she'd been making earlier. She put a hand on the chilled pitcher and then put her palm on her cheek to cool it down. No way would she tell her friend that she and Daniel had tried out that bedpost-tying thing just last night . . .

"So, what's in the blender?" Kelly asked, picking up the lid and leaning over to take a whiff.

"Frozen Banshees. Kind of like a banana shake only with booze in it."

Kelly grimaced and put the lid back on the pitcher. "I'll be glad when we're through with the B's. I'm gettin' awful sick of drinks with bananas in them."

Georgia handed Kelly *The Bartender's Black Book* and flipped the page. "Don't despair. We've got some fun ones coming up. Look— there's a 'Beam Me Up Scotti,' a 'Bible Belt,' and a 'Big Daddy.'"

Kelly studied the book and then handed it back to her with a grin. "Not to mention a 'Bend Me Over' and a 'Belly Button Shot.' But I think we'll leave that last one to you and Daniel, since the recipe says you've got to be naked and on your back to attempt it."

Eyes wide, Georgia stared down at the book. Indeed, the recipe said exactly that. Georgia fanned her heated face and turned back to the blender. "Well, that's just . . . hmm. I don't know. It might be fun," she finally admitted, imagining Daniel lying on her bed while she licked Southern Comfort off his firm abdomen.

"So are you going to pour me one of those or just stand around having sexual fantasies all night?" Kelly teased with a nod toward the blender.

Georgia shook her head to get the image of a whiskey-coated Daniel out of her brain. "Sorry. Here you go." She poured the drink into an oversized martini glass and added a few banana slices and some chocolate curls for garnish before handing it over to Kelly, who took a sip and pronounced the drink, "Not bad."

Georgia heard her front door open just before Emma Rose appeared in the doorway of the kitchen, a box in her hands. "Hey, gals. I thought we could set up shipping operations in the dining room. We're going to need a table and lots of space to spread out."

"Okay," Georgia said, obediently following her cousin down the hall, where she set down her box and started unloading shipping labels.

Behind her, Kelly crunched a piece of ice from her drink and Emma Rose looked up, her eyes narrowed. "What is that?" she asked.

"Banshee," Kelly answered. "Want me to get you one?"

"Is there alcohol in it?"

Kelly squinted at the glass in her hand. "I sure hope so."

Emma Rose reached out and grabbed the drink out of Kelly's hand. "There will be no drinking on the job here," she scolded, taking the glass back to the kitchen and dumping its contents into the sink. She filled the glass with water, took the pitcher from off the top of the blender, and put it into the freezer for safekeeping. As she returned to the dining room, she ignored the shocked looks of Georgia and Kelly as she said, "You can drink later. *After* we're finished working."

Georgia and Kelly exchanged bemused looks.

"What's happening to ya'll?" Kelly groused as she nonetheless took up the spot Emma Rose indicated and started slapping labels on boxes of Miracle Chefs. "First Deborah Lee gets all psycho on us, then Georgia reveals that she's been hiding a secret identity, and now Emma Rose is channeling her inner workaholic. Pretty soon I'll be the only normal one left in the Tiara Club."

"Don't worry, Kelly. As soon as Daniel's show leaves town, this whole Miracle Chef thing will be over and we can all go back to our regular lives," Georgia reassured her.

Emma Rose froze in the process of moving a neatly labeled box from the table and onto the floor and fixed her cousin with such an intense look that Georgia almost took a step back. "What?" she asked.

Emma Rose blinked rapidly, as if she'd just fallen into some kind of trance and was trying to break the spell. She set the box on the floor and turned to the next one. "Never mind," she said.

Deborah Lee and Sierra came in then, Sierra laughing at something Deborah Lee had said. Georgia caught Sierra's eye and they exchanged a your-secret-is-safe-with-me look. Sierra seemed younger than she had the week before and Georgia couldn't figure out what was different until she realized that, for a change, Sierra had left her hair down. It fell in red ringlets halfway down her back, a mass of curls even more wild than Georgia's own.

"Your hair looks good down," she said, moving over to make room for Deborah Lee at the dining-room table.

"Thank you," Sierra said, patting her head self-consciously. "I thought it would get in my way with the kids and all, but it's really not that bad."

"I hope y'all don't mind, but I thought we could go over Sierra's interview questions while we work," Deborah Lee announced, obviously not willing to be swayed from her mission to make Sierra into a beauty queen.

Nobody minded, and they spent the next hour grilling Sierra on current events and her platform—the importance of Headstart-type programs for at-risk children—while pasting a seemingly endless supply of labels on an equally seemingly endless supply of Miracle Chefs.

Georgia had stopped to stretch her shoulders when her phone rang.

Deborah Lee, who was closest to the phone, said, "I'll get it. It's probably someone calling to order a Miracle Chef." Since they'd received three other calls in the last hour, that seemed like a valid assumption.

"Hello," Deborah Lee said.

Georgia rolled her neck and wondered how many more hours it was going to take them to finish this up. She was exhausted from standing on her feet down at the gift shop all day.

"Oh, hey Miss Vivian," Deborah Lee said, making Georgia snap to attention. Dang, what did Mama want?

"Who, us? What are we doing?" Deborah Lee repeated, getting that deer-in-the-headlights-that's-just-about-to-become-roadkill look in her eyes.

Georgia leaped for the phone, but tripped over a box at her feet and went sprawling on the hardwood floor.

"Uh, we're, um, workin' on Sierra. You know, to help her win the Shrimp Queen Pageant this weekend," Georgia heard Deborah Lee stutter as she tried to disentangle her dress from around her legs.

"You're what?" Deborah Lee screeched, then paused for a moment, lowering her gaze to the rug as she said, "I'm sorry, ma'am. No, I wasn't raised by Yankees."

Georgia finally managed to get up off the floor just as Deborah Lee said, "Yes, ma'am. Of course, we'd be delighted." Then she hung up the phone, slowly turned to face the room, and, with a sickly green tinge to her skin, announced, "Miss Vivian offered to help with Sierra's pageant training. She's on her way over."

"Here, I can fit one more into the dryer," Georgia shouted as Sierra ran by with an armload of Miracle Chefs that they were all trying desperately to hide. There were boxes everywhere—stuffed into the icebox, crammed into the hall closet, stacked behind the couch . . . and loaded in the dryer. Sierra tossed a box at Georgia and continued searching for a place to stash the rest of her load.

"Hey, girls. Where are you?" Georgia heard her mother's voice trill from the foyer as she slammed the door of the dryer.

She raced out of the laundry room, skidding in her stocking feet on the linoleum floor as she hurried out to block the doorway of the box-filled kitchen. She draped herself across the doorway, knowing that she looked ridiculous, but hoping that Mama would be too bent on getting her hands on Sierra to notice.

"Hey, Mama," she cooed. "Why don't you go sit in the parlor? We'll be right there."

Vivian eagerly followed Georgia's suggestion, unshouldering the large bag she'd brought with her onto the coffee table so she could start laying out her treasures.

When Sierra ran by again with another load of Miracle Chefs, Georgia grabbed them from her and pushed her toward the front room. "I'll take care of these. You go in and distract her," she whispered.

Sierra took a deep, fortifying breath and pasted a wobbly smile on her face. "I'll do it," she said stoically, straightening her shoulders and looking much like a soldier heading into battle as she determinedly marched toward the parlor.

"Hello, Miz Elliot," Georgia heard her say as she tried to find a place to stash the Miracle Chefs she had taken from Sierra.

"Miss Riley," Vivian greeted back, eyeing her new mission assessingly. "We have a lot to do here," she announced.

"Yes, ma'am," Sierra agreed meekly.

"Do you think you have what it takes to become a beauty queen?" Vivian asked, circling Sierra like a drill sergeant with a new recruit.

"Mama," Georgia protested, having given up and tossed the boxes onto the kitchen floor in order to not leave Sierra alone with her mother any longer than necessary.

"You sit down and hush," Mama ordered, waving a hand imperiously toward the couch where she expected her daughter to sit. "I know what I'm doing," she added as Georgia sat down.

Vivian turned her attention back to Sierra. "Now, answer me. Do you think you have what it takes to become a beauty queen?"

"No, ma'am, I don't," Sierra answered.

Georgia winced when she saw Sierra's shoulders slump, as if she were trying to make herself smaller, less of a target for Mama to hit. And she knew she couldn't do this, couldn't subject her friend to her mother's hurtful comments, even if it meant confessing the real reason the Tiara Club was meeting here tonight. She stood up to rescue her friend, but stopped when her mother put her hands on the top of Sierra's shoulders, looked her straight in the eye, and said, "That's bullshit. You are just as smart, just as pretty, and just as talented as any other girl who'll be up there on that stage. Believing in yourself is the key to winning the crown. If you have the attitude of a winner, you will *be* a winner."

Georgia blinked several times as she sank back down to the couch.

From the doorway, Kelly sniffled. Georgia looked up, amazed to find that Kelly was actually tearing up.

"Thank you, Mrs. Elliot," Sierra said softly, raising her right hand to place it on top of Vivian's hand on her shoulder.

Mama smiled for a moment, then nodded and stepped back, her brusque demeanor returning. "All right. Believing in yourself is all well and good, but that alone won't win you the tiara. Let's get to it. It'll be

nice to work with someone who appreciates my advice, for a change."
She shot her daughter a pointed look that told her just what she
thought about ungrateful children, and said, "Georgia, you run and get
me her swimsuit. Deborah Lee, I have some acrylic shoes in my bag
that should fit her. Would you dig them out for me? And, you, Emma
Rose, would you answer that damned phone? It's already rung five times
since I got here. Georgia, what's going on? Are you runnin' some kind
of phone sex service or something?"

Georgia hadn't even realized the phone was ringing, so intent was
she on the drama playing out in her front room. But as Emma Rose
grabbed the receiver and said, "Yes, sir. Uh-huh. Just one moment
please," before she backed out of the room and grabbed her laptop so
she could take another Miracle Chef order, Georgia began to wonder
just how long it was going to take before this whole thing blew up in
her face.

And as she started down the hall and heard her mother add, "Oh,
and Kelly, would you fetch me five or six of those boxes I saw in Georgia's kitchen, please? I can use them to demonstrate to Miss Riley the
proper way to walk on and off the stage in high-heeled shoes," she
slumped against the wall and prayed that she'd somehow survive this
ordeal.

Twenty~seven

Georgia's fingers stuck to the cardboard box as she slapped the last mailing label on it.

"That's it. We're done," she announced, laying her head down on the dining-room table.

"Please, don't let the phone ring again," Deborah Lee pleaded, her face likewise buried in the heavy pine tabletop.

They'd started work again after midnight, when Vivian had finally been satisfied that Sierra was too exhausted to absorb any more pageant tips that evening and had taken her leave. They'd stopped around three, almost too tired to see the boxes, much less the labels they were supposed to be affixing to them. Most of them had slept where they sat, even Georgia, who was too bleary-eyed to chance the stairs even with the promise of a comfy bed at the end of her journey. At six, Emma Rose had roused them again, and two hours later, they were finally finished. Eight hundred and forty-three Miracle Chefs were packed up and ready to be mailed.

Georgia forced herself to sit up before she fell asleep again. She looked around at the dining room, filled to overflowing with boxes, and it suddenly occurred to her that in order to be mailed, the boxes needed to somehow make their way to the UPS warehouse.

"Um, I hate to ask this, but how are we going to get all these Miracle Chefs out of here?" she asked.

"What?" Emma Rose asked, her voice muffled since her face was buried in her arms.

"Well, we've got to get these boxes out of here. Mama said she'd be back this morning at nine with a training plan for me to give to Sierra. I don't think we're going to be able to hide these Miracle Chefs from her again. But if we call UPS to schedule a pickup, they'll just give us a two-hour window when they can send someone over. We've got to get these things out of here now."

"We could all load up our cars," Deborah Lee suggested.

"It'll take us ten trips each to get rid of all these," Kelly muttered into the tabletop.

Just then a truck rumbled by on the street outside Georgia's front window. A flash of brown sped by and all was quiet again as they contemplated the problem.

"Michael Kingsley just rode by. We could always steal his truck when he's not looking," Sierra joked tiredly.

Georgia sat up even straighter in her chair as Emma Rose raised her head from the table, a calculating gleam in her brown eyes.

"We can't do that," Georgia protested, mostly because she felt guilty enough about hijacking his truck once already.

"He has a thing for me. I'll go and distract him while y'all take the truck," Emma Rose said, determinedly getting to her feet.

"You can't be serious," Kelly said. "I'm an attorney. I could get disbarred for this."

"Then you stay here and just help load up the truck," Emma Rose said. "Georgia, Sierra, you girls come with me. Deborah Lee and Kelly, you start moving the boxes to the kitchen. We'll take 'em out the back way so the neighbors won't see and rat us out to Aunt Viv."

And while Georgia knew this was probably a terrible idea, she was too tired to do anything but follow her cousin out the front door and into the weak morning sunlight.

———

Michael Kingsley had just dropped off another package from Love Pantry at Miss Beall's house when he saw Emma Rose Conover coming up the sidewalk. Although she was older than him by a good ten years and had even baby-sat him a time or two when he was younger, he still thought she was pretty hot. He'd even taken to stopping in at the No Holds Bar for lunch on the days he knew she was working, but she never seemed to treat him with anything but a sort of sisterly affection.

He sighed as she sauntered toward him, her eyes sort of sleepy-sexy and her hair mussed, as if she'd just gotten out of bed. Just seeing her like that made him want to toss her in the back of his truck and kiss her until she saw him as a man instead of just the UPS guy she used to baby-sit.

"Hey, Emma Rose," he called as she started up the walk toward him. He figured she must be meeting Miss Beall this morning. He certainly didn't think she was here to see him.

"Hey, Michael," she said, with a sultry smile curving her lips.

Michael swallowed. Hard. "Uh, you're out visiting mighty early."

Emma Rose kept coming, up the steps and onto Miss Beall's porch, stopping so close in front of him that he could count the freckles on her cute little upturned nose.

Michael took a step back. "Yeah. It's mighty early," he repeated.

"I love mornings, don't you?" Emma Rose purred, taking a step forward.

Michael tried to take another step back, but couldn't since he was pinned up against Miss Beall's door. "Um, yes. I do."

"You know, Michael, I've always wondered what you wore underneath that uniform," she said, raising a hand to the top button of his shirt.

Michael swallowed even harder. "You have?"

"Uh-huh." She twisted the button and slipped her fingers into the vee she'd just exposed at his neck.

"Well, um, I just wear the usual sort of thing."

"Hmm," Emma Rose purred, raising herself up on her tiptoes and making Michael's brain scramble when she kissed him just under his ear and whispered, "One of these days you're going to have to let me see for myself."

He was just about to hand her the keys to his apartment and tell her to meet him there in an hour when he heard a strange rumbling noise. Emma Rose distracted him for a moment when she kissed him again, but when the rumbling continued, he forced himself to open his eyes and peer around her . . . only to see the taillights of his truck disappearing down the block with a blonde in the driver's seat.

He pushed past Emma Rose and started running toward the truck, but it turned right at the four-way stop at Main and Oak and was soon out of sight. "You rotten truck thief," he shouted, shaking his fist at the empty road.

And when he turned back to Miss Beall's to give Emma Rose Conover a piece of his mind for her part in this scam, he discovered that she, like his van, had disappeared.

Pissed off and wondering what exactly he was supposed to tell his boss, Michael started walking down Oak Street toward Main, muttering to himself, "I should have listened to my mama. She always told me to never trust a beauty queen."

By Wednesday morning, Daniel had had enough of Vivian's self-imposed silence and decided to beard the lion in her den, as it were. He found her right where he'd expected her to be—sitting in the middle of her trophy room gazing at the silver cups, jeweled tiaras, and framed certificates.

They had tiptoed around each other politely for the last four days, but Daniel wanted that to stop. He wanted all the secrets out in the open so that the woman he loved could live the life that would make her happy. He knew that telling Georgia that he loved her had been a shock. He knew that she had intended theirs to be a relationship in sex only. But that's not what he'd intended, not even from the start.

From the moment Georgia Elliot had opened her front door and batted her eyelashes at him, he'd been hooked.

But he knew that as long as Georgia continued to agonize about keeping secrets from her mother, she'd never be able to relax her guard long enough to let herself fall in love. Even worse, being in a relationship with him would force those secrets out in the open, whether she was ready for them to be revealed or not.

No, he wasn't a big enough celebrity to have reporters hounding him here in Ocean Sands, but if they were ever spotted together in L.A., everything about Georgia's life would be dragged out as tabloid fodder.

He refused to live that way, praying every morning that he wouldn't walk into some grocery store and see his name attached to some scandal.

Daniel walked to the center of Vivian's trophy room and looked around. Two of the walls were dominated by Vivian's pageant accomplishments, and the other two were filled with Georgia's. Standing in the center of the room, he suddenly noticed that two of the trophies on opposite walls were identical.

"What are those?" he asked, pointing to the two trophies.

Vivian refused to look at him as she answered, "Shrimp Festival Princess. I won mine back when I was fourteen and I saw to it that Georgia won when she turned fourteen as well. The festival always had a special meaning to me."

"Oh?" Daniel asked, sitting down on the red-velvet-covered bench that dominated the room.

"Yes." Vivian refused to elaborate and Daniel didn't push. He was after a different sort of information this afternoon.

"I discovered that it was your Uncle Carter who was holding your hand in that photo I showed you the other day."

"I don't know what you're talking about," Vivian said coolly, although Daniel noticed she had a death grip on the edge of the bench.

"Yes, you do. The man disappeared the day after having that picture taken. You can't tell me that's something a fourteen-year-old would forget."

Vivian's entire body began to shake. "It's been a long time. I don't remember," she said.

"Come on, Vivian. I'm not stupid."

She pushed her chin in the air, her shoulders stiffening. When she answered, her voice had gone, as Daniel termed it, all "la-di-da." He half-expected her to turn to him and say, "Fiddle dee dee." Instead, she drawled out in her most syrupy voice, "Why, of course you're not,

Daniel. You're probably one of the smartest men I've had the pleasure of meetin'."

Uh-huh. "Listen, Vivian, this Scarlett O'Hara act isn't working. I do not for one second believe that you can't recall the uncle who had been visiting with you and your family for nearly a month before he mysteriously up and disappeared. Now, why did you lie to me about that picture?"

Vivian stood, her eyes flashing with such hot anger that Daniel was surprised that he didn't spontaneously burst into flames. He knew he was goading her, but he couldn't stop until he knew the truth. His future—Georgia's future—depended on it.

Then, suddenly, the fire went out of her eyes. Vivian went over to her Shrimp Festival Princess trophy and stroked it lovingly. When she lifted her gaze to his, her brown eyes had gone flat and emotionless.

"Some secrets are best left dead and buried," she said softly, rubbing her index finger over the lettering on the cold silver cup.

Twenty~eight

"Do you think there's something wrong with the phone line?" Emma Rose whispered to Georgia as she and the rest of the Tiara Club stood at the front of the church watching Callie walk down the aisle. In true wedding rehearsal fashion, Callie was carrying the bow-covered paper plate bouquet they'd made for her at her shower and she was wearing slacks and a blouse instead of her wedding dress, but the sight of her walking toward Trey still made Georgia want to cry. Unfortunately, these were not tears of happiness. God, she wished she knew what to do. Share her concerns with Callie and risk losing her best friend forever, or keep quiet and let Callie make what might end up being the biggest mistake of her life?

"Georgia, are you listening to me?" Emma Rose hissed, elbowing her in the stomach.

Georgia sighed and shook her head. She was trapped between the proverbial rock and a hard place, which just meant doing the same thing she'd done for months—nothing.

"What?" she whispered to Emma Rose.

"I said, I wonder if something's wrong with the phone line. We haven't had a call all day, after receiving an average of one hundred fifty-two calls a day for the last four days. I just don't get it."

"To tell you the truth, I can't say that I'm all that disappointed. I like being an inventor, but the business part of all this doesn't really interest me."

"Well, you'd better get interested, and quick," Emma Rose said under her breath. "I ordered another thousand Miracle Chefs yesterday morning to keep up with anticipated demand, but we have less than two hundred orders to fill. If the orders stop and we have to eat the inventory cost, you'll have spent way more money than you made."

"But I can't afford that," Georgia protested, obviously louder than she'd intended since Reverend Jackson hushed her and Trey shot her a disapproving look from his side of the altar.

Emma Rose waited until the preacher started talking again before whispering to her cousin, "I know. That's why you'd better do everything you can to win the next cook-off. If not . . . we may be bankrupt before the week's out."

Georgia was so busy thinking about both Callie and the latest Miracle Chef disaster that she didn't realize until she had her hand on her car door that she had no idea where the rehearsal dinner was going to be held.

"Hey, Callie," she shouted across the parking lot, knowing that if Mama were here, she'd get her mother's "well-bred ladies do not holler" lecture. "Where are we going?"

"Beau's place," Callie shouted back, earning *her* a "well-bred ladies do not holler" look from her fiancé, which she ignored. "He's letting us use his banquet room."

Georgia's hand slipped off the car as Emma Rose gasped from beside her. They looked at each other, horror in their eyes.

"Did you know about this?" Georgia whispered, hoping that Emma Rose did know and had already cleared the first shipment of Miracle Chefs out of the room.

"No," Emma Rose whispered back. "Beau must have figured I knew about it since I'm in Callie's wedding party. Omigod. What are we going to do?"

Georgia rubbed her forehead with one hand, trying to think. "I don't know. No matter how fast we get there, we won't have time to move the boxes before Trey and Callie arrive. I'm not worried about Callie, but you *know* that Trey will tell my mother about this."

"Well, come on. Let's get over there and see what we can do," Emma Rose said, pushing her cousin into the driver's seat as she raced around to the passenger side of the car.

As they sped toward the No Holds Bar, they tossed ideas out to each other.

"We could put a box on each table in the restaurant and pretend they're centerpieces," Emma Rose suggested.

"No, not enough time to disguise them," Georgia said.

"You're right. Maybe we could hide them behind the bar. Beau'll go along with it if I promise to take on a few extra shifts."

"Do you think there's enough room for them all?" Georgia asked hopefully.

Emma Rose blew out a disappointed breath. "No."

Georgia parked haphazardly in a too-small space in front of the restaurant and she and Emma Rose raced inside. The bar was doing a good business for a Thursday night, with over half the tables full and several couples dancing to the music playing on the jukebox. Georgia barely had time to register that Daniel was sitting at the bar talking to Beau before Emma Rose grabbed her arm and dragged her back to the banquet room.

They skidded to a stop just inside the double doors, shocked at the sight before them.

Georgia opened her mouth and closed it again, while Emma Rose put out a hand to steady herself on the doorframe.

"Do y'all like it?" Beau drawled from behind them.

Georgia didn't turn around, instead keeping her gaze fixed on the sight before her. "It's beautiful," she breathed.

"It was Daniel's idea. You should've heard me cussing when I un-locked the banquet room an hour ago to get it set up for Callie's dinner and saw all those goddamn boxes in here. If either of you'd been here, I'd have liked to wrung your necks."

"Daniel did this?" Georgia whispered.

"Yes, I did," the man in question answered, his warm breath stirring the hair at the back of her neck and making goose bumps rise up on her arms.

"But why? You hate it that I'm trying to keep this all a secret," Georgia said, twisting her head so that she could see Daniel.

She couldn't read the expression in Daniel's eyes as he turned toward his masterpiece—an eight-foot replica of a wedding cake draped with linen tablecloths, silvery green grapes, and white roses which, Georgia rightly assumed, hid 250 boxes of Miracle Chefs—and said simply, "Because I love you."

Twenty~nine

Georgia raised the hood on her plastic poncho and pulled her safety goggles down over her eyes as she checked the timer on the Miracle Chef. T minus three minutes.

She picked up the pencil lying next to her blue-lined notebook and scribbled a note. *8:36 P.M., humidity 64 percent. No sign of imminent explosion.* She chewed on the end of the pencil for a moment, then added: *Callie's bachelorette party a smashing success.*

A roar of laughter sounded from her dining room, and Georgia looked up at Daniel and grinned. It seemed as though half the female population of Ocean Sands had shown up for Callie's party and, judging by the noise coming from the other room, the other half was going to regret having missed it.

Daniel grinned back before turning to Shana Goldberg to ask how long they had before the commercial break ended. For the fourth cook-off, Daniel and his crew had opted for a live show. He'd said that there was a difference in the "energy" of a taped versus a live show, and Georgia now understood what he'd meant. Even the film crew seemed more energized than usual, knowing that they had no room for error.

"Four and a half minutes," Shana answered. "And we'd better get this show wrapped up soon before the crowd out there gets completely sloshed."

Georgia glanced at her timer again. Only a minute and a half left to go before the can of sweetened condensed milk was magically transformed into creamy caramel. She had been experimenting with it all week—using the Miracle Chef's dry steam pressure system to cut the cooking time from two hours down to thirteen minutes on low, steady heat. The trick, she'd finally discovered, was to keep the can fully immersed in water the entire time it cooked. If even the rim was exposed to air—KABLAM!—it would blow.

Her phone rang just then and Georgia was careful to keep her eye on the timer as she answered it, thinking it might be her mother, who had been invited to Callie's party but who had yet to make an appearance.

"Georgia, this is Trey," her ex-husband said.

Georgia pressed the phone to her ear as another wave of laughter rolled out from her dining room. "Hey, Trey. What's up?"

"I was just calling to check up on Callie. Y'all aren't doing anything silly like doing shots or downing Jell-O shooters, are you?"

Georgia rolled her eyes. "Of course not, Trey. We're not in college."

"Hey George, where's the tequila? Callie lost a bet and has to eat the worm," Kelly hollered just then from the other room.

Georgia cringed.

"Did she just call you 'George'?" Daniel asked from behind her.

"She does that when she's drunk," Georgia whispered, putting her hand over the phone's mouthpiece.

"What about strippers?" Trey asked.

Georgia held the phone out and frowned. "What about them, Trey?"

"You girls aren't planning to have a bunch of half-naked men jumping out of cakes or anything, are you? I mean, by this time tomorrow, Callie's gonna be the mayor's wife. It wouldn't do to have people see her stuffing dollar bills down some guy's Jockey shorts."

Georgia sighed and closed her eyes in exasperation. "No, Trey, I didn't hire any strippers. But even if I had, it's just harmless fun. It's Callie's bachelorette party, for heaven's sake. Lighten up."

"I'm plenty light," Trey said, obviously irritated. "Besides, when we got married, there was none of this carryin' on. Your mama would never have stood for it, and neither would I. I don't know why y'all couldn't have just met us here at the No Holds Bar for a drink or two and then called it a night."

Georgia felt like screaming into the phone; a long, frustrated, pent-up rant that had been building up in her for a long, long time. She tried not to take out Trey's eardrum, however, when she answered, as calmly as she could manage, "Because that would be boring, Trey. The way I see it, after tonight, you have the rest of her life to bore Callie out of her mind. Tonight, she's gonna have a little fun. Good night." Then she hung up the phone, impressed with herself for not taking the damn thing and banging it against the counter until it shattered into a thousand pieces.

"We're back in one," Shana announced.

Georgia gasped. Oh, no. She'd forgotten all about the caramel again.

"Everybody down!" she shouted. "It's gonna blow."

She squatted on the floor, arms over her head for protection. The typical explosions were bad enough, but with the added pressure of the Miracle Chef, this one was guaranteed to rattle a few windows—or worse.

Georgia hunkered down and waited for the eruption. And waited. And waited.

A pair of expensive Italian loafers appeared in front of her.

Georgia tentatively peeked out around her arms to see the legs attached to those loafers.

Daniel reached down and pulled the safety goggles away from her eyes. "Your timer rang while you were on the phone so I turned off the heat."

"You did?" Georgia asked, standing up from her crouch. The plastic poncho crinkled as she smoothed it out.

"Yes, I did."

Georgia threw her arms around Daniel's neck. "Thank you."

Daniel lowered his head and kissed her.

"Uh, Daniel, we're on in fifteen seconds," Georgia vaguely heard Shana say, but Daniel just kept kissing her.

Her heartbeat ticked off the seconds. When it hit fourteen, Daniel raised his head and smiled down at her. "You're welcome," he said.

Then he stepped back, turned, and smiled into the camera. Be-mused by the way he could morph from lover to TV star so quickly,

Georgia stripped off the plastic poncho and returned to the Miracle Chef to put the finishing touches on her fare for the cook-off. As she opened the can of sweetened condensed milk, the heavenly scent of warm caramel wafted out. She used a spatula to get every drop of it out of the can, then turned her back to the cameras and licked the spoon. Georgia closed her eyes as the sticky treat melted on her tongue. Never before had success tasted so sweet.

This time, the Miracle Chef swept the judges—four out of five voted for Georgia.

"Hopefully, this means I'll be able to unload those last thousand machines," she muttered under her breath as Daniel closed the show, saying, "Tune in Monday at eight for the final episode in our cook-off series. Find out who will win: man . . . or machine."

There was a small pause where the entire film crew and cast seemed to be holding their breath, and then Shana announced, "It's a wrap."

The group in Georgia's kitchen let out a collective sigh of relief and it seemed like the noise level in her house went up another ten decibels. Soon, she and Daniel (who everyone insisted *had* to stay and be their token male) were engulfed in the rowdy crowd.

She was surprised to hear the doorbell ring—both surprised that she was actually able to hear it over the din and also that anyone even bothered knocking before joining the party. Georgia waded through the crowd and flung open the front door to find a shirtless carpenter standing on her front porch.

"Oh, no," she said, holding up her hand like a traffic cop. "I didn't order the Village People."

The man—a handsome blond who Georgia didn't recognize—just grinned at her.

"Hey, who's here?" Kelly shouted from behind her.

And then Callie yelled, "Woo hoo. Show in the strippers."

Georgia whacked her forehead with her palm. "No, no, no."

Unfortunately, she seemed to be in the minority of people who wanted to keep this party relatively tame, because she was unceremoniously shoved out of the way by Miss Beall, who had shown up wearing a flouncy pink hoopskirt that was twice as big as she was. Miss Beall snapped open a lacy fan and set to fanning herself with one hand as she twittered, "There now, aren't you just the cutest thing?" Then she reached out, grabbed the young man's bare arm and yanked him into the house.

Georgia unsquashed herself from the wall and started to close the door, but stopped when another half-naked man—this one dressed as a fireman—came through the door. He was as eagerly welcomed as the construction worker, with catcalls and whistles and, Georgia suspected, more than one pat on those tight young buns.

A policeman came next, followed by a cowboy and a football player. Georgia peeked around the door to make certain that was all of them, then stood in openmouthed shock when Michael Kingsley came up the steps wearing his brown shorts and work boots . . . and nothing else.

"What the—" Georgia sputtered.

Michael glared at her, still angry, no doubt, at the . . . ah, misappropriation of his van on Wednesday morning. "Lots of women have fantasies about their UPS deliverymen. Besides, it's a great way to earn a few extra bucks."

Georgia looked outside to make sure nobody else was coming, a move Michael obviously mistook because he jingled his keys right in front of her eyes and said, "You won't be gettin' your hands on these again," right before he sucked in his impressively flat stomach and— much to Georgia's surprise—dropped the keys into his shorts. Then he pushed past her with a self-satisfied, "Hmph."

Shaking her head, Georgia let Michael pass and then stood back and watched the ensuing chaos. When the doorbell rang again, she began to wonder what the next stripper would be dressed as. Butcher? Baker? Candlestick maker?

Instead, she opened the door to Miranda Kingsley, who peered past her with a wowed expression on her face.

"Hey, Georgia. I just got a call from my friend Roxanne. She said this was one wild party, and it looks like she was right. Do you mind if I join you?"

Georgia held the door open wider. "Come on in. One more drooling female isn't going to make a difference."

"Thanks," Miranda said, stepping into the foyer.

"Oh, wait. Did you know about your brother?" Georgia asked, hoping to spare Miranda the shock of seeing her own flesh and blood doing the bump and grind on Georgia's dining-room rug.

"What? That he moonlights as a stripper?" Miranda asked.

Georgia snorted. "Well, I'm glad to know there are no secrets in *your* family," she muttered, starting to close the front door behind the younger woman.

Only, once again, she was stopped when a man stepped through the door. This time, however, the man was fully clothed. And incredibly annoyed, if the scowl on his face was any indication.

"Trey," she acknowledged coolly, moving to stand in front of Callie's fiancé so he couldn't come any farther into her house. "What are you doing here?"

"You lied to me about the strippers," he said, pushing her out of the way.

"No, I didn't. I told you I didn't hire any strippers and that's the truth." Georgia followed him down the hall, wondering what she could do—aside from braining him with her umbrella stand and dragging him outside—to get him to leave Callie alone on her last night of freedom.

Daniel appeared in the doorway leading to the dining room, as if she had conjured him up.

"Trey," Daniel said by way of greeting, firmly planting himself in front of Georgia's ex-husband.

"Daniel," Trey said, stopping to size up the other man.

Georgia looked from one man to the other—from her past to her future—and it suddenly occurred to her that she was thinking of Daniel not as just the man of the moment, but as something more. Something permanent. He knew more about her than even her own best friend. Even more important, he believed in her. Not in her looks or how her beauty reflected on him, but in *her*. He encouraged her to reveal her secrets, not because it meant anything to him, but because he wanted her to do what she loved without having to skulk about and hide her true passion from those she loved best.

Daniel smiled at her then and Georgia reached out a hand to touch him, to physically connect with this man who meant so much to her.

It was at that moment that things went horribly, terribly wrong. Later, Georgia realized that none of it would have been so bad if one of Daniel's crew hadn't been filming the party just for fun. As it was, the entire fiasco was caught on tape.

And watching it all unfold on the morning news, it almost seemed worse than it had been in person. Almost.

Thirty

"Woo hoo, take it off," Callie encouraged, downing a deceptively mild Barracuda with one gulp and holding her glass out for a refill from the pitcher that was being passed around. She'd never really been much of one for wild partying, but tonight was her last night to try to loosen that awful, smothered feeling that had settled over her.

It seemed the only times she'd ever cut loose, she'd suffered consequences she'd never intended. Of course, that lesson was easily forgotten in the rum-induced haze she was currently enjoying. Right now, seeing this cowboy strip down to his chaps and a well-packed G-string actually seemed like a fantastic idea.

He hooked his thumbs through his belt loops and, in one smooth movement, his jeans disappeared, as if by magic. Well, either magic or conveniently placed Velcro.

The cowboy turned around and wiggled his naked-except-for-a-tiny-string butt at her. Callie giggled. This was a sight she was certain she was not ever going to get to see again and she had every intention of enjoying it to the, ah, fullest. That turned out to be an appropriate word choice as, when the cowboy turned around, Callie realized he had an enormous penis. She had to hope that he had an erection, because if he was this big flaccid . . . Well, she certainly pitied any woman catching sight of something like that heading toward her without any warning.

He ground his hips her way and Callie couldn't seem to take her eyes off that mammoth bulge. He kept getting closer and closer with his giant penis until, finally, he was close enough for her to have reached out and touched it.

Callie guzzled the rest of her drink and took a step back, away from the temptation to do just that.

"Callie, what the hell are you doing?"

She gasped and spun around to find Trey watching her from Georgia's hallway.

Her first thought was, Damn, I am so busted.

Her second though was, Wait a minute, this is *my* bachelorette party. I should be able to go a little wild tonight.

Her third thought was, "I need another one of those drinks."

So, just to spite Trey, she took a five-dollar bill out of her pocket and made a show out of folding it down the middle. Then she put it between her thumb and forefinger, turned back toward the half-naked cowboy, and waggled the money. "Hey honey, come here," she said in her most sultry voice. "I've got a little somethin' for you."

"You got it, darlin'," the man drawled, bumping and grinding his big somethin' toward Callie.

Only, on the way to fetch his reward, he tripped on the dining-room rug and came flying toward her. Callie instinctively reached out her hands to catch his fall, only she forgot she was still holding a martini glass, which somehow ended up getting tangled in the cowboy's costume. He toppled into her and Callie went down, taking his G-string with her.

He squealed like . . . well, like a stuck pig, Callie thought, knowing it was a cliché but unable to think of anything more appropriate. Before he managed to rip the faded brown Stetson off his head and use it to cover his now-dangling parts, Callie got quite an eyeful.

And a whole new perspective on the size-does-matter argument.

"All right, that's enough. You have made a fool out of yourself, Calloway Walker Mitchell. It's time to go home." Trey attempted to push past Daniel, who refused to budge out of the doorway.

"Maybe you should go home," Daniel suggested calmly. "Georgia and I will take care of Callie."

"No, I think it's time that I take care of Callie."

The party goers, who were watching this drama with unabashed curiosity, gasped as one when Beau stepped into the house and pushed his way into the dining room to kneel down next to Callie.

"Are you okay?" he asked, reaching out to remove the G-string and the martini glass from her stiff fingers.

"I can take care of myself," she said, sounding suspiciously like Caroline.

"I know you can." He reached out and pushed a lock of hair out of her eyes. "You take care of everyone."

Trey strode into the room and tried to shove Beau aside, but Beau was having none of that. He stood up, toe to toe with Callie's fiancé.

"What the hell do you think you're doing with my fiancée, Conover?" Trey asked, poking Beau in the chest with his index finger.

"Something you should try. I'm treating her with a little respect. She's not some child you need to keep in line, she's a grown woman who is being crushed under the weight of her responsibilities. Can't you just give her some space to have a little fun once in a while?"

"What the hell do you know about responsibility? You run a bar, which must be like a diabetic running a candy store to an alcoholic like you. I certainly don't need any advice from the likes of you. You're just as much of a fuckup now as you've always been."

Georgia thought she was probably the only one who could see how angry her cousin was, because the only outward indication of Beau's fury was the muscle in his jaw that seemed to pulse with every beat of his heart.

She stepped forward to try to get Trey to shut up and leave before Beau killed him, but she was about two seconds too late. Only, it wasn't Beau who took the first shot, it was Trey. She hadn't seen that coming, but, apparently, Beau had because he ducked just as Trey threw his punch. Without Beau's face there to stop his forward momentum, Trey flew forward—landing a glancing blow on Georgia's chin. Her head whipped back and the rest of her body followed, sending her careening into the folding doors of her hall closet.

She crashed through the thin wooden slats and into the boxes of Miracle Chefs she had neatly stacked there a few days before. Boxes rained down on her, and Georgia put up her hands to ward them off.

Before the last box fell, clattering noisily to the floor of her hallway, Daniel was pulling her out of the rubble.

"Are you all right?" he asked.

Georgia rubbed her jaw, wiggled it back and forth, just like she'd seen in the movies. "I think so."

"Good," Daniel said. Then, without even a hint of warning, he clocked Trey with a right hook that knocked him to the ground. Georgia watched Trey fall like a tree sawed off at the trunk. He tipped, and tipped, and tipped, until, finally, he fell, his head landing at the feet of Miss Beall. Which was rather awkward because with her voluminous skirts around her legs like a pink tulle bell, having Trey's head at her feet meant that he was, in effect, looking up her dress.

Miss Beall screeched and swatted at her dress while Trey just lay there and groaned.

Daniel rubbed his fist. "Damn, that hurt."

"It doesn't feel so good on the receiving end, either," Georgia said, still cradling her own aching jaw.

Beau ignored Trey and helped Callie to her feet. Callie thought about going to see if Trey was all right, but her Barracuda-soaked brain had fixated on the boxes that were scattered throughout her best friend's hallway instead. "What are you doing with all those Miracle Chefs?" she asked, pointing to the articles in question.

Georgia looked around her feet at the evidence of her crime and tried to think up some sort of plausible excuse for all the boxes. She glanced at Daniel, who had crossed his arms across his chest and was regarding her coolly.

"Yes, Georgia. Why don't you tell everyone what you're doing with all those Miracle Chefs," Emma Rose suggested.

As she looked around at the eager faces of her friends and people she'd known nearly all her life, Georgia couldn't, for the life of her, think up a plausible lie. Even worse, she found herself sorely tempted to just blurt out the truth. It would be such a relief to have it out in the open, to pursue her dream of becoming an inventor without hiding up in her attic, hoping that no one would discover her dirty little secret.

Winning the cook-off tonight had filled her with a sense of pride that Georgia hadn't felt in a long time, and it occurred to her then that allowing her mother and her ex-husband to force her into a role she didn't want had cheated her of truly feeling fulfilled. But even that wasn't enough of a reason for her to confess her secret. She couldn't stop wondering what Mama would do when she found out. If her mother tried to commit suicide again, Georgia would never forgive herself. Fair or not, she couldn't make any other choice than the one she had already made.

Daniel let out a disappointed sigh and took a step toward her, but was interrupted when Beau slapped the doorframe with his palm, obviously still full of aggression since *he* hadn't gotten the opportunity to punch anyone yet, and said, "That's it. I'm tired of watching you sneak around town hiding who you really are. If you don't tell them about the Miracle Chef, I will."

Georgia looked at her cousin's dark, dark eyes and knew that he was telling the truth.

Beau was going to out her.

Georgia sighed and pushed a hand through her unruly hair. So much for making her own choices.

"I invented it," she mumbled.

"What?" Callie asked.

Georgia looked up at her friend then—a woman she'd known for nearly thirty years, yet hadn't been able to share her darkest secrets with. She held out a hand beseechingly. "I invented the Miracle Chef. I'm sorry I couldn't tell you about it sooner. I had my reasons for keeping it a secret, but I was going to tell you after your wedding was over. Really, I was. The rest of the Tiara Club already knows."

Callie sighed long and loud and shook her head. "Georgia Marie Elliot, you are a class-A dumb ass. I've known about the Miracle Chef all along. How many times do you think I've driven past this house at two in the morning trying to get Caroline to sleep and seen your attic lights on? Do you think I believed that you were just up there reading? I've known you wanted to be an inventor from the time we were twelve and you made that machine that would automatically turn the pages of your books using the motor of one of those little personal fans and some Popsicle sticks."

"What?" Georgia sputtered, clapping a hand over her chest. "You knew all along?"

"Of course I did," Callie said.

"Well, why didn't you tell us?" Kelly asked, sounding put out.

Callie shrugged. "In the beginning, I figured it was up to Georgia to tell us about her dream. After a while, though, I suppose it became something of a test of our friendship. I knew there was always going to be something between us if she kept that to herself."

Emma Rose snorted and Georgia spun around to look at her cousin, who had her arms crossed across her chest and was tapping one foot with annoyance.

"Well, Callie, you're sure one to talk about people keeping secrets from their friends," Emma Rose said.

Frowning, Georgia looked from Emma Rose to Callie and back. "What are you talking about?" she asked.

"I think Callie has something of her own to confess," Emma Rose answered.

"She does?" Georgia's eyes widened and she blinked rapidly, trying to take that in. She had thought Callie told her everything. Actually, she found herself feeling more than a little hurt that her best friend had kept something from her, even though she knew it was ridiculous to feel that way since she was guilty of the same thing herself.

"Emma Rose, don't," Beau said warningly, that muscle in his jaw jumping again.

His sister whirled on him. "Why? You think it's all right to force everyone else's secrets out in the open except your own?"

"I just don't think this is the right time—"

"That's right, Beau. It's never the right time, is it?" Emma Rose paused for a moment, then said, "I wonder, is that your decision . . . or Callie's?"

Georgia felt waves of anger radiating from her cousin as she glared at Callie and Beau. The tension between them seemed to grow with every breath.

"Emma Rose, maybe it would be best—" Georgia began, only to have Callie interrupt her.

"No. All right. Frankly, I'm tired of watching Beau sneak around town hiding who *he* really is." She threw his earlier words back at him: "Either you tell them or I will."

Georgia watched as a flush crept up Beau's neck, but his eyes didn't waver from Callie's.

"Are you certain you want me to do this?" he asked.

Callie nodded but didn't say a word, her skin taking on a sickly grayish hue which Georgia thought was caused by all the tension flying around the room.

Beau nodded his head, just once. Then he looked over the rapt crowd like a king surveying his subjects and announced, "I'm Caroline's father."

When Georgia looked at Callie, she noticed her friend's eyes looked glassy half a second before she realized what was going to happen. Callie fell toward the floor in a dead faint, Beau caught her, and Trey, who had, sometime during the last few moments, managed to pull his head out from under Miss Beall's dress and stand up, gave them both a disgusted look and stalked out of the house.

That's when Shana Goldberg walked by, clapped Georgia on the back, and cheerfully called an end to the evening by saying, "That's a wrap."

Thirty~one

"Georgia, you have to get up," Daniel said, shaking her shoulder as he pushed a cup of coffee under her nose.

Georgia groaned and rolled onto her stomach, burying her face in her soft, downy pillow. Her head was throbbing as if she were sitting inside a metal garbage can that was being pummeled with rocks.

"I swear, God, I will never touch liquor again if you take away this hangover," she mumbled into the pillow. She thought about swearing to go to church every Sunday, but she pretty much already did that. And she volunteered down at the Ocean Sands Rest Home twice a month and gave money to feed the homeless. She figured she was already as good as she could get while having a full-time job and a mother who depended on her, so making empty promises to God was probably much worse than just offering up the one thing that sounded quite unappealing this morning anyway.

"Here, you'll feel better after some coffee and aspirin," Daniel said, pushing at her shoulder again.

Georgia rolled over and threw an arm over her eyes to shield them from the sunlight shining into the room through the thin curtains. "Why can't you just let me sleep?" she asked grumpily. Was he one of those annoying morning people who couldn't let others sleep when they, themselves, were up and being sickeningly cheerful about starting a new day? If so, their relationship was doomed right from the start.

Although, Georgia reminded herself, their relationship, such as it was, was doomed anyway. With the final Miracle Chef cook-off set for the shrimp feed this afternoon, Daniel could be gone as early as tomorrow morning. For some reason, that thought made her even grumpier, so her voice came out sharper than she intended when she said, "Would you please just go away? I feel terrible."

Daniel surprised her by reaching out to caress her cheek, smoothing her hair out of her face. "I know you do. And, unfortunately, what I have to tell you isn't going to make you feel any better."

Behind the arm shielding her eyes from the light, Georgia blinked. Now what? This sounded serious. Hesitantly, she lowered her arm just a bit so she could see his face. For the first time since they'd met, Daniel didn't look like some just-stepped-out-of-makeup-and-wardrobe movie star. Instead, he looked . . . tired. Haggard. His chin was covered with thick, dark stubble and his eyes were red, as if he'd been rubbing them. Georgia didn't understand why he looked so bad. He hadn't drunk nearly as much as she and the rest of the Tiara Club had after Georgia had shooed all but Daniel and her friends out last night after Beau's shocking revelation and Callie's film-worthy swoon.

The bed sagged near her waist when Daniel sat down on the edge of the bed beside her. He handed her two aspirin and a glass of water. "Here, you're going to need this," he said.

Georgia didn't argue. Obediently, she swallowed the pills and chased them with water. Then she struggled into a sitting position and took the cup of coffee Daniel had brought up from the kitchen.

"We're on television," Daniel announced after she'd had her first jolt of caffeine.

Georgia surveyed him over the rim of her cup. "Of course we are."

Daniel waved a hand in the air, frustrated. "No, I don't mean on the show. I mean, someone from my crew must have filmed last night. It's all over the news this morning."

Georgia sat staring at the smooth surface of her coffee, at the tiny wisps of steam that rose up around the edges and way the color went from dark brown where it touched the sides of the cup to nearly black in the center.

"I'm so sorry about this. I promise that I *will* fine whoever did this."

Georgia barely heard Daniel's apology around the whooshing noise that had filled up her head, leaving no room for thinking or hearing or comprehending. She set her coffee down on the nightstand and, as if in a trance, mumbled to Daniel that she would be all right as she made her way into the bathroom to take a shower.

Hot water sluiced over her as Georgia went through her morning routine by rote. Later, she couldn't have sworn that she'd actually shampooed her hair or brushed her teeth, but she probably had. As she carefully applied her makeup, her brain finally clicked in and began working. She had no doubt Mama would hear about this, if she hadn't already. Georgia had no choice but to confront it head-on and pray that her mother would be able to get through this.

And she knew the one thing she could do that would help Mama cope. She would have to win the Shrimp Queen title, which meant that she wouldn't be able to participate in the final Miracle Chef challenge.

A sharp pain stabbed her in her heart. She fully understood what she was doing, making a choice between her future—a future that included Daniel and her inventions—and her past—which did not.

Georgia rubbed her chest with one hand as she smoothed an extra layer of foundation over the bruise beginning to form on her jaw where Trey had hit her.

She hadn't expected it to hurt so much . . . and she didn't mean the bruise on her jaw.

When she stepped out of the bathroom, Daniel was waiting for her. He was back to being his usual movie-star-handsome self, for which Georgia was grateful. She didn't like to think her personal tragedies were impacting him, too.

"I'm going with you," he announced.

"Hmm?" Georgia said absently, gathering up the supplies she'd need for this afternoon's beauty pageant.

"You don't have to deal with this alone, Georgia. I'm here to help."

Georgia stuffed a pair of pink high-heeled pumps into her pageant bag and then tossed in a roll of packing tape and her makeup bag. "That's just it, Daniel. You're not helping. You're making things worse. You think that by uncovering our secrets, you're setting us all free, but it doesn't work like that. Do you think Callie is better off now that the whole town knows about her and Beau? What if kids make fun of Caroline because her mother isn't married to her daddy? How does that help anyone?"

"But wouldn't it be worse if the secret got out when Caroline was older? She'd hate her mother for keeping that from her. And what about Beau? Doesn't having this out in the open allow him to have a relationship with his daughter? You can't tell me that's not worth the risk that some snotty kid will make fun of Caroline someday. All she has to do is say, 'So what?' and the bully is disarmed. If it's out there, and nobody treats it as if it's a big deal, then it doesn't have a hold on you. Don't you see that?"

"No, I don't. What I see is that your insistence to expose my secret about inventing the Miracle Chef is putting my mother's life in danger." Georgia shoved an emerald green swimsuit into the bag and tugged the zipper closed.

When she turned around, Daniel was angrier than she had ever seen him. He took a step toward her and Georgia had to force herself not to take a step back to get away from the heat radiating off him in waves.

"This isn't about the Miracle Chef. It's about you choosing to hide your true talent, choosing to remain forever in the role your mother has cast you in."

She looked up at him, wishing she could make Daniel understand the pain she'd gone through knowing that her actions had nearly caused her mother's death. No matter how logical his argument sounded, no matter how much he believed he was right, when it came down to being an inventor or seeing her mother lying in a hospital bed, tubes and red lights all around her, Georgia knew what she had to do.

She reached out and took the plastic-wrapped pink-and-white Southern belle gown from her closet. "See, Daniel, that's where you're wrong," she said, the plastic rustling as she draped the dress over her arm. "I don't have a choice."

Georgia found her mother in the middle of her trophy room, surrounded by her happy memories of pageant successes.

"Hey, Mama," she said softly, walking over to the velvet-covered bench and sitting down next to her mother.

"I saw that . . . that spectacle on the news," Vivian said, without turning her head to look at her daughter.

Georgia looked over at her own trophies, trophies she'd been more than happy to let her mother keep, as if they belonged more to Mama than to her. Which, in many ways, they did. If it hadn't been for Mama's insistence that she compete, Georgia would have become one of those kids in school whose noses were always buried in books. She'd have haunted the science lab, and probably been the one to blow up the south wing of the junior high instead of leaving that honor for Kelly's brother, Jefferson. She would have, in short, become a bona fide geek. And who knew if that would have made her any happier than she was now.

She had lots of friends, was active in the community, and, even though she had to tinker with her inventions in her spare time, she at least had an outlet for that aspect of her personality. Before Daniel Rogers had come to town, she had been perfectly happy with her life.

So why, now, was she feeling so dissatisfied?

She only hoped the feeling would go away once Daniel left. And if the thought of never seeing him again made her heart ache? Well, that was just something she was going to have to learn to live with; another secret pain she'd stash away, only to be taken out and examined in the wee hours of the morning when all else around her was quiet.

Georgia reached out to take her mother's cool, smooth hand. "I'm sorry about that, Mama. It won't happen again."

Her mother's back was ramrod straight and it took Georgia a moment to realize that she was silently crying. Georgia scooted closer and put an arm around her mother's shoulders. "Please, Mama, don't cry. It will be all right, you'll see. I'm going to win the Shrimp Queen Pageant and everything will be just like it was before. I promise."

Her mother pulled a handkerchief from her sleeve and dabbed at her eyes. "I saw how Daniel defended you last night. That was very gentlemanly of him."

Silently, Georgia heaved a sigh of relief. It seemed that her mother might not be taking this so hard, after all. "Yes, it was a knight-in-shining-armor sort of moment, wasn't it?"

"Mind you, I'm not saying I approve of men engaging in fisticuffs on a regular basis," Vivian hastened to add. "It's just that sometimes you realize how much a person cares for you by the lengths they're willing to go to in order to protect you from harm."

"Mmm," Georgia agreed.

Her mother turned to her then, her brown eyes intent. "Do you think he loves you?" she asked.

Georgia choked on the breath she'd been inhaling. "What?"

"Do you think Daniel is in love with you?" she asked.

Georgia licked her suddenly dry lips and stood up to pace the room. She thought about what he'd said the other morning in her hall when she had been flippant and he, in turn, asked her if she knew what he loved about her. His answer had stunned her speechless.

"I . . ." She paused. Cleared her throat. "I think he might have convinced himself he does. But it doesn't matter, he'll be gone tomorrow." *Especially after he realizes I've stood him up for the final Miracle Chef challenge,* she added silently. "Besides, can you imagine someone like Daniel being stuck here in Ocean Sands? We don't have anything here that he could want."

"Except you," her mother said thoughtfully.

Georgia went back to the bench and sat down next to her mother. "Mama, Daniel doesn't want me. He may have convinced himself for the moment that he loves this fictional version of me that isn't who I really am." She waved her hand to indicate the trophies and prizes that covered her allotted space in her mother's trophy room. "He doesn't love the woman who won all of these. Not the one who tapes her breasts to get maximum cleavage or knows which swimsuit will minimize that extra two pounds on her thighs or can tap-dance to every song by Sammy Davis Jr."

Her mother frowned. "But that's who you are, dear," she protested. "You are and always will be my little beauty queen."

Georgia squeezed her eyes shut to stop the tears from coming.

"That's right, Mama," she said, finally letting go of her dream. "That's all I'll ever be."

"I am forbidding y'all to serve alcohol at my next bachelorette party," Callie said, sitting on a stool next to Georgia and cradling her head in her hands.

"Is there going to be a next bachelorette party?" Kelly asked, raising her eyebrows.

Callie waved one hand dismissively. "You know what I mean."

Georgia carefully applied adhesive to her false eyelashes and pressed them in place. She blinked at herself in the mirror, trying to convince herself that she didn't look ridiculous with lashes that were nearly an inch long.

"Hey, can I borrow your tape?" Emma Rose asked beside her.

Georgia rummaged around in her bag to find her roll of see-through packing tape, then tossed it to her cousin.

Callie expertly released the curling iron and one perfect spiral curl bounced on the top of Sierra's shoulder.

"I could never do that myself," Sierra grumbled.

"So," Georgia began, knowing that she was about to ask the question that was foremost on all their minds. "Have you talked to Trey since last night?"

Callie snorted in an unladylike manner as she gathered up another lock of Sierra's hair. "Yes. He showed up at my door this morning at seven-thirty sharp."

Emma Rose, having finished taping her breasts together, was now slipping into the dark blue satin gown she'd selected for the final round of the competition. They already tackled interviews, talent, and the dreaded swimsuit portions of the pageant, and only the final evening gown event was left before this year's Shrimp Queen winner was announced. No one had been more delighted than Deborah Lee to see that Sierra's scores had put her in the top ten going into the final round. Now, both Callie and Deborah Lee were working Sierra over to make sure she looked her best. Sierra was just doing her best to stand still as they groped, tugged, and crammed her into shape.

"And is the wedding still on?" Emma Rose asked.

Callie looked around the group then, as if surprised at the question. "Of course it is."

"You mean Trey wasn't upset to find out that Beau was Caroline's father?" Emma Rose asked.

"How did you know, by the way?" Kelly asked, coming up behind Emma Rose to borrow her powder.

"Beau told me one night after he'd had too much to drink," Emma Rose answered with a shrug.

"And you didn't tell us?" Deborah Lee chided.

"I figured it was something Callie would tell you if she wanted you to know. Besides, Beau swore me to secrecy." Emma Rose turned her back to Kelly, who zipped her up without having to be asked.

"Well, thank you for not spreading it around," Callie said. "In the beginning, I was too ashamed to admit the truth and then, after Trey and I got together, he asked me not to let the whole town know. But I guess I took care of that last night," she said, shaking her head with self-disgust.

"You told Trey?" Georgia asked incredulously.

"Of course. It's not something I could keep a secret from him for very long after we were married anyway. Besides, if I didn't tell him and it got out two or five or even ten years from now, what would that do to us?" She didn't wait for anyone else to answer. "It would tear us apart, that's what. I couldn't do that to myself, or to my kids."

"Why do you think you chose last night—the night before your wedding—to let the cat out of the bag?" Sierra asked, crunching down on one of the carrot sticks Deborah Lee had brought for them to snack on while getting ready for the pageant.

"You mean, aside from the fact that Emma Rose was needling me?" Callie said, shooting Emma Rose a look from beneath her eyebrows.

"Sorry," Emma Rose mumbled. "Guess I just got caught up in all the excitement."

Callie shrugged and grabbed a carrot for herself. "I don't know. Maybe . . . maybe because I finally have something good going and I was trying to sabotage it. Maybe deep down inside, I don't feel that I deserve to be happy."

Kelly rolled her eyes heavenward. "Oh, spare me the psychobabble. Did you ever think it's because maybe you were hoping Trey would back out of the wedding? That maybe you're more attracted to Beau than to your fiancé?"

"That's ridiculous," Callie said, her cheeks going red with what Georgia guessed was either embarrassment or anger. "Besides, attraction has nothing to do with it. Trey will make a better father than Beau ever could. I mean, can you imagine Beau as a daddy?"

"Yes, as a matter of fact, I can," Emma Rose said, her own cheeks stained with color.

Callie reached out and took Emma Rose's free hand. "I'm sorry, honey. I know he's your brother and you love him, but I just don't see him being the father I want for my children. Believe me, I've tried."

"But if you *are* more attracted to Beau than Trey, aren't you sacrificing your own happiness for that of your children?" Georgia protested. "I mean, it's not like you aren't doing a good job raising them on your own. Caroline may be a handful, but she's not a bad kid."

Callie leaned back against the wall and stretched out her feet, studying her slip-on brown loafers as if the answer to all the world's questions lay in their seams "I didn't say anything to y'all before, but my mother-in-law is leaving at the end of this month. She said her son needs her more than I do and, while I suppose I might have to agree, you can imagine how difficult this would make things for me if I were not to get married."

"Why didn't you tell me?" Georgia asked, frowning at her friend as she attempted to tug her tight, control top panty hose up her thighs without sticking a fingernail through them.

Callie looked up and smiled. "Because I didn't want you to obsess over how to fix my problems like you've done since we were six years old. There's no magical product you can invent like you did with the Miracle Chef. I need help—human help—to take care of four kids and Trey's willing to do that."

"How much help is he really going to be?" Kelly asked dubiously. "I mean, I don't think I've ever even seen him pick Caroline up, much less fix the other kids peanut butter and jellies or read them a bedtime story. And, as mayor, his salary is a matter of public record. I know for a fact that he doesn't make enough money to allow you to quit your job. So, how is marrying him really going to help?"

Georgia picked up the roll of packing tape that she'd loaned to Emma Rose earlier and cut off a piece about two and a half feet long. She stuck one end under her left arm and drew the strip under her breasts, tacking the other end under her right arm. She looked down to make certain her cleavage was perfect, then carefully put on her bra and turned to her best friend.

Callie shifted uncomfortably from one foot to the other and focused her attention on shellacking Sierra's hair into place with AquaNet. "Well, this is probably something I shouldn't tell y'all, but I will if you promise to keep it between us."

They all leaned in close, while Callie lowered her voice and announced, "Trey's daddy took us to lunch yesterday and, after a few Scotch and sodas, he told us that we're going to be blown away by his wedding present. Now, Trey didn't know exactly what that meant and Mr. Hunter refused to elaborate, but Trey told me later that his daddy inherited quite a large sum when his folks died. Trey thinks his father is going to pass some of that on to us as a wedding gift."

Georgia's brow creased in a frown. If Rock Hunter planned to give Trey and Callie a wad of cash, why had he been so worried last week about trying to find them the perfect gift?

"So, you're marrying Trey for his money," Kelly said, making Georgia shelve her question for a later time. Leave it to Kelly to just blurt out exactly what she was thinking.

The flush was back in Callie's face, but her voice was cool when she responded. "Not exactly. But I'm not going to lie to you. The security that Trey can offer me is not unattractive. And don't get me wrong, I do care for him."

And Georgia, who was convinced—especially after last night—that Callie was about to make a mistake of monumental proportions, finally couldn't keep quiet. "How noble," she said, sarcasm making her voice hard as she eyed her best friend. "So you're sacrificing your happiness for the greater good."

"So are you," Callie said quietly.

Georgia blinked. "No, I'm not."

"You've been hiding who you really are for more years than I can count. Daniel Rogers is the only one you've let see the real you, and I'll bet you've only let him in because you've known from the beginning that when this Miracle Chef challenge was over, he'd be gone . . . taking your secrets with him. You think you can't trust your friends—even me—with the truth about your life."

"That's not true. I told you all about the Miracle Chef."

"Georgia, I know about your mother," Callie announced, her voice loud in the suddenly hushed dressing room. "I know she tried to commit suicide when we were in elementary school and I know she did it again when you were at Ole Miss. That's why you dropped out of school and came back to Ocean Sands."

Georgia sat down, hard, on her own stool. "How did you . . ." She lowered her head, unable to continue.

"I doubt there's anyone in town who doesn't know," Callie said. "Things like that just have a way of getting out. Maybe that's why I felt compelled to tell the truth about Beau being Caroline's father. Because holding it in was hurting me. I knew someday it would get out and then it would have the power to not just hurt me and Trey, but hurt Caroline as well. I'm not ashamed of it. It happened right after Jim announced that he was leaving me. I came home to my parents—like I always did when I needed help. One night, I went out to the No Holds Bar and I'd like to say I had too much to drink, but that wasn't it. Beau was there and he was so nice and so comforting that I just fell apart. Long story short, we ended up making love and . . . well, nine months later, there was Caroline."

Georgia was too stunned about her own secret that turned out to not be such a secret after all to speak, which was just as well. Everyone seemed much more interested in Callie's breaking news than what they considered to be Georgia's old news.

"I can't believe Beau wouldn't accept responsibility for his own child," Deborah Lee said with a disapproving click of her tongue as she expertly swished Sierra's sea-foam green hoopskirts into place.

Callie laughed then, the first genuine laugh she'd had all day. "You've got to be kidding. Beau's been more responsible than Jim has. He was at the hospital when Caroline was born. He's taken care of medical bills, paid child support, and—" Callie thought about not adding this last bit, but was tired of hiding the truth from her friends. And from herself. "And he's asked me to marry him about a dozen times."

"And you said no?" Sierra asked, her romantic sensibilities obviously piqued by this turn of events.

Georgia tugged her own pink-and-white dress over her shoulders and shook the fabric out, turning her back to Deborah Lee and pointing silently to the zipper. She held her hair out of the way while Deborah Lee zipped her up and smoothed out her seams.

Callie shot Emma Rose an apologetic look before turning to Sierra and answering truthfully, "You probably don't know this because you're fairly new to Ocean Sands, but the stories about Beau's wild streak go way back. And now he owns a bar, which is hardly something a man with his past should do. Then there are the women. Beau goes through a new one every month. But the real truth is, I care too much about Beau to have him marry me because of Caroline and then resent me for trapping him. He'd go crazy being stuck with one woman for the rest of his life. So, that's it. Believe me, I've given this all a lot of thought. If I saw any other way to make this all work, y'all have to know that I'd do it."

Callie held her hand out to Georgia, who automatically took her friend's hand.

"You've taught me that sometimes you really only have one clear choice. Even if it means you have to sacrifice your own happiness to make it."

Thirty~two

It was over.

Vivian sat staring at the heavy silver Shrimp Festival Princess trophy she'd won all those years ago and knew that it had to end. All she'd ever done was try to protect her daughter but, in the end, she'd done more harm than good.

She'd never meant for things to turn out this way. She wanted Georgia to be happy, but she realized that in trying to force her daughter into one mold, she had stifled that part of her that made her who she was. And now, Georgia was willing to watch the man she loved walk away because of what she thought her mother wanted.

"I won't let that happen," Vivian said, the words echoing in the quiet room.

Slowly, she got up off the settee and walked to the trophy. The metal was cold against her skin as she reached up and took it off the shelf. This trophy was all the evidence of the lengths her own mother had gone to in order to protect her daughter and keep her safe.

Now, it was Vivian's turn to do the same for her own.

"You do know she's not going to show, don't you?" Callie said from behind him, making Daniel turn from studying his notes.

"Yes. I knew this morning when she packed up her dress and high-heeled shoes that she was choosing the pageant over the cook-off," he said, leaning back against the counter in the kitchen where the final show would be taped.

Callie laughed shortly. "You make it sound so easy. As if she really had a choice."

Daniel crossed his arms across his chest and surprised Callie by admitting, "I know she didn't. She truly believes that if she strays from the path her mother has put her on that Vivian will go off the deep end. And I can't say that I'm certain that wouldn't happen."

"I'm not, either," Callie admitted. "But then why do you keep digging around for answers, when you know what it might cost?"

Daniel ran a frustrated hand through his hair. "Because I didn't know what I was up against until a few days ago. Before then, I didn't know about Vivian's suicide attempts, or realize that the trigger for her depression had to do with her daughter's accomplishments. Even now, I feel that if we knew why this bothers Vivian so much, we might be able to help."

"We?" Callie asked, raising her eyebrows.

"Yes, *we*," Daniel answered. "Do you really think I'm the sort of monster who would make Georgia choose between me and her mother?"

Callie opened her mouth, and then closed it again without saying anything. Finally, she shrugged and said, "I guess I didn't give you credit for understanding what this means to her."

"Well, I do. And even though she keeps hinting that I'll be heading back to L.A. tomorrow, I'm not leaving. I love her and—"

"Daniel, Callie, come quick," Sierra Riley interrupted, balancing a tiara on her wild red curls with one hand and her heavy hoopskirt in the other and breathing hard from having run across the fairgrounds.

"What is it?" Daniel asked.

"It's Georgia. Trey called just as the winner of the pageant was announced. Her mother tried to commit suicide again. And this time, she may have succeeded."

Georgia haphazardly parked her car outside the Ocean Sands General Hospital emergency room, right next to a "No Parking" sign. Frankly, she didn't give a damn if they towed her car or drove it into the Gulf of Mexico right now. All she cared about was her mother.

"I knew I shouldn't have left her," she mumbled, wiping the tears from her eyes as she gathered up her voluminous skirts and extricated herself from her car. A vision of her mother sitting in the middle of her trophy room crying kept running through Georgia's head. Why had she thought that Mama had been okay? All her mother's talk about Daniel had obviously been a smoke screen, put up to try to convince Georgia that Mama, while upset about last night's disaster, was going to be all right.

"I'm so stupid. I should have known better," she sobbed, her breath hiccuping as she flew through the doors of the emergency room and nearly barreled into Trey's father, Rock.

"Thank God you're here, Georgia. Come on, I'll take you back to your mother," he said, taking her arm in his firm grip.

Georgia had to trot to keep up with him, but she didn't mind. She needed to see Mama right now, to know that she was all right. When Trey had called, he'd said that her mother had slit her wrists. She had never done that before, and Georgia couldn't help but envision her mother, lying on the cold bathroom floor, her blood seeping out over the white tile. She couldn't get the image out of her head.

Georgia stumbled and cursed her high heels, but Rock's grip on her arm kept her upright. Their footsteps clattered noisily in the deserted hall as they neared the end with its glowing green exit sign.

And then Rock was pushing open the door, shoving her out into the bright sunshine.

"What are you doing?" Georgia asked. She tried to spin around, to go back into the hospital, but Rock held her fast.

"Shut up and come with me."

Rock was dragging her behind him now, but Georgia found it nearly impossible to fight him with her heavy dress getting in the way. Still, she struggled against his grasp, trying to get him to let her go. Then, instead of resisting him, she threw herself forward, going on the attack. Unfortunately, Rock was prepared for her, easily sidestepping her clumsy charge as he kept his grip on her arm and slammed her into the side of a white van.

Georgia's breath left her lungs with an involuntary "oof." Before she could recover, Rock had handcuffed her arms behind her back and shoved her into the back of the van. He got in behind her and pulled the door closed. Georgia struggled to get up, but tripped on her skirt and fell to the metal floor, breaking the fall with her already bruised jaw. Tears of pain welled up in her eyes, but Georgia refused to let them fall, attempting instead to push herself up again.

Rock grabbed her arms and hefted them up, making Georgia scream in pain. Then something clicked and Rock stepped toward the front of the van.

Georgia lashed out with her feet and caught his ankles. Rock stumbled into the back of the driver's seat, but easily righted himself before turning around and waggling a finger at her.

"Don't make this harder than it has to be," he scolded.

"Make *what* harder? What are you doing?" Georgia felt as if she'd been caught up in an alternate universe. This sort of thing didn't happen in Ocean Sands, and it certainly didn't happen to her. And what did her ex-father-in-law have against her anyway?

Georgia pushed her back against the wall of the van, trying to get to her feet, but found that she'd been tethered to some sort of metal mesh by another set of handcuffs. Frantically, her fingers searched for something, anything, to help her break free. The windows of the van had been tinted such a dark shade that Georgia doubted anyone could see her and she couldn't get far enough off the floor to make herself visible through the front windshield.

She waited for Rock to explain what was happening, like in the movies when the villain takes time out to explain his diabolical plot to rule the world, but Rock remained silent.

Georgia wondered where they were going and just what it was Trey's father had in mind for her whenever they got there. It was obvious that whatever it was, she wasn't going to like it. Georgia did her best to stay calm and pay attention despite the blood pounding in her ears, threatening to make her pass out. She was not going to get through this by panicking.

First, she needed to see where they were going. Georgia got her feet under her and felt the burn in her thigh muscles as she lifted herself up as far as the handcuffs would allow. There. She saw a street sign. Main. Okay. They passed Callie's dress shop and the gift shop, headed west.

Georgia frowned and held on to the metal grate behind her to steady herself when Rock got to the intersection of Oak and Main. He turned right.

What the hell was he doing? Taking her to her mother's house? Was that where Mama was?

Oh, God, no. Maybe she was still lying upstairs in her own blood, already dead.

Then some part of her rational brain intruded. If that were the case, then why this manhandling? Why the handcuffs?

Rock parked the van in front of Georgia's house, in the spot Georgia's own car normally occupied. Then he turned and got something out of the glove compartment, humming under his breath as he took out something Georgia couldn't see. Suddenly, the van was filled with an acrid stench and Rock was coming toward her, a damp rag in his outstretched hand.

Georgia, who had been expecting this, lashed out with one pointy-toed high-heeled shoe just as Rock's groin came within range. Her pink pump connected solidly with his testicles, and Rock fell backward, groaning and clutching himself as Georgia kicked against the side of the van to attract some attention to her plight.

Unfortunately, Rock recovered before Georgia succeeded in doing anything more than making the Talmadge's miniature schnauzer start barking. Rock threw a heavy thigh over her legs to get her to stop struggling, grabbed the rag off the floor, and pressed it to her face as she tried to no avail to squirm away.

It was only as her vision started to go fuzzy around the edges that Georgia realized what it was that Rock had been humming earlier: *Here comes the bride.*

When Vivian arrived at the Shrimp Festival, she was struck by how happy everyone seemed. There were children everywhere, running and screaming like children had a habit of doing, and starry-eyed couples holding hands or shrieking as the Ferris wheel stopped with them at the top.

God, it had been a long time since she had felt that kind of happiness.

Vivian closed her eyes, the picture of that festival so many years ago burned into her brain. When Daniel had shown that photo to her, she thought she might pass out. Or throw up.

That was the last year she recalled being truly happy, a happiness not tinged with ugly secrets.

She clutched her Shrimp Festival Princess trophy tighter to her chest as memories flooded her. Her Uncle Carter's clammy hands on her thighs. His breath hot and sour in her face. Him telling her he'd chosen her over Rose because she was so smart and Vivian, glad that she hadn't picked the little sister she loved with all her heart, was still young enough and selfish enough to resent that she was the "chosen" one. She didn't want to be smart anymore, not if her punishment was to endure this pain and humiliation. But she had no choice. Uncle Carter said if she told, he'd deny it . . . and then he'd turn to Rose. And as much as she hated what he did to her, she couldn't let him do it to her baby sister instead. So she endured it.

Until one day, during that fateful Shrimp Festival when Vivian would go on to win the title of Princess for the first time, Mama came home unexpectedly, saying later that she realized halfway to the fairgrounds, where she was overseeing the preparations for that year's sweet potato pie, that her pocketbook didn't match her shoes. This was back in the day when a fashion faux pas of this magnitude could get your children's children ostracized from the Junior League, and Mother had no intention of potentially handicapping her progeny by her own carelessness.

Vivian still remembered the look on her mother's face when she had peered into Vivian's bedroom and found her daughter in tears and her brother-in-law with his pants down around his ankles.

She also remembered the calm way Mother listened to Uncle Carter's excuses. And then, politely as you please, she'd asked him to put that extra crate of sweet potatoes that Miss Beall had brought over into her trunk for her.

Vivian had felt sick when her uncle left the room, shooting her a look that said he knew what he had just gotten away with. She knew, too, that it meant he would continue abusing her forever. Vivian didn't know how much longer she could endure it.

"You stay here, Vivvie," her mother had said then, in that same calm, polite voice. "And I don't want you to look out your window until you hear my car leave. You understand?"

Vivian had nodded, trying not to cry when her mother told her she was a good girl and silently left the house.

A few minutes later, she heard her mother's voice, saying, "Here, Carter, let me put this tarp down across the trunk first. That crate is so dirty."

She had known the right thing to do would be to obey her mother's command. She tried to stay away from the window, but she just couldn't. She crept along the wall and peered out her window, the curtains stirring slightly when she breathed.

Uncle Carter lifted the heavy crate of sweet potatoes and leaned forward to put them in Mother's trunk. Vivian saw her mother raise her hands. She was holding something wrapped in what looked to be a dish towel. She brought her hands down on Uncle Carter's back and he fell forward, the upper half of his body landing inside Mother's trunk.

Suddenly, Mother looked back toward the window and Vivian leaped back, her head knocking into the shelf Daddy had made for her to display her steadily growing supply of academic achievement awards.

Vivian stumbled into bed and pulled the covers up over her head, waiting for what seemed an eternity for her mother's car to start. Even when it did, Vivian didn't move. It was then, lying in the darkness and shaking in the aftermath of what had just happened, that Vivian vowed never to be known as the smart one again. That afternoon, after she'd cried herself to sleep and woken to an eerily quiet house, she took all of her awards down off the shelf and destroyed them.

At supper the next night, Daddy had asked where Uncle Carter had gone and Mother told him she had no idea.

"You know how your brother is, Jackson. He's about the most unreliable person I think I've ever met."

"Yes, he's always been that way," Daddy said, taking a second helping of Mother's blue ribbon cornbread. His brother's disappearance obviously didn't trouble him much, since he almost immediately changed the subject. "So, how is that new oven working out? Is the pie going to be as delicious this year as it's always been?"

Her mother's laughter, when it came, seemed a bit forced. "Of course not, dear, it will be better than it's ever been. You should know that. Although, it seems that someone accidentally bumped the heat up to its highest setting last night. It's a good thing we were just in the pre-heating stage. Otherwise, our pie would have simply been cremated."

Vivian had frozen with her fork halfway to her mouth, stunned when her mother looked at her when saying that last word, as if she were trying to tell her something.

"Fortunately, I noticed it this afternoon so everything turned out just fine," her mother continued. Then, without missing a beat, she frowned at Vivian and said, "Dear, you look like a trout. Either eat that bite of food or put it back on your plate. And get your elbows off the table. You'd think you were raised by Yankees with manners like that."

Later that month, after the Shrimp Festival was over and she had won the Princess title, and after the police had perfunctorily questioned Mother and Daddy and even herself about Uncle Carter's disappearance, Vivian had crept back to the deserted fairgrounds. She had stood looking at the new oven that the mayor's construction company had built for the city that year. And, with a shudder that shook her down to her soul, she had opened the trapdoor to where the ashes collected and, dreading that she'd discover an arm or a head or something equally awful, she had poked around in the ashes with a stick. When her stick connected with something hard, Vivian had closed her eyes and prayed that it would be nothing.

Slowly, she pulled the object toward her, the sound of it scraping across the cement floor of the oven like sharp fingernails scratching a chalkboard.

It wedged in the opening of the trapdoor and Vivian tentatively slid her arm through the opening, expecting at any second to be grabbed from the other side and dragged into the bowels of the oven. She was so scared, she nearly screamed when her fingers touched the cool smoothness of the object she'd found.

With sweat dripping in her eyes, she pulled the thing out and slammed the trapdoor shut, just in case Uncle Carter's ghost was in there, trying to get out.

In the warm heat of midday, she sat on the hard, sun-baked ground and looked at what she'd pulled out of the oven. It was a knife, or at least, it used to be a knife. The handle had burned off, leaving nothing but the six-inch blade. Vivian slid the pad of her thumb along the blade, her brain not registering that she had started to bleed until a fat red drop splashed onto her bare leg. She knew that she had to hide this last piece of evidence from everyone—from her parents, from the police, from anyone who might come to clean out the ashes years from now and start asking questions that Vivian would not answer.

And so, she had ripped off a scrap of the banner proclaiming the dates of the annual Shrimp Festival, wrapped the remains of the knife in it, and hidden it under her blouse. When she got home, she looked around her room for someplace to put it, and her eyes lit on the gleaming Shrimp Festival Princess trophy that had replaced her "Student of the Year" plaque on the shelves Daddy had made for her.

That's where it had remained, for more than forty years, undisturbed by time or prying eyes.

Only now, in order to set her own daughter free and give her the happiness she deserved, Vivian had to unearth her secret. She couldn't continue to hide it. It was time to let it go.

As if in a trance, Vivian made her way to the oven where this year's sweet potato pie was being served by various residents of Ocean Sands.

Her steps faltered when she saw Rose passing out plates of whipped-cream-topped pie, but she forced herself to continue. She had come this far, she couldn't stop now.

"Sheriff Mooney may I have a word with you?" she asked the uniformed police officer who was serving pie alongside her sister.

He seemed surprised, but smiled in a friendly fashion and handed his apron to a waiting volunteer before steering her out into the picnic area adjoining the fairgrounds. "What can I do for you, Miss Vivian?" he asked when they were seated on plastic chairs that wobbled when she shifted her weight.

Vivian pushed the gleaming trophy toward him. "My mama killed my Uncle Carter with the knife that's in here. I saw her do it, and I know how she disposed of the body. I thought . . . I thought it was time someone knew."

The sheriff frowned at her and pushed a hand through his hair. "Well, now, Vivian, you're talking about something that happened quite a long time ago. Are you sure? You were just a kid back then. Your memory might not be as accurate as you may think."

Vivian laughed shortly. "I can assure you, it's not the sort of thing a person is likely to forget."

Sheriff Mooney's gaze slid to the brown grass baking in the sun and then his kind hazel eyes met hers. "I knew your mama, Viv. Not well, of course, but she was a force in this town until the day she died. She was a tireless volunteer and never caused any trouble. Why would she have just up and killed her brother-in-law one day?"

Vivian stared at the well-polished trophy, noting the way the sun glinted off the metal. She could see her own reflection in the silver surface. Distorted by the curved shape, her face looked wide and flat, her eyes bulging and enormous, her chin pointed. She blinked back tears, knowing that the only way she could be free of this terrible burden would be to tell the whole truth, not just pieces of it.

"Because she found out that he was molesting her daughter," came the calm answer.

Both Vivian and Sheriff Mooney whipped around to see Rose standing a few feet away, near the edge of the eating area. Rose slowly came closer, ignoring the sheriff while keeping her eyes fastened on her sister.

"Because the day Uncle Carter disappeared was the day I told Mother that he was abusing me."

Vivian sprung up off her chair and it toppled over into the dying grass. "What?"

"When Mother left for the Shrimp Festival that day, she found me hiding in the backseat of her car, crying. She'd left me alone with Uncle Carter again that morning when she went off to the grocery store with you. Uncle Carter took advantage of me that day for the first time. Before, he had always scared me. He seemed to want to get closer to me than other grown-ups and he touched me a lot but, until that morning, he hadn't done anything worse. But that day, he nearly did. If you and Mother hadn't come home earlier than he'd expected, he would have raped me. At first, I didn't know what to do, so I just ran and hid in the tree house in our backyard. When I saw Mother getting ready to leave again, I wanted her to take me with her, so I ran and got into the backseat. When she was a few blocks from home, she heard me crying and pulled over to the side of the road. When Mother found out what had happened, she told me to go to Lottie Talmadge's house and not to come back until supper time. I remember being so frightened. I was only six at the time, and I had no idea what Mother would do. It was only when I was much older that I began to suspect that Uncle Carter's disappearance might have been more than just a case of Daddy's wayward brother running off."

"No," Vivian breathed. Her legs didn't feel strong enough to support her, so she sat down on the grass next to her toppled chair. "He said he wouldn't touch you if I didn't tell."

Rose stepped in front of her sister, her tennis shoes spotted with dirt. "What are you talking about?"

Vivian swallowed, then put a hand up to shield her eyes as she looked up at her younger sister. "Uncle Carter had been molesting me since he first came to Ocean Sands. He warned me that if I told, he would deny everything and start in on you. I couldn't take the chance that he might make good on his threat, so I never said a word. I couldn't stand the thought of him hurting you."

Rose crouched down in the grass beside her. "Oh, God, Vivvie, no."

Vivian felt tears start to well up in her eyes. "I never said a thing. He told me he had chosen me instead of you because I was the smart one."

Rose held out her arms and wrapped them around her sister's shaking shoulders. "Oh, Viv," she whispered. "That's what he said to me, too."

Thirty-three

She's not at Ocean Sands General," Callie shouted, even though she was only a foot away from Daniel in the passenger seat of his rental car.

"Try the other hospitals in the area. Do you know anyone who works down at the police station? Maybe they would know where the ambulance might have taken Vivian," Daniel suggested. Agitatedly, he rolled through the stop sign at Oak and Main without bothering to come to a complete stop. Both Sierra and Callie were working their cell phones, trying to find out where Georgia may have gone. With no leads, Daniel had decided to come back here to see if anyone was still at the scene who might be able to tell them what was going on.

Daniel parked across the street from Vivian's house, halfway between her house and her daughter's. "I'm going to go check out Georgia's place to see if there are any clues as to where she's gone. Would one of you go see if anyone's at Vivian's?"

"I'll go," Callie said, already out of the convertible with her cell phone still pressed to her ear.

Daniel wasn't certain if Kelly, Emma Rose, and Deborah Lee knew what had happened but he was willing to bet that if they did, it wouldn't be long before they showed up here, too. Sierra had known what was going on because she and Georgia were standing at the front of the stage waiting to hear which of them had won the Shrimp Queen crown when Trey had called.

Since he didn't have a key, Daniel tried the doorknob of Georgia's house, hoping she hadn't locked the door. The knob turned easily in his hand and Daniel rolled his eyes. So much for security. It was a good thing Georgia didn't live in L.A. She'd have been robbed blind or murdered in her sleep by now.

The front door creaked when he pushed it open and stepped into the house.

"Georgia," he shouted. "Are you here?"

There was no answer, so he rubbed his forehead, trying to think of where he might find some clue as to where she might be. First, he checked her phone to see if she had any messages. Then he looked at the pad next to the phone, holding it up to the light and hoping for the sort of magic etchings like he'd seen in a million movies.

Nothing.

He turned and ran upstairs, thinking maybe she had stopped here to change out of her dress and into more appropriate hospital attire. But when he got to her bedroom, everything was as she'd left it that morning—the bed hastily made, several high-heeled shoes strewn about the floor.

Damn. No clues here. Maybe she had just gone straight to Vivian's house.

Daniel raced out of the bedroom . . . and felt his head explode as something hit him from behind.

"Look, I'm going to need you two to come in so I can file a formal report, but the truth of the matter is, there's nothing that I can do. Everyone directly involved in this case is dead. I suppose some might say that you were required to come forward and tell what you had seen to the police, Vivian, but I don't think there's a jury in this country that would have blamed you for keeping quiet. Why don't you two come by my office on Monday? Say two o'clock? I think it's safe to say that you've both earned some closure in this matter."

Sheriff Mooney picked Vivian's trophy up off the table and said, "I'll just take this with me down to the station. You can have it back when it's determined we no longer need it for evidence." Then he waved and walked away, leaving Vivian and Rose huddled together on the grass.

Vivian sobbed silently into her sister's shirt for a long time after the sheriff left. Rose let her cry, rocking her gently and feeling a lifetime of resentment seeping away with each tear her sister cried.

"I'm so sorry. I never knew," Rose said. "All those times you talked about what you'd sacrificed and I thought you were just putting on airs. Why didn't you ever tell me?"

Vivian shook her head and breathed in several hiccupping breaths. "I couldn't. Not without telling you everything about Mother. At first, I didn't want to burden you with the truth. You were too young and I wasn't certain you could understand why Mother did what she did. If I'd known Uncle Carter had tried to hurt you, too . . . Well, I guess now all of our secrets are out."

"God, Vivvie, I didn't tell you about what had happened to me for the very same reason. Look at what these secrets have stolen from us. We threw away a lifetime of being a family for this."

Vivian sniffled and—Rose couldn't believe she was seeing this— dabbed at her nose with the back of her hand. Rose pulled a handkerchief out of her jeans pocket and handed it to her sister, who stared at the white square of fabric as if unsure of what it was for.

"I know that now, but I just couldn't see it before. You know, I hate to admit this, Daniel being a man *and* a Yankee, after all, but he was right. All those years I kept this bottled up inside me and it turned me into someone I don't want to be. When I saw that news report this morning and saw that my daughter is smart enough to invent something like the Miracle Chef but couldn't tell me because she was afraid of what I might do, I realized that I wasn't protecting her at all. Instead, my fears were forcing her into the same unhappy, unfulfilled life I've lived. I couldn't do that to her any longer. That's why I had to tell the truth. And now . . . to find out that Uncle Carter had been lying all along, that he didn't single me out because I was smart, that he just said that for his own sick purposes. I can't believe I let him do this to me. To us all."

Rose reached out and enfolded her sister in a heart-squeezing, bone-crushing hug. "I'm so proud of you."

Vivian started crying again. "I love you, Rose."

Rose patted her sister's back. "I love you, too, Vivvie."

"Well, I'm glad to see that somebody's having a good time at this stupid festival," Shana Goldberg said, plunking down on the seat that Sheriff Mooney had vacated and digging her fork into a piece of sweet potato pie.

Rose gave her sister a final pat and then pushed herself to her feet, holding out her hand to help Vivian up.

"Something wrong in la-la land?" Rose asked.

"My stars have disappeared," Shana said glumly, spearing a bite of whipped cream.

"What do you mean?" Vivian asked. She wiped away the last of her tears and dabbed at her eyes with Rose's hankie, hoping her waterproof mascara had stayed put.

"I mean, *your* daughter"—she jabbed her fork in Vivian's direction—"chose some silly beauty pageant over the final cook-off, and Daniel just dashed from the set, telling me that we'll have to fill this slot with a re-run. Doesn't he understand a thing about ratings? We've hyped this silly cook-off thing and viewers are clamoring to know how it's going to end. We can't just give them some stupid rerun. The network execs are gonna have my head for this." She gave a disgusted sigh and stabbed her fork into the remainder of her pie, glaring at it balefully.

"Is it still possible for the show to go on?" Vivian asked, tilting her head and squinting at the spike-haired producer.

"Well, yeah, if I actually had stars," Shana answered, as if Vivian was too dumb to have understood the problem.

"Yes, of course. What if my sister and I volunteered to do this final cook-off? I mean, I owe it to my daughter to prove that the Miracle Chef is exactly that—a miracle for working men and women who want to feed their families nutritious, delicious meals. I've watched Georgia use the thing a dozen times, and God knows Rose and I both learned how to cook from one of the South's best. Our mother won blue ribbons for everything from her barbecued shrimp to her sour cream biscuits and everyone will tell you her cherry cobbler was enough to make grown men weep. Isn't that right, Rose?"

"It surely was. Why I remember the time—"

"Okay, can it with the trip down memory lane, would you? The film crew has already started packing up. If you two are serious about this, we need to get you into makeup right now."

Vivian held out her hand to her sister. "What do you say, Rose? You want to do this?"

"Absolutely," Rose answered, taking her sister's hand. "Let's go show the world what the Hughes girls are made of."

Thirty~four

$\mathcal{D}$aniel, wake up. We've got to get out of here," Georgia said, and then spritzed him in the face with some water, which she figured was far more polite than slapping him. Not that she could have reached him anyway, since Rock had secured her hands behind her back.

Daniel groggily opened his eyes. "Wha—?"

"Look, I don't have time for a long explanation. Trey's father has rigged this place to blow. We have to figure a way out of here."

Daniel blinked and tried to orient himself, but felt as if his brain had somehow been detached from his skull. His head throbbed and he tried to raise his hands to touch the aching spot, but discovered that he'd been handcuffed to the leg of a workbench in Georgia's attic laboratory. Georgia was across the room, similarly trapped, although she'd managed to scoot around so her back was to him and had maneuvered her squirt bottle well enough to spray him in the face.

She shot at him again, and Daniel shook the water out of his eyes before saying, "I'm awake. You can stop squirting me now."

Georgia scuttled around so that she was facing him again. "Good. Now how do we get out of this?" she asked.

Daniel thought for a minute. "Okay, I've read enough of the movie scripts my parents have been sent over the years to figure this out," he said, sounding surprisingly convincing.

At least he hoped he had.

"How much time do we have?" he asked, looking around the room to see what sort of James Bond-ish tools he had at his disposal. Unfortunately, he didn't think Georgia's marinade vacuum seal and butt-sticking fabric were going to be of much use in their escape.

"I don't know. Rock activated the timer over there after handcuffing me to the table. I assume he was giving himself enough time to be long gone once the place exploded. But it could be just a few minutes."

"All right, look, here's what I'm going to do. I need to get my hands in front of me so I can pick this lock. Can you try to find something like a paper clip or a small screwdriver?"

"Sure," Georgia said, pushing herself up using the metal table leg to see what she could find on her workbench. She had paper clips at her desk, of course, but that was too far away for her to reach, even with her feet. She spied a small screwdriver and contorted herself to try to get a leg up on the workbench to kick it over to Daniel, but her skirt kept getting in her way. Finally, she managed to kick the tool off the bench, only she kicked too hard and it went flying out of reach of them both.

"Damn," she swore, letting her leg fall back to the floor. Now what?

She glanced over at Daniel, who somewhat resembled a pretzel with his legs draped over his arms. His certainty that he could get them out of this increased her resolve to not just stand around like some air-headed blond sidekick. Damn it, she could kick some ass here, too.

Think, Georgia, think, she ordered herself, desperately looking around the room.

That's when she spotted her wedding gift to Callie lying neatly wrapped on the edge of her workbench. A set of Francis I silverware from Reed and Barton. A gift for the woman who wants it all. There were twenty-eight pieces of fruit on the knife handle alone, and almost no end to what one could buy in that pattern. With her budget, Georgia had had to settle on a dinner knife, fish knife and fork, soupspoon, butter knife, dessert spoon, iced tea spoon, ice-cream fork, salad fork, dinner fork, and—her personal favorite—a cocktail fork, with its tiny tines and intricate multifruited handle. Georgia leaned over and knocked the box to the floor with her head. Then, using her feet, she scooted the box up between her knees and clamped it tightly so it wouldn't move. She ripped open the wrapping with her teeth, sending up a silent apology to

Dr. Steve, her dentist, who had reminded her since birth that, "Your teeth are not tools." Finally she had the box open, all eleven pieces of silverware lying in her tulle-covered lap. She spread her legs wide and bobbed for the cocktail fork amid yards of pink-and-white fabric. When she had it in her teeth, she looked over at Daniel, who had miraculously managed to get his hands out in front of him.

"Here, toss it to me," he said.

Georgia took careful aim and jerked her head up, watching, as if in slow motion, as the cocktail fork landed right in front of Daniel.

"Good job," he muttered, picking it up with his cuffed hands.

"Do you really know what you're doing?" Georgia asked dubiously as he jiggled the fork in the lock of his handcuffs.

Daniel didn't waste time looking up at her. "Sure. My dad had to learn how to do this for a movie he made a few years ago. *One Man's Army.* Did you see it?"

"Uh, no. I'm more of the chick-flick type," Georgia admitted.

"Now there's a surprise," Daniel muttered.

Georgia was tempted to throw the ice-cream fork at him, but she managed to resist, and was especially glad she had when he looked up at her and grinned, holding his uncuffed hands up in the air. He didn't waste any time getting her cuffs off and they both raced to the door.

Georgia had her hand on the doorknob when Daniel slammed his palm on the door next to her head. She let out a yelp of surprise.

"Come on, let's go," she said.

"He's rigged the door. Look, see that wire down near the floor?"

Georgia pressed her skirt against her legs and, indeed, saw the wire running across the doorframe. Her heart rate immediately quadrupled. Then her eyes widened when she heard footsteps on the stairs outside.

"Georgia? Daniel?" Callie yelled.

"Don't open the door," she and Daniel shouted in unison, pressing their palms against the door as the doorknob rattled.

"What's going on?" Sierra said from the other side of the door.

"It's Trey's father. He rigged this room to blow," Daniel said. "You guys get out of here. Call the police and tell them to send over a bomb squad."

Georgia snorted. Right. A bomb squad in Ocean Sands.

"Are you two all right?" Callie asked.

"Yes, just go," Georgia encouraged. She could almost feel her best friend's hesitation, but then heard footsteps retreating back down the stairs.

Georgia turned to Daniel. "Okay, Mr. Bond, what do we do now?"

Daniel pinched the bridge of his nose. "Hell if I know," he said. Then he traced the wire that had been stretched across the door to see if there was some sort of timer or anything that would tell him how many minutes they had left. When he found the bomb, it looked deceptively simple, with a digital timer attached to a small box. Unfortunately, his secondhand stuntman training didn't include disabling bombs—especially ones that didn't have red or green or blue wires that had to be cut. Even then, Daniel wasn't sure which was the right one to slash. That seemed to change with every movie.

The seconds were ticking by at an alarming rate as Daniel looked around at the windowless room and tried to think of a way out. Finally, he shook his head sadly, walked back to Georgia, reached out to brush a lock of hair from her eyes, and said, "We have fifteen minutes and twelve seconds left. I'm sorry, but I'm all out of ideas."

Georgia looked around her lab, at the inventions she had worked so hard on, even knowing that she was the only one who would ever know that this was her secret passion. And now, she thought, looking at Daniel, she had two secret passions—him and inventing. God, she wished things could have turned out differently between them. She wished she'd been able to be the woman he wanted, strong enough to face her devils and win out in the end. Instead, she had hidden behind her fears and her love for her mother and chosen this half-life instead.

Still, she couldn't leave this world without telling him the truth. She loved him. Even though she couldn't be who he wanted her to be, he was the first man who had ever tempted her to want more than she had been given.

She reached up and caressed his cheek. "I love you, Daniel," she said.

He pulled her close, but then surprised her by saying, "I know you do. I love you, too. But this really isn't the time for long, romantic speeches. How the hell are we going to get out of here?"

Georgia blinked up at him, bemused by his pragmatic response to her declaration. Sheesh, you'd think he'd at least act a little more surprised than this. Cocky man.

She stepped back and tripped over the hem of her dress, her elbow crashing into a stack of cans on her workbench behind her. "Ow," she said, rubbing her elbow. This damn Eagle brand sweetened condensed milk was the bane of her existence. If it wasn't exploding all over her kitchen, it was—

"I've got it," Georgia shrieked, leaping on one of the neatly stacked boxes of Miracle Chefs in the corner and ripping at the box with her hands.

"What?" Daniel asked, clearly perplexed.

"I'm going to blow a hole in the wall so we can escape," Georgia said. She yanked a brand-new Miracle Chef out of its box and set it on the burner she used in her experiments. She turned the heat on high and then ran over to the canned milk and tossed them to Daniel. "Here, put those in the Miracle Chef and seal the lid," she ordered.

"Yes, ma'am," he answered. When he'd done as directed and turned around, his jaw dropped open to see Georgia tugging her arms out of her dress. "Georgia, this is no time for, ah, whatever it is you had in mind."

She rolled her eyes and whipped off her bra. "Right, because you're so hot that all I can think about is sex at a time like this."

Daniel grinned. "Hey, you said it, not me."

"Give me a break." Georgia, however, did notice that Daniel's gaze had become fixated on her bare breasts. She closed her eyes, grabbed an edge of the tape she'd used to push her breasts together to give her beauty queen cleavage, and ripped it off. "Jeez, that hurts," she said, opening her eyes again.

Daniel looked as if he were about to clutch his own chest in agony.

"This is the price you have to pay to be a member of the Tiara Club," she said, hastily putting her arms back through her sleeves as she walked over to the Miracle Chef and put the tape she'd just ripped from her breasts over the pressure release valve. This, she figured, was the key to getting an explosion that would do more than just spew hot caramel all over the place. Once those cans built up enough pressure, they should be able to blow a good-sized hole in her wall. At least, that's what Georgia hoped.

"How long do we have?" she asked.

Daniel glanced over at the digital timer. "Ten minutes and forty-one seconds. Is that enough?"

Georgia worried the nail on her left index finger. "I don't know. It took thirteen minutes for a can to cook in the Miracle Chef on low without exploding. I'm hoping this won't take as long."

"Well, that's the best we can hope for. We need to shield ourselves in case this does work," Daniel said, waving her over to her desk and shoving everything off onto the floor while Georgia hugged her laptop.

She sighed. All the work she had saved on her hard drive would be gone. Years and years of careful notations entered into notebooks and then transferred to her computer. All gone.

Of course, if this didn't work, she'd be blown to bits anyway, so what did it matter?

Daniel upended the desk. "Here, get behind this," he said.

Georgia did, but realized they were still completely exposed from the top. She glanced around, looking for a piece of wood or anything that might help keep them safe, but found nothing except the bolt of fabric she'd tested for use in making pageant swimsuits that wouldn't ride up.

Well, she figured, it was better than nothing. If scalding hot caramel came raining down on them, at least they'd have some protection.

She leaped out from behind the desk, only her skirt caught on one leg and her leap turned into something more like a nosedive. Daniel grabbed the material around her hips and hauled her back behind the table.

"Get down," he ordered.

"I was going to use that fabric over there to shield us from the caramel," she explained.

"Oh. Good idea," he grudgingly admitted. "You stay here, I'll get it."

Georgia let him go, figuring he could move faster than her anyway. He grabbed the bolt of fabric and turned back toward her.

And that's when she heard it. An ominous hissing, getting louder and louder with each passing second.

Oh, no. It was going to blow.

"Daniel, duck," she screamed.

Then several things happened simultaneously. First, Daniel lunged toward the desk. Second, her world went dark. And, third, an enormous explosion rocked her house, the floor beneath her seeming to buck and twist until, finally, all was quiet.

Thirty~five

"Let's get out of here," Daniel yelled, trying to extricate himself from the sticky fabric that wouldn't let him go. Damn, that's right. They needed water to get this stuff off.

Well, they were just going to have to escape like this. The bomb Trey's father had set was going to go off any minute.

He hauled Georgia up off the floor. The fabric stuck to every inch of their exposed skin, but fortunately, that left their legs mostly free except for the extra yards of cloth draped around their feet.

Georgia had already leaped over the table, but Daniel found himself dragged down by an unexpected weight. He turned to see that the fabric was sticking to the metal legs of the table, too. Great, so the stuff adhered to metal as well as to human flesh.

"Hand me a knife," he shouted. Stuck together as they were, it was going to take some cooperation to get out of here.

Georgia stretched as far as she could away from Daniel, reaching for the pocketknife that had fallen from her workbench onto the floor. Her fingernails barely touched it. "Lean forward," she told Daniel, who did so without question. She grabbed the knife from the floor and handed it to him. She heard the fabric rip when Daniel tore into it, frantically trying to free them.

Suddenly, the fabric gave and Daniel toppled over the table, inadvertently pushing her to the ground.

"Okay, I've had about enough of this," Georgia grumbled.

Daniel's fabric-covered hand grabbed hers as he pulled them both up off the floor. The caramel explosion had blown a hole the size of a person in the wall of her attic. They were going to have to squeeze out single file.

"You go first," Daniel said, pushing her toward the opening. "Try to land on your feet with your knees soft instead of locked."

"How do you know that?" Georgia asked.

"My dad did his own stunts whenever he could," Daniel answered, then helped her punch through a bit of the wall that was still in the way.

Georgia looked out into her front yard and realized she must not have heard the sirens of the Ocean Sands fire and police departments over the sound of the explosion. "The fire department's coming," she said excitedly, turning back to Daniel, who turned to look at the timer counting down the seconds until they were both goners.

"No time," he said in verbal shorthand. "Jump."

Georgia looked down at the roof covering her front porch, and realized they were not in for a soft landing. Still, it beat standing here waiting to get blown into a million tiny pieces. She grabbed Daniel's hand as he squeezed into the opening behind her.

And then they were flying.

A huge boom sounded behind them as they landed—ker-thud!—on the roof. They did not, as Daniel had hoped, land on their feet. Instead, Daniel, perhaps because he was heavier, landed on the roof first and Georgia landed on top of him, shoving the air out his lungs with a giant "oof."

Then they rolled, gravity doing its part to make them one with the earth.

Over and over they went, until Georgia didn't know which way was up.

Then they were falling and Georgia couldn't seem to manage to get her hands unstuck from the fabric to break her fall with the onrushing cement. Only, at the last second, just as she closed her eyes and envisioned herself lying on the walkway leading up to her house, her head cracked open like a bleeding watermelon, she jerked to a stop.

Daniel groaned, and Georgia opened her eyes.

He had stopped their descent by grabbing on to her metal gutter, and her body-sticking fabric had adhered to it. That, in addition to

Daniel's own grip on the gutter, had stopped them from plummeting to the ground.

Suddenly, they were surrounded by people. Firemen, Sheriff Mooney, the Tiara Club.

When Georgia was back on her feet again, she didn't waste any time, turning the water hose on them to get the fabric to release its hold. Then she turned to her friends and asked, "What about my mother? Where is she? Is she all right?"

"I can answer that for you," Sheriff Mooney said before anyone else could say anything. "She's fine. I left her at the Shrimp Festival, making peace with your Aunt Rose. Now, you tell me, what happened here?"

"Trey's father," Georgia panted. "He tried to kill me."

"Where do you think he is now?" the sheriff asked.

"I don't know," Georgia answered, a frown creasing her brow.

"I think I might know," Callie said. "He and Trey were supposed to meet up at the fair this afternoon at four o'clock. Then they were going to go back to Rock's house to get ready for the wedding at eight."

"What time is it now?" Daniel asked, his own watch having stopped during the two explosions it had recently endured.

"It's three forty-six. Let's get back to the festival," Callie yelled.

"No, wait. I'll take care of this," Sheriff Mooney hollered, but by then it was already too late. The women of the Tiara Club were already on the move—with Daniel on their heels.

"And what do we have here?" Rock Hunter asked, smiling wide for the cameras and turning so that they could get his good side.

"I made my mother's world-famous spicy barbeque shrimp, red beans and rice, corn bread, and cherry cobbler for dessert." Vivian set an appetizing-looking plate of food in front of the man who'd been chosen as the fifth judge for today's cook-off. Vivian wanted to win this more than she'd ever wanted to win any tiara or crown or silver trophy in her life. She wanted the world to know that her daughter was an inventor; that she was smart and tenacious and had a heart so big that all she ever wanted to do was to help make other people's lives better.

Vivian felt her eyes getting watery again and sniffed. Behind her, Rose slipped her a tissue and Vivian squeezed her sister's hand gratefully.

"I hope you win," Rose whispered, quietly enough that no one else could hear.

"I hope Georgia wins," Vivian corrected.

Rose shrugged and, with a smile, said, "Either way."

"All right, judges, are you ready to vote?" Shana Goldberg asked.

The first judge was Miss Beall, who voted for Rose, making Vivian fight the urge to stick her tongue out at the old woman. "She never liked me," she muttered under her breath.

Young Jason Broussard was the second judge and he made Vivian nearly jump for joy when he voted for the Miracle Chef.

Next was Jefferson Bremer, a boy Vivian was certain had a crush on her daughter back in the fourth grade. "Yes," she said, clenching her fists at her waist when he, too, voted for the Miracle Chef.

Here it was, two to one for the Miracle Chef.

Come on, come on, Vivian prayed. Please, let Georgia win.

The fourth judge was Velma Boleen, a woman Vivian knew was fond of her daughter. Surely, she'd cast her vote the right way. "I'm sorry, Vivian, but the shrimp was just too spicy," Velma said, voting for Rose's meal instead.

Vivian wanted to reach out and wring the woman's skinny neck. Too spicy, indeed. What sort of Southerner was she, anyway?

All eyes were now on Rock Hunter, who held the deciding vote.

"We-e-ell," he began, drawing the word out as if he were about to make a lengthy speech.

Vivian wanted to scream, but instead, she clasped Rose's hand and squeezed as the tension mounted.

"Rock Hunter, you are under arrest."

The crowd gasped and Vivian turned to find Sheriff Mooney actually holding a gun on Trey's father. She couldn't believe it. This had to be the first time in Ocean Sands' history that the sheriff had actually pulled his gun out of its holster.

"What are you talking about, Doug? I've been here for the last hour. I have all these witnesses who can tell you so," Rock said smugly, taking a sip of the iced tea Vivian had poured him earlier in an attempt to get on his good side.

It was Vivian's turn to gasp when Georgia—who looked as if she'd just survived the second coming of General Sherman—stepped beside the sheriff.

Iced tea spurted out of Rock's mouth. "But you . . . you . . ."

"Yes, me. Your plan didn't work." Georgia stayed back behind Sheriff Mooney while she made her announcement. Then she glanced at her mother and her shoulders started to shake. "Mama, I'm so glad you're all right."

Vivian frowned. "Well, of course I'm all right, dear. Why wouldn't I be?"

Georgia swiped the tears from her eyes and gulped in a sobbing breath. "Rock told me you were hurt again."

"Why in the world would you say such a thing?" Vivian asked, spearing Rock with her gaze.

"Because he wanted to lure me to the hospital so he could try to kill me," Georgia said. "Only it didn't work. Daniel and I escaped. As you can see, I'm still very much alive."

"He tried to kill you?" Vivian asked.

Georgia nodded.

Rock chose that moment to try to escape, but he didn't know what he was up against. As he vaulted over the table set up for the judges, Vivian picked up the Miracle Chef and Rose picked up her cast-iron skillet and they each took a side. Rock fell to the floor like a . . . well, a rock, and Georgia had to guess that he'd probably hear ringing in his ears until the day he died.

As pandemonium broke out, Georgia ran to the set only to stop dead in her tracks when her mother and her Aunt Rose looped arms and, looking down at Rock Hunter, Mama said, "And that better be the last man who tries to fuck with the Hughes girls."

"Amen," Rose added.

All Georgia could do was gape, shocked more that her mother had used the forbidden f-word than with the fact that Mama and Aunt Rose had just knocked a man out cold.

Thirty~six

$\mathcal{I}$ 'm sorry, Daniel, you know that men are not allowed at Tiara Club meetings," Vivian announced.

"Especially not ones who are prettier than we are," Kelly Bremer shouted from the dining room, making Daniel grin.

"Your movie-star smile has no effect on me whatsoever," Vivian said, crossing her arms across her chest.

"Aw, come on. This isn't even a regular meeting," Daniel protested. "Besides, I wanted to tell you all what Sheriff Mooney found out about Trey's father."

"Y'all," Vivian corrected. "It's not two words, honey, it's one."

Daniel laughed. "Okay. Y'all," he drawled.

Vivian pushed herself away from the doorjamb and frowned. "Hmm. That wasn't too bad. Maybe you'll learn to fit in here after all."

"I have a strong motivation to do just that," Daniel said softly, looking past Vivian to see Georgia coming down the stairs, looking like a princess with a diamond tiara on her head. The look was somewhat spoiled by the sky blue flannel pajamas she was wearing. Daniel wasn't sure, but he even thought he saw fuzzy pink bunny slippers on her feet.

Now this was his kind of beauty queen—one who didn't take herself, or her looks, too seriously.

"All right, you can come in. But just so you can tell us what in heaven's name Rock Hunter was thinking."

Vivian stepped back to let him in and Daniel stepped over the threshold, his senses immediately assaulted by the wonderful smells coming from the kitchen and a cacophony of giggling from the parlor. He immediately saw the reason for the laughter, since Callie's three boys had tiaras perched on their heads and looked decidedly unhappy about it.

"They said we had to wear these," the oldest boy mumbled.

"I'm a prince," one of the twins announced, obviously deciding to make lemonade out of lemons.

The third child remained silent, but Daniel guessed that had more to do with the cookie he'd stuffed in his mouth than any lack of opinion on his part. Callie, he noticed, kept a close eye on Caroline, on guard for whatever mischief her littlest imp might have up her sleeve next.

Daniel followed Vivian out into the dining room where all the "girls" were gathered. Even though they called themselves that, Daniel—having been raised on the West Coast—had a hard time thinking of any woman over the age of twelve as a "girl."

He sat down in one of Georgia's creaky old dining-room chairs and smiled when Georgia, plate heaped with all manner of goodies, sat down beside him on the floor and crossed her legs. She offered him up a cracker filled with a sort of orangy goo, and Daniel took it without asking what it was. He'd learned that he liked Southern food better if he didn't know that the dish he thought was heaven on a spoon was made with pineapple, cheddar cheese, butter, and Ritz crackers. He had, after all, studied under one of the greatest chefs in America. This was not the sort of thing his former mentor would exactly approve of.

As he swallowed the gooey mess, he nudged Georgia's shoulder with his knee and she scooted closer. He tangled one finger in that long, curly hair that he loved so much and brought the strand to his lips.

God, he loved this woman, who always seemed to be surrounded by people she cared about . . . and who cared about her in return. It was almost as if she were the switchboard operator in an ancient telephone system, plugging everyone in to one another, connecting them. And when he was with her, he felt connected, too. In this place, with Georgia at his side, he felt like he belonged.

And for that, among a million other things he could list, he loved her.

He looked up to find everyone watching him, so he smiled awkwardly, cleared his throat, and let Georgia's hair fall back into place.

Right. They wanted to hear what had happened.

Daniel coughed. "So, seeing as how you all—that is, y'all—ran me off earlier, I found myself over at the No Holds Bar with nothing much to do besides wait. After a while, my waiting paid off when Trey and Sheriff Mooney showed up. The sheriff made a beeline for your fiancé, Kelly, and Trey made a beeline for the bar. I gave him a few minutes to get properly loosened up, and then moseyed on over to see if I could get any information out of him."

"We don't really say 'mosey,' " Georgia informed him, handing over another cracker.

"Sorry," Daniel said around another mouthful of heaven.

"Was Trey all right?" Callie asked hesitantly. "He hasn't even bothered to call me after I told him that we'd have to postpone the wedding. Since the father of the groom was going to be in jail and all, I figured that would be for the best."

"He seemed fine. A bit shell-shocked perhaps, but not too bad, considering," Daniel answered, sugarcoating the truth just a bit. The truth was, Trey had looked like shit. Before Daniel left the bar, he had helped Beau pour Trey into a cab. But Callie didn't need to know that. By tomorrow, things would look a lot better for everyone.

"How did the sheriff look?" Vivian surprised him by asking. She tried to act nonchalant, as if it had just occurred to her to ask, but Daniel, having grown up in Hollywood, could spot a fake a mile away.

"He looked great. Fit. Young. Didn't I overhear him asking you out on a date next weekend?" Daniel said, calling Vivian's bluff.

She gasped and started fanning herself with her napkin. "Well, well . . . yes." She squared her shoulders. "Yes, he did. And I accepted. And before anyone decides to inform me that he's a decade younger than I am, you can rest assured that I already know."

"Good for you, Mama," Georgia said, grinning up at her mother from her seat on the floor.

"Thank you, dear."

Vivian looked like she was about to burst into tears and Daniel decided he'd seen enough waterworks for the day, so he got back to business. "Okay, so here's what I learned from Trey. Rock was stonewalling the sheriff. No pun intended." Daniel paused to see if anyone got his joke, and Georgia pinched his calf, so he figured that she, at least, had. "Anyway, after they got Rock locked up, Trey and Sheriff Mooney went to Rock's house to see if they could find anything."

"And did they?" Sierra asked, leaning forward intently, the Shrimp Queen crown she'd won that day listing dangerously to one side.

"Yes. Apparently, they found an old will of yours, Georgia. One from when you'd still been married to Trey. One that left everything to your ex-husband," Daniel added.

"But I've got a new will now. One that doesn't even mention Trey," Georgia protested, turning to frown up at him.

"From what I gathered, the sheriff suspects that your new will may have mysteriously disappeared from your attorney's office. That's why he went looking for Stuart Grainger, so they could find Alexander Wright. That's the name of your lawyer, isn't it?" he asked.

"Yes. I didn't want to see Stuart or Kelly because . . . well, sometimes it's just better not to do business with your friends. But, my God, I can't believe Alex was in on this. I mean, it's not like I'm worth a lot of money. Everyone knows that." Georgia shook her head.

"No, Georgia. It's not like you *were* worth a lot of money, but that was before the Miracle Chef," Daniel corrected.

"Oh, big deal. So I'll sell a few thousand of the things. That'll go to help pay off Mama's bill down at Callie's dress shop and pay the deductible for the new roof I now need, but that's about it."

Daniel smiled down at her. Then he started laughing, until tears came to his eyes. "You have no idea, do you?" he asked.

"What?" Georgia's brows creased as she set her plate on the floor next to Daniel's feet and slapped his shins. "Stop laughing at me. What's so funny?"

Daniel tried to contain his mirth. "What's so funny is that you have no idea what sort of response we've been getting to the Miracle Chef. In the last several days, our switchboard has routed over seven thousand calls to GME Industries. Only you weren't getting them because Rock, who works for the phone company, was rerouting the calls to another number so that he could keep you thinking you had no money until he could figure out a scheme to get you out of the picture."

"Seven thousand calls?" Georgia's skin took on a grayish hue that Daniel had never seen before. Then she brightened up and turned to her cousin, who was sipping a Bat Bite with a Battered Bruised and Bleeding floater. "Emma Rose, how would you like to be the new CEO of GME Industries? I'll offer you a share of the company and pay you five times what Beau does."

Emma Rose swallowed her drink and, as nonchalantly as if Georgia had just asked if she wanted the blue sandals or the green, said, "I'll sleep on it and let you know tomorrow."

"Oh my God," Callie said then, dropping the glass of wine she'd been holding. The wineglass fell onto Georgia's dining-room rug, but didn't break. "Don't you remember," she said, turning to look at Georgia. "I told you Trey and I had lunch with Rock on Friday before my bachelorette party. He said we were going to be *blown away* by his wedding gift to us."

"That's a terrible joke," Emma Rose said.

"Well, apparently Rock had an awful problem with gambling and he was barely scraping by financially. He saw this as a way to give his son a helluva wedding present and probably fund his own retirement as well. On top of the Miracle Chef and the profits you can expect to see from that, I'm going to make a guess that someone's going to be pretty interested in that fabric you invented," Daniel said.

"Well, it's a product with a limited market. I mean, who wants a swimsuit that rides up when it's wet?" Georgia said, shaking her head. "Pageant participants are really my only market."

Daniel looked at her incredulously. "Georgia, that stuff saved us from being blown to bits in a major explosion. Don't you think that maybe the government or a defense contractor or two might have some use for it?"

Georgia blinked up at him, apparently too stunned to speak.

There were various choruses of "I can't believe it" and "Who would ever have thought" and then Daniel found himself being escorted out the door by Georgia's mother. He wasn't quite certain how it had happened so quickly, but she pushed him out into the night with a polite, "Thank you for letting us know the latest developments," and then she shut the door behind him.

Daniel shook his head with disbelief as he started down the stairs. The way he figured it, he had the rest of his life to figure out how to handle Georgia's mother. And wouldn't *that* be the accomplishment of a lifetime? He had come to Ocean Sands to prove something to himself, only what he'd ended up winning was far more than a cook-off. He'd won a life of his own where what he did mattered, not just to himself or to Georgia, but to an entire community.

It was, by far, his greatest achievement.

"So, how's the party?"

Daniel drew up short, surprised to find Beau Conover standing in the darkness, just outside the glow of Georgia's porch light.

"Raucous," Daniel said, thinking of the first word that came to his mind.

"Yeah, these Southern girls . . . they know how to party."

Daniel grinned. "They definitely seem to know how to have fun," he agreed.

"Thanks for helping me with Trey. I could have handled getting him into a cab by myself, but it's a lot easier with a second pair of hands."

"You're welcome. Anytime." Daniel blew out a breath, surprised to find that he could see it hanging there in the air. He hadn't realized it had turned cold this evening.

"You got plans for the rest of the night?" Beau asked.

Daniel wasn't sure why he was so surprised. Probably because Beau seemed like such a loner that him going out of his way to try to be friendly seemed a bit unnatural. "No," Daniel admitted. "What did you have in mind?"

"Well, I figured since tonight was supposed to be Callie's wedding night, she's probably feeling a little disappointed by this turn of events. I . . ." Beau shifted his feet, rubbed his hands together. Coughed. "I thought it would be nice if I took the kids off her hands, so she could just let loose and have some fun. I volunteered to watch them last night during Callie's bachelorette party, but she said her mother-in-law was taking care of it. I figured I'd give it another try tonight, but to be honest, the prospect of baby-sitting all four of them at once has me terrified. I'd really appreciate a little help."

Daniel scratched his head. Then he thought of those three little boys, trapped inside that den of perfume and makeup, and wondered what the long-term effects of such a horrifying experience might be. He shrugged. "Sure. We could get some movies and video games. Order out for pizza. How tough could it be?"

Beau shuddered. "Don't ever ask that question."

Daniel laughed, then followed Beau back to Georgia's front door.

After some protestation by Callie, and some incredulous looks by the rest of the women, Callie handed over her children after Beau assured her that he and Daniel would take good care of them.

"Besides, we'll take them back to your place where there are lots of toys and things for them to do. You can even come down and check on us if it'll make you feel better," Beau said.

Callie seemed dubious but the rest of the Tiara Club won her over.

And that's how it was that Daniel found himself walking down the sidewalk with two six-year olds attached to his hands. Beau carried Caroline and Callie's oldest boy walked stiffly, a bit ahead of the group.

"So, how is it you have the night off?" Daniel asked, as if this were a casual question.

"I took it off to go to Callie's wedding," Beau said darkly.

"Were you going to object? You know, when the preacher asks if anyone knows any reason why this man and this woman should not be joined?" Daniel asked quietly.

The night was full of sounds Daniel didn't recognize—probably crickets and frogs and a whole host of things he'd never heard growing up in L.A. As the silence between the two men lengthened, he thought Beau wasn't going to answer.

Beau stopped at Main Street and took Callie's oldest boy's hand.

The boy looked up at him and Daniel saw Beau nod. As they started to cross the street, Beau's answer drifted back in the quiet of the night.

"Hell yeah," he said.

Daniel smiled and shook his head, then stopped when another sound reached his ears. He twisted around to see Georgia leaning out of her bedroom window with her hands cupped around her mouth.

"Hey, Daniel. Daniel Rogers," she shouted.

"Yes?" Daniel yelled back.

"I love you."

Daniel looked down at the two little boys whose hands he held. They seemed shocked that grown-ups were hollering at each other down the street, but Daniel just squeezed their hands and grinned as lights went on down Oak Street. He knew exactly what Georgia was doing and his love for her expanded even more. She was making sure that how she felt about him was no secret—that even if he left, the people of Ocean Sands would know that she had loved him enough to trust him with her heart.

And Daniel, knowing he had no intention of ever leaving, yelled back, "I love you, too, Georgia Elliot."

Then he turned back toward Callie's house, unable to hold back a laugh when he heard Vivian shout, "Georgia, you get back inside. And, Daniel, you stop hollering like a banshee. Do you two want people to think you were raised by Yankees . . ."

READING GROUP GUIDE

1. Georgia appreciates the benefits of her small town, but living there means she also has to make sacrifices. Do you empathize with the lengths she goes to in order to conceal her secrets? If not, why? What would you have done?

2. Georgia's mother is obsessed with holding on to her power over her daughter—in the little as well as the big things. What do you think of the straightforward and the sneaky ways Georgia evaded Vivian's control? At the end, do you believe that Vivian really changed?

3. What did you think of the irony of Georgia forming a group of close women friends as a method of taking attention away from herself? Do you and your friends often talk about what's most important to you? What about you and your significant other, parents, or children?

4. The Tiara Club is a wonderfully supportive group of friends, but there are jealousies and faultlines that run through their relationships. Do you think it's possible for a group of women to always be supportive of each other? Why or why not?

5. Did your idea of beauty queens change after reading *The Tiara Club*? What did you think of them before? What do you think of them now?

6. What did you think of Callie's reasons for marrying Trey? Do you think she was right to value stability over true love? Would you have felt differently if she didn't have children?

7. Georgia's inventions are aimed at making the lives of women easier. The Miracle Chef, however, has a much deeper aim than just cooking quickly— it's about family. If you could invent something, what would it be? Why?

8. Georgia tells herself she's keeping her secrets in order to protect her mother, but, in truth, having a life no one else knows about also allows her to maintain a distance from those around her. Have you ever caught your-self telling one of these emotional lies? If so, did realizing that you weren't being truthful (if only to yourself) make you change your behavior? Why or why not?

For more reading group suggestions visit
www.stmartins.com/smp/rgg.html

St. Martin's Griffin

Chetco Community Public Library
405 Alder Street
Brookings, OR 97415

WITHDRAWN